The UNDOING *of* SAINT SILVANUS

the

UNDOING

of

SAINT SILVANUS

BETH MOORE

Tyndale House Publishers, Inc.
Carol Stream, Illinois

Visit Tyndale online at www.tyndale.com.

Visit www.BethMooreNovel.com for bonus material, background, and a discussion guide.

TYNDALE and Tyndale's quill logo are registered trademarks of Tyndale House Publishers, Inc.

The Undoing of Saint Silvanus

Designed by Julie Chen

Edited by Kathryn S. Olson

The Undoing of Saint Silvanus is a work of fiction. Where real people, events, establishments, organizations, or locales appear, they are used fictitiously. All other elements of the novel are drawn from the author's imagination.

Library of Congress Cataloging-in-Publication Data
Names: Moore, Beth, date, author.
Title: The undoing of Saint Silvanus / Beth Moore.
Description: Carol Stream, Illinois : Tyndale House Publishers, Inc., [2016]
Identifiers: LCCN 2016011410 | ISBN 9781496416476 (hardcover_
Subjects: LCSH: Boardinghouses—Fiction. | Interpersonal relations—Fiction. | GSAFD: Christian fiction.
Classification: LCC PS3613.O5545 U53 2016 | DDC 813/.6—dc23 LC record available at http://lccn.loc.gov/2016011410

ISBN 978-1-4964-2023-7   (International Trade Paper Edition)

Printed in the United States of America

22	21	20	19	18	17	16
7	6	5	4	3	2	1

To my dear friend and co-laborer Evangeline Williams,
a gorgeous gem washed onto Houston shores
by the horrors of Hurricane Katrina.
God knew we wouldn't have wanted to miss you
for anything in this world.

This book is the fruit of your prayers, your faith, your hugs,
and your constant encouragement.

I love you.

Prologue

CHRISTMAS EVE 1921

REVEREND R. J. BRASHEAR dipped the bread into the wine. He lifted his chin and stared at the stained-glass image of Jesus, the rocking boat, and the daring disciple. Then he took the bread.

Not a single ear was open when the gun went off.

CHAPTER I

Sergeant Cal DaCosta glanced at the digits on his dashboard as he threw the car into park. "Sheesh. Eighty-four degrees and barely daylight. That body's going to be ripe." Several patrol cars were already at the scene, zigzagged all over the pavement. The lights were flashing but they'd saved themselves the sirens. As he shut the door and walked toward the small circle of officers, he took a few seconds to absorb how odd the ordinariness of it was. Only a handful of spectators were lurking. The few people on their way to work at this hour took the other side of the street to avoid the inconvenience. This was the nocturnal side of town, where the night was as the day. The patrol officers seemed almost as detached, chugging down weak coffee from a convenience store and eating something unidentifiable out of clear wrappers.

Sure enough, he got hit by a whiff of the body from twenty feet. "How do you guys do that?"

"Morning, Sarge. How do we do what?"

"How do you eat with that smell? Can't you taste it?"

One of them mumbled as he stuffed the last bite of a sticky bun into his cavernous mouth. When the man licked his fingers, Cal decided he'd pass on breakfast.

The odor radiating from the sidewalk wasn't so much the smell of death. Not yet anyway. It was the smell of filth, blown his way by a hot, humid gust that seemed to belch from the underworld. Frank Lamonte, Cal's closest friend and former partner, said what all of them were thinking. "Finally drank himself to death."

Cal imagined those five words etched beneath his own last name on a granite marker. At least half a dozen family members on his daddy's side were vying for the same epitaph. He'd considered going to a couple of meetings to try to dodge the family fate, but opening up to people wasn't exactly his strong suit. Anyway, his alcoholism wasn't in a glass. He was scared it was in his blood.

"Any chance we've got a name?"

Frank took off his hat and tried to rub out the permanent dent it had made in his forehead. "No, but I've seen him around here enough to tell you that this was his corner. He held that old cardboard sign over there and sat right here with his back against these bricks."

Cal glanced over at the sign and saw the usual scrawl with a black permanent marker. *Out of work. Hungry. God bless!* The words *need a job* had been scratched out with a blue ballpoint.

Another officer joined them, out of breath. "Hey, guys. Sorry I'm late. The light's out at Canal."

Frank nodded at him and continued. "To tell you the truth, I've seen him passed out in that alley as many times as I've seen him awake. I'm not sure how anybody could tell he was dead."

But he was dead alright. He'd probably been dead a long time. His lungs were just the last to know. He had that look a person gets when he's tried too long to make friends with the sun and enemies of his organs. Concrete made a poor cushion no matter how drunk you got. Cal squatted down beside the crumpled corpse, gave a firm grip to the right shoulder, and turned him faceup. The eyes were half-open and the teeth were almost as dark as a rotted pumpkin.

The late-arriving officer suddenly heaved and coughed until everybody still on their feet scattered like mice. Why Bully couldn't do them the courtesy of turning away when he pulled that stunt was a mystery to Cal. He said it was because he never actually vomited—he just had a weak gag reflex.

Bully was a two-hundred-and-fifty-pound anomaly. He had the sensitivity and the stomach of a nine-year-old girl. All of them had seen him cry on the job at least once. This was first on the list of top-ten reasons Billy Bob La Bauve was the most picked-on member of the NOPD. And, some would say, the favorite. For Cal, it depended on what day it was. It wasn't today. Honestly, if he started sniffling, Cal was going to send him home.

Once they recovered, Frank bent over toward Cal and the corpse. "You've seen him before, haven't you? I've threatened to haul him in a few times for harassing people for money, but these days there are so many just like him, who knows where to start? The old rules don't hold near as well this side of the levees." Frank forgot every now and then that Cal had joined the force after the hurricane. This was the only New Orleans he knew from behind a badge.

To Cal, cops didn't get much better than Frank. He'd never once caught him in a lie. He didn't have a foul mouth about women. He had a wife he apparently liked going home to. He worked with Midnight Basketball for kids at risk and was the closest thing some of them had to a father. He'd told Cal recently that he was studying up on soccer because the YMCA had asked him to coach a team. He'd never played, but no one else would volunteer. Frank actually had a life outside the force.

Cal answered Frank's question. "Yeah. I've seen him around here. How old a man do you think he is?"

Bully had pulled himself together by now. "Well, he looks a hunerd."

"He's not nearly as old as he looks. He's only gray at the temples and beard." The thick mop of matted hair looked out of proportion on the body's slight frame. Only God knew what color the man's hair was naturally, but the sun had turned it some faded shade of auburn. He was wearing a pair of black sweatpants and an old plaid Western shirt with snaps on the pockets. No shoes.

"We've got everything we need here. Y'all want to let us at him or do you want to carry him to the morgue yourself?"

The officers stepped aside and watched the coroner's team lift him onto a stretcher like he was a five-pound sack of Idaho potatoes. Cal was particularly impressed that one of the heavy lifters was a woman. He knew a lot of faces on the response teams since they were destined to gather at the same scenes, but names were another story.

Cal's big brother, a politician from diaperhood, had tried to teach him how to make name associations at a barbecue one Sunday. It was particularly humiliating because he'd had to go around the picnic table and practice associating the names of a few of their family members with memorable images. Maybe it was his imagination, but his aunt on his dad's side had acted cold ever since the word *horse* popped out when he got around to her. It was the dentures, his mom explained later. Either they were a size too big for her or the front teeth needed filing down.

"Sarge, anything else you want done here?" Bully wanted to know.

"Yeah. You and Sanchez ask around and see if you can get a few of the others who hang here to tell you anything about him once we've cleared out. They usually network. Maybe we'll get lucky and his prints will turn up a name pretty quickly. I'll head back in and handle the paperwork."

Some days Cal would almost rather shoot off his little toe than fill out forms. At least he'd be indoors with the AC. He and the rest of them already had sweat rings halfway to their belts and it wasn't even midmorning. With all the talk about cutbacks and financial woes in the department, he was glad no one had cut back on the air-conditioning. Raw meat would keep for a solid week on his desk. AC was something to be thankful for in a triple-digit June, and lest people forget, the cantankerous unit would freeze up and shut down at least two or three times a summer. It was no mystery to Cal why crime spiked in the sweltering summer. Heat sometimes made him want to haul off and hit somebody too.

CHAPTER 2

"RAFE IS DEAD."

Jillian might have found a better way to say it if she hadn't been caught off guard. Her mind was still whirling from the phone call, and her mother had picked that day of all days to stop by the restaurant where Jillian worked.

She knew Jade wouldn't be grief stricken. It was just that the two of them never spoke of him. They hadn't in years. Somewhere along the way—by high school, if Jillian's memory served her right—they'd come to an unspoken agreement to simply act like he'd never existed. It was easier. But now that he was dead, Jillian felt strangely compelled to face the fact that he'd been, all that time, alive.

Jillian waited for her mother to respond, but she didn't make a sound or move a muscle. She'd have been easier to read without her sunglasses on. It wasn't particularly sunny, but Jade never walked out the door without a pair of expensive sunglasses on. She teased that sunglasses made it harder to tell how old a woman was. Jillian seated her at one of the patio tables so they'd have a small hope of privacy and asked the assistant manager if she could take her fifteen-minute break early.

"Mom, did you hear what I said?"

"I heard you."

A chilly breeze swept a small stack of cocktail napkins off a nearby table. Jillian jumped up to grab them and saw Jade rub her bare arms. "How about a cappuccino? I've gotten pretty good at making them. Want one?"

"Nonfat milk?" Jade responded.

"Got it."

Jade added, "Extra foam."

"Coming up. And I'll make it extra hot. I probably should have seated us inside."

Sigmund's was a privately owned hot spot perched like a bird-of-paradise in the hub of Pacific Heights with a spectacular view of San Francisco Bay. If a person aimed to eat healthy, their chefs made it more than bearable. The food was downright ambrosial, but a customer would be a fool to confuse that with affordable. Even with her employee discount, Jillian could only afford to eat there a couple of times a week, but nobody made a black bean burger like Sigmund's. The sandwich was stacked nearly four inches high with perfect slices of California avocado—never mushy, never rubbery—sprouts, Swiss cheese, and garlic-herb mayo on a toasted whole-wheat bun with lightly grilled plantains on the side. Depending on the number on the scale that morning, sometimes she'd substitute a side of sweet potato fries. All that and a glass of iced tea tallied up to fifteen bucks.

Jillian considered herself fortunate to have a job here, and she needed to keep it. As it was, the assistant manager resented Jillian for having a personal gig with the owner, so she had to work twice as hard and watch her back, especially when he wasn't around. She glanced at the time. She had nine more minutes before she had to get back to waiting tables. She steamed the extra foam, wiped off the frother, and headed to the patio with Jade's extra-hot, imperfectly coiffed cappuccino.

"When I'm not in a hurry, I can make a double-heart shape in the foam. This looks a little more like a boiled egg. Sorry."

Jade took a sip. "It's perfect. I've just got a few more minutes before my appointment. A new client at the gallery wants me to take a look at her office and make some art recommendations. It's a bay view near here. If there's something you need to tell me, you'd probably better go ahead." Jade wrapped both her hands around the cup like she was warming herself around a campfire, leaned forward, and sipped as casually as if the deceased were no one she knew.

"Do you want to know?"

"No, not particularly. Nor do I want you to know. But since you do, you may as well tell me."

"About two hours ago I got a call from an area code I didn't recognize, so I let it go to voice mail. The woman left a pretty cryptic message saying Rafe had been found dead and there would only be a private burial. No service or anything. Just said she thought I should know and it was up to me what I wanted to do about it."

"I truly believed we'd moved on a long time ago, Jillian. Have you been in touch with those people without me knowing about it?"

"No! Absolutely not. I haven't had any contact with them since we moved to California. What was I, six years old? I hardly remember them."

Jillian and Jade seldom argued. Jade had always been the live-and-let-live kind. Whatever Jillian wanted was fine with her, as long as whatever Jade wanted was fine with Jillian. But somehow bringing up any part of the past, distant or recent, that could in any way call Jade into question, was completely off-limits. She lived by the philosophy that the past was exactly that, and the only relevance was *now*. Anything else would invite an onslaught of negative energy. Jillian usually agreed. She hadn't come to work that day looking for skeletons. They'd dropped by unexpectedly, just like Jade had.

"So Rafe's mother called you today out of the blue? How on earth did she know where to find you, Jillian?"

"Well, it wasn't actually her. It was a woman who works for her," Jillian tried to explain. "This woman said she was calling me because her boss was overwhelmed with the arrangements. She also said, word for word, 'Your grandmother will cover the expenses.' I could go for free."

"Your *grandmother*. Well, she was some grandmother. I'll tell you that. And this woman found you *how*?"

"Okay, this is where it really gets weird. She did one of those searches online. The kind you pay something like ninety dollars for. It listed where I work and she looked up the number and called here. She said there had been a family emergency, so the assistant manager gave her my cell number."

"And now they have your cell number and can get in touch with you anytime. Perfect." Splotches of red surfaced on Jade's neck, the usual sign that her mother was trying to remain controlled on the outside but was simmering hot underneath that thin layer of skin.

"Why are you freaking out?"

This time Jade's emotions permeated her pores. With uncharacteristic volume, she blurted out, "What do you mean, why am I freaking out?"

A woman at a nearby table shot them a glance, but the gentleman with her was more concerned with his empty glass and shook his ice annoyingly. Jillian was probably out of time since the waiter who'd agreed to cover for her was nowhere in sight. She got up, grabbed a pitcher of blackberry tea, poured the customer a refill, threw in some fresh mint, and picked up a credit card from a corner table.

When she slid back into the chair opposite Jade, her mother said, "Jillian, I dropped by here today to surprise *you*. I wasn't looking for you to surprise me. You tell me you've heard from the Wicked Witch of the South and that Rafe is dead and some stranger has your personal contact information, and you want to know why I'm unnerved?"

"I know. I get it. Can't we just talk about it? I need to sort it out. Don't you?"

"No. Actually, I don't. You're not telling me you're upset over this, are you? Are you suddenly all grieved over him?"

"Are you kidding? I have zero feelings for the man. But it's a little intriguing, don't you think? I mean, a few days in New Orleans? I haven't been since I was a little kid. I have a few vacation days. If you did, too, maybe we could go together and you could show me where I—"

"*We?*" Jade stood up from the table, grabbed her purse, and pulled the strap over her head to her left shoulder. "*I* am not going to New Orleans. And if you know what's good for you, neither are you." She placed both palms on the table, leaned forward, and spoke in a whisper. "Anyway, how is Vince going to feel about all of this? Since when is he going to let you that far out of his sight?"

That one hit home. Vince owned Sigmund's. At this point, Vince basically owned Jillian. He'd hired her a year ago, and not long after that, they began seeing each other on the side. Those were the good days. He'd talked her into moving in with him about two months ago, but at work, he still acted like he hardly knew her. He said it was to keep things professional.

Jillian hadn't had to deliberate for long when he first suggested she move in. It was so nice to have someone take care of her for a change. She'd felt like an adult all her life. Vince was ten years older, established and confident, and the idea of not being stressed over money was as big a lure as the man himself. Her mom understood how lucky she was. The guy was way out of her league. He was gorgeous and loaded with cash and could have anyone he wanted. He'd chosen her, and she needed him to keep choosing her.

"Are you listening to me?" Jade's tone softened a little as she lifted Jillian's chin with her fingertips. "Answer me. Would Vince mind you going to New Orleans?"

"He's out of town for a few days trying to close a deal for a location in Los Angeles. Why would he care? And anyway, he's been so aloof, he probably wouldn't know I was missing even if he was home."

"Jillian, don't risk what you have here for those backward people. They aren't worth it. They'll poison you."

"But he's dead."

"That's just it. He's been dead to you for nearly two decades. He had nothing to give you. Never even tried. He was a total loser in every way."

"I know he was," Jillian responded, standing. "You've got to go and I've got to get back to work." She stepped around the table and hugged Jade. "Thanks so much for dropping by. I was so happy to see you walk through the door."

Jade returned the embrace and whispered in Jillian's ear. "You don't owe those people anything. Put yourself first. Your future needs to be with Vince. If I were you, I'd hang on to him at all costs."

When they let go of one another, a few strands of Jillian's hair got caught in Jade's sunglasses. "Oops! Sorry about that, honey!"

"No problem." When Jade turned to wave good-bye, Jillian caught a glimpse of her own black hair plucked by the roots and sprouting from the hinge of her mother's shades. In a way Jillian couldn't exactly explain, something about the sight seemed fitting.

Jillian sighed as she cleared her mom's half-empty cup from the patio table. Jade was probably right. She would be an idiot to risk a conflict with Vince to fly halfway across the country to bury a man she didn't know. A man she couldn't care less about.

When she grabbed her apron from behind the bar, one of the other waiters piped up. "I can't believe that was your mom. I guarantee you my mom doesn't look like that. She looks more like your sister."

"Yep. I get that a lot."

"You must look more like your dad."

This was a mistake, Jillian thought for the fifteenth time since boarding the plane. The dead meant nothing to her. All she wanted was Vince's attention—and she got it just long enough for him to twist into a tornadic rage. She'd tried to call him during her hour layover in Houston but he hadn't answered. She knew he wouldn't.

The pilot announced their final descent and asked the flight attendants to take their seats. From the middle seat, Jillian craned her neck to see the edge of the city from the window. She felt panic rise like poisonous floodwaters all the way from her feet to her throat. When the wheels bounced onto the runway at Louis Armstrong, she pressed her feet to the floor like she was slamming on the brakes. She knew what she had to do. She had to go straight to a ticket counter and book the next flight back.

"I can get you to Houston today, but I may not be able to get you back to San Francisco. The flight's already delayed and may be canceled. They're expecting a serious late-afternoon fog to roll in."

The woman's fingernails kept clicking on the computer keyboard the whole time she addressed Jillian. "Want to go to Houston? You could stay for the night and catch a flight out tomorrow. But I'll need your credit card. There's a charge to change your flight."

Jillian's heart sank. What if her grandmother didn't reimburse her after all? And why should she if Jillian didn't even bother to show up? "Thanks anyway." She threw the strap of her carry-on over her shoulder and headed down the terminal with tears burning in her eyes. As she took the escalator down to baggage claim, she panned the crowd for anyone who might be looking for her. Not that she would recognize her grandmother even if she tripped over her broomstick and tumbled into her lap.

"Miss Slater?"

Jillian jumped. Standing beside her was a chocolate-brown woman of medium stature and middle years, with a white, toothy smile that swung from the east to the west. Her eyes were dark and bright at the same time and full of mischief.

"Hey. Yeah, I'm Jillian Slater. And you . . . well, you are not my grandmother."

"You are mighty right about that, young lady, but I am about to stick you in my chariot and drive you to her. Anyway, you're safer with me behind the wheel." The woman pitched back her head and laughed and then reached forward to give Jillian a proper handshake. "I'm Adella. We met on the phone. For a minute there, I was afraid you'd backed out."

Jillian fought the urge to say, "I tried." Instead, "You work for her, right?"

"Yes, ma'am, I do and have for going on eight years. She and I do right well together. I run that big old house of hers and manage the tenants. My sons are thankful. They say it keeps me from managing them as much as I'd have a mind to. My mama claims I was born bossy. That one bag all you've got?"

"Yeah, this is it. I'm only staying the two days."

"Well, women from the South have been known to average about one large piece of luggage a day. I'd say you're traveling light. That's good then."

"Oh. Well, not me. Not from the South."

Adella looked like she might be inclined to argue that point, but all she said was "Come on. Help me find my car. It's somewhere over there. It's the silver economy."

Jillian attempted a weak smile as she cased the overstuffed parking lot. Only about twenty cars in close eyeshot fit that description.

After finding the right car, Adella made several stabs at light conversation as they navigated the traffic, but Jillian put on her sunglasses and hoped her driver would take the hint.

The farther they drove from the airport, the more magnificent the houses became. The thick two- and three-story columns, the ornate European trim, and the vast porches were like pages turning in a pop-up history book as they drove quickly past. Many of the houses had clearly withstood the ambitions of modern architecture and the ire of Gulf winds for well over a century. Some of the live oaks arching over them must have been six and seven times their seniors, lurching up from trunks wider than a woman is tall.

The longer they drove, the closer Jillian drew to the window. Her nose was nearly pressed to the glass. She'd landed on another planet. That much was certain. And it was hot.

After what felt like next to forever, Adella finally pulled over. The tires squeaked and squealed along the curb, bumping up and over and back down before she came to a stop. With a jolt. Alarmed, Jillian pulled off her sunglasses and said, "Where are we? Why are we stopping here?"

Adella opened her car door and glanced back in at her, looking puzzled. "This is it!"

"But this is a *church*."

"No," Adella responded, "this *used to be* a church. It's a house now. Has been for years. Renters live here—three right now. And of course your grandmother, who owns the building."

Jillian shoved her glasses up the bridge of her nose and pulled her bag close to her chest. No way was she going into that place, whatever Adella wanted to call it.

The woman circled around the car and headed toward Jillian's door. She paused at the curb for a moment, obviously waiting for Jillian to open it. "In your dreams," she whispered under her breath. When Adella reached for the handle to open it herself, Jillian locked the door. Adella threw her hands onto her hips, tilted her head, and gave her a look that suggested she might consider growing up. Exasperated, Jillian hit the button and unlocked the door.

Adella opened it and swung out her left hand. "After you, my dear."

"This isn't a house."

"It *is* a house. Or an apartment building, anyway. If you take one step inside the door and spy a pulpit, I promise to drive you right back to the airport. Deal?"

Jillian slammed the door harder than she really meant to.

CHAPTER 3

Sparing the original front doors of Saint Sans had come at no small price. Even after considerable refinishing, the wet heat kept them swollen all summer, and an ample arm was required to open them. The renters and more familiar guests opted to bypass the wrestling match and head straight for the back. The dramatic effect of the building, however, was woefully diminished by entering through the back, and right about now, Adella was looking for enough drama to make a twenty-five-year-old snob glad she'd shown up.

Jillian stepped through the front door, and instead of feasting her lucky eyes on the startling collection of antiques, she gawked at the gargantuan stained-glass window on the upper back wall, which had at one time been the front of the chapel. She looked squarely back at Adella like she'd been kidnapped. Adella cased the giant room, trying to see it through her reluctant traveler's eyes.

As house manager, she'd grown so accustomed to treating Saint Sans as a business that she'd let herself lose sight of what, with fresh eyes, was a rather glaring history. The leaded glass depicted a wind-tossed wave, the tip of a boat, and Jesus robed and standing on the water, his hand extended to Peter. When the room was shadowy, the scene brooded with the dark pigment of fear, but let a beam of the sun catch it just right, and faith would find its feet.

They could have used more sun that day.

Of the actual furnishings, only a few pieces were distinctly ecclesiastical, and all of them had been repurposed. In fact, the organ was the only other giveaway to the untrained eye, and if Jillian had a trained eye for church wares, Adella was a little green man from Mars.

The pine altar still had its original white marble top, but the sterling tea and coffee service captivated most of the attention. And what little was left for the taking, the china cups and saucers robbed blind. The parson's bench just inside the front door looked like a regular settee, and the baptismal font was out on the back porch with a fern growing in it.

"Well, do you see a pulpit anywhere?"

If a look could cause a kidney stone, Adella would have doubled over.

"As you can imagine, the shape of this room might have made an adequate sanctuary a century ago, but it was a nightmare of a great room. Hard as petrified wood to furnish."

"Why? Because it's shaped like a big coffin?"

"Girl, what are you talking about? Haven't you ever been in a church shaped like this before?"

"You said it wasn't a church."

So it was going to be like this, was it? Adella fought the urge to ask if Jillian had been raised by hyenas. Instead, she'd take the high road, ignore the girl's insolence, and get her revenge by giving a less abridged version of the tour. "The fireplace and mantel were added, of course, when Saint Sans was refurbished as a house. It's limestone. Impressive, isn't it?" And it was. Placed in the center of the long wall along the left side of the room, it was seven feet wide at the base and the hearth jutted out two and a half feet. Three or four people at a time could sit on it, and when it was cold enough outside to build a fire, many a cup of hot cocoa had been consumed right there. The limestone blocks were stacked all the way to the ceiling, providing the central attraction in the oblong room.

The problem with a den of these dimensions was the necessity of arranging three stations, one right after the other, and on a hardwood floor. Just inside the front door was a couch so gloriously comfortable that, once you sat down, you couldn't soon stand up. And when you did, you were liable to need help. They called it the Snapdragon because it had a way of swallowing its happy victims whole. A dark-brown leather recliner was to one side of it and a deep-red overstuffed chair with an ottoman to the other, all on one Persian rug.

The fireplace and its surroundings comprised the second, central station, the most formal, with wing chairs, a delicate antique love seat, two tables and lamps, all on a second spacious rug.

Deepest in the room, on the left, was a long dining table that seated eight. A late arrival, of course. Once upon a time, congregants had probably been fed with the Word and the elements from a dark wooden lectern right there. With the remodel, a generous kitchen had been built along the right wall, across from what was now the dining area.

"Afternoon, Adella. Who've you got there?" It was David, coming in through the back door.

Startled by the sight of him, Adella glanced at her watch. "Are you home already? It can't be that late!"

David Jacobs had rented apartment 2A for the better part of

Adella's tenure as manager. The man was the consummate tenant. His rent was automatically withdrawn from his bank account on the first of every month. He complained little, lived rather quietly, and was meticulous with his grooming and his belongings. Adella tended to think most folks were half-crazy and sanity simply meant you spent more time living out of the other half. As far as she could tell, David kept his mad side mostly to himself.

He had a highly evolved palate for fine art and antiquities without an equally evolved budget. Never married and nearly forty, he said that he found the surroundings of Saint Sans altogether worth squeezing himself into little more than a one-room dwelling with a kitchenette. In Adella's opinion, if Jillian had a fraction of David's taste, she'd have seen that Saint Sans was a veritable museum. All the renters got to enjoy the main room, even to entertain guests on occasion, as long as the other residents weren't put out. They could use the large kitchen freely—first come, first served—as long as they used their own food and left the counters cleaner than they found them.

The young woman walked over to David and extended her hand, taking Adella by complete surprise. "Hey, I'm Jillian." It was the girl's first sign of life in fifteen minutes. David was obviously less alien to Jillian than Adella and this church-turned-house.

"Oh, goodness, where are my manners? David Jacobs, this is Jillian Slater. She's from California and she'll be staying with us a couple of days. Jillian, David teaches music at the biggest public high school in this district. He's a talented—"

"Nice to meet you," Jillian interrupted.

"Likewise. Do tell me what part of California. The coast?" And they were off to their own tête-à-tête as if Adella had fallen through a trapdoor. Not a bad idea. She felt queasy. Time was running thin and she knew it. She pulled her phone out of her purse and looked at it hoping someone with a hint of empathy might call her with an exit strategy.

"Are you going to the burial?" Jillian's question to David nearly jolted the sense out of Adella, but he responded before she could think exactly how to hijack it. Clearly she could have used a few more days to work out the kinks.

"Burial? I'm sorry. I don't know what you mean. What burial?"

At that moment, Jillian jumped like she'd stepped on a live wire. Her eyes shot to the floor. With one foot still wrapped around the other ankle, she offered a bare explanation. "Sorry. I don't like cats."

Clementine had appeared on the scene. That blasted cat could mean only one thing.

"Adella?"

At the sound of that familiar voice, Adella's stomach lurched into her throat. Every pair of eyes except hers darted toward the hallway opposite the apartment wing. Adella's mind spun like a wobbling top, but she turned around in slow motion, trying to buy a few extra seconds and get control of her expression. How long exactly had the woman been standing there? She wasn't due home for almost an hour.

Everyone in the den seemed bound and gagged, so David played the gentleman. "Mrs. Fontaine, it's good to see you. I haven't run into you in the last several days. I thought maybe you'd gone out of town, but I'd seen the car. But then again, I hadn't seen you out on the grounds. Of course, it's so hot. I thought maybe you'd flown somewhere. Are you well?" David didn't usually talk so much, or at least quite so fast. He was acting like a kid who'd been caught cheating on a spelling test. Adella took it as a moment's mercy and left him to fry while she scrambled for words.

At the next dead silence, she jumped in, hoping everyone would mind themselves. "Olivia, look who's here! Say hello to Jillian! How long's it been since you two . . . ?"

Jillian looked at Olivia, but Olivia's gaze never wavered from her employee's face. "Adella?" she posed again with the same unsettling, upturned pitch, each syllable distinct.

Some folks had a knack for making people nervous. An uncanny gift for running every perfectly reasonable explanation out of another person's head. In one fell swoop, yesterday's inspiration had become today's perspiration and Adella, for one, didn't appreciate it. She couldn't think of a single thing she liked less than sweating, and here this blouse was, fresh from the cleaners. Olivia owed her three dollars and fifty cents and she was lucky Adella had more manners than to tell her so.

CHAPTER 4

ADELLA WOULD HAVE FELT BETTER if Olivia had bitten her head
off. But she just stood there stoically, black eyes boring a hole
through her, letting Adella dig herself a grave. She knew the dirt
was about to fly when Olivia refused to acknowledge Jillian and
said instead, "Adella, may I see you in my quarters, please?" She'd
followed her with the enthusiasm of a woman walking off a diving
board into a drained pool.

David had thrown his Korean stir-fry on the kitchen counter
and run for his life. The man had the sense to recognize the primal
danger of placing himself between two unhappy women. They
were like the blades of a pair of scissors, getting sharper by the rub,
held together by the tight screw of territorialism.

After ten of the longest minutes known to man, Olivia uttered her
first words. "What hotel did you put her in? We're at full capacity."

Adella tilted her head and looked at Olivia, pleading wordlessly for her to be reasonable. "We have the guest room, Olivia. Let her stay in it."

The discourse didn't get loud, exactly, but what it lacked in volume, it made up for in tension. Olivia was the kind who yelled the loudest when she got the quietest. She carried an authority that was a little undoing if she wasn't on your side. And really, she didn't seem to often be on anyone's side.

"You had no right." Still, she never raised the volume, but Adella could hear Olivia breathing deep and hard and she could almost feel the reverb of her employer's heart through the hardwood floor. "You know it's impossible for her to stay in there. You had no right. You have overstepped your bounds, and I . . ." Olivia let the last word hang in the air.

As Adella steadied herself to accept the loss of her job, Olivia turned around, walked into her bathroom, and closed the door behind her.

Adella found Jillian in the front yard on the concrete bench. In this temperature, its surface had to be almost as hot as an iron. Even under the shade of that monstrous live oak, the young woman was sweltering, her carry-on bag still clutched in her lap.

Jillian didn't give her time to utter a word. "You lied."

Adella was taken aback. In this part of the world they tended to beat around the bush before they plowed it up by the roots. "I prefer to think I helped."

"Helped?" Jillian raised her voice. "What part of manipulating me here without her even knowing I was coming is helping? Did you see the look on her face? She's a witch!"

Adella gasped. "Young lady, don't you talk about your grandmother that way. Why, you ought to be ashamed of yourself."

"What grandmother? Did that look like a grandmother to you?

Don't you dare shame me. Shame her! She's a hateful old stone. She doesn't even want me here."

"Yes, she does. She . . . just doesn't know it yet." After the face-off she'd gotten in the house, Adella figured she'd probably lied again and guessed God could as easily forgive two fibs as one.

For the first time she realized how much the child favored her estranged grandmother in both looks and temperament. She couldn't charge Jillian with silent stoicism, however.

"I'm calling a cab," the young woman stated. "And I'm going to stay in one of those dives by the airport. You couldn't pay me a thousand dollars to stay in this . . . *house*."

The magnitude of what Adella had done was settling in on her, and she felt fresh out of remedies and twice her age. All the progress she'd made with Olivia in the last six months had sprouted wings and flown like a hawk. "I can't let you do that. After the mess I've made, the least I can do is offer you a room at my house. You can catch a flight out tomorrow. I'll cover the costs of the ticket change. We have a comfortable home and you'll look a mighty long way to find a man as fine as my Emmett."

"I'm not staying at your house. I'm staying by myself."

"Jillian, I'm asking you nicely. Please don't do that. Don't put yourself in harm's way in a strange city."

"Strange is right. That may be the first truthful thing you've had to say to me. I'm an adult. I can take care of myself."

Adella blew out a long sigh. "Let me go get my keys and I'll take you wherever you want to go. But Mrs. Fontaine will have my hide if I don't pay to put you somewhere decent."

"I bet," Jillian quipped with a disrespect Adella didn't run into every day.

Adella had retrieved her purse and was heading back toward Jillian with her keys dangling from her hand when two police cars pulled up to the curb, one in front and the other behind her vehicle. The back one blocked the driveway. "What on earth? Officers, can I help you?"

There were four of them. Two men had gotten out of the first car, and another man and a woman crawled out of the second.

"Yes, ma'am. I'm Sergeant Cal DaCosta. This is Officer Frank Lamonte."

"Good afternoon, ma'am."

"And Officers Bill La Bauve and Carla Sanchez."

Officer Sanchez reached out to shake Adella's hand. She responded in kind, though she didn't want to. She preferred knowing their business to holding their hands.

"We need to see a family member of Mr. Raphael Fontaine. This is the address we tracked down for nearest of kin when he was found deceased," Sergeant DaCosta explained.

"We already know he is deceased, officers. Two others brought us the news several days ago. So unless you have further business here, I'll need you to move your cars from right in front of Saint Sans. You're illegally parked." Adella knew she'd lost her mind to talk in such a way, particularly since hers was the car between theirs. But she was at least a decade older than all four, and the last half hour had frayed her nerves to threads.

"Yes, we are aware that there's already been a visit to this address, ma'am, by patrolmen from this district." Officer La Bauve was talking now. He sounded like a man who was used to defusing tense situations. "We're awful sorry for the difficult circumstances. We're from the Eighth, where the body was found. We're only over here now because we have additional information. What did you say your name was?"

"I didn't say. My name is Adella Atwater. I manage this place of business. I feel certain the owner would have me serve as a go-between." Her heart started pounding. She wasn't sure how much more turbulence this day could take. "What is the news?"

Sergeant DaCosta was kind but insistent. "Are you a relative of Mr. Fontaine's, Mrs. Atwater?"

"No, technically I am not, but I can relay any pertinent information to his kin. Surely you would spare her further indignity."

"I'm afraid we need to see a family member if at all possible."

Jillian stayed put on the concrete bench but Adella could clearly see in her peripheral vision that she'd shifted her position enough to catch every word of the interchange.

Officer Sanchez spoke up. "Mrs. Atwater, the officers talked with a Mrs. Olivia Fontaine. I understand that she is the mother of the deceased. Is she in?"

Adella realized there was no deflecting. Whatever news they had, Olivia was going to have to hear it. "Officer Sanchez, you can come in the house with me. Gentlemen, you can pull your cars into the driveway around back and we'll meet you at that door."

"Come on, boss." Officer Lamonte put his arm on Sergeant DaCosta's shoulder, and after a slight hesitation, the sergeant turned and walked with the other men toward the cars.

As Adella walked to the front door with Officer Sanchez, she said to Jillian without glancing her direction, "Miss Slater, I'm sure you heard all that. You may as well come in the house and rest a minute. That ride to a hotel will have to wait."

Out of curiosity more than anything, Adella supposed, Jillian followed them. She went straight to a barstool at the kitchen counter and sat down, holding on to that same tired piece of luggage.

After letting the other officers in, Adella tapped on the door to Olivia's suite and soon Olivia appeared, looking as inconvenienced as possible. When her eyes met Jillian's, the young woman turned her head and stared coldly out the window.

"Officers, this is Mrs. Fontaine," Adella said, gluing herself to Olivia's side.

All four greeted her as cordially as they could, apologizing for the intrusion. She nodded at them but said nothing.

Sergeant DaCosta took the lead. "Mrs. Fontaine, Mr. Raphael Fontaine is your son, correct?"

"Yes." Her voice was low. She spoke as if each word would take a year off her life.

"We have learned that your son died as a result of a stab wound rather than natural causes."

Olivia looked directly into his eyes. She'd never been much on making anything less difficult.

Adella jumped in, horrified. "What are you saying, Officer? Are you saying that Rafe was killed?" She could hardly force herself to say the right word. *Murdered?* Her voice cracked as she reached over and held Olivia's wrist.

"Yes, ma'am. I'm afraid so."

"How could you not have known this when you found him?" Adella was incensed.

"That's why we asked to be the ones to come today. We felt we owed it to you for the oversight."

"Oversight? Did you say oversight? How could you not have known?" One tear slid down Adella's cheek and then another. Her voice quivered but she intended to hold them accountable and to say everything Olivia couldn't.

"Not our oversight. Our mistake, Mrs. Fontaine. We missed it. Everything about the condition of his body looked textbook for natural causes that typically claim lives on the streets. The abdominal wound was several days old, so there wasn't the bleeding that—"

"Oh, my Lord in heaven, help us." Adella was still doing all the talking. Olivia had yet to add another word but she was no longer looking in Sergeant DaCosta's eyes. She stared blankly toward the wall.

"Mrs. Fontaine, we won't pretend we know how hard this is. Within only a few hours, we were able to identify him by his fingerprints and the officers were dispatched to inform the nearest of kin. Your name appeared on a court record for paying his bail a couple of times. There was a mix-up between the district and the morgue over a second John Doe. A drug overdose that took priority. Word didn't get to us about the stab wound until today. He might have had some chance of making it—" the sergeant paused and took a deep breath—"had he reached out for help. Probably not much chance, I'll admit, but he wouldn't have died on the concrete. At some point after the stabbing, he must have been sober enough to change clothes, unless someone else changed him. We deeply regret the delay on this information reaching you."

Hardly above a whisper, Olivia asked, "Who?"

The sergeant looked at Officer Sanchez like he could use some help, and she stepped up instantly. "Mrs. Fontaine, perhaps you could sit down."

"I'll stand. I trust you won't be staying long. Is that all?"

"Ma'am, in answer to your question, no, we don't know who the perpetrator was." Sergeant DaCosta looked at the floor and then once again met Olivia's cold glare.

Adella never had more trouble buttoning her lip than when she got a verifiable invitation to bear some indignation. "Well, are you even going to bother to find out?"

Officer Lamonte put his hand on his boss's shoulder and took up the charge. "Mrs. Atwater, you know that's exactly why we're here. We fully intend to get to the bottom of it, but we have to start right here. At this point, we suspect it wasn't personal. He might have had some money on him or—"

"A bottle." Olivia finished his sentence for him.

"Maybe. Yes. Sad things happen out there on the streets.

Desperate things. We'd all seen him around, ma'am. Some of us for years."

At that, Olivia turned and walked back to her room without another word.

"I'll need to see to Mrs. Fontaine, Officers." Adella grabbed a piece of paper from a kitchen drawer and scratched her cell number and the main number for Saint Sans on it. Noticing the unoccupied stool at the end of the kitchen counter, she realized Jillian was gone. "Here's our contact information. I don't live on the premises, but I'm here Monday through Thursday during normal business hours and half a day Friday and occasional Saturdays."

As the officers let themselves out the back door, Adella rushed to the front in time to see Jillian climbing into a cab. "Jillian, wait! Don't go yet!" The door slammed and the driver pulled onto St. Charles and, seconds later, out of sight.

Adella realized Officer Sanchez had followed her when the woman spoke.

"Mrs. Atwater, I saw that young woman when we drove up and then again inside. Is she a resident here?"

"No, Officer. That was your dead man's daughter."

CHAPTER 5

Thick hot air clung to Adella like a wool coat in late summer. Not a whiff of wind. Tears and sweat ran together in thin streams down her neck. She could feel the layer of hair closest to her head frizzing by the minute and resisted the urge to smooth it down, rubbing her hands together instead.

She'd have known better what to say to Olivia a few years ago. The lines had been clearer. More formal. There was something to be said for formal. She hadn't thought so then, but she did now. The woman was Mrs. Fontaine then, her employer, and using words like *condolences* would have been sufficient. The sparing of words would have been the sparing of a woman who saw transparency as debility. But this side of the Great Divulgence, the awkwardness was as heavy as the casket in front of them.

Just the two of them stood beside it, facing the funeral director on the opposite side. Others would have been there in a heartbeat if they'd been permitted. Emmett had insisted, "Honey, let me come. She could use a safe man to lean on. I've still got a pair of shoulders on me, don't I?"

"Don't you think I want you there, Emmett Atwater?" Adella had said. "She won't have it."

David had begged Adella to let him attend, but Olivia wouldn't consider it, especially after the unfortunate way Jillian had let the cat out of the bag. Adella was sure that one of the five flower arrangements at the interment was from him and, knowing his taste, expected it to be the one splashing with white roses and amaryllises. The bright, multicolored one was probably from her and Emmett but it didn't look like what she'd ordered. She wasn't sure who might have sent the other arrangements. Adella made a mental note to gather up the cards on the way out if Olivia made no move toward the flowers. They weren't likely from Mrs. Winsee or Caryn, the residents of 1A and 3A respectively. Not because they didn't care, but because they didn't know. Had they been told, both of them would have wanted to take their places at the graveside today too.

Of course, whether or not Mrs. Winsee would actually know she was there was a toss-up, or whether she'd come without Mr. Winsee, who'd been dead for a decade. She missed most events, waiting for him to get showered and readied. She rarely lost her cheerfulness no matter how long she waited in the den with her purse in hand. "He's always had an allergy to timeliness," she'd explain with a chuckle. "Sometimes I wait all day." And they all knew she did. They'd given up trying to gently remind her that he was gone because she'd grieve his loss again with such fresh, raw emotion, such wails of soul, that they could not bear it. By the next day, she would have forgotten all over again.

Curiously, some things Mrs. Winsee never forgot. At the top

of that short list was her weekly hair appointment Wednesdays at straight-up noon. Sometimes she couldn't remember the way to her room at Saint Sans, but not once had she forgotten how to get to the salon and back on the trolley. Of course, every conductor knew her name because Adella had made certain of it. Olivia told her to. Mrs. Winsee thought they were all familiar with her because they'd seen her perform in community theater. Never mind that she hadn't darkened a stage in twenty-five years. In Adella's book it went without saying that good hair improved mental health, so they'd dared not tempt fate by trying to change Mrs. Winsee's routine. That's not to say it was without challenges.

Just last week Mrs. Winsee had emerged from her room like clockwork at exactly a quarter till with her purse over her forearm and her lime-green coat on. It was hot as blazes outside, so Adella had done the only responsible thing she could do. And as it turned out, somebody should have thanked her. "Oh, now, Mrs. Winsee," she'd said. "As fetching as you look, I can't help feeling you'll be too warm out there in that lovely coat. Let me help you take that off. I'll go hang it up and you head on out to your appointment."

"You think?" the old woman asked, chipper as a woodpecker. "Maybe you're right." Mrs. Winsee flung the coat onto the floor and headed for the front door like greased lightning in nothing but her longline bra and girdle. That half of Orleans Parish hadn't been privy to the sight was, in Adella's opinion, a testimony to her new supplements. She'd landed on that woman like a duck on a june bug.

It was days like those when Adella questioned the wisdom of a woman with such delicate sensibilities staying on at Saint Sans indefinitely. Olivia insisted Mrs. Winsee had never been formally diagnosed with Alzheimer's or even classic dementia. She just seemed perpetually stuck in the time of her prime.

Caryn, on the other hand, was a young medical student with

enough brains for her and Mrs. Winsee both. Between school loans and the rent at Saint Sans, Adella doubted she'd have the extra funds for flowers—even if she had known to send any.

It was a crying shame that Olivia didn't want anyone to come and that she had gone so far as to ensure their absence by keeping the time private. In all, Adella could well picture fifteen or twenty people showing up at that burial if Olivia had allowed herself a little comfort.

Adella had told Emmett the night before, "All the fuss makes her feel worse somehow. I think the pain on our faces makes it harder to keep hers covered. Lord knows she has to do that at all costs. And then there's the fact that I betrayed her trust."

"You did not betray that woman, Dell. You were the only real friend she had."

"She thinks I did. She won't get over it, either. Not if I know her at all."

"But you know that God—"

Letting him go on was like salt in the wound. "Right now she's got God and me both strapped in the same boat and we'll be lucky if she doesn't sink it with her own big feet. I'm sure she doesn't like him any more than she likes me. Wherever she and I had gotten, we're highways and byways from it now."

The wonder was that Olivia had let Adella come. The fact that she still had a job and was the only one standing next to her boss at that graveside kindled at least a fool's hope that Olivia would consider forgiving her conniving.

It had been the longest, darkest week of Adella's employment at Saint Sans. The homicide ruling delayed the body's release to the funeral home, making all of Adella's efforts to woo Jillian to her grandmother's side for the burial a colossal waste of time. She couldn't have stayed that long anyway. But maybe the anvil of waiting had crushed open Olivia's heart and she could accept the compassion behind Adella's actions. Then again, she'd probably ask for the keys the second they got home. She might forgive her, but there was no doubt in Adella's mind that Olivia would never trust her again.

She squeezed her eyes shut and flashed back half a year to the morning of the Great Divulgence. A wave of nausea shot through her. It had been a while since the guest room in the private wing of Saint Sans had been thoroughly cleaned. She'd had it on her to-do list for a couple of weeks and the housekeeper was there unusually early that morning. Adella didn't possess a key to Olivia's private quarters, but this one dangled from her large silver ring for those rare occasions when the room was used. They called it the guest room, but it was Rafe's. Every year or so, he'd land on the back steps, sometimes rolled up in a ball. Or Olivia would pick him up on the street. He'd stay a night or two, and they would try again to see if they could make it work without disturbing the peace. They never could.

Adella had considered Olivia fortunate that Rafe customarily flew the coop with the first sign of sobriety and without tearing up the place or robbing her blind. This had been a grace in the affliction, but one she'd left Olivia to discover for herself. Adella's job was to cover for them but act like she wasn't, and then retreat to her usual distance, never to speak of it again. That code of conduct had worked for nearly seven years.

That morning she swung open the door to Rafe's room with the housekeeper right next to her, vacuum cleaner in tow. She shut the door as soon as her mind absorbed the sight, but she was sure the housekeeper had gotten an eyeful.

The most controlled and private person Adella Jane Atwater had ever met was sprawled across the bed half-dressed. The hair she'd kept neatly swept back into a wide barrette every day that Adella had known her was wild and tangled. A swath of it was stuck to the

vomit dried on her cheek. Adella had never seen Olivia near a glass
of wine, let alone a bottle of bourbon, but one was empty on the
floor. She'd obviously pulled out a box of old family photographs
because pictures were strewn around the room, some of them torn
to pieces. A chair was turned over and the vanity mirror was broken
at the upper right-hand corner, looking like a spiderweb of glass.
Maybe the heel of a shoe, Adella thought to herself.

After Adella waved the housekeeper from the hall and sent her
to the other wing, she opened the door just enough to slip through
it. "Mrs. Fontaine, you okay?" she whispered. There was no
response. She sat softly on the edge of the bed so she could lean in
closer. "Mrs. Fontaine, it's Adella. Let me help you up."

With that, Olivia's eyes cracked open and she flopped like a
rag doll from her back onto her side, dropped her head in Adella's
lap, and held her with both arms around the waist and began to
sob. Adella had held a horde of crying folks in her arms in forty-
five years but not this one. Not one remotely like her either. She
couldn't remember ever purposely touching the woman in all their
years together.

Her heart pounded so hard, she was half relieved Olivia was
drowning it out. Over the next solid hour, Olivia spilled more
beans than Adella could have shoveled back into a ten-gallon can.
Some of what she said was incoherent and some of it fragmented,
but the part about her son spoke a language between two mothers
where words were unnecessary. Olivia would pick herself up on one
elbow, grab a photo of Rafe, and fall back into Adella's lap with it
wadded in her fist. Adella knew that she meant for her to unfold it
and comment on how beautiful he was.

It was not hard to do. He was as beautiful a light-skinned lad as
she'd ever seen. The boy in those pictures was almost wholly absent
from the man she'd seen stumble and mumble in and out of that
room. Out of Olivia's volcanic stupor erupted several searing

streams: she'd hated her husband and loved her son and stood by her husband and left her son. How all of that played out in detail was anybody's guess right then, but it had not been pretty. Olivia also kept saying the word *curse*, and since it was in the same jumble as her husband's name, she supposed she was cursing him. Right then, Adella would let her.

Adella had held so still and tight with Olivia draped over her that her right thigh began to cramp and twitch. When she could get Olivia's voice down enough to slip her into the hall and back to her own bedroom unnoticed, she threw a bathrobe around her and made haste.

Thick, strong coffee with a cloud of real cream had always been Olivia's drink of choice. Adella felt like she was having a dream as the electric coffee grinder buzzed and whirled. She poured less grounds than usual into the French press for fear it would come right back up after Olivia swallowed it.

While she waited a couple of minutes for it to steep, she saw the edge of her red Bible sticking out of her purse on the back counter. It was Wednesday and she had a prayer meeting right after work and it was far enough to the church without having to run by home. "Have courage, weak woman o' God. It may be now or never." She slipped the Bible under her arm as she carried the coffee tray into Olivia's room.

And she read out of it. And, would wonders never cease, Olivia did not stop her. She also never told her to keep going, but Adella had always considered that a door cracked was a door flung wide open. Maybe off the hinges. She read a segment of Psalm 18 until it got to the part where David said, "According to the cleanness of my hands he has recompensed me." She wasn't exactly sure what had happened in the Fontaine family, but she didn't think clean hands had much to do with it. But recompense did, at least in the mind of the woman in that bed.

Then Adella read just one more thing. She read every word of Isaiah 53. Sometimes all you could do for the suffering was to make sure they knew someone was suffering right there with them. Someone who had also felt stricken, and smitten, and afflicted.

Olivia sobered up that day, but she stopped short of returning to the previous code. A loosely knotted tie looped the lives of the two women. As long as Adella picked her times carefully and privately, she could slip Olivia a Scripture or a quote or even a book of inspirational readings—if it wasn't too preachy. Snooping was second nature to Adella, so she'd watch to see if the bookmark was moved, and it often was.

Sometimes Olivia would seem stiff and chilly again and Adella would think they were getting nowhere, but other times the woman looked downright cheery. Well, maybe *cheery* was stretching it. But that summer Adella had seen a little peace wash over Olivia's face like dew on a thirsty petal. She had even heard Olivia humming a few times while she gardened. David had heard it too. "An alto," he observed one day as he walked through the back door.

"Would either of you like to say something?"

Adella was jarred from her memories when the funeral director spoke. Adella hated awkward silence almost worse than anything. When Olivia shook her head to decline, Adella's mouth fell open like someone had pitched a ten-pound weight on her tongue.

"Well, I—"

All Olivia had to do to shut her up was lift the fingers of her right hand.

The funeral director cleared his throat. "Then I'll close with these words that have brought comfort to the mourning for centuries. 'The Lord is my shepherd; I shall not—'"

He got more than a few fingers. He got Olivia's whole hand right out in front of him, like she was stopping traffic. Adella looked at his indignant expression and wanted to whisper to him, "Indeed, you shall not."

Olivia paused for a moment. Then she turned and started for the car without even touching the coffin. The pity was, Adella knew how much she wanted to if only she were the kind of person who could. She leaned over and patted it for her. "Rest in peace, troubled soul. Jesus, I'm hoping you got this one."

Adella was the only one still at the graveside. The director had dearly departed so that he could fetch the workman to lower the casket into the ground. She gathered up the cards from the flower arrangements, thinking how she hated these old New Orleans cemeteries. The aboveground vaults gave her the willies. They looked like concrete changing closets, like something a mummy could step out of at any minute. She also imagined somebody lurking behind one nearby, spying on her, about to scare her half to death. She'd probably lunge into that opening in the crypt and hit her head on the concrete and pass out and they'd shove the coffin right on top of her. She'd be stuffed in that big drawer alive and have to beat on the wall for a week till she finally starved to death.

She shook off her overactive imagination. "Get a move on, woman. Your boss is going to bake like a country ham in that hot car."

As she walked to Olivia's sedan, she opened the cards. She was right about the one with the amaryllises. *Sorrowfully, David.* She was also right about the multicolored one, but she thought she'd made herself clear how she felt about carnations. Adella slid the small card out of the third envelope and stopped dead in her tracks. It had only one word printed on it.

Atonement.

CHAPTER 6

THE CORNERSTONE OF Saint Silvanus Methodist Church was pressed to the soil more than a century after the first circuit rider of like devotion tied his horse to a post a few miles from there. The forty or so adult congregants who gathered for the groundbreaking held all the hope within them of the early spring that surrounded them, cordial but with might enough to wrestle the winter from the trees. God willing, buds would soon swell from these simple stems and burst into blooms, as fiery as a burning bush.

The ground had been flattened for several weeks and stakes pounded at the corners, displaying the first tangible flecks to stick to the surface of the vision of those gathered. The plans were ambitious, but no less so than the men who had drawn them. This was no country for those of anemic will.

41

That celebratory morning, the women spread makeshift tables with embroidered linens, anchored down against the March breezes by plates of fried chicken, crispy and cold, and slices of fat, pink ham, blackened in iron skillets. Perfect for cupping redeye gravy. Mounds of buttermilk biscuits were covered by dish towels, and black-eyed peas, thick and smoky, threatened to cool despite the heavy lids on their pots.

The children, who outnumbered the adults by a long shot, insisted on roughhousing particularly close to the dessert table. Even before the meal could begin, they had swiped most of the oatmeal cookies, and several fruit pies were missing chunks of crusts along the edges.

Urged by his own stomach, the parson finally put the faithful out of their misery—and the reprobates with them. The latter, after all, could be particularly generous tithers. With food and property blessed, Saint Silvanus Methodist Church kicked within her new crib with the life of a robust newborn, full-term and lungs full.

CHAPTER 7

JILLIAN STOOD IN FRONT OF the picture window on the seventeenth floor, counting the white sails adrift on the sapphire bay. She was still mesmerized by the view from Vince's loft.

She liked looking out more than facing in. The loft was impressive and always immaculate, but she never knew exactly where to sit. The couch cushions were so stiff she might as well recline on an ironing board. All the furnishings were contemporary and angular and the colors, brisk and cool. The whole place was a feast starving for touch. Jillian loved the granite fireplace, though, and when Vince wasn't home, she sat in the accent chair closest to it, draped her legs over one of its arms, and lost herself in a good book. The outside temperature was irrelevant. Vince had kept the thermostat at a frosty sixty-five degrees all summer long. The gas logs lit at the flip of a switch and she could turn the fireplace off faster than he could turn a key in the entryway door.

Jillian hadn't been sure what to expect when she moved in with Vince. She knew he went out a lot. He said it was necessary if he intended to carve out a noticeable name as a business owner in San Francisco. He only asked her to accompany him occasionally, but avoiding the stress of trying to look and act worthy of him was almost worth being left out. He'd also made clear from the very beginning that he liked to keep his private life separate from his professional life. But if she had to stay home, she supposed this was the place to do it.

Turning her back to the window, Jillian took a fresh look inside. "Home." She said the word out loud with an uncertain tone like she was trying it on to see if it fit. She wanted it to fit in the worst way. She wanted to be happy here. If a woman couldn't be happy here, a woman couldn't be happy. She didn't need her mother to tell her that. Maybe the only thing missing was some semblance of permanence. Getting married was off the table. In Vince's very vocal opinion, marriage was the stupidest financial decision a man with money could make. Jillian would settle for an occasional reassuring reference to *our place*. All these months later, Vince still called it *his* place and, of course, it was. Anybody looking to prove Jillian lived here was out of luck without searching the medicine cabinet in the master bathroom or thumbing through the small section of women's clothes in Vince's closet.

Two nights ago, when he'd darted in just long enough to change clothes, she'd come up behind him, wrapped her arms around his waist, and said, "Stay home this evening, please? Let's spend it together. We could watch a movie or something."

He'd responded with a chuckle. "You're not about to ask me if I want to play cards again, are you?"

She'd never hear the end of that. She'd chalked up more than her share of memorable embarrassments along the way, but she'd never known until then that liking a good round of gin rummy could leave you red-faced.

"You can come with me if you want," he'd offered, unwrapping Jillian's arms from around him. She'd been on her feet all day at Sigmund's, but they needed an evening together. She was just about to tell him she'd like to when he'd turned around, studied her face, and said, "But you look exhausted."

He'd brushed his chin across her forehead with what she supposed he'd call a kiss and told her to get some rest. He'd then sauntered out the door and left her staring in the mirror, feeling old enough to be his mother. The whole last month had been like that, the newness wearing off to a dull nub. Jillian wasn't sure if his most recent coldness was genuine disinterest, or if he was still punishing her for heading off to New Orleans on a whim.

Jillian felt sick at the prospect of the relationship dismantling. She'd given up so much for Vince, even her best friend. She and Allie had been inseparable for the past few years, as most of their other friends moved away or got married. They'd had a huge fight over Jillian's moving in with Vince.

It *was* unfortunate timing. She and Allie had put down a deposit on a vintage apartment they could only afford together. They'd gotten a couple pieces of furniture from secondhand shops and painted them in the garage at Allie's parents' while the music blared and the two of them sang at the top of their lungs. The pieces turned out so well, Allie's parents threatened to fund a furniture store and force them to run it while they retired off the fortune in Cabo. Then just before Jillian and Allie got the keys to the new place, Vince told Jillian he wanted her to move in with him.

She'd never forget the things that had come flying out of Allie's mouth in her fury. She said Vince wasn't just possessive, he was psychotic. She said Vince wasn't in love with Jillian and that he patronized her in front of people. She said he was arrogant and conniving and that he'd intoxicated Jillian with all sorts of perks, and that soon he'd get sick of the game and drop her like a hot coal. "Don't you get it, Jillian? Money is a wild card that can make a joker look like a king. Is it worth it to you? Don't you see the way he gawks at other women when you're standing right in front of him?"

Jillian had—and of course she hadn't liked it—but didn't all men do that? Allie's final words in the wet sand of anger hardened into concrete in Jillian's head. "He came on to your best friend, Jillian! I can't believe you would take his word over mine."

That was the end of it. Jillian didn't believe her. She couldn't afford to.

At least Jillian's mom had been supportive in the wake of that fight. "A true friend would have understood, Jillian. Who on earth wouldn't choose a man over a girlfriend?"

Vince had been so good to her in the beginning, telling her what a natural beauty she had and how different she was from everybody else he'd been with. *Everybody else.* Even his compliments had a way of making her feel insecure.

Jillian was a hundred and eighty degrees removed from a stereo-typical Southern California blonde. She had raven-dark hair, cut short and left naturally curly at the nape of her neck. With enough humidity, it looped around a tiny tattoo she had just behind her right ear as if the whole presentation was planned that way. The black-and-white dragonfly with a wash of pale pink inside its wings was ink at its most feminine. She had big, round Christmas-green eyes that caught the light like a prism when she laughed and broke the banks of a river when she cried. Or, at least that's what someone had told her when she was a little girl.

Jillian had never been bone-thin, but she'd been okay with how she looked until Vince started dropping a string of remarks about her weight. Long-waisted, her stomach was as flat as a kitchen counter, so what she ate slid right over it and landed squarely where she sat. These days she mostly ate behind his back so he wouldn't glare at her like she was an old sow.

Jillian missed Allie terribly, especially on a day off. She was the best friend she'd ever had.

The ring of the phone in her back pocket was a welcome red light to Jillian's racing thoughts. It was Garrett, a fellow waiter at Sigmund's, in a fast-talking, high-pitched panic. He was hands-down her favorite person at work, but he could manage to make a nap dramatic. They needed her at work ASAP to help with a party of sixteen, he said. Casey was on the schedule, but according to Garrett she was indisposed, so they were shorthanded and overwhelmed. He said Vince indicated that Jillian had better get down there posthaste if she knew what was good for her.

In fifteen minutes flat, Jillian flew through the door of Sigmund's, grabbed her green apron, tied it around her waist, and spun around, looking for a table set for sixteen. Garrett and Sam, another waiter, were standing at the end of the bar, making peculiar faces.

Jillian was flabbergasted. "Why don't you guys have the table ready? Are you crazy? What time is their reservation?"

Garrett and Sam stared at her wide-eyed without saying a word.

"What is wrong with you two? Let's start moving tables!" Jillian wasn't often the one barking orders but she was in no mood to hide how annoyed she was. "I can't believe you guys didn't get started. What have you been doing for fifteen minutes?"

Garrett shifted his eyes toward Vince's office and tilted his head, clearly trying to signal Jillian's attention that direction.

"What?" She had no idea what was the matter with him, but if he didn't shake out of it, the party of sixteen was going to be a disaster.

He shifted his eyes a second time with unmistakable insistence.

"Is he mad at me or something?" This time Jillian didn't wait for a response. When she took the shortcut behind the bar to get to Vince's office, she caught a glimpse of Casey's purse. "Are you guys kidding me? She came in after all and you didn't bother to save me a trip?" Jillian felt like punching Garrett when she walked past him.

The second she saw Vince's office door closed, Jillian knew. In that very moment she could have scripted the next scene with stunning precision. She grabbed the doorknob and tried to turn it. It was locked.

Of course it is, she said to herself, her head feeling like it would explode. She beat on the door with her fist, and when her knuckles throbbed, she banged with her palm. After what seemed to Jillian like minutes, Vince opened the door, severely annoyed. "What?" he demanded, almost shouting. From the expression on his face, Jillian was obviously the last person he expected to see. His annoyance escalated into anger.

"What, Jillian? I'm in a meeting. What are you even doing in today?" He spit the words out, offering no pause for an answer. "You're making a spectacle out of yourself. Give me a minute, will you?" Before he shut the door in Jillian's face, he looked her up and down like she disgusted him.

Jillian staggered into the kitchen, her mind whirling. Everyone but the chef scattered like mice, and he studied his saucepan as if he'd never seen onions simmer. When she heard the door of Vince's office open several minutes later, she steadied herself and stepped back into the hall, trying to muster the courage to be unavoidable. Casey emerged first and headed for the dining room. Then came Vince, as cool as a California cucumber. Jillian thought he was going to walk right past her as if she were invisible, but he didn't. He paused next to her and, without so much as a glance her direction, said, "Go home, Jillian."

Home?

He'd spoken to her like she was a child. No, worse than that. He'd spoken to her like she was a repulsive child, and loudly enough for anyone paying the mildest attention to hear. The instant he hit the dining area, he turned on the charm, stopping by tables to say hello and to ask the customers if they were being well taken care of. Jillian had never in her life met a man so smooth. If he'd offered them his palm, she was pretty sure they'd eat right out of it.

He slapped one of the regulars on the back, a big spender at Sigmund's, and called Garrett over to the table. "Make sure this man's dessert is always on the house, will you?" The customer beamed and the waiter awkwardly nodded. It was the only time Garrett's gaze met Jillian's. Maybe what she saw on his face was regret. Maybe it was pity. Maybe it was too late to make a difference to Jillian.

After Vince garnered sufficient praise, he pulled out his keys, put on his sunglasses, and walked out the door of Sigmund's like a man exiting a Broadway stage after a standing ovation. Almost instinctively, Jillian shifted her attention to Casey. The young woman watched every step Vince took toward the curb, where his car was parked, and then she carefully watched him climb inside, shut the car door, and drive off. Jillian didn't bother wondering what Casey was looking for. She'd been there too many times. She was looking to see if he'd glance back at her.

He didn't. He never looked back at either one of them.

CHAPTER 8

ADELLA CAUGHT HERSELF walking on tiptoes again through the great room at Saint Sans. She felt like she hadn't walked with her heel to that hardwood floor since the day Rafe was buried. It was as if the world within those walls was so delicately balanced that the least tremor would bring the whole thing down. They were a shattered window waiting for one faint tap to send it falling to the floor in a thousand pieces.

September had finally dragged its lazy girth through the door but with no relief from the summer swelter. That was normal this far south. A cool spell by now would have made the morning news, and if the digits dropped a lick lower than sixty even by October 1, that city full of Chicken Littles could celebrate because the sky would be falling.

Everyone at Saint Sans was in mourning, but rather than calling it what it was, they had all cloaked themselves in the sackcloth of quiet cordiality. All of them were pallbearers, bearing the weight of Rafe's lifeless body, finding no fitting place to lay him to rest.

Adella had been around the block enough times to know such things happened, but she still wondered how a man could live and die on a sidewalk within one day's walking distance of this big, fancy house. Some people were just too sick to come home. Or others weren't well enough to let them.

David told her they rarely heard music wafting from Mrs. Winsee's room in the late evening, as they'd all grown accustomed to. She'd said Mr. Winsee's back was out and there had been little dancing. Caryn had made herself scarce, restricting her studies almost entirely to the Tulane Medical Library. Adella actually missed coming in on occasion in the early morning and catching Caryn cleaning up the mess of textbooks strewn over the kitchen island after an all-nighter.

The dense weight upon Adella's soul wasn't only from the death of their proprietor's son or even from his unsolved murder. It was also from the secrets. She'd never told Olivia about the cryptic card on the flowers at the grave site. Nor had she told her about the blue baby rattle she'd found on the doormat outside the back door of Saint Sans a few weeks ago. She chose to believe Clementine had dropped it there like a dead mouse. She hadn't mentioned it even to David.

Between the unsolved murder, that stupid card, and the baby rattle, Adella was herself as nervous as a cat. She looked over her shoulder every time she got in or out of the car in the dark. A woman of God knew better than to fear superstitions and omens, but this town had a way of turning anything unexplainable into something paranormal. Anyway, Adella didn't feel much like a woman of God right now. Emmett had commented on Sunday how she'd clammed up at church. All that conniving and secret-keeping had made her feel what her mama would've called sin-sick.

The only bright spot during the past weeks had been an unexpected, out-of-season cardinals' nest in the formal garden outside the great room and Olivia's suite. It had proved to be just the distraction everyone in the house needed.

When David came in after school on the day two eggs had been spied in the nest, Olivia was hovering in the den and Mrs. Winsee was fussing around the kitchen, looking for her tea bags. The afternoon sun was at just the right spot to spill every color in the large stained-glass window over the floor like water. The deep blue of the tossing waves under the disciples' boat fell in a lighter shade across Olivia's legs.

"Good afternoon, Mrs. Fontaine." David's words were directed starboard but his eyes shot toward Adella, who raised her eyebrows to show equal bafflement.

"Afternoon, David. Have you heard we have new boarders?"

"Caryn's leaving? Where is she going? And right in the middle of a semester?"

"Caryn's not going anywhere, at least as far as I know." Adella took it upon herself to explain. "Mrs. Fontaine is talking about a nest of cardinal eggs right there in the formal garden."

David made an odd face. "In autumn?"

"Well, now, aren't we all quite the bird experts in this house?" Olivia looked unusually pleased with herself and had become so conversational that Adella wondered if she was nipping on a little something in her room.

A voice from the kitchen: "Surely it would come as no surprise to any of you that a pair of doves was released into a perfect blue sky from a gilded cage at the garden wedding reception of Mr. and Mrs. Waylon Randall Winsee III."

"No surprise at all, Mrs. Winsee. I can only imagine the

romance of it all," David replied, walking over to the window to see the nest for himself.

"And you know they mate for life, don't you, dear David?" Still Mrs. Winsee and, with that, she giggled and for just a moment her deep-rose lip pencil appeared to align with her lips. She joined him at the window, tea sloshing into the saucer.

Olivia had stood next to them, clicking the nail of her index finger on the glass. "Right there. Do you see it?"

"I hate to spoil the party, you three, but if you want that mother to come back to those eggs, you better move away from that window. The last thing you want is for her to abandon that nest."

And just like that, it happened. Like she'd jinxed it by speaking it. Adella was supposed to be off today but she couldn't keep from going to Saint Sans to save her life. It had been twenty-four hours, and if the mother bird had not returned, she was sure the two speckled eggs were lifeless by now.

"Adella, what are you doing here?"

She caught Olivia off guard and in her housecoat in the kitchen. She rarely ever emerged from her quarters without being neatly manicured from head to toe. She wasn't fancy per se, but she well surpassed presentable. Her makeup was understated but always in place and her earrings were small but never missing. And almost never cheap, at least as far as Adella could tell. Adella had only ever seen Olivia barefoot that one time, drunker than Cooter Brown in Rafe's bed. Of course, she wasn't barefoot now but her slippers said it all.

"Well, I just wanted to see what supplies we were running low on. I'm headed to the supermarket for my own family and I might as well pick up the things we need here."

"Suit yourself." Olivia turned and walked down the hall without a passing glance to the left for a roll call in the camellia bush. That should have been all Adella needed to know but she headed to the window the second Olivia's door closed. Two speckled eggs. Nothing more.

To make less a liar of herself, Adella checked the cabinets in the laundry room for cleaning supplies. "It's just nature's way anyhow. Isn't there enough to worry about with humans? That oldest boy of yours, for instance. Does he or does he not have a midterm biology exam today and has he or has he not made every excuse for why he can't concentrate? ADHD, he says. I'm going to give him a dose of ADHD, alright, with a knot on his head."

"Adella, are you talking to yourself again? Tsk, tsk, tsk. Do you answer yourself, too?" It was Mrs. Winsee sweeping past her in the hall. Well, if that wasn't the pot calling the kettle black. Things were obviously worse for Adella than she feared. It was the change of life, and day after tomorrow she guessed she'd no longer remember where she worked. That might be a relief.

"Your hair looks nice, Mrs. Winsee. That's a good shade for your skin tone." Adella had barely seen it out of the corner of her eye, but she had the manners to be kind to the elderly and nothing made Mrs. Winsee happier than a compliment. Maybe it was a tender mercy of God that the old woman saw someone wholly different in her vanity mirror. Not a different person really. Just another era.

"Well, Mr. Winsee would have me blonde again if he could. You know how men are. But I think Hint of Chestnut goes best with my naturally dark eyebrows."

Adella knew those hadn't been naturally dark eyebrows in three round decades, but the way things were going, she might bleach her own hair blonde next week. Then it would all break off the next. She added Pine-Sol to her list as Mrs. Winsee chattered away in the great room. Adella had overheard her talking to her dead husband no few times but this was the first time she'd heard her talk to her dearly departed mother. "Poor, lost thing," she murmured, shaking her head. "Lord, let me keep my mind."

Adella pitched down her pen. "Wait a minute." She spun around the corner, where she could see Mrs. Winsee and concentrate on what she was saying.

"Where have you been, Mommy? We've been watching for you!"

Adella nearly tripped over her own feet making her way to Mrs. Winsee, a yard shy of the window. "Well, I'll be a striated pardalote," Adella whispered. "Would you look at that?" There she was, feathers bristled as big as she could get them, two speckled eggs hidden from sight, snuggled safe and sound underneath.

Before Adella walked out the back door to finally have a decent day off, she picked up the pen, tore the blank part of the page off her grocery list, scratched two words on it, and slipped it under Olivia's door:

She's back.

Adella was right there in the aisle between the kidney beans and the sweet relish when it happened. Without a hint of notice, tears squirted from her eyes like she was shooting a water gun. She couldn't stop herself. Her whole head drained like a tub. She felt a howl coming from her inner regions, like she was about to bay like a hound—and all this over a pair of eggs no bigger than thimbles. She tried to fend it off with a snort just as a woman turned the corner sharply with her grocery cart and stared at her.

Adella snatched the wax paper from Emmett's apple fritter, blew her nose into it, and cried, "Will these prices ever break? A dollar seventeen for a can of shoepeg corn? Criminals, all of them!"

The woman hugged the pickle shelf as tight as she could as she moved past Adella and on down to dairy. The condition she was in, Adella felt it the better part of wisdom to wait on those two dozen eggs even if they were on special. Maybe the chicken livers weren't a good idea either.

As she unloaded groceries from the plastic bags onto her kitchen counter, Adella was at a complete loss about what a woman could conjure up for supper from this ugly conglomeration. She glanced into the refrigerator to make sure she had some fresh mayo. At the welcome sight of it she said, "BLTs. They'll love 'em. Thank you, Jesus."

"Is it safe to come into the house this afternoon?" Emmett was peeking around the door with a grin so sheepish and handsome, Adella couldn't even play mad.

She'd flown all over him that morning for poking fun at her for activating the church prayer chain over eggs. "Here's you a pair of eggs to pray about!" she'd said and commenced scorching his over easies in the iron skillet until the kitchen smelled to high heaven.

She and Emmett had tied the knot five years ago in a real, live church with a bona fide minister. All day long she'd said, "If I'm dreamin', nobody better wake me up." And no one had. Adella had known her share of heartache, but over the last several years—even swimming in the hormones of two teenage boys—she'd been about as happy as anyone she knew. And she'd tell you she was blessed if you'd listen.

Now the man grabbed her up in a bear hug so tight, she'd have stayed there all night had the boys not come in right behind him. "I found a couple of scallywags on a corner and brought 'em home with me. They threatened to starve before I could get them home, so I was held at gunpoint until I pulled into the Circle K." The oldest boy was plenty old enough to drive, but Adella was of the mind-set that a kid would make it to destruction slower if he had to walk there. She'd have to give in soon, but it wouldn't be this week.

Each of her sons strutted toward the refrigerator with a king-size bag of corn chips under an arm. With "Hey, Mama!" flecks flew from both mouths. Soda cans popped open simultaneously.

"Have those teeth been brushed this year?" Adella asked as she kicked the refrigerator shut. She held their faces in her palms one at a time and kissed each one on the cheek with a loud smack.

"I know I brushed mine in April for my birthday!" quipped the younger, and all four of them laughed.

"I tried calling you a couple of times, Dell. You had me worried."

That was the first Adella had thought about her cell phone in a couple of hours. She told him where all she'd been as she dug around in her purse for it. "Four missed calls! Emmett Atwater, since when did you start stalking me?"

"Since when does two phone calls qualify as stalking?"

"Three voice mails? I never even heard it ring. Pipe down so I can listen to them."

Adella waved for Emmett to hush as he said, "One's from me."

She could barely believe her ears. She was shaking her head, still stunned, as she set her cell phone on the counter.

"Who was it, Dell?"

"Jillian Slater. Twice. Needs me to call her right away. Lord, she sounds awful."

"Well, what on earth did she say?" Emmett pried.

"Please."

CHAPTER 9

"Now, LET ME SEE if I understand what you're telling me."

In less than three hours, Adella was looking at Jillian across the kitchen table. The smell of maple bacon still floated through the room even with the skillet scrubbed clean. "You and your boyfriend had a fight. Hold on a second." She twisted in her chair and yelled, "Emmett, you and those boys get that confounded TV turned down! I cannot hear myself think! And all this noise with company in the house!" Turning back to Jillian, she continued, "And instead of taking a break for a few days and refusing to see him, you hopped on a plane all the way to New Orleans."

She wanted to throw in an additional "Did you change your mind about a city full of 'cavemen'?" But she had to admit the young woman looked a bit haggard, and who knows, maybe she really did misunderstand the word *Cajun*. She settled for offering to make a cup of tea to busy Jillian's hands before she plucked that lock of hair right off the back of her neck.

"I guess that could be good. Do you have a white loose leaf? It settles me down and helps me center."

"Uh, no. I am fresh out of loose leaf." It was a good thing strings weren't longer on tea bags. "But I have chamomile. Or how about some Sweet Dreams blend?" She pulled out several boxes and set them on the counter. "I'd say you could stand to relax."

Jillian agreed to give it a try and Adella lit the flame under the kettle. "Honey, tell me something. How long were you planning to stay? You surely have little more than nothing in that bag."

"I left in a hurry and didn't really get to pack."

"And headed to the airport?"

"Yes."

"With no plane reservations and no idea when the next flight was?"

Jillian hesitated before she answered. "That's right."

"Why? Can you help me with that?" Adella had no intention of letting up until she got the full story.

"Because I didn't want him to catch me."

"And by *him* you mean . . . ?"

"Vince. His name is Vince." From Jillian's expression, she hadn't counted on this kind of interrogation. She took a deep breath and started talking. "Garrett, one of the waiters at Sigmund's—that's where I work—called me yesterday afternoon. He said Vince wanted me to get down there right away. I was annoyed but I went anyway. Our loft isn't far from the restaurant."

"Your loft or his? Or by *ours* do you mean yours and a roommate's?"

"Mine and Vince's! I'm trying to explain what happened, but you're getting me off track. It's his loft, really. I've been living there with him. He pays for it."

Oh, I bet he's not the only one. Adella followed the thought with the words "Okay, I'm getting the picture." Adella felt conviction well up in her. She knew better than to cast a stone. She well remembered herself at that age and could only imagine where she'd be today if not for Jesus and Emmett Isaiah Atwater. Emmett was a man who still believed in marriage. A man who believed in a woman and her two fatherless sons. Believed in them enough to navigate the boys' stormy preadolescent years with the patience of Job, taking it slow until they accepted him.

She softened and said, "I've been there. No condemnation here. Go on ahead with your story."

Jillian looked at her with confusion and Adella realized *condemnation* wasn't even in the young woman's vocabulary. Adella urged her again, waving off the distraction. "Go on, now, child."

Adella had no idea where this was going, and she remembered right then that she hadn't asked that boy of hers how his biology test had gone. Eventually Jillian got to the point, something about her boyfriend fooling around with another waitress in his office. "Are you sure something shady happened? Sure it wasn't really a meeting?"

"Uh, yeah, I'm sure. I was the one in that office less than a year ago. I thought Casey was my friend, too! She's the one who covered my shift when I came here in June. Now I know why. She's not even that great-looking."

"I'm not sure it's always about great looks, but I do hear what you're saying and that's not how a good man treats his woman. There's no denying that. What did Vince say to you?"

"He said, 'Go home, Jillian.' Like I was the one who had done something wrong. Then he took off."

"And so that's when you decided to fly here? I don't necessarily think that's a bad thing. I'm just trying to get the sequence of events straight." Adella set the young woman's tea in front of her.

"Well, yeah. I made it to Houston late last night but then I spent the night in the airport." Jillian held the warm mug with both her hands just under her chin and stared into it.

"You spent the night in the airport?" This woman surely made life harder than it had to be.

"Yes."

"You couldn't go back to the loft because you didn't want to run into Vince, right?"

"Right." Jillian set down the mug, put her elbows on the table, and rubbed her face. Adella wondered for a moment if the young woman was going to cry, but when she lifted her chin, her eyes weren't cloudy.

"What about your mother? If I'd been you, I'd probably have saved myself all this trouble and gone to my mama's house." Both boys walked into the kitchen with expressions a mother could read faster than a magazine cover. "May I help the two of you?"

"We're thirsty."

"Both of you?"

"Yes, ma'am." What they were was lovesick—or as lovesick as two teenage boys could get over a darling, mysterious female visitor in one short evening. Something about a slightly older woman who was a planet out of their reach could make a pair of boys act like the biggest fools. From the smell of things, Adella could have sworn one had even shaved, and not the one that needed to, either.

"Get you some water and go then." Adella tapped her fingers on the table while they hemmed and hawed. "And don't drink too much. I'm not in the mood for any of that bed-wetting tonight." That did it. They didn't show their faces in the kitchen again all evening. Adella heard Emmett in the den bust out with a laugh and then turn it into a cough as both boys passed him by, muttering all manner of offense. She worked to keep from grinning.

"Your mother, Jillian. We were talking about why you didn't go to your mother's."

Jillian paused a moment before answering. "Vince would have known I was there."

"Would that have been so terrible? I'm thinking men would have left me alone at my mother's. Of course, my mother was the kind that would get a frying pan after an unwanted guest and all the faster if it was still hot, but most mothers would give their daughters haven from a madman, wouldn't they?" Adella knew she'd crossed the boundaries of most acquaintances, but this was the best story she'd heard since her goddaughter got saved.

"I didn't want to stay there. That's all. It's the first place he'd look. There or at Allie's. I didn't even call Allie. She's my other friend. She doesn't work at Sigmund's. She's jealous of Vince anyway and I don't want to hear all that right now. Jade—my mom—wouldn't have been all that excited to have me land in on her. She would have told me to do what it took to keep him. Anyway, she likes her privacy, and we free each other to live our own lives."

Both of them sat quietly for a moment, Jillian rubbing her index finger along the rim of the mug. The young woman picked the conversation back up with a totally different tone. "And I don't have any money for a hotel."

"Well, sister, you probably could have stayed in a hotel for a solid two weeks while this all blew over on what you just spent for a same-day flight halfway across the country."

With that, Jillian stood up from the table and said, "I knew I shouldn't have called you. I thought maybe I'd misjudged. I'll call a cab. I can stay at that same old motel by the airport . . . if it hasn't been condemned." She picked up her bag and fished out her cell phone.

"Oh, no, no, Jillian. I'm sorry. I didn't mean any offense. I was just being nosy. I'm glad you called me. You did the right thing.

I don't know what's going to happen, but things like this have a way of working out."

Jillian looked off into the distance through the kitchen window.

Adella had no choice at all. She had to say it. "But I think you remember all the trouble I got in with your grandmother for lying about you last time. It's a wonder I still have a job. I have a room for you tonight. A good soft bed and a hot shower. But in the morning, I've got to go over to Saint Sans and talk to Olivia."

Adella knew something was off when Jillian nodded and said, "Okay."

CHAPTER 10

OLIVIA'S HANDS WERE FOLDED on the table, her gaze boring such a hole through them that Adella wondered how they didn't catch fire. Adella resisted the urge to oversell the point. She'd said what she came to say and now Olivia needed to think.

Adella didn't have a single notion how the whole thing would go. She could be talking her employer—and, despite the last few months, her friend—into a center-stage production of *Family Nightmare: The Next Generation*.

"Here? It has to be *here*?" Olivia asked.

Adella needed to choose her words carefully and rein in any negative attitude or excessive emotion. Either of those would elicit an automatic *no*. "Well, she doesn't have money for a hotel and, needless to say, she lost her job. She literally brought the clothes on her back and a couple of shirts she bought in the airport."

"I have money," Olivia stated matter-of-factly.

"Yes, you do, and that's one option. You could pay for temporary lodging."

"Or I could pay you to keep her."

"Olivia, you're not boarding a pet." *Easy, Adella Jane.* "Whether or not she can admit it or even consciously think it, she's here in New Orleans because you're here. You're the only family she's got."

"I most certainly am not. She has Jaclyn."

"Who's Jaclyn? Are you saying there's another relative around here?"

"No, Adella. She has a mother." The disdain on Olivia's face was impossible to miss. "Jaclyn." She said the name the way Clementine would cough up a hairball.

"You mean Jade?"

"No, I mean Jillian's mother. Jaclyn!" Her face was turning red.

"Sorry. I'm new to the family tree. Jillian called her mother Jade."

"Oh, so it's Jade now, is it? That figures. It must suit her most recent persona. I seem to recall her insisting at one point years ago that we all call her Jac-*leeeen*."

Adella's curiosity roused but she'd hold it off until another time. If she didn't get this conversation refocused on Jillian, they'd get nowhere. "How about a week? Invite her to stay for a week. That wouldn't be so bad, would it?"

Olivia took that intense stare of hers and shifted it right to Adella's face like a spotlight from a prison tower exposing an escapee. "Would I have to eat with her?"

You have got to be kidding, Adella thought. *We're back in elementary school and it's nearly lunchtime in the cafeteria.* "What do you have against this child? Can you just tell me that?"

Another round of interminable silence. *Don't speak, Adella. Make her answer you.*

But she didn't. All she said was "Okay. Let her come."

"Are you going to be decent to her?" Adella had lost her patience and, right about then, couldn't care less if she lost her job with it.

"For one week." Then Olivia stood, smoothed her pant legs, and walked out of the room.

Adella decided not to sugarcoat to Jillian what she could expect at Saint Sans as they headed uptown. As much as she hated to, she decided that the only way to spare the child in the long run was to alert her to the dim forecast. She took a deep breath, looking straight ahead, both hands squarely on the steering wheel. "You have the room for a week. I wish it were longer, but don't you think that will buy you a little time to think?"

"That's fine." Staring out the passenger window, Jillian continued, "I'll keep my distance. No trouble."

"I wish I could say I didn't think that was a good idea. But as it is, yes, I think the more you look at this offer as simply a free room where you can have a little quiet and hear your own thoughts for a week, the easier you'll get through it. This is not 'Over the river, and through the wood, to Grandmother's house we go.'"

"I know." The young woman sounded worn and weary. Adella had hoped she'd get a good night's sleep in that guest room bed at Emmett's and her home, but the mattress was as old as Methuselah.

"You know what, Jillian? The temperature might be a bit on the cool side at Saint Sans, but that bed in the room where you'll be staying is heaven on springs. You're not going to want to get out of it."

Not a word.

"And don't feel the need to make your flight arrangements back to San Francisco right away. Let your head clear a bit. You can come back to my house for a day or two when your week is up . . .

if you think you can stand the smell of aftershave." Adella was hoping for a smile.

"I don't have any money, Adella. I told you that last night. I don't have a way to buy a return ticket. I'll spend the week trying to think of where to go and how to get some work."

Adella wondered what in God's creation the girl had done with the money she made from a full-time job and no rent, but those kinds of questions needed to wait awhile. First things first. They needed to survive the move-in.

When they pulled into the driveway of Saint Sans, Adella reached into the backseat. "Jillian, I took the liberty of bringing those pajamas I lent you last night. I know they nearly swallowed you whole, but jammies that fit tight are no fit jammies at all. On the way back to get you, I ran by Penney's, and well, I got you these."

Jillian opened the bag to look inside.

"It's unders." Adella stated the obvious. "White ones. I just went with your basic white. I guessed at the size—"

"Thank you, Adella." For the first time all day, Jillian postured herself toward Adella. "I appreciate what you're trying to do." She didn't hand them back to her and Adella took that as a good sign.

And just like that, Adella would've emptied out her checking account for Jillian if she hadn't been up to her eyeballs in sons and house payments. "How about tomorrow we go grab you several changes of clothes and some groceries?" she asked as they walked to the back entrance. "Emmett gave me some mad money, and I can't think of anything I especially want right now. You won't need to spend a dime. Oh, and you have a small kitchenette in the room, but the boarders also have access to the main kitchen. As long as they clean up after themselves." She just couldn't leave off that last part, no matter how weak she was feeling, or she'd be washing the dishes at Saint Sans three times a day before the weekend was out.

Adella pulled out her key to open the guest room door and

realized it wasn't locked. She opened the door, smiled at Jillian, and said, "After you, young lady."

"Adella?"

"Yes, honey?"

"Is there not an empty room down there in the other wing, where the rest of them are?"

Who could blame her for not wanting to be just across the library foyer from Olivia? "I'm afraid not. The house is full to capacity. You haven't met the others yet, but Caryn is a med student at Tulane and she's in 3A. David is in 2A, you may remember. He's the high school choral teacher. And we try to keep Mrs. Winsee a little closer. She's in 1A. There are five suites in all. Of course, Mrs. Fontaine's is a bit more like a traditional one-bedroom apartment. Her part is the biggest." Adella was so peeved at her right that moment that she refused to insult Jillian by referring to her as *grandmother*. "Originally, this was a freestanding parsonage, but during the remodel it was attached to the main building."

"All well here?"

Adella nearly jumped out of her skin. Olivia was standing at the door. She wasn't exactly smiling, but she also didn't look like she was about to rip somebody's gizzard out.

"Yep," Adella answered, "I'd say so. I was just telling her who all lives in the house."

"Yes, I heard you. Thank you, Adella." A pause, then, "Jillian, how are you?"

"Fine." She wasn't rude. Just uninformative, an instinct she must have inherited.

"Wooooeeeee, look at the time! I better get to it!" Adella wasn't sure what "it" was, but it had to be better than hanging on to two icicles with sweaty palms.

"I'm sure Jillian has better things to do than talk to two old women anyway," Olivia commented.

Adella had to twist her tongue into a pretzel not to say, "Yeah? Like what?"

"Oh, one more thing." Olivia looked at Jillian but pointed her question to Adella. "She'll know not to make much commotion by the windows, won't she?"

CHAPTER 11

JILLIAN DECIDED TO VENTURE OUT of her suite on the third evening of her week at Saint Sans and make use of the laundry facilities. She emerged to find David with a young black woman who couldn't have weighed 105 pounds soaking wet and the palest old woman she'd ever seen. All three had their backs against the wall in the hallway and were peeking around the edges of two windows at a spot in the garden.

"Jillian! Finally!" David blurted out in a loud whisper, motioning her to his side of the window. "The mom's flown the coop for a minute. You've got to look while you can! Have you seen them yet?"

Jillian shook her head. She followed the direction of his index finger until her gaze landed in the middle of a perfectly shaped nest only a couple of feet from the glass. The setting sun reflecting off the deep-green leaves served as a spotlight on its miniature contents.

"Ohhhhh. Wow."

"Mother calls them Virginia nightingales," the elderly woman whispered.

"But we call them Egg A and Egg B, don't we, David?" said the younger woman.

"That's a fact. And we don't know which is which. Jillian, meet Caryn. The phantom of Saint Sans. She only comes out after dark." Caryn grinned and shoved him. "Think of her as our resident vampire."

"Hey, Jillian. I've heard a lot about you." Caryn started to extend her hand but Jillian kept her arms wrapped tightly around her small pile of laundry. So the elderly woman must be Mrs. Winsee.

"When will they hatch?" Jillian asked in a whisper.

"I looked it up," David explained, "and they incubate for just under two weeks, so we're figuring sometime next week." Jillian's seven days would be up before then.

"David's all into it," Caryn said with a grin.

"She's right. It's pathetic."

"Looks to me like you're all pretty into it." Jillian barely got the words out of her mouth before Mrs. Winsee grabbed her by the arm and pulled her close, spilling the pajamas Jillian had borrowed from Adella onto the floor.

The elderly woman put her icy hand underneath Jillian's chin and raised it several inches. "See there in that tree, Jaclyn? Right there on that branch, as red as a geranium? That's the daddy. He's guard over the garden till those babies die or fly."

Jillian broke away from her and reached down for the pajamas. "My name is Jillian. Excuse me. I need to get some things in the wash if no one else is using it."

"I've gotta get back to the books anyway, y'all." Caryn followed Jillian down the hall and then on past her as Jillian entered the laundry room.

When she walked back through the kitchen, David greeted her again. "Jillian, how are you doing? What brings you back to New Orleans?"

Jillian wasn't sure she wanted to answer, even if she'd known what to say. Instead she changed the subject. "That old woman creeps me out."

"Which one?" David looked perplexed.

It wasn't until then that Jillian noticed Olivia sitting in a white wrought-iron chair on the back lawn near the trellis. Her back was to the house and Clementine was rubbing against her right ankle while Olivia scratched the tabby's head. She had a fan in her left hand, steadily cooling herself with it. The sight of someone using a folding hand fan that was anything more than a stiff piece of paper on a Popsicle stick was foreign to Jillian. This was a real one. A black one at that.

"Midsixties gets younger to me all the time," David was saying, "so Mrs. Fontaine's not exactly what I'd call old, but to you, I'm sure she's ancient. What are you, midtwenties?"

Jillian gave a noncommittal half nod.

"But I'm guessing you mean the much older of the two. Mrs. Winsee." He chuckled. "She's harmless. Wait till you get to know her. She's actually pretty fascinating."

"She's crazy. And scary-looking."

David smiled warmly. "I wouldn't say she's crazy. I'd just say she spends a fair amount of time in a parallel universe. You'll like her in no time. Just see if I'm right about that. Hey, I'm starving. What are you planning to have for supper? If I order a pizza, would you eat some of it?"

She paused to consider. "If it was whole wheat crust maybe. Paper thin. Is their vegetable pizza organic?"

David's eyebrows rose. "Well, I tell you what. I'll just call them up and ask them."

"That's okay. I've got some pepper salmon and tabouli in the freezer. I think I'll just have that."

"If that's what you'd rather do, would you eat here at the counter with me after my pizza gets delivered?" When she hesitated, he added, "Listen, middle-aged man here with no ulterior motive. I hope the women around Saint Sans could tell you that I'm not a freak. Not even desperate for friends." He grinned. "Just offering some supper conversation."

Jillian shrugged. "I guess."

Since she refused to use the microwave, she pulled her frozen meal out of the oven piping hot within a few minutes of David's pizza delivery. The Canadian bacon and pineapple hand-tossed pizza was deliciously aromatic. She blinked toward it with every bite of tabouli.

"You sure you don't want a slice, Jillian? It's more than I can eat."

"I'm sure. This is great. Just what I wanted." She'd scattered so many flakes of peppered salmon over her plate that, if a gust of wind had blown through the house, fish would have flown like feathers. By the time thirty minutes turned to ninety, Jillian had not succumbed to a single slice of pizza, but she'd eaten every bite of crust left in the cardboard box.

Wonder of wonders, Olivia stopped by the kitchen island while the two of them were eating. All she said was "It looks like the two of you are getting along famously." That neither one of them knew how to respond was a moot point because Olivia patted the corner of the granite counter, said, "Well, good then. Good night," and proceeded to her room.

Jillian emerged from her room at nine the next morning with her purse over her shoulder. David had insisted that she visit Jackson Square before her week was up. "What do you mean, you've never been? You can't say you've landed in New Orleans if you haven't stepped foot in the French Quarter, Jillian."

He'd jotted down exactly where to get off the trolley and then how far to walk. Jillian needed to get out of these four walls anyway. Maybe some fresh air would help her figure out what to do next.

Adella was nowhere to be found, and Jillian's stomach sank when she saw Olivia in the kitchen with her back to her. She knew there was no way to escape without being noticed, so she did what any grown-up would do. She feigned a cough.

"Well, Jillian. Look who's here." Since clearly no one else was in sight, Jillian supposed Olivia was talking to Jillian about Jillian. How was she supposed to respond to that?

"Yes, it's me alright," she answered with all the naturalness of a plastic knife.

"I was just steeping some coffee. May I pour you a cup on your way out? I can see you're in a hurry. I won't keep you." With the quick draw of the time boundary, Jillian wanted in the worst way to say no, but Olivia's wide sleeve seemed to catch a waft of coffee and sweep it across the room so delectably that she caved.

Olivia's expression betrayed her bafflement at Jillian's assent. "Well, now," the older woman said, walking over to the large, open pantry. "I wonder where Adella keeps those Styrofoam cups she sends Caryn to class with?"

"Actually, I don't drink out of Styrofoam." She'd be darned if she'd let Olivia cross her convictions, but still Jillian was determined to have what was in that glass pot if she had to drink it out of scalded palms. "I have a moment. I'll just take a regular mug if that's okay."

Olivia looked at Jillian starkly, blinked a few times, and answered, "Yes, of course. Now, let's see." With this she reached up and opened a cabinet full of carefully placed cups and saucers of various delicate patterns.

When Jillian heard the sound of the china cup clicking rapidly against the saucer, she knew Olivia's hand was shaking and decided to soften a bit. "That smells good."

"A coffee drinker, are you?" Olivia's question seemed sincere enough.

"Oh yeah. I can't remember when I wasn't. Mom said she used to pour it into my baby bottles when I'd drained the milk and cried for more."

"Good mom, sounds like."

Was that sarcasm Jillian heard in her voice? She didn't know whether to take offense or to say, "Thank you, she was."

"It's all in the precise roasting. Ground coffee should be outlawed," Olivia declared, looking as if she might actually shiver. "Whole beans only, ground to perfection no sooner than the water is boiling. There's never been a drip coffeemaker in this kitchen. Never will be, not as long as I have my right mind. I've come close a few times to getting one of those expensive machines, but then again, I'd miss the French press. I still achieve a fair enough crema and it makes coffee the perfect weight. Heavy. Just like the cream." Olivia laughed, deep and throaty like maybe she'd been a heavy smoker at some point. "For supreme enjoyment, fine coffee should only be poured into a thin-lipped cup like this one. Mugs belong in diners. But that should go without saying."

Jillian's eyes bugged. She had no idea Olivia had that many words swirling around inside her—or that much passion about anything. And never mind that the Bride of Chucky had just chuckled. Before Jillian could object to the calories, Olivia pulled a carton of whipping cream out of the refrigerator and poured what looked like a full ounce of the white gold into a cup of coffee as dark and thick as mud. Without stirring it, she presented it to Jillian on a silver tray with china handles that matched the cup and saucer. Jillian reached for a spoon.

"Ah, no, no, mademoiselle," Olivia said as she tapped Jillian's hand with a mock reprimand, touching her for the first time, if only with the tips of two fingers.

It was love at first sip. And it was everything Jillian could do not to say so. Sigmund's boasted its own special house roast and made a small fortune selling it by the half pound. She'd consumed gallons of it as she'd waited tables there, particularly over the last six months since, for all practical purposes, she'd given up eating. But never in her life had Jillian tasted anything like the brew Olivia set before her.

After the first good swallow, she'd had to control herself from shaking her head wildly like someone who'd just thrown back a first shocking sip of bourbon. Instead, she picked up the delicate cup in the palms of both hands and cradled it like a baby until she rocked the last sip onto her tongue. She stopped just short of patting the bottom of the cup. Then she walked to the trolley stop nearly high.

The weekday morning left sparse crowds on the square that day. A handful of plein air artists speckled the sidewalk with easels. The gray spires of the St. Louis Cathedral pierced a spotless cerulean sky. The church was impressive from an architectural standpoint, but Jillian had no interest in going inside a dead monument to man's ignorance. It was enough that she was having to bum a room in a house that looked like a church. She passed the entrances to the museums David had told her about, the Cabildo and the Presbytère, but she wasn't in the mood for museum strolling.

The Mississippi River flowed thick and muddy in the mid-morning sun, lapping the bank with a faded Coke can. It was a floating parking lot to barges on the opposite shore and, on this shore, to party boats that looked like leftovers from a long-lost era. Only the bridge to the distant right bore any similarity to the San Francisco world Jillian had escaped. She did not want to be here, not on this concrete bench, not in this eccentric town.

She was in acute withdrawal from her phone, but after she'd texted her mom and told her she was going away for a little while, she'd turned it off to avoid Vince. He paid her cell bill, so it was only a matter of time until he'd have a record of every number she'd called. Her only choice was to kill it.

Jillian hated leaving Allie in the dark, and as soon as she could figure out how to get a new number, she knew she should call and tell her what had happened. Jillian was in no hurry for that phone call. It would be the biggest I-told-you-so in the history of friendship.

Have fun! That's all her mother had texted back. *I'm not having fun, Mom. Why can't you just be a normal mother for once?*

They'd always been close, but not in a typical mother-daughter kind of way. Between the hardships of single parenthood and a couple of broken marriages, Jillian's mom had been treating her like a peer as long as she could remember. On occasion, she came close to treating her like the competition. But Jillian loved her and took up for her ferociously. "She's a free spirit," Jillian always said. "She doesn't live by the rules. To her, they make you common." Jillian's high school friends had been wild about her. Nobody else's mom would let them party like that. Jillian never had the guts to tell her but she wished the surcharge wasn't her partying with them.

Blood was thicker than water, but not always thick enough to blanket every issue. Jade made pretty decent money at an art gallery in the theater district. She lived in a great condo that she'd let one man after another trash for her. She just couldn't stand to be alone. Jade had no idea who she was apart from a man. But Jillian figured no woman did.

If only she had a brother or a sister or even an aunt she could move in with for a few weeks. Or a dad. How was it possible to have so little family? Were they all inbred or what? Her mother was an only child and both of Jade's parents were dead. To her knowledge, Jillian's entire extended family consisted of one lone grandmother who put the *strange* in *estranged*.

The bronze statue of Andrew Jackson, the centerpiece of the square, caught more of Jillian's attention than anything framing the park. The appeal wasn't in the hero of the Battle of New Orleans and the War of 1812. She had her own battles to fight and no hero in sight. It was the sculpture of his horse, reared back on its hind legs, that caused her to stare upward, blocking her eyes from the sun. Horses had fascinated her as a young girl, but as a woman dwarfed below the monument, all she could think about was being caught underneath that horse when its front hooves hit the ground.

Jillian had been too lost in her thoughts to see the bum wander up to the concrete bench where she was sitting. "Dat ol' man river."

"What?" she asked, startled.

"He mus' know sumpin', but don't say nuthin'. He jes' keeps rollin', he keeps on rollin' along." The man stood close enough to touch her, but his gaze was unfocused. She could see the dirt under the fingernails on his huge hands.

"I don't know what you're talking about, mister." Her heart was pounding.

"Spare a few bucks fo' a man down on his luck?"

"Oh, Crawley, get on out of here. You are scaring that girl to death." The middle-aged woman seemed also to come out of nowhere, but Jillian was so relieved to see her, she could have hugged her.

"Here," the woman said, pulling a couple of wadded dollars out of her shoulder bag. "Go get your breakfast." She stuffed the money in the man's hand, looking at him like he was more of a nuisance than a threat.

He grunted and limped off, saying, "Ah gits weary an' sick of tryin'. Ah'm tired of livin' and skeered of dyin'.'."

"Don't mind him." The welcome stranger smiled at Jillian. "He's harmless."

"You know him?" Jillian asked.

"Oh, he's been around here for years. The cops occasionally shoo these guys off, but eventually they all make their way back to their corners."

"Is he homeless?"

"Well, if you asked him, he'd probably tell you that you were sitting in his home and on his couch right this minute."

When Jillian jumped up from the bench, the stranger laughed and asked, "Where on earth are you from, girl?"

"California. Actually San Francisco." Jillian was still clutching her purse and glancing over her shoulder.

"Huh. You look like you're from here. Look like you could have been raised here."

"Well, I wasn't. I'm Californian. I still live there. I'm just here for—"

"You sure you couldn't lay a little Creole on me?"

The woman's forwardness began to make Jillian antsy.

"Oh, now, don't go getting offended. That would be a compliment to a lot of people around these parts." She stuck her hand out. "My name is Stella. And who might you be, Miss San Francisco?"

Jillian didn't want to tell her, but she couldn't think quickly enough to avoid it. "I'm Jillian." She wished she hadn't seen the woman's hand touching the homeless man before she shook it.

"Come on. I'll buy you a cup of coffee."

Perhaps Jillian had been alone so much she was desperate for company. On the other hand, maybe this woman Stella was so forceful that she couldn't say no. Whatever the reason, in less than three minutes they were sitting in a large, open-air café right on the corner of the square.

"Two café au laits," Stella said to the waitress. For a flashing moment, the woman's brashness reminded Jillian of Vince. He almost never asked her what she wanted. He just ordered for her and it annoyed her. "You hungry, Jillian? Want an order of beignets?"

"Maybe I'll glance at the menu." Jillian might have let Stella get away with ordering her coffee, but she intended to decide on her own food.

Stella laughed. "Jillian, beignets *are* the menu. That's all they've got. See the name? Café Beignet. Do you want some or not?"

Jillian glanced around the restaurant and saw small mounds of powdered sugar on several tables that hadn't been cleared and shoe prints caked in dusts of it on the concrete floor. "No thanks. I'm not hungry."

The coffee wasn't bad, but it sure wasn't Olivia's. The company turned out considerably better, however. To a slight degree, the woman on the other side of that round Formica table resembled Jade. Her hair was brown but streaked with highlights that hadn't been retouched in a good three inches. It was long, naturally curly, and wild, like it hadn't had a brush through it in months. The look was intentional, of course, and as far as Jillian was concerned, it worked. Stella looked the part of this gritty rectangle called Jackson Square.

Stella was striking in a mysterious sort of way, but she had a rough edge to her. She wore a colorful ankle-length gauze skirt, a tube top, and lots of costume jewelry. Jade was more refined and her version of the same outfit would have been at least five times as expensive, but at first impression, Stella was the strong, independent free spirit that Jade pretended to be.

"So you need a place to work and a place to live." Stella summed up the story that had taken Jillian two refills, one orange juice, and one trip to the ladies' room to tell. Even then, she'd abbreviated it.

"Yeah. That's about it." Jillian twisted a curl at the back of her neck. The heat and humidity had swollen her coarse black hair to twice the size it had been when she left Saint Sans this morning.

"Well, maybe I can help you out. I live nearby—in the cheaper section, of course—but I can keep an eye out. As for a job—" Stella grinned—"ask and you shall receive." She pointed at a sign tacked on the wall close by. *Wait Staff Wanted. No Experience Needed.*

"Here?" Jillian was indignant.

"Let's see. You're a waitress who can't get a job reference because you're in trouble with your lover who also happens to be your boss and you've got no permanent address. What do you want from me here? Can you dance? The pay would be better by a long shot."

Jillian had passed enough of those seedy establishments on her walk over to the square to know exactly what Stella was talking about. "No," she said emphatically. "Yuck."

By the time Jillian caught the trolley heading back to Saint Sans, she'd filled out an application to make minimum wage peddling deep-fried dough, and she was clutching a piece of paper with a stranger's name and number on it like it was a life preserver.

CHAPTER 12

DURING THE WEEKS following the groundbreaking, the foundation was finished and the frame began to rise from the ground almost by itself, sleek and tall and taller still to the eye than it could actually be. The standing-seam metal roof, as handsome as it was, only served to condense the structure. Capping was inevitable, of course, but all the hammering hunched its shoulders somehow.

This nascent city church resembled its rural Methodist sisters in shape and, some might say, in modesty of size. Vieux Carré had yet to catch the plague of Protestantism, but on this side of town, churches of like persuasion were popping up like Louisiana cotton. Let no one claim this patch of ground was city backwash. A thriving college was only a few blocks away and one of the charter members of this fine fellowship hung his hat every weekday morning at the door of Gibson Hall. This was prime real estate, and with reputations to uphold, rural wood siding was snubbed in favor of brick, baked till the red was streaked with brown like a tongue after a chocolate drop.

The public applauded imagination in its hotels and theaters but, more often than not, found consolation and propriety in a church that looked its part. For those, Saint Silvanus delivered. Not counting the abbreviated entryway, the chapel was of typical dimension, twenty-five feet wide and fifty feet long. It was topped by a high roof, rising majestically to a twelve/twelve pitch.

Ten tall Opus Francigenum windows stretched up the walls of the chapel, five on each side, all trimmed in thick planks, painted white. With the exception of one large stained-glass picture at the front of the sanctuary, they'd opted for Queen Anne style—clear glass edged with green, red, and yellow squares that directed armfuls of antiseptic sunshine onto the laps of listeners. The arsenic-green storm shutters framing each window were ordered by necessity more than aesthestics, but they were surprisingly pleasing to the eye. A miniature pair of the same Gothic windows, shorter and squatter, were set eye level in the double cypress-wood doors.

Long before the sanctuary was finished and furnished, children boosted one another up in laced palms to peek through those front windows. Churches held mystique for children in those days. Did religious men build a place and hope God would move into it, or did they sense God there on the barren soil and try to cage him in like a wild beast? And once he was inside, did he brood there all night by himself? Eat wafers and drink wine? If a soul were brave enough to sneak over here at midnight, could he catch a glimpse of the Holy Ghost sweeping across those floors, like a white vaporous tablecloth pinched up at the center? Most children were as scared of an empty church as a cemetery after dark. But on Sundays even God seemed to play nice. The subject was moot anyway. To church they would go because their parents said so. And better to make a friend of God than a foe.

CHAPTER 13

"WHY ON EARTH didn't she apply for a job around here?" Olivia demanded of Adella, as if the woman had all the answers. Goodness knew she usually spoke as if she did.

"I don't know. Probably because the restaurants around here are upscale enough to be put off by a young adult applicant who can't supply a reference."

"So she's not planning on going back to California anytime soon?" That didn't make any sense to Olivia. These things usually blew over, and even if this one didn't, it was a big state. Jillian could live a hundred miles from the man and never lay eyes on him again. "This all seems so rash." She paused, hoping to no avail that Adella would say something. "Well, then, if she insists on staying in New Orleans indefinitely, I can get somebody over here closer to hire her. I have enough connections in this area to—"

"That's kind of you," Adella interrupted, "but you know she won't let you do that for her. And anyway, she can't afford to live remotely close to this place and you know it."

"I do not understand why her boss can't just act like a professional and let her list his restaurant as a reference."

"I don't either," Adella agreed, "but there you have it. She says she can't. Now that her week is up, I offered to let her move in with me and Emmett and the boys for a while, until she can get the money together to find a place to live. She said thanks but no thanks. I don't know what she thinks she's going to do."

"But why does she want to live here in Louisiana where she doesn't even know anybody?"

Vida Winsee burst through the door to Olivia's private quarters at just that moment, nearly scaring the life out of both of them. "Girls, hurry! In here! Quick!"

The three women came close to getting wedged in the doorframe as they scrambled into the hall like the house was on fire. Instead of finding someone asphyxiated, there was Jillian, back against the wall next to a window to the garden. Her index finger was over her mouth.

"Shhhhhh," Jillian cautioned with a smile that made her look like a shy little girl. She pointed out the window and there, no bigger than a pair of thumbnails, were two squirming creatures. If they hadn't been cradled by a nest and surrounded by pieces of cracked shell, none of them would have known they were birds.

By sundown, all six of them—Olivia, David, Vida, Caryn, Jillian, and even Adella—were hiding in the hall, taking turns peeking around windows like amateur spies. "This just beats all," Adella whispered.

David had a big pot of chili with beans simmering in no time. As he set out bowls and corn chips, he commanded, "Somebody turn down the thermostat and we'll play like a northern's blowing in!" No one was surprised when Jillian insisted on one of her own frozen meals, but she'd at least joined them in the food genre and chosen a spicy black bean burrito.

Everybody ate in the great room that night. They kept the lights off and candles lit and their voices low. Adella told them that they needed not go to extremes since the cardinals were accustomed to the regular goings-on in Saint Sans, but they'd all been hit upside the head by a happy hatching.

The chatter over supper was heavily imposed upon by every conceivable bird idiom, none of which would have been remotely funny under less auspicious circumstances. David started it when both Olivia and Vida insisted on saltines with their chili instead of corn chips. "It's clearly true. Birds of a feather flock together."

When Jillian asked Caryn why she wanted to be a doctor and she said it was all she'd ever wanted to do, Adella chimed in, "I guess you could say she's gone and put all her eggs in one basket."

Jillian was accused of crying "fowl" over the meat in the chili, and when David called her a vegan, she responded, "I'm a vegetarian, birdbrain. There's a difference."

Though Olivia didn't add much to the conversation, she did catch herself holding back a smile now and then, shaking her head over the foolishness. When Adella asked her teasingly why she didn't get herself a houseful of decent renters, she finally brought the house down. "Well, I suppose because a bird in the hand is worth two in the bush."

But Vida stole the show. "Say what you will, all of you, but it was I alone who performed in the musical *Bye Bye Birdie*."

"Oh, do tell!" David egged Vida on, clapping his hands and winking at Jillian, who was far too young to have the least familiarity with the title.

Vida stood and took the center of the room. "I played the part of Mae Peterson, Albert's mother, to rave reviews of course. It was a terrible shame that she had not one solitary solo. Everyone said so. But Mr. Winsee always maintained I could have played the part of young Kim McAfee magnificently. I memorized all her lines in the event that they might need an understudy."

Then right before their eyes, Vida did it. She cleared her throat and sang every word of "How Lovely to Be a Woman" from memory, complete with dramatic hand gestures. The only time she missed a beat was when she dropped onto the Snapdragon for theatrical effect and had considerable difficulty getting up. Once David pulled her back to her feet, she regained her momentum and brought the number to a grand finish.

"Right he was!" David exclaimed with shameless flattery but not a hint of ridicule. "Bravo, Mr. Winsee! A talent scout of the highest order."

Jillian joined in the applause, looking a little shocked, but grinning.

"Life at Saint Sans does not get better than that, Jillian Slater. If you need more than that, you'll have to pass this old house by." David was so caught up in the moment that he didn't realize the awkwardness he'd invited center stage until it was too late.

"Oh, that's right, Jillian. You're leaving soon, aren't you? Where are you headed?" Caryn inquired innocently.

"Yeah, I'm packing up. I'm going to stay with a new friend for a while." The next few minutes were loaded with questions no one in the actual loop felt prepared to answer.

Olivia cornered Adella at the kitchen sink, rinsing chili out of the bottom of the bowls. "Tell her she can stay another week. Or until she finds a place."

"You tell her!" Adella insisted in an equally strident whisper. "She won't believe it's sincere unless you tell her yourself."

"I can't."

"Yes, you can!"

"You're the house manager."

"You're the *grandmother*." Adella nearly growled the last word as she shut the back door on her way out, leaving Olivia no choice.

"Jillian?" Olivia said as she tapped the door to Jillian's suite. "Can you open the door for just a moment?"

She'd almost given up when Jillian cracked the door. When Olivia saw what her granddaughter was wearing, she almost lost her train of thought. The pajamas seemed a little out of character for a young woman with a dragonfly tattoo, but admittedly, Olivia hardly knew her. "There's no sense in you packing up all your stuff and moving two times. Why don't you just stay a little longer, until you find a more permanent place?" Olivia could feel the heat in her face and wondered at that moment why she had to make everything more difficult.

"It's not that much stuff. I can get all of it in one suitcase. Adella let me borrow one. You could be charging for this room. I have a place to land for a few days. It's fine." Jillian folded a pair of jeans and placed them on the end of the bed.

"I never charge for this room." Olivia immediately wished she hadn't said that, but she had, and Jillian looked at her for the first time since she'd opened the door. "I keep it for my own guests. I sometimes have—well, *guests*. They come and go." She had a feeling Jillian could tell she wasn't really the guest-having kind. But the girl would have to admit it was a lovely room, furnished to the last touch with antiques, the true value of which might be beyond her appreciation. "I don't need to rent this room. It's fine for you to stay a bit longer." She defaulted to her blunt side.

Her progeny returned the sentiment. "I don't need your pity."

"It wasn't pity," Olivia responded, taken a bit aback. "It was—"

"Or your guilt," Jillian interrupted.

"*Guilt?*" Her face burned hot. "And what exactly would I feel guilty about?" She was incensed, but she did not intend to give

Jillian the chance to answer the question. "Very well, then. Suit yourself. You're a grown woman."

She turned to walk across the foyer to her room.

Jillian surprised her with her next words. "Maybe a few days? If it wouldn't matter a whole lot, if I could just stay a few more days, that would really help. I should find out soon if I'm going to get hired at that donut place."

Olivia had her hand on the doorknob to her own suite, but after a moment's pause, she turned around to face her only child's only child. She saw Rafe standing there.

No, it really wasn't Rafe she saw so vividly in Jillian's face. She saw herself standing there in that doorway as if the antique mirror in that very room had been pulled into the hall and rewound forty years.

She took a deep breath as if to push something down and responded with a thin tone coming from the top of her throat, "Yes, yes, of course. I mean, no, it wouldn't matter. Please do, until you find a suitable place. That shouldn't take terribly long."

They each nodded slightly as if the strings of two puppets were held in the same set of hands. Then they simultaneously turned around and closed their doors.

CHAPTER 14

HAVING SOME OF THE PRESSURE OFF to move right away worked wonders for Jillian. She had been bluffing when she told the others she had an invitation to stay with Stella. She had planned to throw herself on the woman's mercy, but she was glad it hadn't come to that—at least not yet.

She knew Adella's offer of her guest room was sincere, but when she left Saint Sans, she wanted to make a clean break, a fresh start. She'd gotten the job at Café Beignet and was scheduled to begin the first of next week. It had crossed her mind that her enthusiasm over such an abysmal paycheck was itself pathetic. But at least it wouldn't be difficult to memorize the menu like she'd had to do before. Full order or half order? That was the only relevant question. "Of course, I'd never eat one," she declared when she told the others she'd gotten the job.

"Goes without saying!" David responded with his palms out. "Unthinkable!"

Jillian rummaged through the pantry, setting items on the counter one by one. "I'm going to show you bunch of Creoles how to eat a breakfast that won't kill you by lunch. This is what we served at Sigmund's and we couldn't keep them on the shelf. I've been craving them all week and grabbed the stuff at Langenstein's a few days ago."

"Need some help?" David asked.

"Are you kidding? And let you take the credit? I don't want a single Southerner in this kitchen. *Out.*" Over the next hour, Jillian stirred up homemade bran muffins chock-full of raisins, apple chunks, walnuts, and fresh shredded carrot. Even the dubious couldn't hold their noses high enough to escape the smell of heaven as the muffins baked. When she pulled them out of the oven, deep brown and glistening, they'd peaked a full inch and a half above the tin.

"They don't need butter," she said as Olivia set out a cold stick on a china plate.

"Maybe *they* don't, but *we* do," her grandmother replied. "A Louisianan could be thrown into septic shock from sudden butter withdrawal. We'd have to taper off slowly to avoid a seizure, but most of us would not want to risk it." Olivia, Mrs. Winsee, and even stick-thin Caryn sliced their muffins shamelessly right down the middle and stuffed them with enough butter to drip down the sides in thick golden tears. Half a stick of butter was gone before a single crumb passed a lip.

"Well, from the look of things, it must be colon-cleansing day at Saint Sans. And to think I nearly missed it." Adella had thrown open the back door and was standing behind them, a sight to behold. The usual red purse hung on her shoulder, but her top and her jeans each sported a little extra bling. She had on open-toed heels and white tissues woven between her toes to guard a fresh pedicure.

"Adella! The door!" Caryn cried out, but it was too late. Clementine flashed through the six-inch crack like she'd been a missile aimed for launch. All five of the residents nearly ran Adella down as they dashed out the door.

Jillian took stock of the situation and tried to bring some order to the chaos. "Someone head for the bush and stand guard! The rest of us, snare that cat!" And the chase was on. Domestic feline turned African cheetah, and by the time they were in hot pursuit, she'd left a cold trail.

At one point David managed to grab the end of her tail as she darted over the gate but she whipped around and bit him until he screamed like a girl. "I'm bleeding!"

"Get some hair on your chest and run, boy!" Adella shouted.

In the furor, Olivia had gone purely manic on them. One second she'd try her sweetest cat-speak to coax her companion gently into outstretched arms and the next second she'd threaten something like, "I'll have you stuffed like a Christmas hen!" and "Get over here before I get the weed-eater out after you, you glorified possum!"

Caryn flew around the house to guard the camellia bush in the formal garden and broke the necks of a whole patch of daylilies en route. She slid nearly flat to the concrete in the water feature and sent the box turtle that lived in it flying like a torpedo into the chrysanthemums. The rest of the crew darted through the gate to follow the escapee as she showed clear intent to break for the front yard and, no doubt in their frazzled minds, to bag up some fresh baby bird. By the time they got to her, she'd be stretching in the sun and picking her teeth clean with a feather.

For the briefest moment, they had her cornered in a crape myrtle by the carport, but she outsmarted them again. Instead of jumping down, shooting through the driveway, and risking a tag, Clementine shimmied up a limb, ran right over the roof, and headed straight for the garden on the opposite side of the house.

"Caryn, catch!" Mrs. Winsee hurled a small rake at the med student, who caught it like an Olympian and waved it wildly at the eave of the house where the cat was arched up and hissing.

The nest was no longer oblivious to the clatter. Both hatchlings' necks were stretched as thin as shoestrings and their beaks were wide-open, crying foul with all they could rally. The bright-red daddy was darting in and out of the scene, forsaking his usual *purdy* for a hoarse caw. And all this fuss over one confounded twelve-pound cat. Instead of heading back over the roof, Clementine launched onto the grass and streaked like lightning out of the formal garden, through the legs of her pursuers, and up the soaring oak in the front yard.

As the whole lot of them gathered at the trunk of the tree, staring up at a limb two stories high with a wild-eyed cat glued to it, Jillian noticed a patrol car pulling up and parallel parking in front of the house. It was one of the officers who had been there before—Officer La Bauve, she thought his name was.

"Well, if it isn't an angel unawares," Adella called out to him. "I am assuming policemen can still get cats out of trees or can't they, Officer La Bauve?"

"Pardon, ma'am?"

"You heard me. Can you get that cat out of the tree?"

"With all due respect, are you thinking of a fireman, ma'am?"

"Well, since I'm looking at you, I'm talking about you. Fireman, policeman, what's the difference? Public servants, aren't you? Well, we're public and we need some service."

David jumped in. "I think that cat-out-of-a-tree thing might be what they call an urban legend. But the technical difference is, a fireman has a ladder and a tree is tall. That's why I think you mean a—"

"David," Olivia interrupted, "would you be so kind as to go to the garage and get the ladder? Jillian, why don't you help him steer it around the house so he doesn't take out a window."

Before Jillian could respond, Caryn spoke up. "That's okay, Mrs. Fontaine. I'll help him."

"Officer La Bauve, I realize you're here to see me, but I can't concentrate until *that* cat is out of *that* tree overlooking *that* nest." Olivia punctuated every *that* with the directive point of her finger. "*Comprenez-vous?* Once you've gotten her down, tap on the front door. We'll wait for you inside." She called out behind her, "David, you better get him that thick pair of gardening gloves while you're at it lest she draw blood a second time today."

Officer La Bauve winced.

"Vida, come on with me. Let's get you out of this sun. You were brilliant today. All are safe and well, thanks to you." Olivia took Mrs. Winsee's arm in a rare physical gesture and escorted her toward the front door. Mrs. Winsee smiled and nodded and mumbled. Jillian had begun to suspect that Mrs. Winsee brought out the best in Olivia, almost like she owed the old woman something.

"The rest of you, come on inside. Let's leave the apprehending to the officer. It's his job to keep the neighborhood safe. And, Officer La Bauve, although I am admittedly a bit perturbed at Clementine, to be certain it will be short-lived. She is my closest companion. See to it that you do not hurt her."

Officer La Bauve seemed transfixed, staring up into the tree. Jillian and the others made it inside as far as the nearest window. "Olivia," Adella said without ever turning around, "if it's been too long since you've seen a rerun of *The Three Stooges*, you might want to get over here without meandering. Caryn must not have believed David could handle it by himself, so there she is, all eighty pounds of her, holding down one side of the ladder."

After a good bit of lengthening and posturing, head-shaking and nodding, Officer La Bauve began climbing the aluminum ladder. Since the three had no choice but to straddle the ladder over a massive tree root, Officer La Bauve's knee knocking proved only to reiterate the rocking. David was on the far side of the tree, leaving Caryn and the officer by themselves in eyeshot of the great room window.

"Now, this is a sight you don't see every day. Come look, Olivia. It's an elephant balancing on the nose of a mouse." Adella threw back her head and howled. By the time she collected herself and turned to see why Olivia hadn't joined them, there came a *tap-tap-tap* at the door. "Well, I'm sure they've gone and lost her."

Jillian opened the door to find Clementine, practically purring in Officer La Bauve's big arms, and him without a drop of blood to show for it. "Well, I'll be a monkey's uncle," Adella said when she took in the sight.

When Olivia and Officer La Bauve stepped out on the back porch to talk privately, Adella cornered David for an interrogation. "How'd he do it? That's what I'd like to know. If I'd been a bettin' woman, I'd've put my money on Clementine, not the scaredy-cat."

"You wouldn't have believed the man's skill, would she, Caryn?"

"Not in a million years!" his cohort chimed in.

"Skill?" Adella exclaimed, making the word two syllables. "He looked to have all the cat skill of an overgrown puppy. I know!" Adella started guessing. "He offered her some food. I've got it! I bet he held out the end of a Slim Jim. Cops love Slim Jims, don't they? I bet it was stuck right in his shirt pocket like a ballpoint."

"That wasn't it," David said, clearly baiting her.

"Well, for crying out loud, what was it?"

"Big Boy got about two rungs from the top, steadied himself right good, held out both his arms, and, Adella Atwater, if I'm lying I'm dying—"

"Get at it before I land you on that limb by your drawers, David Jacobs."

"Well—" the story picked back up—"he held out both his arms and he said . . ." David left Adella hanging right there long enough to clear his throat for a key change and take it up a good octave and a half. "'Heeyah, kitty, kitty! Heeyah, heeyah, kitty, kitty! Kitty, kitty, kitty, kitty, kit-tee.' And lo and behold, here she came like she was running into the arms of her long-lost love."

CHAPTER 15

"Pssssst. Adella! Come in here!" Adella heard Jillian whisper through a crack in the door as she neared the mouth of the hall. The young woman looked like she'd seen a pair of ghosts. She'd slipped away to her room as soon as Olivia had stepped outside.

"Girl, make it fast. There is no telling what on earth is happening out there on the porch between the officer and your grandmother and I've got to get someplace where I can spy on them. On second thought, maybe this is just the spot. I bet we could hear them through your window." Adella made a beeline to the plantation shutters in Jillian's room.

"I know what's happening out there, but I can't figure out how they know! How did they find out?" The girl was in an obvious panic.

"What are you talking about? Did Olivia tell you something I don't know?"

"No, she couldn't have known! I think the cop is telling her right now! The woman already hates me. She just started acknowledging that I'm even in the room. This is it. I'm going to be put out on the streets."

"Wait. I'm not getting this. Have you got some information on Rafe? Something the officer is telling her right now? But how did you—?"

"Adella, stop talking and listen to me! This isn't about Rafe. The police must have found out about the money. Oh, my gosh, I think I'm going to throw up."

"Save your throwing up and start explaining, and I don't mean maybe. What money?"

"I borrowed it from Vince when I left."

"I've got so much spinning in my head right now, it's about to hurl my wig into the neighbor's yard like a Frisbee. Let me see if I can change tracks here and follow. You borrowed some money from what's-his-name. So what?" Adella was confused and a little perturbed over the timing. "But I'm trying to picture you borrowing money from the man right after he betrayed you. I'm assuming this happened before your last day of work."

"No, it actually happened that day. And, well, that's the thing. I didn't exactly borrow it. I took it. I sort of—"

"Whoa, Nellie, sister. You stole it? You stole money from your boyfriend?" She took Jillian by the arm and sat her down on the bed, positioning herself in front of her like a nose tackle across from a center. She bent over and looked into her eyes for a few seconds. When she knew she had the young woman's attention, she took the classic Adella stance: hands on hips, feet about twelve inches apart, and heels sunk into the floor like they were melded an inch deep into concrete.

The tissue woven between the toes on Adella's newly pedicured left foot hadn't survived Clementine's hegira, but the one on her right foot wasn't liable to go anywhere soon. One end was adhered to the fresh nail polish on her big toe, and as she patted her foot impatiently, the rest of it dangled like a slightly crumpled white streamer. "Do you think I'm standing here for my circulation, child?"

"I was so mad. I wasn't thinking. I knew where he kept cash in his office drawer because I'd seen him pull out small stacks so many times. I also knew where he hid a key to it." Jillian's tanned neck was beginning to splotch with crimson.

"Okay, now, let's think really straight here." Adella puckered her lips and shoved them to the right for a few seconds to help her concentrate. "So that means you didn't just take money from your boyfriend. Technically, you took it from your boss. How much did you take, Jillian? It couldn't have been that much."

"All that was in there."

"And how much was that?"

"A thousand dollars."

Adella dropped onto the side of the bed. "Keep going."

"I was so upset, I couldn't even think. I mean, he'd been locked away in that very office with my friend not ten minutes earlier where they were—"

Adella waved her hand quickly. "I do not care to know what they were doing. And you don't know for certain either, so let's just move on with the story and invite all our vain imaginations right on out of this."

"After he sped off, I was stunned. And I felt stupid. I didn't know what to do. I wanted to get back at him. But you can't go head-to-head with Vince. He's scary and cold when he's mad. That stack of cash I'd seen in there just dropped into my head and it seemed like the next move. Even before I could think of where I'd go, I knew it would take some money. I didn't have any money of my own since Vince was taking care of my finances."

Adella didn't know what to say. She had a pretty good idea of how that snake might have been "taking care of" this poor girl's finances, but that didn't justify her stealing from him.

Jillian kept plowing through the story. "I don't know why, but right after he left, I just thought *money*." Jillian cupped her face with both hands and looked at Adella with an expression that morphed from anxiety into anger. "He's such a jerk! He deserved it! He owed it to me! But I don't get how the cops found out! Do you think he called them or something?"

"Okay, now, you calm down and pull yourself together. I can tell you with near certainty that Officer La Bauve's arrival here today had absolutely nothing to do with you. That's just your guilt arresting you. You are over twenty-one, and he wouldn't have bothered going through your grandmother. He'd have come asking for you. Anyway, your crime was in California. Not Louisiana."

With that, Jillian threw herself back on the bed and exclaimed, "I'm a criminal!"

"Get back here." Adella took her by the arm and pulled her up. "We've got to think with a pair of level heads. Has Vince tried to call you about it?"

"I don't know. I don't have guts enough to turn on my phone. But I had to take the money. How else was I supposed to get out of there? There's hardly any money in my bank account. He has all my account numbers and my passwords."

Adella blew out a puff of air. Not bothering to hide her exasperation, she asked, "Jillian, why does a man you're not married to have all your passwords?"

"He asked for them."

"He asked for them, did he? And did it ever occur to you to tell him they were none of his business? Now, what on earth did Mr. Bidness need with your passwords?"

Jillian dropped her chin and shrugged her shoulders.

"Control. That's what." Adella answered her own question because she'd lived long enough and hard enough to know.

Jillian blurted out, "I'm a fugitive!"

"No, you're not. But I don't mind telling you what you are. Because you're what I used to be. You're what Paul called a weak-willed woman, laden down with—" Adella stopped herself from finishing the sentence, knowing it was too much.

Jillian took offense anyway. "I don't care what Paul said! And anyway, he doesn't even know me! Is he your oldest one or the one that stunk? Didn't you say they liked me?"

Adella hadn't had to think this hard since the Great Divulgence. "What are you—?" Then she caught on. "Child, I am not talking about my sons. I was talking about . . . Oh, for heaven's sake. Never mind that. Does AJ ring a bell? That's the oldest one's name, and the one that stunk is Trevor Don. And yes, I'd say they both liked you aplenty, but we've got bigger fish to fry here. Jillian, tell me something. You had a full-time job and you were living with Vince, I assume at his expense. Where did the money from your paychecks go?"

"I don't know. Vince told me not to worry about finances. He was good at that kind of stuff, and it was a relief to let somebody else take care of things for a change. I know some of it went to pay for putting my stuff in storage, because none of it went with his stuff. And I needed nice clothes to go out in public with him and, gosh, to even get out of his car. And I'd also finally lost some weight and needed a smaller size, and—" Jillian's eyes narrowed. "It costs a fortune to live there! Don't you get it?"

"Okay, okay, I get the picture. You need to get busy changing your passwords and I've got to talk to Emmett. He's real wise about stuff like this and he wasn't raised under a rock. Neither was I, for that matter. And we need to pray about it."

"I don't want you and Emmett to 'pray about it.' I want you to tell me what to do to get out of this mess! Knowing Vince, he has a hidden camera somewhere in that office and I'm probably viral on the Web by now, stealing that money." Jillian fell back on the bed again, flopped over on her side, and pulled up her knees. "Oh, my God." She lay there long enough to picture the whole thing. "Oh, my God! I'm on the Web. I just know it."

"Girl, I'm going to jerk a knot in you if you take the Lord's name in vain one more time. Now, sit up here with me and take some ownership. Think with your head instead of your fear." This time Adella sat Jillian up like she meant for her to stay. "The first thing we need to clear up is why the police dropped by here today."

Adella got up and walked over to the blinds and peeked through them. "Well, that's just dandy. They're not even out there on the porch anymore. Now I've gone and missed the whole conversation. A lot of good that's gonna do us. Now I'm going to have to sink to the straightforward approach, and that's about as effective with your grandmother as a foot with no toes in a jumpin' contest."

They heard someone walking down the hall outside Jillian's room. Jillian grabbed Adella's arm and held it in a vise grip. "See? They're coming to arrest me."

"Young lady, you better brew you some of that loose tea of yours and get ahold of yourself while I go out in that hall and find out how much it's gonna cost us to bail you out." Jillian looked at her with horror. Adella came close to smiling as she patted Jillian's leg. "I'll be back in a minute. Don't crawl through a window or anything. You've done right to tell me. It all starts with the truth. Hold on here. And blow your nose. That whistling it's doing is gonna call every dog on the block." She reached for the doorknob.

"Adella? One more thing."

She looked back at the frazzled young woman with bright-green eyes rimmed by this time in a ribbon of red. "What, sister girl? You know I need to get out there and get in on all the goods between your grandmother and Officer Big Boy."

"I think I'm pregnant."

CHAPTER 16

"I CALLED THE OFFICER myself and asked him to come by when he could."

Olivia's words left Adella slack-jawed. To Olivia, the system was something to be tolerated more than respected, let alone requested. For starters, her late husband and his associates had a checkered history with law enforcement. Accusations had usually evaporated for lack of solid evidence, but rumors flew nonetheless in a town where all things underground added depth to the mystique.

A handful of criminal charges had been brought against him, mostly money-related, but he had always slithered through one loophole after another like he'd been greased on both sides. Folks liked to say he'd been involved in more suits than a menswear manufacturer. Olivia's father-in-law was a legend, notorious among his contemporaries for being an out-and-out crook but so irresistibly charismatic that those who accused him usually ended up working for him. Unfortunately, Olivia's late husband had inherited no such charm. Any shred of public favor came to wrack and ruin when he won a well-publicized lawsuit and his opponent left the courthouse bankrupt, drove straight home, and hanged himself by his belt from his bathroom closet door.

Adella had come into the Fontaines' employment innocently, knowing nothing about the family history. When several people at church raised eyebrows over who'd hired her, she'd made a conscious choice not to pry open a single closet where she suspected a hanging skeleton. But that didn't stop people from filling her in on the gossip over the years.

The financial books at Saint Sans were as clean as a whistle. Adella knew that firsthand. No crimes were being committed under that metal roof. Not that she knew of anyway. She'd have quit on a dime if she'd discovered anything legally iffy. The objections of a few stuffed shirts were based on old conjecture, and God didn't hold one person responsible for another's sins. That Olivia had personally invited the law over to this property should have made Adella feel better. But it didn't.

"You had just cause—there's no doubt in my mind—but for the life of me, Olivia, I can't rightly picture you making that call."

"Well, it's been three months, and I have yet to hear any further word about the investigation." Olivia's explanation might have been completely expected and rational from anyone else, but it fit her about as well as a grown man's water ski would fit a toddler.

"I didn't know you were all that anxious for the details. I mean, of course, you should be. You have a right to know. Do they have any leads?"

"No. I doubt it's a big priority. Officer La Bauve said they'd asked questions there on the street, but everyone either claimed not to have seen anything or talked too much nonsense to pay any attention to." Olivia stared off into space as she talked. "The people that were closest to him out there aren't the most credible witnesses."

"Has the officer not kept in contact with you like he promised? Them showing up here in June en masse irritated me to no end, but they seemed sincere enough about Rafe's case. I'd asked them to contact me instead of you, but of course, they refused. Confidentiality and all."

"I've heard from them several times, yes."

Adella drew down her brow and held her peace for a few moments because she knew Olivia hadn't told the whole story yet.

"Adella, I did ask the officer here to see if there was any new information on the case, but that's not the only reason. I also asked him to come by because something seems off around here. I think someone's been on the property, right on the back porch. And maybe more than once."

The possibility frightened Adella more than it should have, but she covered it with rationalizations. "People come and go all the time from the back of Saint Sans: the residents, repairmen, the pest control guy, the lawn man. Only a stranger knocks at that old frozen front door. You know that. I don't understand your concerns." *Then why did your pulse just spike?* Adella asked herself silently.

"I get feelings about things. Call it intuition, if you like. Items keep being moved around, but only enough for me to notice, I guess."

"Like what? What kinds of things are getting moved around?"

Olivia shot Adella a look highly suggesting that the whole conversation was about to shut down if she didn't stop interrogating her.

"Now, wait a second. I believe you. I'm just trying to get the full picture."

"My chairs will be rearranged. I always have them just so. Once they were entirely switched around in order around that table. A pot of flowers will be shoved over maybe six inches. A spade that

I know full well I left in the garage will just be lying on the porch table on a day when there's been no gardener in sight. And anyway, it's all happening at night."

"Lord, have mercy. Maybe Mrs. Winsee's gone to sleepwalking. I've always feared . . . Maybe we'd better—"

"It's not Vida. I know it's not."

"How do you know?"

"Because that was my first thought, too. So after she turned in for the night a couple of times, I put a strip of clear tape on her door down at the bottom where no one could see it. The next morning, I'd purposely get up before her and the tape would still be adhered."

Adella was astonished. "Well, I'll be. You've gone all Sherlock Holmes on us here, Olivia Fontaine." So that was why she'd caught Olivia up and moving around the kitchen on so many early mornings. "Girl, why didn't you say anything?"

"Take one look in the mirror at your expression and you'll answer your own question. Because all of you would think I was imagining it or doing it myself but forgetting it. And I didn't want to spook anyone."

"Well, we're all adults here at Saint Sans. I hardly think you've told me anything that would actually scare us." Adella lied through her white teeth. "I mean, what can Officer La Bauve do about some rearranged chairs?"

Fire shot through Olivia's eyes. "Oh, give me some credit! Do I really strike you as the kind who would call the police over shifting chairs?" She dug into her pocket, pulled something out, grabbed Adella's palm, and slapped the object into it. "This showed up on the porch table a few days ago with its edge tucked under the flower arrangement. You still think I'm imagining things?"

Adella's heart nearly jumped out of her chest. It was a picture of Rafe. "So, someone's been in your stuff? Into your pictures?"

"That's not my picture. I've never seen it before. I am well acquainted with every picture I have of my only child." Olivia's tone dropped an octave and became hoarse. "I assure you I'd recognize it."

The picture wasn't recent, but neither was it old. It had to have been taken sometime over the last decade and during a fairly sober stint. His eyes were as clear as water and his expression looked, if not overtly happy, at least pleasant. Somebody else had been in the picture because it appeared to be a three-by-five print that had been torn—not cut—slightly off center.

The baby rattle Adella had found atop the doormat on the back porch nearly started shaking itself in the bottom of her purse. She moved the bag from her shoulder to her chest and guarded it with both arms. "Okay, Olivia. You've got my attention. Where do you think it was taken? And by whom, for heaven's sake?"

"I don't know. But somehow it feels too shady to be friendly."

Adella had to give her that. "I know you've resisted a house alarm up to now, but maybe it's time we got one installed. And maybe even a security camera."

Olivia rolled her eyes. "Must you always fly to a ten when a five will do? I'm willing to talk about an alarm, although no telling how often it's going to be set off by this scatterbrained bunch. But I'm not about to start putting us all on film."

Olivia had never agreed to an alarm on Saint Sans before, arguing that she refused to live in fear in her own well-lit house. Adella always suspected the real reason was her fear that Rafe would show up on the back porch in need and too drunk to knock. He'd force a door open and every resident would be up and the police on their way before Olivia could slip him out of sight.

"What did Officer La Bauve recommend?"

Olivia hedged for a moment before answering, "A security camera."

Adella threw her hands in the air.

"Or a big dog! But I'm not getting either one. I told him that.

Not unless I have to. Think what a dog would do to my flower beds. First La Bauve recommended that I let him put me in touch with law enforcement in this district, but once I showed him the photograph, he said it connected with his case enough to warrant his involvement a little longer."

"Well, that's some good news, I guess," Adella commented. "He can at least make himself useful and whisper Clementine out of trees when need be."

"It's him or somebody new. You can surely understand that I want a new pride of police on this property as much as I want a liver transplant. He said at this point the picture doesn't prove trespassing since it could have come from the house, which it most certainly did not. But he does agree that it is . . . Well, he called it creepy. Imagine a man his size using the word *creepy*. He's going to talk to that Sergeant DaCosta we liked so much the first time around. It should be fun to see him again, don't you think?" Olivia was never more at ease than when she was sarcastic.

"Some answers will at least bring understanding. Maybe a little peace," Adella said.

"That all depends on what pans out to have happened. I don't know how finding out who stabbed him in the gut can bring any peace, but I guess we'll see about that."

Adella wasn't about to argue with her. She had been around enough people in the throes of grief to know that there was very little that could be said by an outsider, especially one that Olivia would consider "religious." Besides, she suspected Olivia had not yet figured out exactly what she had lost. If a relationship wasn't healthy in the first place, it was a whole lot harder for the grief to be healthy when it was over.

They both stood silently for a moment, first one drawing a deep breath, then the other. When Olivia's nails started tapping on the small table next to her, Adella knew they were done. It was like a

drum roll announcing somebody's exit, and since they were standing in Olivia's quarters, it was obviously going to be Adella's.

"Well then, I'll get back to the tasks at hand. Let me know what
I can—"

"How's Jillian?"

Scared out of her wits of getting arrested for stealing and she's proba-
bly pregnant and all but penniless and has two detached kinfolks to her
name, but beyond that, I'd say she's peachy. "I think she's okay. She
seems to have inherited a distrust of the police. Go figure that."

"The muffins were pretty good, don't you think, if you can
tolerate a whole hay bale of bran in one sitting?" That was classic
Olivia. Every compliment showed its backside.

"Maybe that's what's wrong with my stomach."

"Adella, you didn't even have one. That's what's wrong with the
rest of our stomachs. What's wrong with your stomach is that you
sent Clementine out the back door bird hunting. And for heaven's
sake, pull that wad of tissue off your big toe. It looks like the
world's worst aim had a shoot-out in the ladies' room."

"Atonement?"

"That's right. *Atonement.* That's all the card said. It's a Bible
term." Adella heard Emmett come in from work through the
kitchen door, so she stepped out the back door for privacy.

"I am aware of that much, Mrs. Atwater, but thank you,"
Sergeant DaCosta responded, clearly struggling to be polite.

"Officer La Bauve is the one who's up-to-date on the case.
Perhaps you should just have him call me," Adella suggested,
not bothering to hide her own irritation. She hated having to
explain a bone to a dog. "This is what you policemen do, is it not?
Investigate cases? Consider the evidence?"

"Of course it is, ma'am. We're just understaffed here in the busiest crime district in New Orleans. One of the busiest in the nation, I might add. We might need your patience. The phone is ringing off the wall with the flavor of the day. Today it's car thefts. I will certainly pass word on to La Bauve, but several of us are involved in this case. I'm overseeing it, so let's keep talking here for a minute. If it's any consolation, I don't think you're making too much of it by reporting it."

"Well, that's a relief. Hold on a sec." Adella opened the back door and yelled, "I'm out here, Emmett! I need another minute. It's business, not pleasure! Eat an apple or something." Was it two boys she had or was it three?

"Mrs. Atwater? Are you there?"

"I am here. Speak up!"

"I understand why you didn't show it to Mrs. Fontaine the day of the burial, but why haven't you told her since then?"

"Well, how exactly do you suggest to a grieving mother—and that's what she is, no matter how strange she's acting—that, by some sick person's estimation, your son's death was meant to 'atone' for something? Huh? How would you suggest I bring that up? The whole thing gives me the creeps."

"Those are good points, but it's time she knew. She may be the only person that can shed light on why somebody would want to take revenge."

"Atonement and revenge are not the same thing, you realize, Mr. DaCosta?"

"Semantics. Listen, I'm trying to help here. I really am. But I wonder if we could forgo the competition and move to the same side."

Adella wanted to ask him who was competing with whom, but she was afraid she'd overplay her confidence and start getting all convicted. "I'm a reasonable person, Sergeant, and I've always been easy to get along with."

"I'm sure of that, so consider us officially getting along." He paused, and Adella imagined him rubbing his temples. "Let's do a little strategic planning. When should you tell Mrs. Fontaine about the card? Tomorrow morning or afternoon?"

Adella sighed. "I guess at the same time I tell her about the baby rattle."

"What baby rattle?"

"The blue one I found on the back porch welcome mat not that long after the burial."

"I don't get the connection," Sergeant DaCosta said. "Where would a baby toy fit into all of this?"

"I don't know. I was thinking it was because Rafe was Olivia's only child. You know. The kind of child that starts as a baby. A *boy* baby." She felt like an idiot. "And babies play with rattles." As Adella heard her own explanation, it seemed ludicrous.

"Understandable," the officer responded. "To tell you the truth, we still need a lot more to go on. Trespassing is a long way from murder. My guess is that the two things won't turn out to be related. But in the remote chance they are, if there's an unwanted visitor to the place, someone there might catch the person in the act. Then we could question him."

"Or *her*. So you're saying that we need to catch the person committing the crime, and then we can move forward? We should put ourselves in harm's way to help the case. That's it, is it?"

The sergeant was silent.

"Fine, then. We're set to go with our part around here. What's your part?"

Adella looked through the screen door to see what her menfolk were up to. By this time, all three of them were circling around the kitchen like vultures, dive-bombing anything remotely edible. That's when Trevor Don accidentally knocked his mother's big red purse from the kitchen counter to the tile floor, sending contents flying. As he and AJ dove for a couple of quarters rolling on the floor, all three sets of ebony eyes focused on a single point on the floor. Adella didn't have to see it to know what they were looking at: a small rectangular box labeled *Early Pregnancy Test*.

Both boys jumped to their feet like they'd been electrocuted. Each of them took a giant step back and stared in horror at Emmett. AJ's expression took on a disgust so palpable, it looked like something would project from his mouth any split second. Trevor Don, on the other hand, turned into something resembling a mad, rabid dog about to take a chunk out of somebody's thigh. Had Emmett been a foot shorter and considerably less broad, he might have been in harm's way.

"What? Don't look at me! I don't know anything about this!" Emmett was clearly horrified and on his way to petrified.

That's when Trevor Don took what, with generous imagination, might vaguely resemble a swing at Emmett. AJ grabbed him by the other arm and slung him out of the kitchen. The last word Adella heard one of the boys say was "Sick!"

CHAPTER 17

PASSERSBY SEEMED MOST IMPRESSED by the construction of a copper-topped belfry rising above the ten-by-ten entryway. Within it hung a heavy bell, slightly undersized to the critical eye but one that made a particularly impressive effort in the right hands. The four corners rose another ten feet above the chapel's roofline, meeting at the tip, hinting at a steeple but stopping just short of a full commitment. Saint Silvanus was a sight for the sore eyes of its visionaries and, as it turned out, no eyesore at all for its community. Those with ostentatious tastes might have found it underwhelming, but it was sturdy, color-rich, and pristine. They'd come a long way from the one-room churches of their older fellows.

At the front of the chapel, beyond the organ, a corridor of slight unintended decline led off to the right, where four meeting rooms could be found. To have such a wing for Sunday school classes was a luxury to a petite congregation and a considerable source of pride.

On the opposite side of the church from the classroom wing was a detached parsonage, small but quaint. Its lower half echoed the church's brick and mortar and its upper half was wooden siding, painted a glossy white. Matching wooden railings enclosed the house's small front porch, and a cedar swing hung from two chains, wooing a couple to come and sit a spell and watch the world go by. Its roof was made of the same standing-seam metal as the church building's. All told, the parsonage was a fine home for the family of a man of Methodist cloth.

The family who would first call it home was the Reverend R. J. Brashear and his wife, Evelyn Ann, and their young daughter, Brianna. The child had a sweet, tender disposition and a swath of freckles across her cheeks. She'd been crippled by polio for the better part of two years and was almost entirely reliant on a wheelchair to go any farther than from the parsonage to the church. Her father carried her there and back for each gathering as she latched her arms around his neck.

CHAPTER 18

CAL GLANCED AT HIS PHONE and shot a text back to Frank. **Meet you there in 5.** It was close to midnight and he could use a cup of coffee.

They'd gotten a panicked call from a woman whose ex promised to make good on a threat that night. Cal had provided the documentation for the woman's protective order and he intended to catch the guy violating it before the maniac got his hands around her neck.

Cal had taken responsibility for watching for him at the woman's apartment while Frank eyed her workplace. Bully and Sanchez were parked down the street from his house and five minutes earlier reported that he'd arrived and gone inside. Until he reemerged, Cal and Frank could grab some coffee.

The French Quarter was famous for bringing out the worst in

people. The Eighth District had the smallest land mass of any in Orleans Parish but the highest number of officers assigned to it. In Cal's opinion, this band of officers took it in pretty fair stride. The Eighth also encompassed the Central Business District, Canal Place, Bourbon Street, and the casino, so their days were rarely monotonous. And despite the area's reputation, they still got to serve some decent citizens.

Heading up the sidewalk on Decatur, Cal heard a loud clang coming from the alley behind Café Beignet. The beam of his flashlight landed on a young woman in an employee's uniform picking up the lid of a stainless steel trash can. Just beyond her, a dog scurried out of sight. "Oh, man!" the employee exclaimed. "I nearly had him!"

"Didn't mean to startle you. I'm with law enforcement." Cal lowered the flashlight. "That stray been getting in the trash?"

She set the lid back on the trash can. "No, I was looking for something to feed him. I can usually find a leftover hot dog in here or part of a sandwich. Otherwise, it's just gross, soggy beignets. He'd be hungry enough to eat one but I'd rather give him some meat." She took a good look at Cal, tilted her head with a hint of disapproval, and said, "Are you going to arrest him?"

He smiled. "That's not really my job. Mongrels on four legs don't worry me much. It's the ones on two legs I'm interested in. Has he been begging here for a while?"

"Oh, he doesn't beg. He's too skittish to be any trouble. I've caught him snooping around the trash can several times, but every time I try to get close to him, he runs off."

Cal leaned over and looked past the young woman's shoulder and then motioned for her to look behind her. A scruffy medium-size dog with wiry gray-and-white fur stood in the entryway to the alley. Cal knelt down on one knee. "Here, boy. It's okay. Nobody's going to hurt you." After several rounds of those same words, the stray slowly inched its way over to Cal and sniffed his open palm, even letting him scratch behind his ears. Without taking his eyes off the dog, Cal whispered to the woman, "Did you see anything while you were rummaging around in there?"

"Nothing but beignets."

"Well, that'll have to do tonight. Can you take that lid off—*quietly*—" Cal glanced up and grinned—"and hand me one?" She did as he asked, but when she stepped toward Cal with it, the dog darted off again. "Just wait a second." As if on cue, the stray soon made another timid approach. As he swallowed the large piece of fried bread whole, a car alarm went off close by and the dog scrammed with his tail down, the way a coyote would.

As Cal got to his feet, the young woman gave him a puzzled look. "How'd you do that? I've been trying to get him to come to me for two weeks."

"Give it time. He'll come around. The old boy just knows me a little better."

"You've seen him before?"

"Yeah, he's been running these blocks for, I guess, a year now."

"How does he stay alive? And out of the pound?"

"He's warmed up to a guy who lives on the streets around here and sings for cash when he's sober enough. The two of them mostly roost in that abandoned eyesore on Iberville. I guess the reason animal control hasn't picked him up yet is because some people around here feel the same way I do. It seems wrong to take a man's dog. It's all he's got."

She paused for a moment and stared into the distance behind Cal. "So what's the secret?" she whispered.

"Patience. And you've gotta get down eye level and talk gently to him."

Cal could hide neither his surprise nor the twinge of endearment she provoked in him when, right on the spot, the young woman did exactly as he'd suggested. Why did the woman seem familiar to him? He knew he hadn't seen her here before.

"Here, boy. It's okay," she said, crouching down, her hand extended with a second beignet in her open palm.

The dog crept around Cal and took several steps toward the young woman. "That's a good boy," she said with a wide smile, raising her eyebrows toward Cal. "It's working!"

Cal reciprocated the smile and nodded. She continued to coax her reluctant dinner guest, parroting Cal's exact words. "It's okay, boy. Nobody's going to hurt you." The trembling stray took the food right out of her hand and tarried long enough to lick the powdered sugar off her palm.

The back door of Café Beignet swung wide open and a woman in similar attire bellowed, "Jillian! What's taking you so long?" She jumped to her feet like she'd been caught swiping candy. "You're ten minutes over," the woman chided. "I need a smoke."

Before Cal could say a word, the dog disappeared from the alley and the girl disappeared through the door. Her coworker pulled out a pack of cigarettes, smacked the bottom of it on her palm, and slid one out. The cigarette between her lips, she flicked on a lighter and, from the corner of her mouth, mumbled, "Need something?"

"No," he answered. "Just wanting to grab a table for a cup of coffee."

The woman cocked her head at him disapprovingly. "You planning to walk through the kitchen?"

"Nope. Heading around front right now."

She lit the cigarette, took a deep drag, and blew a puff of smoke. "Alright then."

When Cal entered the open-air café, Frank threw his hands in the air, looked at his left wrist dramatically, and asked, "What took you so long? I'm starving here."

"Sorry, buddy. Why didn't you go ahead and order?"

"Because I was waiting on my date." Both men chuckled. Frank was as good a comrade as a man could maintain in the madness of urban law enforcement. That their friendship had remained largely undisturbed in the wake of Cal's promotion was something he hadn't taken for granted a single day. He credited Frank entirely for that.

"Hey, sit down here," Frank insisted. "You're not going to believe this. See that girl? I'm nearly positive that's Rafe Fontaine's daughter. Remember? We saw her at the Fontaine place that day, and Sanchez told us that's who she was. Gotta be. Dead ringer. Don't you think?"

"Doesn't she live in California?"

Frank shrugged.

Jillian was wiping off a Formica table close to the kitchen. Cal studied her carefully as she pushed through the kitchen door with a stack of dirty dishes, then seconds later, came back into sight with a plate stacked high with piping-hot beignets. She placed them in the middle of a table of four, pulled a green order pad out of her pocket, and headed their direction.

She was only five feet from their table when she looked up from her order pad. She came to an abrupt stop and stared. It was her, alright. From the look on her face, she wasn't remotely comfortable with them turning up at one of her tables. Just because Cal had seen her in the alley, or did she recognize them from the case?

"You think we could order when you get a minute?" Frank sounded uncharacteristically impatient at Jillian's hesitation.

She dropped her pen and it bounced under their table. When Cal picked it up and handed it to her, her face was crimson against the white neckline of her uniform. She avoided his eyes and looked at Frank.

"Sure." She pressed the ballpoint against the pad. "So it's true what they say about cops and donuts, I guess."

"Well, your management has always welcomed a few officers dropping by late at night since it gives your café here some free security," Frank countered. "But you're obviously new since you still don't know the difference between a beignet and a donut, *I guess.*"

Cal grimaced.

"Fried dough," Jillian responded, rolling her eyes.

"Sharp edges and no holes." Good grief, Frank sounded like a fifth grader. Maybe Frank even heard it in himself because the next thing out of his mouth came with a more familiar jovial tone. "But call it whatever you want. I'll have two orders and a café au lait. What's your pleasure, bro?"

Cal glanced at Jillian. "Just coffee. Black's good."

"Suit yourself."

Frank shook his head as she walked away. "That girl's got a little attitude, doesn't she? She's gone and hurt my feelings."

"Save your hurt feelings for the creep we want cuffed before dawn. He'll show you some sharp edges. He'll be cussing a blue streak from the backseat all the way to jail and calling you everything but an altar boy."

They both chortled as Jillian approached with their order on a brown tray. All it took was one look at her and Cal knew she assumed they were laughing at her.

"Here you go, gentlemen." She clapped the plate of beignets in front of Frank and set his cup down with a slosh. The slight jolt unbalanced the tray, splashing blistering hot coffee across Cal's lap. He jumped to his feet with a loud yelp.

"Oh no! I'm so sorry!" Jillian grabbed every paper napkin out of the stainless steel dispenser on the table and threw them toward Cal, her face scarlet. She grabbed another stack from a nearby table, squatted down, and started soaking up what had spilled on the floor.

Wincing, he blotted his soaked pant leg. "I'm good. It'll dry. No real problem."

"That's right, my man," Frank said, sounding amused. "You've never been bothered by a good third-degree burn."

"I'll go get you another cup." She was clearly grappling for an exit strategy.

Frank slapped Cal on the back. "He's had enough coffee for one night. He can just wring his pants out if he wants any more."

"Leave it alone, Frank. Yeah, absolutely. I'll have another."

As Jillian turned on her heels and headed back to the kitchen, Cal said to Frank, "Stop giving that girl a hard time, man."

Frank stuffed a beignet in his mouth, still tickled enough to blow a cloud of powdered sugar down the front of his shirt. When Jillian set the second cup of coffee on the table in front of Cal, Frank swallowed, cleared his throat, and asked, "How have you liked New Orleans so far, Miss . . . Is it Fontaine? You must like it pretty good, since you came back."

She made no attempt to mask her shock. "How do you know who I am?"

Frank seemed surprised she didn't remember them. "We're working the case involving your fath—"

"*Family,*" Cal finished for him.

Astonishment swept over Jillian's face and she fixed her gaze on Cal. "Is that why you were spying on me?"

"I wasn't spying on you. I heard a noise, and—"

"You knew it was me?"

Frank looked back and forth between the two of them. "Am I missing something?"

Cal ignored him and tried to answer Jillian's question. "No. I thought you seemed familiar, but I wasn't sure where I'd seen you until Officer Lamonte here made the connection."

Jillian turned her gaze to Frank. "Miss *Slater*. My name is Slater, not Fontaine. And what makes you think you have to like a place to come back to it?" She hesitated for a moment and then slapped the check on the table and walked off in a huff.

"That's not a bad point," Cal responded to the back of her head. Then he said loud enough to hope she heard, "Hey, I really did know that stray!"

"What are you talking about?" Frank might have pressed the point had he not simultaneously turned over the check. His eyebrows flew up. "She charged us! Didn't even comp us after scalding you."

Cal took the check from him, read it, and slapped it back into his palm. "She didn't charge *us*, Frank. She charged *you*. My burn was free."

"Gah, that's girl's crazy. Crazy's in her bloodline."

"If a bloodline could make you crazy, we'd all be nuts."

Frank countered with his mouth full. "Yeah, maybe, but those Fontaines are their own kind of crazy. They're criminal crazy."

"If that's true, they've sure done a good job of dodging prosecution."

"I didn't say they weren't smart. Slick as greased pigs, with lawyers just as oily. Of course, that corpse couldn't have been too smart." Frank threw back the last of his coffee. "Let's go, boss."

Cal had told his old partner repeatedly not to call him that, but the man had a mind of his own.

As the two left the open-air café, four guys were heading toward them on the sidewalk, not stumbling drunk but too happy and with mouths too coarse to be stone-cold sober this time of night on the square.

"Fraternity pledges," Frank offered.

Cal directed his attention and volume toward them. "What has you boys out tonight?"

The young men couldn't have seemed less intimidated.

"Looking for a bite to eat, Officers," one said as he tipped his base-ball cap and tried to go around them. "Top of the evening to you keepers of the peace. Good job you're doing there."

Cal stepped squarely in front of him. "Where have you gentle-men been?"

"Oh, just doing a little sightseeing." All four of them laughed. "Is that against the law?"

"Well, I guess that depends on how old you are, now doesn't it?" Cal knew they were old enough to get into those illicit clubs but he still didn't like it. He hadn't even liked it when he was their age. "Why don't you boys get a cab and go back where you came from?"

The same one spoke up again with fearless sarcasm. "If it's all the same to you, can we eat first?"

Cal glanced over his shoulder. He could see Jillian mopping underneath their table at the café.

"Go somewhere else."

"Why can't we go *there*?"

"They're closing." Cal shifted his weight toward the one who'd stepped off the sidewalk.

"No, they—"

"Go somewhere else."

Cal decided to take a detour on his way back to his post. He lagged as far back from the trolley as he could and still keep it within eyeshot. When it screeched to a halt on St. Charles across from Saint Sans, he pulled over to the curb and turned off his lights. He watched Jillian sprint across the street and halt at the front door, digging into her purse. She withdrew what he was certain was a key but then she stood there longer than it should take anybody, in Cal's opinion, to unlock a door, especially a woman at 1 a.m. He leaned forward against the steering wheel, squinting for a better look, and saw her trying to turn the key with one hand and push the big door open with the other. His eyes might have been playing tricks on him, but he suspected she was crying.

"You can't just sit here, you idiot. You'd do this for anybody," Cal grumbled to himself. As he cracked open the door and started out of the car, his right elbow landed on the horn hard and long enough to wake all but the dead. Jillian looked frantically the direction of his car. Then she shoved the stubborn front door with her shoulder, causing it to fly open. The only thing louder than the horn of his car was the quick slam of that door behind her.

CHAPTER 19

IT WAS LATE THE NEXT NIGHT. Stella stopped by the café just before Jillian clocked out and persuaded her to come by when she got off.

Stella was growing on her. She came to the café almost every night for coffee. She asked Jillian a lot of questions—some of them pretty personal—but maybe that's the way people were around here: in your business. At least the woman seemed genuinely interested in her. Jillian was tired, but she could use a friend, and so far Stella was the closest thing to qualify on the muddy banks of the Mississippi.

Jillian asked her if she could wait a few minutes so they could walk over together, but Stella insisted on going ahead. "Let me get a jump on you and get things tidied up a little. Sound good?"

Actually, it didn't. Jillian put on a brave front, but walking by herself at night in this town gave her the creeps. All seemed shadows here. She longed to go home. In the six months she'd lived with Vince, she'd tasted a whole different life. Everything was new: the loft, the furniture, the cars, the clothes. The sidewalks outside Sigmund's were spotless. Sour smells didn't assault one's senses. The bay was beautiful. The people were beautiful. The view from the loft was beautiful. A wave of nausea tightened her throat as the memories of the good life were swallowed in an avalanche of images replaying the brutal end. The same butterflies flew into her stomach. The same emotions sent heat waves through her chest.

She slipped her purse strap over her head and told the night manager she was leaving. The woman nodded and waved. "See you day after tomorrow then."

Everything in Jillian wanted to answer, "I hope not," yet she knew in the pit of her stomach she'd be right here, right in this town, right on this square, in this uniform, making minimum wage.

Stella's apartment was only four blocks away, but the moonless night left the streetlamps to small circles of light. On the weekends, people traipsed up and down the sidewalks until the early hours of the morning, but this was a weeknight and a slow one at that. The few people she saw were each sitting alone on the sidewalk with a bottle. She circled as far around them as she could. *Keep your head up and look confident,* Jillian told herself. *Don't look like a victim. Anyway, you'll be living down here soon yourself.*

She stopped in front of an old four-story redbrick building with tattered green awnings and checked the address Stella had written with a felt-tip on the inside of her wrist. *301. This is it.* She opened the door and took two flights of narrow stairs. "The last apartment at the end of the hall on the left," Stella had told her. "Easy to spot. It's the one with a green vine painted on the door." Jillian found it and tapped at it tentatively.

"Entrez, s'il vous plaît." The door swung open, Stella motioning dramatically with her left hand. Jillian crossed the threshold to a

densely furnished room lit only by candles. Wooden figurines were perched on the higher surfaces like sentries standing watch over the room. A clear glass bowl filled with strands of colored beads was on a small table. A door to a second room was closed. Besides a small kitchen and dining area, that seemed to be the extent of the place.

Jillian had secretly hoped the apartment would turn out to have two bedrooms so that it wouldn't be too awkward if she asked Stella if she could stay with her until she found a place of her own. She was on borrowed time at Saint Sans, and she wasn't about to stay long enough for Olivia to have to ask her to leave. The last thing Jillian wanted was to stay in New Orleans permanently, but one thing was clear: after pocketing a thousand dollars from Vince's desk drawer, she wasn't going back to California anytime soon.

Jillian's eyes cased the room. The walls to her right and her left were painted a dark solid color—maroon perhaps—and in odd contrast to the rest of the clutter, each void of a single picture. A swath of fabric was draped over the window. The wall opposite the entrance was overlaid by a large painted mural.

"You like my secret garden?"

"Yeah," Jillian answered, shrugging her shoulders. "Yeah, I do."

"A friend painted it for me. I closed my eyes and described what I saw in my mind's eye and voilà. When I opened them, there it was."

"It looks like you could get lost in there and never come out."

"But, my new friend, who'd want to?"

"You're a reader." Books, mostly old with torn spines, were stacked vertically and horizontally any way they'd fit on the shelves of a small, ornate bookcase.

"You could say that. How about you? You like to widen your mind, Jillian?"

"I like reading okay. Magazines mostly."

"Not me. I love the smell of an old book. I want pages to crack when I open it. I've got a friend who owns a secondhand bookstore a few blocks over. He lets me know when he gets something he knows I'll like."

Jillian was curious. "So what do you like?"

She wasn't sure what was funny about the question but Stella responded with a bit of a laugh. "Hmmm. I guess history might sum up my taste in books. There's some history around these parts, Jillian."

"I'm not much of a history person."

"Not even your own history?"

"Especially not my own history." They both chuckled. "But I do like art. My mom is an artist. She sells art mostly, but she also paints."

"I'd love to know about your mother, Jillian. What's she like? She must be lovely. I mean, look at her daughter. Is she dark like you?"

"You think I'm dark?"

"Dark-headed. Does she have that gorgeous black hair like you?"

"No, not really." Jillian felt an unexpected wave of emotion at the thought of Jade. "I'm sorry. It's just that I haven't talked to her in a few weeks. I miss her."

"I know what you mean. I was never close to my mom, but my dad was my whole world. He died several years ago. But he's still here with me. I often feel his presence."

Jillian had no interest in feeling the presence of a dead man.

Stella continued. "Are you close to your dad?"

"No." The room fell silent except for an antique clock on a small buffet ticking like a bass drum. "It's a little later than I realized. I better keep an eye on the clock."

"Oh, don't be silly. You just got here. The trolley runs all night. We stay up late and sleep late around here. You know what they say: When in Rome . . ."

"So, what's this?" Jillian walked over to the square wooden table in the dining area next to the kitchen. Candlelight flickered on the shiny surface of a deck of oversize cards.

"Ah, that. Have you ever had your fortune told with cards?"

Jillian laughed. "No. I've never even seen any of those."

"It's fun! Want to do it? You can't work down here and never have your fortune told. That's not right."

"How long does it take?"

"Jillian, quit being such a spoilsport. Relax a little. You sit. I'll pour us each a glass of wine."

Jillian pulled out a chair and sat down.

Stella reached over and took the deck off the table. "Forget the cards. We'll just talk. There's so much I still don't know about you. Tell me about your dad." She poured two glasses of deep-red wine and set one of them in front of Jillian. She sipped out of the other one as she took the chair opposite her guest.

The prospect of recounting any more of her miserable life or missing relationships to Stella was intolerable. "Let's do the cards. Sounds like fun." It was a diversion, and she needed one.

"Okay." Stella placed the stack of cards back on the table. "You shuffle them."

With her first try, Jillian sent cards all over the table and a few on the floor. "I'm all thumbs with these. They're enormous."

Stella laughed. "You'll get it. Keep trying."

"These look medieval or something." Jillian finally managed to come up with a decent shuffle and placed the cards back on the table.

"Now, cut the deck," Stella instructed.

"When exactly does your part kick in?"

"Oh, soon I'll turn into Marie Laveau. Just give it time."

"Who is that?" Jillian asked.

Stella swallowed another sip of wine and cackled. "She's the witch queen of New Orleans. Boy, you truly are from another planet." She shook her head. "I'm teasing. We're just playing cards here. Nothing crazy."

After Jillian cut the cards, Stella slid the deck facedown across the table toward her. "Okay, now choose five cards from the deck."

"Any cards I want?"

"Yes, any five cards. Keep your cards facedown after you draw them."

Jillian chose the first two slowly. "Oh, what the heck. This is just for kicks anyway." She pulled three others together from the stack. "Who cares?" She laughed and tried to loosen up, imagining how ridiculous her stiffness must have looked in Stella's eyes.

Stella smiled and arranged the five cards in a semicircle facing Jillian. "While we do this, set your mind free to course over your life. Not just your past but your future. Think of a gate and open it."

Jillian nodded and tried to set her mind free, whatever that meant. "Gate officially open."

Stella turned over the first card. It was a rider on a horse with sticks of some sort around it. "A six of wands."

"What does that mean?" Maybe this was going to be intriguing after all. Jillian leaned forward toward the cards, both elbows on the table, her chin in her palms.

"This one is speaking to your finances."

"Well, then it's telling you I'm broke."

"Maybe not for long. It looks to me like you may have some cash coming."

As Jillian repositioned herself, the chair creaked. She wondered if somehow Stella possessed a peculiar power and could see her taking the money at Sigmund's. Maybe she was seeing her past instead of her future. "That one's clearly off. Let's go to the next one."

Stella stayed with it, tapping the face of the first card with her fingernail. "An inheritance maybe?"

Jillian burst out laughing. "No. That can't be it." With her certainty that the card was wrong, Jillian decided to relax a little and have fun. Obviously it was just a game. "Can I flip the next one?"

"Sure. We'll go at your pace. You're not much for elaboration, are you?"

Jillian grinned and turned over the second card.

"Another six! Six of swords. How about that?"

Jillian studied the boat on the card. At least it wasn't religious like the one in the stained glass at Saint Sans, and there were no waves. Just calm rowing. "So what does it mean?"

"You're on a journey."

"Well, that's insightful." Jillian sipped out of her glass. "Aren't we all?"

"Yes, that's true. But if you'll listen, you might learn where you're headed. Do you want to know?"

"Only if it's good."

"I'd say so far, so good. Want to keep playing?"

The room was beginning to get a bit warm and the smell of the candles too sweet. Jillian had only had a few sips of the wine but she already felt a little light-headed. She turned over the third card. This one was unnumbered.

"The fool." Stella spoke quickly. "But no worries. In tarot cards, the fool can be very fortunate. The draw can just mean that you're off to a new start and you're experimenting with things. That fits, doesn't it?"

Jillian's head was beginning to spin. She didn't want to have to tell Stella that she was having an odd reaction to the wine. She was sure Stella would think she was an idiot. She squeezed her eyes shut and opened them, attempting to regain her focus. The candle threw an ethereal light on the edges of Stella's untamed hair. She was moving her mouth but Jillian couldn't make out what she was saying. She tried to break her gaze by looking past Stella to the mural behind her but her eyes kept blurring. The vines looked like they were moving, winding around the gate. The lamp in the mural seemed to flicker and the small, dark clearing in the center of the garden yawned.

Jillian could feel a single bead of sweat roll between her shoulder blades. Her body jarred rhythmically to the pounding of her heart. Now nothing in the room was still. Those figurines. She could not see them but she could feel them. They were staring at her. Small ghosts frolicked on the wicks. Jillian's palms were flat on the table but something tugged at her hands. She could no longer see Stella's face, but the aura around her remained, looking like the edges of a silhouette burning. She could smell the soil of the garden. She could feel a tickling vine looping around the fingers of her right hand.

Breakers of terror and exhilaration crashed upon Jillian with such equal force that she could not tell them apart. A soundless voice called her.

CHAPTER 20

JILLIAN AWAKENED to an earsplitting pounding. She sat up quickly, head throbbing. Disoriented, she blinked her eyes and cased the surroundings for a semblance of familiarity. Couch pillows were scattered on the floor but she had no recollection of putting them there. She blew out a breath of relief as she noticed the bookcase she'd seen last night. There were the rickety chairs and that garden mural. The room looked so different in the daylight, but at least Jillian knew where she was. *Why* she was there was another question she'd try to answer when she was thinking straight.

The pounding continued. "Stella! Somebody's at the door!" There was no sign of Stella.

"Just a second!" she howled toward the commotion. She steadied herself on her feet and walked dizzily over to the door that she assumed led to the bedroom. Beating on it with the palm of her hand, she yelled, "Stella!"

A man's voice called from the hall. "Miss Slater, is that you?" More knocking.

Jillian felt like she'd been caught doing something wrong, but in the blur of confusion, she couldn't sort out why. She tried to open the door to the bedroom but it was locked. She yelled one more time, "Stella? You there? Open the door!"

"Miss Slater?" It was a woman's voice sounding from the hall this time, insistent and loud.

Jillian glanced in the antique mirror over the buffet. "Look at yourself." She licked her fingertips and tried to wipe away the mascara caked under her eyes and then brushed through her dark hair with both hands. She needed to use the restroom in the worst way but she was afraid the apartment door would come off the hinges before she got back. "Alright, already!"

"Miss Slater, are we ever glad to see you. You remember us? Officer La Bauve, here, and my partner, Officer Sanchez."

"Okay." Jillian's mind was still in a fog. She remembered them all too well, but she had no idea what the two of them were doing in Stella's doorway. "The owner—I mean the renter—is not here. Well, I don't think she is. Maybe she's in the bedroom but the door's locked. Her name is—"

"Actually, we're here to see you," Officer La Bauve explained cheerfully. The man was happier than anybody ought to be at this time of the morning. What time was it, anyway? His sidekick looked considerably less cheerful.

"Me? Why?" Jillian glanced at the clock and saw that it was just shy of ten o'clock. She smoothed down her shirt and realized she still had on her white work uniform. Embarrassed, she glanced around the floor for her shoes.

"Well, your family was worried about you."

"My family? Are you talking about my mom? How did my mom get your—?"

Officer Sanchez picked up the dialogue. "The people over at Saint Sans. They were pretty worried when you didn't come home last night."

"Are you arresting me?" Jillian was confused and unnerved.

Officer La Bauve smiled warmly. "Oh no, ma'am. Of course not. This is not even an official missing persons call. Hasn't been long enough for that and you, an adult and all. Just a courtesy to Mrs. Fontaine."

Officer Sanchez chimed back in. "Mrs. Atwater called. We've gotten to know her through the other case. You know, the one concerning your dad. She isn't one to take no for an answer."

"He wasn't my dad."

"Either way," Officer La Bauve interjected, resting his hand on his partner's shoulder, "we're just glad to see you're fine. How about a lift home?"

"In a police car? Are you out of your mind?"

"It's a free ride. And we won't make you wear the handcuffs or anything." He laughed heartily at himself.

Jillian was not amused. "No thanks." She looked around the room until she found her purse and her shoes. She sat down on the couch to put them on. The surface was as stiff as bare boards. No wonder her neck hurt so badly. "I'll take the trolley. How did you people find me?"

The two stepped through the door like Jillian had just handed them a written invitation. La Bauve kept talking and Sanchez circled behind Jillian and glanced into the kitchen. "Mrs. Atwater started calling the station at five this morning. By eight o'clock, our boss had us asking questions at the café and around the square."

"Oh, great." All Jillian needed was to lose her job. She'd need to call the café as soon as she got to Saint Sans. "Did you make them think I was under arrest?" She was too frazzled to mask her anxiety.

"Oh no, ma'am," Officer La Bauve responded. "We just said your people were worried because you hadn't come home last night."

"They're not my people. I'm just staying there until . . . well, until I can move."

He continued as if he hadn't heard a word she'd said. "Sarge isn't usually one to jump the gun, seeing it hadn't been long you'd been unaccounted for. But he said we weren't overloaded and for me and Sanchez to give it the morning. And it was uncanny how fast it all pieced together. One person saw you go this far. Another picked up from there. We just kept picking up the breadcrumbs kinda like—"

"I get it."

"Like me and Sanchez were—"

"Hansel and Gretel."

"That's exactly right! See there? You and me are tracking this morning. We woke up a man sleeping right out there on the sidewalk and asked if he'd seen anyone by your description. Would you believe he told us right where we could find you? How about that?"

"Fabulous." Jillian was back on her feet and slapped her purse strap on her shoulder. If she'd known she was going to end up spending the night, she'd have brought a change of clothes. In her opinion, only one thing looked worse than her uniform and that was her uniform after she'd slept in it.

"Miss Slater." Officer Sanchez came around Jillian from the back. "Do you want us to check on your friend? You say she's in there?" She glanced at the bedroom door. "Do you have any reason to suspect she's not okay? You want us to try to pry that door open?" She tried to turn the doorknob.

"No! She's not in there. At least I don't think she is. Or if she is, she's asleep. She was fine last night. We're not prying any doors open around here. I think you're already more company than she was looking for."

The truth was, Jillian was as confused about Stella as the officers were. If she was in that room, she was the soundest sleeper on the planet. If she wasn't, why had she locked the door? And why didn't she leave a note? And what on earth had happened last night to knock her out for so long?

Jillian picked the pillows up off the floor and set them on the couch. For the life of her, she could not remember how they had been arranged.

"If she doesn't touch base with you pretty soon and you start getting concerned, how about you let us know?"

"That won't be necessary."

Officer La Bauve jumped back in insistently. "You sure you don't want a ride?"

As much of a caricature as this guy seemed in Jillian's eyes, she had to admit that his persona was so well perfected, he almost came across as sincere. "Positive. I don't need any more help, thank you."

Officer Sanchez shook her head. "Ma'am, we're just trying to—"

"Don't call me *ma'am*. I hate that. It's backward."

"Backward? Are manners backward where you come from? And forgive me for asking, but what exactly do you *not* hate?"

Jillian was slack-jawed. "I'll tell you what I don't hate. I don't hate being left alone!"

"If alone is what you want, Miss Slater, you may have come to the wrong city." The officer opened the apartment door and said forcefully, "After you."

Jillian was uneasy about leaving the apartment unlocked, but Stella had left her no choice. She had enough problems of her own, including what she was going to say to Adella when she got back to Saint Sans. For starters, she was going to tell her she was a grown woman. What she couldn't offer Adella was an explanation for why she ended up spending the night on that short, awful couch. But it was none of Adella's business anyway.

Jillian walked down the two flights of stairs behind the officers, balancing herself with her right hand on the wall. Officer La Bauve was so tall and broad that, when he stepped through the building's doorway to the bright midmorning sun, Jillian stood in the shadow of a solar eclipse. When she stepped out onto the sidewalk she was relieved that at least there was no police car double-parked at the curb with lights flashing. She tried to gauge which way the pair of policemen were going to turn so she could dart in the opposite direction. Considering they had obviously asked about her all over the square, she had no intention of being seen with them. She didn't care if she had to walk five blocks out of the way to catch the trolley.

Officer La Bauve flashed a big smile and waved good-bye like they'd all just enjoyed a champagne brunch. Officer Sanchez hesitated for a moment. Then she dug into her back pocket and pulled out a card with a New Orleans law enforcement logo on it. "Miss Slater, here's my card if you ever need anything."

"What would I need?" Jillian answered defensively.

"I don't know. Probably nothing. But you're new in town. It doesn't have to be business. Just if you need anything."

"I won't." Even with Jillian's sharp tone, the officer maintained her stance and held out the card for several awkward seconds until Jillian took it and threw it in her purse. With that, the two officers turned to the left and headed toward Jackson Square. Jillian took that as a signal to go right as fast as her wobbling legs could take her. She had no memory of drinking enough to have the kind of hangover she was fighting. Then again, much of the night was a blur.

As she turned the corner at the end of the block, she glanced over her shoulder and caught a glimpse of a woman facing her direction, sipping coffee out of a mug at a sidewalk café. There was no mistaking all that hair. It was Stella.

CHAPTER 21

"Well, that went well." Carla Sanchez retied her thick hair in a ponytail as they passed Café Beignet on the way to their car.

As usual, sarcasm was wasted on Bully. "I don't know. She seemed surprised to me."

"I'd say that's an understatement, Bully. She's got some kind of mouth on her, doesn't she?"

"You know how it is, Carla." It was rare that anybody on the force called Sanchez by her first name, and if they even came close, it was usually *Carlitos* just to get on her nerves. "She's just scared."

"Scared of what? I think she could use a little more fear than she seems to have. She's gonna get herself in serious trouble."

"Oh, she's scared alright. Give her some slack."

Bully's words often had a gentle edge to them, but this time he sounded downright sappy. Sanchez stopped in her tracks, put both hands on her hips, and stared at him. "William Robert La Bauve, take those sunglasses off and look me in the eye or I'll take them off for you."

"Why?" Bully grinned and held both sides of his glasses in place.

"You think she's cute!"

"No, I don't! I mean, it's not that. She *is* cute. Anybody can see that. But that doesn't have anything to do with me taking it easy on her. She seems lost. You know, like a lost puppy."

"You better listen to me well, partner. Puppies turn into dogs, and dogs bite."

"I'm starving." That was the most convincing way to change the subject in a city that boasted the best food on the planet with waistlines to prove it. "How about I grab us two orders of these?" Bully motioned toward the café where Jillian worked. "That might hold me over till I can get my hands on a shrimp po'boy for lunch."

"I'll pass on the beignets, but don't think I don't know what you're doing. You're gonna make sure they know she's okay."

"I could just let them know at the to-go window that it was a false alarm. You don't want them to go thinking something's up with her."

A few minutes later, Bully joined her at the curb with a white paper bag in his hand. The grease spots on the bag suggested the beignets were fresh out of the fryer, hot and tasty. She resisted telling him she believed she'd have one after all. A breeze swept an empty paper cup down the sidewalk toward them. She closed her eyes for a moment and felt the gust against her face. "If I didn't know better," she remarked, "I'd think the first winds of fall might be blowing in."

"That'd be nice, wouldn't it? Not unheard of this early either. But you know we don't usually get a north wind down here that doesn't come riding in on a storm."

Sanchez glanced off to the right and mumbled under her breath, "Yeah, and I feel a storm brewing. I feel it in my bones."

Bully called Adella as soon as he shut the patrol car door and turned the ignition. While he listened, he adjusted the air conditioner vents on his side of the car so they'd blow directly in his face. Adella's tone was spirited enough that Sanchez heard most of what she said from the passenger seat but she couldn't resist asking Bully to recount it. "So, how'd she take the news?"

He quoted Adella in his best female pitch. "'What do you mean she was asleep? Asleep! I'll show that young lady some sleep! I'm gonna knock her to kingdom come! She won't wake up for a month!'"

They both laughed.

"Did she bother to thank you?"

"Yes, as a matter of fact, she did. Right before we got off the phone. 'Officer La Bauve,' she said. 'Yes, ma'am,' I said. 'Thank you.' I said, 'You're mighty welcome,' but I think the phone was dead by then."

Sergeant DaCosta had a string of questions as long as a fishing line once they arrived, but most of them were left dangling. "The good news, boss, is that she is safe and sound and headed back to Saint Sans," Bully said.

"That's good," Sarge responded. "Yeah, that's good. Now maybe we can get to work around here—if it's alright with Mrs. Atwater." His words sounded like he'd found the whole thing to be a nuisance, but his expression differed.

"She wouldn't let us take her home, Sarge. We tried."

The sergeant's phone rang and he gave Bully and Sanchez a quick nod. "Gotta take this. Thanks, guys. Good work."

Half an hour later, Sanchez had her face glued to the screen of her laptop when Bully approached. "Did Sarge say we had to write a report?" he asked. "I was hoping we wouldn't have to do paperwork on a courtesy call."

"Nah, that's not what I'm doing. Come over here and look at this."

Bully walked around the desk and looked over her shoulder. "What are you—? Are you playing cards?"

"No, dork. You know better than that. This isn't a computer game. It's the tabletop at that apartment. While you were talking to Miss Slater, I took a few steps to look into the kitchen to see if anything seemed out of the ordinary. Everything in there looked fine, but this caught my attention. These cards were laid out on the table. Tarot cards, all faceup. See?" She tapped her finger on the screen.

"You took a picture?"

"Yep. I did. If she'd caught me, I was planning to tell her that I was texting Sarge."

"Tarot cards." Bully pronounced the silent *t* on the end of the word. "You've seen one, you've seen 'em all. Not unusual around these parts."

"No, you're right about that. But I wonder if our Miss Slater went over there to get herself a reading."

"Did you happen to get a good angle on a crystal ball?" He slapped his thigh. Nobody got a bigger kick out of Bully than Bully.

"I'm serious. Look here." Sanchez rolled the chair out beside her and patted it, motioning for him to sit down. As he did, the chair protested with a long squeak. "That's what you call a five-card horseshoe spread."

"Is that kinda like a five-card flush?"

"Bully, don't even act like your mama has ever let you play any poker."

"Don't be talking about my mama now." Bully grinned. His mother had her own reputation on the force for sending copious batches of cookies to work with him like he was having a first-grade class party. She had cookie cutters for every season. Any day now, she'd be sending iced sugar cookies in the shape of ghosts and pumpkins, and in fifteen minutes flat, there would be nothing but crumbs.

Sanchez stared pensively at the screen, unwilling to get sidetracked. "Bully, my great-aunt read cards. Growing up, I was completely infatuated with her. She was exotic and eccentric. She scared my big sister, but somehow I was enamored by her. My mom would tell me not to pay any attention to all that nonsense, but she didn't stop me from going over there. It got me out of her hair for a little while. Anyway, I didn't think it was nonsense. And I promise you that my great-aunt didn't. Those cards were a bible to her. I can still picture exactly the way her hands looked when she held them. Two rings on each hand. She was thin, so her hands were really bony and she wore her nails long and painted dark red and they'd be chipped most of the time on the edges."

"You might have missed your calling, Sanchez. Maybe running a nail salon was in the cards for you."

Sanchez ignored his attempt to lighten things up. "Funny how you keep some images in your head all your life. And sounds, too. I can still hear the sound of her long nails clicking against those cards. As she got older, she increasingly lost touch with reality. And I lost touch with her. I felt so bad at her wake that I'd let go of that relationship. My uncles kept kidding that 'she should have seen this coming.' But I didn't think they were funny."

"Weird. So you're not about to tell me you're a palm reader, are you, partner? Because I'd like to see you read this palm." His pale, outstretched hand was the size of a dinner plate.

She punched him in the shoulder. "No, I'm not a palm reader. But, Bully, I can read that draw. I'd sit right at my aunt's side and she'd go through those cards one by one, telling me their stories, like she was reciting nursery rhymes. She'd try various hands on me and get me to tell her how I'd read them. She'd ask things like whether the cards in that draw were speaking to the future, the present, or the past. She really believed in the whole thing, said I had a knack with them and that only gifted people got the nuance. I started to get taken in by the whole thing until my mother finally told me she'd better not catch me over there again. To a large part, their use relies on the power of suggestion over a willing victim. They can be dangerous, but mostly they're just creepy. This morning when I saw these things, it all came back to me. My stomach flipped like I was back in that musty room with the dark drapes. There's no telling how that woman might have interpreted these cards for Jillian, but I can tell you how my great-aunt would have interpreted them."

"I'm listening." Sanchez had Bully's full attention at this point.

She pointed to them one by one, slowly and in order. "That one involves money. That one—" she circled it on the screen with the mouse—"signals doom. The middle one is the fool. It can be a wild card, but in context with the rest of them, my aunt would say it lived up to its name." She moved to the fourth one. "This one here? Betrayal."

"And that one?" Bully asked, pointing to the fifth card.

"Death."

CHAPTER 22

As the trolley came to a stop, Jillian could see Adella standing at the front door of Saint Sans with her hands on her hips, steam coming out of her ears.

Adella started in before Jillian's foot hit the curb. "You've got thirty seconds to start explaining, young lady."

"Explaining what?" Jillian attempted to walk around her. "Why is it any of your business? My own mother never made me answer to her like that, even when I was in high school."

Adella blocked the doorway with her arm. "Well, has it occurred to you, Miss Thing, that she should have? Huh?"

"I'm an adult, Adella. Treat me like one."

"Girl, I'll treat you like an adult when you act like one. Take some responsibility. You had your grandmother worried sick. Just look what she's done to the flower beds." Wilted summer flowers and weeds had been pulled out by the roots and piled up in heaps under the oaks. "For that matter, you had us *all* worried sick. She called me in the middle of the night when you didn't come home. I got here before dawn this morning and every light in the house was on. Mrs. Winsee was up half the night and was fit to be tied, saying Mr. Winsee couldn't get a wink of sleep. For all we knew, your cold dead body had been thrown into the Mississippi mud."

"Oh, please. Don't act like you guys all care like that. I can't believe you're mad at me."

"You better be glad you have some people in your life who care enough to get mad at you. I don't know what I'm going to do with you. I'm about to enroll you in a class with Miss Manners. You'd qualify for a scholarship."

"I'll tell you what you're going to do. You're going to get out of my personal life!"

"That is precisely what I am *not* going to do. That much you can take to the bank. As long as you're under this roof—"

"It's not even your roof!"

Adella didn't back down. "I'll have you know that I may not own this roof, but I hire every single person who touches it, *and* I have a strong say in who lives under it."

"Well, then you will be relieved to know that I will not be under it much longer." Jillian ducked under Adella's arm into the great room. Adella marched right after her, heels clicking on the hardwood floor.

"Young lady, you're lucky I'm in the mood to overlook an offense since our day wasn't ruined by a call to the morgue. Turn around here and pinch those smarty lips of yours and listen to me."

Jillian was headstrong but Adella had a way of barking orders that unearthed an involuntary compliance in a person. She faced Adella with as much annoyance as she could capture in one expression.

"People in this house do care about you, Jillian. Some of them are just better at showing it than others. You could have called and eased some minds around here. It's just common decency. Consideration. Do you get that?"

Jillian almost let a *yes* slip from her tongue but thought better of it and sharpened her edge. She wasn't going to let these people control her. "I went over to a friend's apartment after work. That's it. That's all that happened. And then I fell asleep on her couch. Are you satisfied?"

"*Her* couch." Adella didn't even try to mask her relief.

"Yes, *hers*. I wasn't with a guy. But if I had been, it still wouldn't be any of your business. Are you people stuck in a time warp here or what?"

"Need I remind you, Jillian Slater, that we have all the man problems we can handle right now?"

"*We* don't have anything."

"I'll tell you what we have." Adella whispered the loudest of anyone Jillian knew. "*We* have a pregnancy test in my purse and the one of us who still has a uterus is about to take it."

Jillian's stomach rolled. She walked through the door of her room and set her purse on the bed. "I don't want to take it yet."

Adella closed the door behind them. "That's what you've been saying for the past two weeks. What I don't understand is why not?"

"I don't want to take the test until I have some money to do something about it."

Adella started to speak. Then she stopped and seemed to change gears. "Now, let's just simmer down and take one step at a time. Don't go making those kinds of plans even in your head right now. Every baby is—"

"Don't say *baby*!"

Adella took a deep breath. "Let's just take the test and see what it says. Then we'll go from there." She pulled the box out of her purse, put her glasses on, and squinted to read the instructions.

"Oh, just give it to me. I know how to do it." Jillian took the test out of her hand and went into the bathroom, slamming the door behind her. Her hands were shaking as she took the stick out of the box. She set it in the dry sink and steadied both hands on its edge. "Please," she whispered into the air, speaking, she supposed, to Fate.

Staring into the mirror over the sink, she flashed back to the reflection she'd seen in the restroom of a clinic eight years earlier. The girl in that mirror was seventeen. Her hair was long back then, her natural black but with two strands of blonde highlights framing her face. The bridge of her nose had broken out from the stress and her round face was slenderer than usual. She'd lost nearly ten pounds. She'd known for about a month but hadn't gotten the guts to tell her mother until a few days earlier.

Jade had done almost exactly what Jillian expected. She'd handled it. She made the appointment for her, drove her to it, kissed her on the cheek, and said, "Call me when you're ready for me to pick you up." Jillian had gone through that door all by herself. Even though Jade had always claimed to love being a single mom, Jillian had to wonder if she had regrets about going through with her own pregnancy. Otherwise, why would she have been so quick to arrange the termination of Jillian's?

The memory of the expression on that face in the mirror had never left her. The girl in that reflection wore a mask of raw fear. She was scared of the pain and terrified of the sight of blood. And she was alone. Nobody was in that reflection with her. She hadn't told the guy. She really liked him and she was afraid it would be the end of the relationship.

Jillian remembered curling up that night under a crocheted blanket on their couch with the sound of popcorn popping in the microwave. Jade had rented a movie for them to watch together. "It's a comedy," she said cheerfully. "What we need to do is laugh."

Jillian couldn't recall the movie title or who was in it. A few days later, she went back to school with a note from her mom saying she'd had the flu. The two of them never mentioned it again. She and the guy quit seeing each other soon after that.

"Girl, do I need to bring you a gallon of water to drink? How long can this take?" The sound of Adella's voice jolted Jillian back to the present.

"I need a few more minutes. Go work. I'll come find you when I'm done. You're making me nervous."

When Jillian finally opened the bathroom door, three people were standing side by side in her room staring wide-eyed at her like she was an apparition. "What in the—?"

Caryn blurted out, "Well? What did it say?"

David was as red as a beet but spoke up next. "We're just here for support, whether it's positive or negative."

Jillian glowered at Adella. "Thank you for being so trustworthy."

"I didn't exactly tell them. Well, not in so many words. Wouldn't you two say y'all kinda figured it out?"

Caryn and David looked back and forth between Adella and Jillian, apparently unsure of the safest way to answer.

"Anyway," Adella continued, "you didn't tell me not to tell, and sometimes you need people more than privacy."

"Oh, really? Like when?"

"Like *now*! I was so upset this morning when we couldn't find you that I let it slip that we didn't just have *one* missing person. And Caryn—well, she might as well be a doctor. David has a school holiday. He was ready to drive the whole mess of us to your aid today if we found out you were in trouble somewhere." Adella paused and lowered her hands to her sides. A certain vulnerability crept into her voice. "To tell you the truth, I was afraid maybe you had done something rash."

Jillian didn't feel well enough to be as mad as she wanted to be.

"I guess Mother Mary was ready to throw me out over it. She's so maternal and all."

"Olivia doesn't know. I didn't say a word to her."

"Well, give yourself a medal." Jillian drew a deep breath. "It's negative, anyway."

"What did you say? Exactly how do you mean *negative*?" Adella pressed.

"Negative as in *I'm not pregnant*."

Adella, Caryn, and David flopped down in perfect unison on the edge of Jillian's bed and the mattress popped up on the opposite side. Adella slapped her knee and said, "Shout hallelujah, somebody!"

It was unlike Jillian to refrain from snide remarks under the circumstances, especially with the outbreak of religious talk, but she was dead silent this time. Then her eyes widened into hula hoops and she slapped both hands over her mouth.

Adella stood up and stepped toward her. "Child, what is it? What's wrong with you? You look a little peaked. Are you—?"

Jillian bent over and vomited on Adella's shoes.

CHAPTER 23

JILLIAN PULLED THE SHEET DOWN from her face and forced her eyes open. She rolled onto her side and turned the digital clock on the bedside table toward her.

"Seven o'clock," she whispered, dropping her head back on the pillow. "Morning or night?" She sat straight up in the bed, hit by the thought that, if it was evening, she needed to get to work. Or didn't she have an early shift coming up this week? The first thing Jillian would have to do was figure out what day it was. She'd never felt more disoriented.

She set her feet on the floor, now vaguely remembering Adella helping her into pajamas. The image of Adella's bare feet popped into her mind, her toenails painted in bright contrast to her brown skin. The bottom edges of her feet looked almost pink. "Oh, gosh," Jillian muttered, rubbing her head and replaying the scene that had left Adella conspicuously shoeless. If half the house hadn't been in her room when she projectile vomited, she might have had a shred of dignity left. *These people have no boundaries.*

Jillian jerked up her feet at the recollection of what had been on the floor in that spot. Both the hardwood and the edge of the rug that had been in the path of destruction were perfectly unsoiled. Someone had cleaned up after her. "Please somebody tell me it wasn't David. Or Caryn." Then she recalled David shooting out of that room like he'd been blown from a cannon. She hated that she was probably going to have to thank Adella. Then again, maybe she'd make Jillian mad before she got the opportunity.

David was in the kitchen sitting on a stool at the island, blowing on a spoonful of something hot when Jillian came in. He dropped the spoon in a bowl when he saw her and rose to his feet. "How are you feeling, sleepyhead?"

"Embarrassed. I'm sorry you had to see that."

"Oh, no worries. I'm a high school teacher. I've seen worse. Not a lot worse, I'll admit." He grinned warmly.

"You did make a pretty quick exit as I recall."

"Ah, but for the sake of your honor alone."

"I bet." They both smiled. "I only remember having one glass of wine. I don't even remember finishing it but I guess I did. And I guess that wasn't all I had. At first I assumed I felt sick because, well, you know. But when the test came out negative—"

"Not for me to judge. Maybe it was a bug. I'm just glad you're better now. You feel like eating? You're not going to believe how good this is." David sat back down and pulled up a spoon heaped with small bits of carrots and celery.

Surely that meant it was evening, but she wouldn't have been surprised if these people ate fried gator for breakfast with a side of tart green tomatoes.

David kept talking. "You think you slept it off? You've been

dead to the world all afternoon. I only know that because Adella
stuck her head in there a few times, but she locked the door of
your room behind her the last time before she left."

That meant it was the same day. Jillian was relieved. She wasn't
on the schedule for work until tomorrow then. She spied a half-
empty sleeve of saltines a few inches from David's right elbow.
Maybe she could eat a few of those.

"The soup is homemade," he explained. "I added salt and pepper to mine because it was intentionally a little bland for the sake
of the sick."

Jillian sat down beside him on the next stool. "I can't believe
you did that. Thank you, David."

"I wish I could take credit for it. Your grandmother fixed it.
Even boiled a whole chicken for the broth. She said there was plenty
of it and for me to help myself. Mrs. Winsee had some too. I think
Caryn had lost her appetite though." David elbowed Jillian gently.

"You're kidding me."

"You surprised? Your grandmother is a fabulous cook, Jillian.
Granted, she doesn't usually make a pot of anything that isn't so
spicy you need to be carded to eat it, but there is no denying the
woman can cook. She was in here chopping up vegetables for
at least an hour earlier this afternoon. Then as it simmered, she
headed to the backyard and pulled weeds. She went back to her
suite a few minutes before you came out and told me that she'd
come put it all away before bedtime."

"She said it was for me?"

David looked up and squinted his eyes, obviously trying to replay
the conversation. "No, not exactly, but who else would it be for?"

"Herself?" Honestly, Jillian couldn't picture the woman that
benevolent.

David laughed. "You see this bowl?" He clinked his spoon
against the edge for emphasis. "If she'd cooked for herself, instead

of that clear golden broth, there would be a thick elixir from a roux as dark as mud. And see that chicken?"

Jillian nodded, unsure of where this conversation was headed.

"That would be a deveined shrimp nearly as thick as your little finger, boiled to a perfect opaque white. Take your spoon a little deeper on the next round and you'd come up with some lump crabmeat—maybe even a claw—or maybe what you'd score is an oyster." Jillian made a terrible face. "On second thought, your stomach may not be up to that image. Increase your rice ratio in that bowl for now and pass on the oysters. There'd be some celery just like this but it would play second fiddle to the okra."

"I get it. At one time, believe it or not, I really did waitress where we served more than donuts. But I'm not a big fan of gumbo."

"Jillian, forgive me, but you have never seen a bowl of filé gumbo in California like I'm talking about unless it was straight from the soup pot of a homesick transplant. Girl, this is Louisiana gumbo. And your grandmother is the Justown Wilsown of Saint Sans, I guar-ron-tee."

"What's a justown?"

"It's really Justin, but he pronounced it that way. Justin Wilson was a famous Cajun chef. A storyteller with the comedic wit of a world-class stand-up. He sort of crafted it all together, and with an accent so thick, anyone past the state line would need an inter-preter. He had a cooking show on PBS. Been dead awhile now. Of course, he was famous for chicken and andouille gumbo. You know why de sheecken cross de road, haaah? Really, to run away from dem Cajuns, I tell you dat right now, 'cause Cajun will eat mos' any-ting, an' dey love to cook sheecken."

Jillian had to smile. David was so proper and well-spoken that the accent was delightfully absurd coming from him.

"Mrs. Fontaine is more of a seafood purist when it comes to her gumbo. I am too, but from this side of the bowl. Never made any of my own. How'd you manage to get me to go off into all of that?"

Jillian shrugged her shoulders, her stomach gurgling.

"Oh yeah! I was saying that's how you know she didn't make this homemade chicken soup for herself. Face it. It's for you." David scooted out his stool. "Let me spoon you up some. Sound good?"

David twisted the lid off the pressure cooker and dipped a ladle in it, stirring the soup several times. Jillian trailed behind him and peered over his shoulder as he scooped toward the bottom of the pot and lifted the ladleful of white meat chicken, carrots, celery, and small cubes of potato. Jillian wasn't sure whether she'd feel better if she ate or worse.

"Hmmm," she said. "I don't eat much meat. Do you know if that chicken is organic?"

"That I couldn't tell you." David looked at Jillian with a trace of bewilderment.

Mrs. Winsee stuck her face right in between theirs, startling Jillian. "And how is our patient? I wore my washable slippers just in case you weren't done. See?" Mrs. Winsee pulled up her satin robe a few inches, exposing an ankle so white, it shone like a naked lightbulb. Her slippers were solid gold sequins with plastic black bows.

"You sure those are washable, Mrs. Winsee? They're pretty fancy." David always found some way to compliment the old woman.

"The gentle cycle. I'm sure of it." She was having a perfectly lucid moment, it seemed, although she'd been gently banned from the laundry room since an unfortunate incident involving an entire gallon of Tide. She'd blamed it on Mr. Winsee. The washer had bubbled up like a volcano for days every time somebody threw in a load. "These remind me of the matching pair Maude Anne and I got from Mother on Christmas Day 1942." Mrs. Winsee was still staring at her feet. "We also got matching gowns and robes. We felt like princesses in them. We twirled and twirled for Father."

Jillian tried to steer the conversation from turning into a Norman Rockwell painting. What Mrs. Winsee needed, Jillian figured, was a realist, and if Jillian was anything in her own eyes, it was a realist. "It doesn't matter. You're safe. My stomach's too empty to be a threat." She sighed, accepting her unavoidable fate as the laughingstock of Saint Sans over the baptism of Adella Atwater's favorite heels.

"But nothing surpassed the Christmas of '45. That was the year we tore red foil wrapping and satiny ribbons from matching pairs of ruby slippers. They were glittery patent leather. Oh, how we squealed and clicked our heels." Mrs. Winsee closed her eyes and tapped her heels together counting to three. "There's no place like—"

"Holy cow, is this soup ever good!" David spoke up before Jillian could say anything cynical and stuck a ladleful of broth right under her nose.

"I don't think I can eat it after all."

Mrs. Winsee offered cheerfully, "She said you wouldn't."

"What do you mean she said I wouldn't? Who?"

"Olivia. She said, 'Now watch her not eat a single bite of it.'" Mrs. Winsee smiled ear to ear as innocently as if she'd just paid someone a thousand-dollar compliment. "I sound just like her, don't I, David? I could play her on the silver screen."

Jillian threw open the cabinet and pulled out a bowl. "Give me that," she ordered David as she snatched the ladle from his hand. She dipped it deep into the pressure cooker and splashed its contents into her bowl, flinching as drops of near-boiling liquid splattered her hand. On her way out of the kitchen, she grabbed the saltines and, hands full, headed for her room.

As she reached the door to her suite, she heard Mrs. Winsee say to David, "Well, I suppose a woman has a right to change her mind, but I wonder why she didn't want to eat in here with us."

Jillian made no attempt to hear his response. She elbowed through the door she'd left ajar and slammed it behind her with her foot.

Before Jillian could decide where to set her bowl of soup, she saw a cell phone on her bedside table with a handwritten note:

Jillian—

Please use this while you are in town. It's an extra one I have on hand. It's a year or so old but still works fine. I took the liberty of having it reactivated. It's already on my bill.

Olivia

The phone number with a local area code was written at the bottom and a wall charger was draped next to it. Jillian sat down on the edge of the bed and picked up the phone and held it. As much as she hated to accept the charity, especially from Olivia and especially right now, the humiliation of giving the landline at Saint Sans for her contact number at work had been almost more than she could stand. It was a wonder she'd withstood the temptation to turn on her cell phone from San Francisco, but she was too afraid she'd find out that there was a warrant in California for her arrest. She plugged in the phone, ate a few crackers, and pressed the On button.

If anyone had ever texted from this phone, the log had been wiped clean. Only three contacts were stored: Adella Atwater, Olivia Fontaine, and Saint Sans Apartments.

CHAPTER 24

THE MALADY disabling young Brianna Brashear had left her mother limping as well, though her infirmity was not as clear to the eye. Evelyn Ann doted day and night on her ailing child. She'd taken the pain personally when her daughter's recovery was not all they had hoped and prayed it would be, and she determined to devote the rest of her life to easing the child's burden.

Naturally this left her less available for ministry in the church than many expected. She hosted the occasional ladies' tea but only reluctantly. She cooked adequate but simple meals for visiting missionaries but added little conversation to the table she painstakingly set. Despite frequent pointed suggestions from the faithful, she felt no obligation to the choir nor a summons to the piano bench.

What Mrs. Brashear lacked in congregational servitude, her husband worked tirelessly to compensate for. Reverend Brashear was gregarious, warm, and so unflaggingly energetic that he could wear on the nerves.

Most of the time he seemed unaffected by his helpmate's detachment, but on occasion, a keen observer could see him look toward her with pleading eyes, begging her to spring to life and amaze their community with her wit and wisdom. In his rare quiet moments, he couldn't shake the feeling that Evelyn Ann blamed him for Brianna's condition, although for the life of him, he couldn't fathom how. He chose to stay busy, and she chose to let him.

CHAPTER 25

"RAFE ADORED THAT CHILD."

Adella was taken aback by Olivia's unexpected declaration—
both by what she said and the fact that she was there saying it at
all. Adella was in the utility room early the next morning when
Olivia happened by and dropped that bombshell. And apparently
that wasn't all she had to say because she went right on without
even noticing Adella's reaction.

"She was his whole world. His whole face lit up when he talked
about her."

Adella gathered her wits and replied, "I had no idea you remembered her so well."

"Well, of course I remember her. She was the daughter of my
only child." Olivia somehow managed to always dodge the word
granddaughter. "He loved her mother for that matter, though God
only knows what he saw in the woman."

"I'm sure Jaclyn was beautiful."

"I despised her so much that I really couldn't tell you. But I don't think he was hung up on her because of her looks, and it certainly wasn't her winsome personality. I think it was a case of rejection making the heart grow fonder. Jaclyn didn't want Rafe, so he wanted her twice as much."

"How old was Jillian when Jaclyn started pulling back from him?" Adella popped the door of the dryer open so it would stop turning. She meant to hear every word.

"Oh, that started before he even knew Jaclyn was pregnant. She told him she didn't have the same feelings for him that he had for her and that she didn't want to see him anymore. That he'd taken it more seriously than she had. I didn't know all of this until later, needless to say. Communication has never been a Fontaine family trait. He still tried to pursue her after that, but she managed to avoid him and dropped out of sight."

"But she was already pregnant at that time?" Adella struggled to keep the timeline straight.

"Yes, she was. He pined for her for several months and tried to move on. Then, about the time he started pulling out of his misery, he caught a glimpse of her from a distance at the airport when he was about to fly out on a business trip."

Adella had only known Rafe in his severest destitution, so she'd never imagined him living a normal life. Taking business trips. With every sentence tumbling out of Olivia's mouth in that utility room came a new frame to try to force his picture into.

Olivia continued. "He was about to board a plane but stepped out of line and hauled off after her like it was going to be one for the movies. He finally caught up to her outside of baggage claim. He grabbed her by the arm just before she got into the backseat of a cab. She jerked her arm away from him, called him something insulting, ducked into the car, and slammed the door. He stood there with his chin hanging. She looked nearly full-term, from what he described."

"He was sure the baby was his? Just like that?"

"I asked him that, as you can well imagine. I certainly wasn't. Not until later. He found her again about six months after that. She'd moved to Baton Rouge. He tried the gracious approach. Showed up at her apartment and asked if he could see the baby. She denied the baby was his."

"And he didn't believe her."

"No. He'd have done better to have been poorer at math. I wish he had taken her word for it. But instead he saw a lawyer and got a paternity test ordered. DNA testing was just getting started, but Rafe had the money to have it done, and the results showed that the baby was his. He told Jaclyn he was going to court to request parental rights to see Jillian. Jaclyn caved because she was running out of money to fight him, so it never went that far."

"Whew. That's a hornets' nest." Adella was trying to think what she would have done if her boys' biological father had wanted to be a part of their lives. Emmett Atwater had been the best thing that ever happened to them. She'd get glimpses here and there of the boys' wounds of abandonment—often when she least expected it. All in all, however, they'd managed to navigate the absence without excessive fallout. God had been good to them. For a split second she wondered where on earth his grace was hidden in this mixed-up Fontaine bunch.

"You have no idea how big a hornets' nest. Rafe's father was livid at him for not letting it go. He said they'd go after every dime we had. I wasn't happy with him either. It looked to us like he had the spine of an inchworm. He begged that woman for that child over and over again. Told her he'd do anything."

"So Jaclyn finally agreed to let him see her some?"

"Yes, but she left no doubt how put out she was about it. She managed to convince Rafe not to sue for legal custody, saying it would be too disruptive for Jillian. I didn't buy it. She had the maternal instincts of a bullfrog."

Adella tried not to let her face give away what she was thinking about the pot calling the kettle black. Anyway, she didn't want to interrupt. Pieces of the Fontaine family puzzle were flying through the air in that conversation with the speed of light, and she meant to catch them while she could.

"That's not to say the baby adapted well." Olivia paused long enough to close her eyes and shake her head with exasperation. Her expression betrayed how much she resented the right of those memories to surface from that deep vault. "She screamed her head off the first few times Jaclyn dropped her off, and I surely don't have to tell you that Rafe didn't know the first thing to do with that baby." She sighed. "But he learned. And Jillian eventually seemed to adapt to him. He bought her everything under the sun. Clothes. Toys. The whole place looked like a nursery."

Olivia smoothed her palm over the surface of a folded bath towel, looking like she was trying to keep herself composed. "Once he asked me if I'd ever consider getting a swing set. I didn't know why on earth we needed one, when there was a perfectly good park within walking distance. Mr. Fontaine never remotely warmed up to the idea of Rafe parenting a child. He refused to accept the 'scientific hoodoo' that said she was his." Olivia stared out the window in the utility room for a moment. Then, right before Adella's eyes, the woman seemed to shake off every ounce of emotion like a dog shaking off suds.

"But you?" Adella asked.

"I wasn't blind. I caught a glimpse of the three of us in a full-length mirror walking out of a restaurant once. The resemblance was unmistakable."

A lump welled in Adella's throat. "She looked just like him, did she?"

"No, Adella. She looked just like *me*."

Both women went dead silent for several moments. It was Adella's turn to stare out the window. Olivia blew out a breath and stiffened her lower back against the washing machine. Adella knew that if she didn't say something quick to detain her, Olivia was going to make an exit and the subject would never come up again. "Well, I wish this was when you could tell me they lived happily ever after."

"It is clear enough that they did not. They had several years of this odd arrangement, but at least Rafe got to see the child. Jaclyn wouldn't let her refer to him as Dad. Jaclyn had a number of men in her life in this period of time, according to Rafe. But everything changed when one of them moved in with her. I think the long and short of it was that Jaclyn wanted Jillian to attach to the new guy. She poisoned that child toward her father. Lied to her about him. By this time she was old enough to be brainwashed. Jaclyn told her Rafe wasn't her father and that things would be better if he'd leave them alone."

"But she loved him by this time, right?"

"She had, I think, before that, but she turned on a dime. I don't know if you have ever seen a six-year-old with disdain on her face. She'd throw fits. She'd demand to go home. She'd say, 'We hate you!'"

"She was just a child, Olivia."

"Well, yes. A child with the power to break a grown man. One day he went to pick her up for a scheduled visit and stood knocking at the door for fifteen minutes. A man stuck his head out of the apartment next door, mad about all the racket. Rafe learned from him that they'd moved all their stuff out the day before. He went to the manager's office in a tailspin, demanding to know if there was a forwarding address or contact number. Would you believe Jaclyn had the forethought to leave a letter in the manager's hands with Rafe's name on it? I saw it later in some of his things. She said they were moving to California for a fresh start, and if he cared about the child, he'd leave them alone. 'She doesn't want you to be her father,' she'd said."

Adella's stomach turned. "And he accepted that?"

"If you want to call it that. That's when a man who drank a bit too much on occasion picked up a glass and never set it down. He was just too sensitive for it all."

Olivia had only one thing left to say. "Jaclyn and Jillian killed Rafe long before he was dead. They might as well have put a gun to his head. He never got over it."

The morning sun was bleeding through every crevice in the plantation blinds when Jillian's alarm went off. The sound persisted as she repeatedly slapped the top of the clock on the bedside table. Sitting up in bed, she remembered that it was the alarm on her new phone. She turned it off and fell back on the pillow.

"Get up, girl," she whispered to herself. "A world of dough awaits you."

Jillian climbed out of bed and turned the knob on the shower almost all the way to the left. As the temperature warmed and the bathroom mirror fogged, she splashed cold water from the sink on her face. She felt almost normal, a small miracle considering the last forty-eight hours. Maybe her stomach wasn't quite ready for Olivia's French press, but she could probably handle some coffee when she got to the café.

Jillian realized that morning how much she missed music. She never got ready for work back home in San Francisco without it, and music played continually over the speakers at Sigmund's. After her shower, she opened the app on the phone Olivia had given her and found nothing stored. For a moment she considered transferring the music stored in her old phone to the new one, but then again, to turn it on was to chance discovering a host of vicious voice mails.

She put on a few coats of black noir mascara and some lip gloss, both of which she'd purchased at the grocery store. They weren't her favorite but they weren't so bad either. Slipping on a pair of hoop earrings, she glanced in the mirror over the antique vanity and tilted her head. What she needed was a haircut. If she was going to have to wear this white getup to work five days a week, she at least owed it to her customers to keep her dragonfly in view. She made a mental note to ask Caryn for a recommendation or, on second thought, Stella, if she ran into her. Jillian had no idea if a stylist who worked with a black woman's hair could also tame hers. Maybe she'd ask Adella.

She grabbed her purse and stuck her new cell phone in its side pocket. As much as she hated to have to talk to Olivia this morning, she'd need to say something about the phone, especially since she planned to use it. Or maybe she'd leave her a note. Perfect idea. That's what Olivia had done. Jillian headed into the kitchen and found a pad of paper by the phone and a pen in the drawer below it. The ballpoint appeared to be dry but she made circles on the pad until the ink began to flow.

Mrs. Fontaine,
Got the phone. Thanks. I will pay for it myself when I can.
I will try not to be here much longer.

Jillian paused a moment and considered how she could tell Olivia that she'd eaten the soup just to prove her wrong.

Mrs. Winsee told me—

Maybe that wasn't a good idea. She scratched out those four words and jotted down two instead.

Jillian Slater

As she propped the note against a large bottle of olive oil on the kitchen counter, she heard voices down the hall. One voice was easy to identify. It was Adella's. Thinking the other might be Caryn's, she rounded the corner to inquire about a low-cost hair salon. It wasn't Caryn after all. It was Olivia talking in a low voice to Adella in the utility room. She got within a few feet of the doorway just in time to hear Olivia say, "Jaclyn and Jillian killed Rafe long before he was dead. They might as well have put a gun to his head. He never got over it."

Jillian went cold. She swung around to get out of the hall before they caught her, stepping on the end of Clementine's tail. The cat yowled loud enough to crack a glass. Jillian flew through the den toward the front entrance without glancing back to see if they were following her. She flung open the door, and as she stepped through it, she tripped, tumbling to her hands and knees.

Clementine scurried past Jillian onto the front lawn as she caught her breath and scrambled to her feet. Both Olivia and Adella were standing in the doorway with their chins dropped but neither of them were looking at her. Jillian followed their gaze to the all-weather doormat where she'd tripped. All three women glared at a baby doll wrapped in a light-blue blanket.

"Is this somebody's idea of a joke?" Jillian was stunned. "Who did this?"

Olivia was shaking her head. "We have no idea who, but some-body's been—"

"You people are sickos! I told you I wasn't pregnant!"

Olivia looked at Jillian with confusion. "What?"

Adella stepped over the doll toward her. "Jillian, calm down a minute and let's all get our bearings. Come back in here and let's sort all this out."

Jillian glanced down St. Charles and saw the trolley in the dis-tance heading their way. "I'm going to work. I wish I never had to come back to this place again." She stormed across the lawn and then the street without looking back, even though both women were calling her name.

Once she was on the trolley, Jillian turned up both of her stinging palms, scraped from catching her fall. She heard the muffled sound of a phone ringing and realized it was the one in her purse. Pulling out the phone, she saw the caller ID: Saint Sans Apartments. Jillian declined the call, silenced the ringer, and threw the phone back into her purse.

CHAPTER 26

ADELLA STARED AT THE UNCLOTHED DOLL lying on the dining table and the blue baby blanket crumpled beside it. Olivia was back in her suite, waiting to hear from Officer DaCosta. The morning's events had not been the circumstances under which Adella wanted to tell Olivia about the arcane card on the flowers at the burial and the baby rattle on the back mat. But she'd promised Officer DaCosta she'd spill the beans, and she needed to do it before the man showed up himself.

"Why *atonement*?" Olivia had asked with a look on her face that suggested she wasn't sure she wanted an answer.

"I was hoping you might know. Any idea at all?" Adella had begun to wonder if the two women had ever had a single conversation that wasn't uncomfortable.

Olivia had hesitated for a moment and then responded, "None."

Adella still wasn't sure what atonement had to do with baby paraphernalia and things moving around on the back porch, but that picture of Rafe showing up out of nowhere made the whole thing so spooky that the hair stood up on her arms.

Maybe the police could help make sense of all of it.

Waiting for her to emerge with some news, Adella replayed in her memory the conversation earlier that morning between her and Olivia in the utility room. The one Jillian had caught the tail end of before running out the front door and tripping over the doll. No wonder the poor girl was always on the defensive. The whole house had gone crazy. There wasn't a single rug she could stand on that didn't get jerked out from under her. From the sound of things, that had been the story of her life.

"I swear to goodness, it's like the woman is amphibious," Adella railed to Emmett that evening. "She pulls the girl in with her right hand and pushes her back with the left, all in one move."

"*Ambidextrous*, you mean," Emmett replied.

"And Jillian is no better. She's just a younger version. We're all getting the silent treatment from her now. The very idea that she thinks we'd plant that doll on the front porch."

"Dell, you better give me that knife before you amputate one of your fingers with it."

She pinched her lips together, hacked the blade through the raw onion, and sent slices flying off the cutting board.

Seven hamburger patties were simmering in a giant skillet of brown gravy, two for each of the boys in the house and one for her. Emmett was apparently too hungry to sympathize properly with the latest from Saint Sans. Knowing him, he'd been thinking about that smothered steak all day. He gathered up the slices of onion and threw them into the skillet. He stuck a fork through a chunk of potato boiling on the stove to see if it was tendering up. It must not have been, because he turned up the flame.

"Are you cooking this or am I?" Adella turned toward him with her hands on her hips.

"You are, thank you, ma'am, but not fast enough for my appetite. You know what you need, woman? You need a hug." He threw his arms around her, squeezed her, and kissed her forehead.

"I do most certainly not need a hug." Adella's words were muffled as her face pressed into Emmett's shirt. "What I need is some peace of mind!"

"You know as well as I do, Adella Atwater, that peace of mind isn't about peaceful circumstances. There'll always be some conflict or calamity as long as we're trudging along on this side of Jordan's shore. Peace of mind is about trust. You take too much responsibility for all those people over there anyway. You can't save them. Give them to Jesus."

"What was it Pastor said just last Sunday? From the book of James, I think. No, it was Jude. 'Save others by snatching them out of the fire.' You heard him yourself. I know I can't save their souls, but if somebody doesn't do something, resentment and distrust are going to rub together like two dry sticks and the sparks are going to burn that whole house down."

Emmett pulled back from Adella so he could look right into her eyes. Holding her face in both his hands, he said, "You can't snatch somebody out of a fire who's refusing to budge. And you're getting yourself burned trying."

Water sizzled on the hot stove and Adella looked up to see the potatoes boiling over. She turned down the burner and stirred them briskly. "Oh, now look what you've gone and made me do!"

Adella lay awake for a long time after Emmett started snoring. She couldn't get her mind to stop replaying all the events of the last few days. She was fitful about having been so preoccupied with the reality show over at Saint Sans that she'd come in two weeks late on Trevor Don's love life—the topic of conversation at dinner, thanks to a less-than-accidental slip of the tongue by AJ. Apparently he'd been keeping company with Tonya Thompson, a girl from church. Much to her boys' dismay, she had insisted on reading every word of every text on Trevor Don's phone. "I intend to steal it regularly from now on," she had assured Emmett before he dropped off to sleep.

"I don't find that hard to believe," he responded.

"And the same goes for AJ's, too."

At that, Emmett had reached over on the bedside table, picked up his phone, and handed it to her. "You might as well read mine, too."

She pushed his hand back, laughing. "You happen to be the one man in the house I trust farther than I can throw him. Anyway, your texts bore me to tears. Give me back that phone. Let me read you a perfect example. This was just yesterday. Me: 'I am in enough traffic to give a civil woman a murderous case of road rage. Those idiots have got all the lanes closed down but one. I'm going to try to exit Poydras and take the feeder road. Can you stop by the store on your way home from work and get some hamburger buns? If I stop, I may never get back on. I've got fresh meat in the fridge but I forgot the buns because a woman with a behind the size of a barn hogged up half the aisle at baked goods while she squeezed every bun on the shelf. By the time she finally moseyed on to the fruits and nuts where she belonged, I forgot what I was there for. You know how the boys hate it when I use regular bread on a burger. And all I've got is that wheat bread that I bought on Tuesday in a vain attempt to save all our arteries and you would've thought I'd committed a domestic crime the way they acted about it. You got off earlier than I did today and Jillian has nearly sent me into a nervous fit so can you get some?' And here's you." Adella put the phone right under his nose but he was too tickled to read it. It didn't matter because she was certain he remembered exactly what he'd texted back: **K.**

In all the excitement of the evening, she realized now, she hadn't looked at her phone a single time, and she wondered whether anyone from Saint Sans might have called with an update on Jillian. The way the girl hightailed it out of there this morning, Adella worried she might decide to stay out all night again.

She crawled out of bed and felt around for her phone on the dresser and then on the bathroom counter. She tiptoed downstairs and flipped on a lamp and searched the den to no avail, and then the kitchen.

"I bet I never brought the darn thing in from the car," she whispered to herself. She started to leave it until morning but decided it could be stolen by that time. Her pajamas were decent enough that she didn't bother to go back upstairs for a robe. She grabbed her car keys and slipped out the back door. The neighbor's German shepherd startled her nearly out of her wits, barking like he was about to take the ankle off an intruder. The bulb in the porch light was out, but the light from the kitchen was enough for her to see her way to the car. The motion detector over the garage door would come on once she got out there.

She pressed the button on her key as she opened the gate and she heard the car door on the driver's side unlock. When the motion detector switched on the light, she nearly put her foot down on a raccoon tearing into a McDonald's bag for leftover fries. She squealed and the raccoon took off, hissing. Adella put her hand over her pounding heart and tried to catch her breath. "If those boys don't quit leaving the lid off the trash can, I'm going to pull every hair out of their heads." Opening the car door, she caught a glimpse of the phone on the floor on the passenger's side, just under the seat. Rather than go around to the other side in her bare feet, she got into the driver's seat and bent all the way over to retrieve it. With her head down in front of the seat and her feet hanging out of the car door, her mind tried to read what her eyes were seeing on the screen.

Missed Call: Raphael Fontaine

She jumped up and lunged out of the car, running headlong into a man's chest.

It was the kind of thing that could make a grown woman nearly wet her pants.

The man turned out to be a neighbor from the end of the block who said he was on a late-night walk when he saw the light on in her car and her feet sticking out of the driver's side. He said he just wanted to make sure she was okay.

Adella wanted to respond, "I was perfectly fine until you showed up without announcing yourself," but she refrained. *Who takes a walk at midnight?* she thought. *Who wouldn't just call from the end of the driveway, "Hey, lady! You okay?"*

She never shut her eyes all night. Her heart was racing like it had something to run from.

CHAPTER 27

JILLIAN CLOCKED OUT at the café at ten thirty, glad to head back to Saint Sans at a decent hour. It was Halloween night and Jackson Square looked like an audition for the world's biggest freak show. The waitstaff back at Sigmund's and a few regular customers came in costume on Halloween, too, but these people were a whole different caliber. They looked more like they'd taken off the costumes they'd worn to their day jobs and come as themselves.

One of the other waitresses teased Jillian as she left. "Get home before midnight. You know what they say about this city and vampires, don't you?"

No, and she didn't want to know. She'd already watched one bizarre guy down a whole order of beignets in about three bites with his vampire teeth still in place. Another gulped at least four cups of café au lait with a noose dangling around his neck. And there was no counting the witches. The square might as well have been a Wiccan convention.

"And people raise their eyebrows when I tell them I'm from San Francisco," Jillian answered the waitress.

When she got off the trolley across from Saint Sans, all seemed quiet on St. Charles except the wind. She tried to rub the chill bumps off her arms from the northern blowing in. As she pushed through the front door and adjusted her eyes to the dim light of the great room, she reminded herself she only had to face this place for a few more days. It had taken a couple weeks of well-placed hints, but Stella had finally agreed to let her stay at her place for a while. She planned to split her time between working at the café and looking for a better-paying job.

There was no comparison between Saint Sans and Stella's place. Only a glutton for punishment would leave the bed in her room here for Stella's couch. But sometimes it was too expensive to stay somewhere for free. She stared for a few seconds at the boat in the stained glass, the waves around it alive with the moonlight. She needed to tell Adella, David, and Caryn she was leaving. Maybe she'd leave Olivia to figure it out when she shut the door on Clementine's tail on her way out.

David walked into the room. "I thought I heard you," he said. "Figured I'd see you in."

"You still up?" Jillian liked David. He'd be the only one she'd really miss. Caryn had been friendly to her, too, but Jillian always assumed it was insincere. After all, how could somebody going to medical school not look down on somebody like Jillian?

"The Winsees have been dancing for the last half hour. It won't be any use to try to sleep until they tire out." David smiled warmly.

"What do you mean, *dancing*?"

David motioned to Jillian. "Come here. Real quietly now."

She slipped off her shoes and tiptoed down the hall with him until they were right across from Mrs. Winsee's door. David took Jillian by the hand and pulled her down to the floor, where they sat with their backs against the wall. Music wafted from the room and David quietly sang with it.

"Some day, when I'm awfully low
When the world is cold
I will feel a glow just thinking of you
And the way you look tonight."

"Hey, you can sing!" Jillian whispered loudly.

David grinned with unfeigned affection. "Well, that would be helpful, seeing that I teach chorale."

"What if she opens the door and finds us out here?" Jillian giggled.

"She won't. She's too happy doing what she's doing. Anyway, she wouldn't care. She'd probably just sit down here with us and ask us who we're eavesdropping on."

The sound of Mrs. Winsee's laughter lifted above the music.

"The woman's nuts, David. How can you be so tolerant of her?"

"Don't call her that. She just lives much of the time in a world that her mind spins out of the yarn of her past. But she's a delightful woman if you give her the chance. Let her talk sometime. Ask her about herself and hear her out. And who wouldn't want a marriage like that, anyway?"

Jillian whispered, "But it isn't real!"

"Oh, make no mistake, Jillian. It's real to her." They could both hear Mrs. Winsee talking to her dead husband.

"Sheesh. Can you imagine what the poor man was like?" Jillian shook her head.

"Adella once told me that he helped Mrs. Fontaine sort out some legal issues about her husband's will after he passed. He was a lawyer, you know. I think he already had cancer at that time."

"Did they strike up some kind of deal over the old woman?"

"Business deal, you mean? I don't think you'd call it that, though he left more than enough money for her care. Adella made it sound like he'd been a true friend to Mrs. Fontaine when the state of Louisiana tried to lay claim to every dime her husband had made. Then she was a true friend to him after he died."

"After somebody dies is a little late, don't you think?"

"I suspect she'll oversee Mrs. Winsee's care for the rest of her life. I'd say that's not too late."

A lower voice trailed from Mrs. Winsee's room. A man's voice. "Oh, gosh, is that her doing his voice now? I'm creeped out!"

"I've never heard her mimic Mr. Winsee's voice. It does sound a little odd." David chuckled. "But remember, much of her life was spent on the stage. Think of it like she's reading both parts."

"Whatever. It's giving me goose bumps."

They leaned closer and closer to the door to try to decipher the dialogue. David almost had his ear next to the knob when a loud slamming sound jolted Jillian to her feet. "What was that?"

David looked a little unnerved himself but said calmly, "No worries. I bet the gate is unlatched in the backyard and the wind banged it shut."

A shrill scream came from Mrs. Winsee's room. David jumped to his feet and beat on her door with his palm. "Mrs. Winsee! It's David. You okay? Mrs. Winsee? Let me in." She made an indistinguishable but unsettling sound. He dashed into the utility room and started throwing open the cabinet doors.

"What are you doing?" Jillian wasn't whispering anymore.

"There's a key to her room in here. It's in one of these cabinets or drawers. Help me find it!"

As Jillian scrambled through several drawers, David ran his hand along the top of the cabinet over the washer and dryer. They both heard the banging sound again.

"Got it!" He was back at her door in a flash. "Mrs. Winsee, it's your friend David. Grab your robe if you need to. I'm coming in and I mean right now." He turned the key and swung open the door.

Mrs. Winsee was standing with her back to them, facing an open window, her gown and the curtain sheers whipping with the wind, her shoulders shivering. David grabbed her robe off the rocker, draped it around her shoulders, and ordered Jillian to shut the music off.

When he turned Mrs. Winsee around, her face was awash with fear. She mumbled something imperceptible, saliva bubbling on her lips. Before David could lower the window, they heard one of the iron chairs scoot across the back porch. "That's no wind doing that! Stay with her!"

He darted out of Mrs. Winsee's room toward the back door. When Jillian turned toward Mrs. Winsee, she saw a large man's head and shoulders framed by the open window. He was wearing a ghoulish mask that looked like melted flesh and a shirt that looked splashed in blood. Jillian screamed and Mrs. Winsee froze in fear.

Jillian pulled Mrs. Winsee from the room and charged out the back door just as the whack of a broom handle hit the man. The man moaned and turned toward David with a growl, grabbed the broom, and pitched it to the ground. As David started to lunge for it, the man threw a blinding punch to his left cheek.

Before Jillian could run to his aid, a strong arm grabbed her around the waist and jerked her back into the house. "Oh no, you don't. Get yourself in here and call the police!" It was Olivia. She pulled a handgun out of the pocket of her robe, held it with both hands, and aimed it into the backyard, yelling with the mouth of a sailor.

"Don't shoot!" David was flat on his back and covering his head. "It's me!"

The wind caught the door and it slammed with such force that Jillian was certain the gun had gone off. She looked up to see the front door wide open and Mrs. Winsee standing on the porch, trancelike, her arm outstretched, her index finger pointing toward something. "Mrs. Winsee, what are you doing? Get in the house!" Jillian grabbed her phone and headed toward her. Reaching the porch, Jillian gazed in the direction Mrs. Winsee's trembling finger indicated. The intruder was running with long strides into the blackness of Audubon Park.

"911. Where is your emergency?"

"S-s-s-saint Charles." Jillian was so frightened she couldn't remember the street number.

"Caller ID says Raphael Fontaine, ma'am. Are you calling from his residence?"

"Raphael? No! Yes, I guess! His mom's—" Flustered, she hung up the phone and threw it on the Snapdragon and grabbed the afghan to wrap around the frightened old woman. "Mrs. Winsee, it's me, Jillian." She spoke with a gentleness the walls of Saint Sans had never before heard from her. "You did so good. You spotted him. You saved the day. Come on back in. Let's get you warmed up." She sat Mrs. Winsee down on the couch and knelt in front of her and swept the old woman's tumbled hair out of her eyes. Mrs. Winsee stared straight ahead, her lips moving, but nothing audible coming from her mouth.

"Jillian, I'll get her medicine." It was Olivia coming in with David, each appearing as stunned as the other. "Get some ice for David, will you?" The pocket of Olivia's robe sagged with the weight of the handgun.

"Blood," Mrs. Winsee said.

"On the man's shirt? Yes, I saw it, too. But I don't think it was real," Jillian responded. "It was just a costume."

"Blood!" Mrs. Winsee insisted loudly.

"Jillian, your foot," Olivia said with alarm, circling around the couch. "Sit still. I'll get a towel."

The cut hadn't stung until Jillian saw it. It didn't look disturbingly large but the sight of that much blood made Jillian dizzy. She glanced around and saw splotches of crimson on the floor behind her.

David joined Jillian in front of Mrs. Winsee. He patted the older woman's hand as she stared wild-eyed at him with a question she couldn't find the words to ask. "You're alright, Mrs. Winsee. We all are. Let's see if we can get Jillian fixed up here." He reached toward Olivia for the damp hand towel and dabbed it on the bottom of Jillian's foot. "It's not so bad. See?" He pulled back the cloth to show Mrs. Winsee a clean slice in the tender arch of Jillian's foot. It was an inch wide but not deep. When he applied some pressure to it, Jillian winced. "How'd this happen? Do you know? Did you walk out in the front yard?"

"I got no farther than the porch. I have no idea how it happened. But you're the one who's really hurt," she said, still shaking. "The rate you're swelling, your left eye is going to be shut within the hour."

David's cheekbone was already purple. "He was huge. I don't think I came to his shoulders."

"Well, you went after him like he'd met his match."

"Pure adrenaline. By the time I saw how big he was, I was committed. You're going to need a bandage. Sit still and I'll go get one."

"I've got it, David." Olivia handed him a small box of Band-Aids. "And I've got the medicine. You two give me a little space and let me see if I can get Vida to take this."

When Jillian heard the siren down the street, she remembered that she'd hung up on the emergency operator. She hobbled through the front door, and to her relief, a police car pulled up at the curb. The flashing lights were so blinding that a policeman was halfway up the sidewalk before she could see that it wasn't any of the officers they knew. Her heart sank. Only one thing was worse than having to deal with the police—dealing with new ones.

"This is our district, ma'am. Why don't you tell us what happened and let us take a look around and we'll contact that district if we need to."

Jillian's grandmother put it bluntly. "You can go ahead and contact them now and we'll wait until they get here. As you can see, no one has been mortally wounded and we clearly aren't going to bed anytime soon. You can call them or I will. Jillian, why don't you go get my purse? I have the sergeant's number in there. And go ahead and get my handgun license too, to show the officers."

The absurdity wasn't lost on Jillian. She had no idea where Olivia kept her purse and she wouldn't know a handgun license if she had one tattooed on the palm of her hand. As Olivia anticipated, they made the phone call.

Thirty minutes crawled by before two more police cars pulled up in front of the house and officers with familiar faces walked through the front door. Officer La Bauve got up to speed with the policeman that Olivia had ordered to a halt, Officer Sanchez checked on Mrs. Winsee, and Sergeant DaCosta headed for Jillian and the others.

"Tell me what happened. Every detail. Maybe it was just a Halloween prank that went south, but let's start ruling out some other possibilities." He turned to David. "Mr. Jacobs, you first."

After hearing David's story, the officer stepped out onto the back porch to have a look around.

"This belong to any of you? Mr. Jacobs?"

Jillian peered through the door to see what he was referring to and caught a glimpse of metal just to the right of the doormat, reflecting off the porch light. It was an open pocketknife.

"Never seen it," David answered. "I'm more of a broomstick man."

"Miss Slater, did you come out this way?"

"Only a few steps. I was trying to run after David when Olivia pulled me back in."

"Well, it's at least pretty clear how you sliced your foot. Does it make sense to you that you could have stepped on it when you darted out the door?" Jillian nodded. "Have Sanchez look at that before we leave tonight and see if you need a couple of stitches. A tetanus shot might not be a bad idea either."

"Was he planning to stab someone?" Jillian asked, alarmed.

"Maybe, but my gut says no. I'd expect a man with violence on his mind to come equipped with a more serious weapon." He must have seen the terror of possibilities spread across Jillian's face. "Miss Slater, look at me."

She turned her eyes up to him, trying to hide how vulnerable she felt.

"No, I do not think he came with that kind of intention," he said. "But I will tell you this. We *will* find him and we *will* sort this out and everybody around here is going to be safe. You hear what I'm saying?"

"It's Rafe's." All three sets of eyes shot to Olivia's face. Her olive complexion was ashen. "Your eyes are younger than mine, Sergeant. Look at the base of the blade. Is anything engraved there?"

He shone a small flashlight on it and inspected one side before turning the knife over. Even Jillian could see the faint but unmistakable *F* engraved exactly where Olivia told him to look.

Olivia sat down in a chair at the dining room table, tapped her forefinger to her lips several times, and with remarkable composure said, "It's Rafe's. His father gave it to him when he was eleven or twelve."

"Who would have had it?" the sergeant asked.

"I have no idea. I haven't seen it in decades. Haven't thought about it in that long either, but it was his alright. It was one of the only personal things he ever got from the man. It had belonged to Mr. Fontaine's own father. There's a picture of him with it in a box in the closet of his room. Well, Jillian's room right now."

Jillian was speechless. All this time she'd been at Saint Sans, she'd stayed in Rafe's room? Pictures of him were in the closet where her clothes were hanging. He'd slept in that bed. Her stomach rolled. She leaned over and stared closely at the knife, studying the sterling silver and mother-of-pearl handle. For a few seconds, Jillian imagined him about eleven or twelve. Maybe he'd gotten the knife for his birthday or maybe it was a spontaneous gift. He'd admired it and his father simply handed it to him. She tried to shove the picture out of her mind. She'd never let herself think of Rafe in personal terms. Even since she'd met Olivia, she'd refused to imagine Rafe as anyone's son. A terrible father had to be a terrible son, she'd thought. Rafe was a loser. A bum. A skeleton in a closet. But for the first time, the skeleton had some meat on it. She pulled out a chair and sat down with a thud, her mind spinning.

"Could he have pawned the knife, Mrs. Fontaine?" David asked. Olivia didn't answer, but Jillian saw her jaw tighten.

"That's a fair enough question," Sergeant DaCosta responded. He pulled out a third chair at the table and nodded at David to sit down in it and he did so with the third thud in the course of five minutes. "But of all the residences in New Orleans, it just happens to turn up on this back porch? What is the likelihood of that? Nope, I'd say someone's messing with y'all. We don't have much to go on, but it's a far sight more than we did. We know we're looking for a male over six feet tall and maybe substantially so. That helps. Now, why did he have your son's pocketknife, Mrs. Fontaine, and why is he trying to—at the very least—harass you?"

The words of the 911 operator replayed in Jillian's mind like a padlock on her brain had been broken. She blurted out toward Olivia, "You gave me Rafe's phone! You gave me a dead man's phone!"

CHAPTER 28

"What on God's green earth is going on in here? A slumber party?" Adella had come into Saint Sans and found Caryn and Jillian sound asleep on the Snapdragon with their heads at opposite ends. Jillian was wearing the pajamas Adella had given her, and Caryn was in scrubs. Their hair looked like they'd both stuck their fingers in light sockets. Before she could get a coherent explanation out of either of them, David walked into the great room sporting a shiner the size of a saucer. Seconds later, Olivia emerged in her bathrobe from the wrong end of the house.

"Vida had a spell last night," Olivia said dryly. "I gave her some medicine and put her to bed in my room and I slept in hers."

"With Mr. Winsee, or did he join her in your room?"

"Adella, I'm not in the mood for any extra mouth this morning."

"I'm just trying to make out the fruit-basket turnover is all.

Somebody better start talking. The sight of David in this condition is working me into a hot flash. Have you taken up gambling? What have I said, over and over, about these casinos coming to Louisiana? From the very pit of hell. Yep, I said it and I meant it."

Olivia opened a cabinet door in the kitchen. "No one is saying another word until I've made some coffee. I mean *no one*."

It took three carafes and a half pint of whipping cream before Adella got the full story. "A Peeping Tom?" She was aghast.

"This was no run-of-the-mill Peeping Tom, Adella. Unless this is the biggest coincidence this side of the river, we think he's the one pulling all the shenanigans on the back porch," Olivia continued, glancing across the table at Jillian. "And the front porch. That doll on the front porch recently, Jillian? It has to be tied up in all of this insanity somehow, though God alone knows how. Or why." She looked back at Adella. "Last night he left us another little trinket."

Adella sat mesmerized as Olivia recounted the discovery of the open pocketknife. Caryn propped Jillian's bandaged foot up on the table as proof of collateral damage. If they were to have any luck putting the pieces together, the time had come to spill the beans. After last night, every resident at Saint Sans had the right to know. Starting with the ominous card on the flowers at Rafe's burial, Adella began recounting every strange discovery she and Olivia had made over the last several months. The torn snapshot of Rafe appeared to be the clincher: Olivia was the obvious target. Reminders of her deceased son were being used to make sure the arrows made it past the surface to lodge in her heart. This was personal. The haunting question was why.

The air felt thick. Everybody around the table knew that Olivia despised the spotlight. The only thing she could have hated more was standing in the brightness of it with her vulnerability showing. As Adella spoke, Olivia maintained an ironclad veneer, staring into her coffee cup and running her index finger slowly around the rim.

The floodgates opened at the table, and the others all shared things they'd felt were out of the ordinary around Saint Sans recently. None of their stories involved concrete evidence, but it was clear that everyone had the sense that something had been off. The only time Olivia looked up was when Caryn used the word *foreboding* to describe the sense she'd had around there recently. The word carried weight because Caryn was the scientific kind, not the sort to be superstitious.

Jillian blurted out, "Maybe the house is haunted!"

Adella tried to nip that thought in the bud. "Jillian, take a good look at David. Does it look like he's been punched in the face by a ghost? Or would you say that whatever hit him had knuckles? What you saw last night was flesh and blood."

"How do we know that? He was wearing a mask! Or what if it wasn't a mask? What if that was his real face?" Jillian looked panic-stricken.

Adella got her by the hand and tugged her back into the chair. "I think everybody at this table has had too much caffeine. You're all scaring each other half to death. Now, let's quit feeding fire sticks to one another's imaginations here and try to keep to the facts." She said it to herself as much as to them.

When a knock came at the front door, everybody froze affright like twelve-year-olds telling spooky stories who'd just heard a bump in the night. There was only one man at the table—and him with only one good eye. When he got up to answer the door, Caryn called out, "Whatever you do, David, do not turn the other cheek!"

Officer La Bauve walked through the entryway with a mile-wide smile on his face and a white cardboard box in his hands. "Top of the morning to you! Just coming to check on y'all before work."

Adella glanced at Caryn and whispered, "I'll swear to goodness, this house is too weird for reality TV. It's like a passel of cartoon characters under the same roof."

Officer La Bauve set the box down on the kitchen bar and opened the lid to reveal a dozen plain glazed donuts.

"True enough, Adella, but this character is having one." Caryn pulled a donut out of the box and took a bite. David followed suit.

If they hadn't been hot and steamy, Adella might have been able to resist. "Well, I did leave the house this morning too early for my shredded wheat. I guess one wouldn't hurt."

Olivia put her hand up to indicate that she'd pass. When Jillian started to reach into the box, the officer stopped her.

"I thought you might like this one," he said sheepishly, handing Jillian a small white paper bag. She opened it and pulled out a cake donut with pink frosting and multicolored sprinkles. "That's my favorite. Well, I usually get the blue, but it's the same flavor."

The whole table went silent. Adella swallowed hard and tried to think of something awful to keep her from getting tickled because once she got started, she wasn't liable to soon quit. All eyes were on Jillian, who was clearly flummoxed. "Well, thank you, Officer. I don't usually eat donuts, but since you went to all this trouble, I guess I'll go ahead—"

"Y'all can just call me Billy. Or Bully, if you want. That's what they call me on the force. I don't mind."

Caryn broke the silence. "Thank you, Billy La Bauve. They're wonderful. Best thing I've eaten in ages. It's nice to officially meet you." She stuck out her hand and he shook it enthusiastically. The contrast of their skin color was matched by the color of his flushed face against his blond hair.

"Officer La Bauve," Olivia interjected impatiently, "was this just a donut delivery or do you have something for us?"

"Oh no, ma'am. I'm just the donut man this morning, but we hope to have something for you soon. Sarge was pretty heated about it last night. From the sound of things, he intended to give it personal attention. I heard him say that he'll have a squad car sticking pretty close around here for a few nights."

"Perfect," Olivia retorted with a sarcasm that went right over Bully's head.

"Well, I guess I better get on my way to work then." His words said *go* but his body language definitely said *stay*. "Well, there is one more thing. I'm turning thirty Sunday week, and we're having a crawfish boil at my house that evening. A lot of people are coming. Ask anybody in this town how my mama cooks and you'll know why. You won't want to miss it. You'll know a few people there because of your friends on the force."

Olivia rolled her eyes.

"All of you are invited. I brought this so you could stick it on your fridge with a magnet." Bully reached into the pocket of his jacket and pulled out a bent-up party invitation with a bright-red crawfish on it with his smiling face photoshopped right into it. "The directions are on the back. See?" He turned it to the other side to show them a small map.

Olivia looked at him incredulously, as if she'd sooner skin a pig than stick something to her fridge.

The awkwardness of Bully holding out an invitation and nobody budging to take it from him was more than Caryn could bear. "Sounds like fun, Billy. I'll see how my schedule is going to turn out. When do you need to know? Do we need to RSVP?"

"You can. There's the number right there, but it's not necessary. It's my mama's way to have enough food for everybody on the invitation list and a few that ain't. She says it's the *ain't*s that eat the most."

David piped up, taking the invitation from Caryn's hand. "I just don't think I can pass this up. You might have to count me in, too, if Caryn's coming. How about you, Jillian?"

Jillian swallowed a big bite and said, "Who, me? Oh, I think I have to work. All I do these days is work."

Bully was undeterred. "I bet you could switch shifts with some-body this far in advance. Anyway, my mama's is only about ten minutes from your café. Fifteen minutes max, depending on the traffic. I could swing by and get you."

"No, no! No need!" Jillian eyed everybody at the table for help. The next words must have flown out of her mouth before she could think what she was saying. "I'll ride with David and Caryn!"

"You sure?" Bully asked.

"Absolutely positive."

"Okay, then!" He was so happy every tooth in his head gleamed like they'd been silver polished. A text came in on his phone. "That's Sanchez. I better get going before she puts out an APB on me."

Olivia cleared her throat. "I can only imagine how distracting all the birthday plans will be, but if you and your colleagues end up with any news about our perpetrator, do try to work in a call."

"Oh yes, ma'am. We will let you know first thing." Bully patted Olivia on the back, causing her posture to freeze up like a Popsicle.

Adella couldn't resist. "Jillian, why don't you see our kind keeper of the peace to his car?"

Jillian had her back to Bully and shot Adella a look that could have curdled the whipping cream. "I'm in my pajamas."

Adella answered, "They're plenty decent. I ought to know. I've raked leaves in them in my own front yard without raising an eyebrow."

Jillian scooted out the dining room chair, got to her feet, brushed the crumbs off her pajama bottoms, and feigning some fine Southern manners, said, "Right this way, Officer La Bauve."

As if on cue, David, Caryn, and Adella corrected her. *"Bully!"*

CHAPTER 29

SIX AND A HALF MONTHS after the cornerstone celebration, the new bell applauded a finished work and the heavy double doors, arched like praying hands, swung wide and embraced every comer for the inaugural service. Believer, beleaguered, or bedeviled, all were welcomed.

Evelyn Ann Brashear and her daughter, Brianna, took their proper places on the front row, dressed in their finest. The elder wore a wide-brimmed hat, the younger a bonnet. Both were beaming, Evelyn Ann uncharacteristically so.

The pews, dark and shiny, could accommodate one hundred and fifty. The chapel was two-thirds full that first Sunday, and during the opening hymn, few eyes were dry and fewer chins failed to quiver.

Come, ye thankful people, come,
Raise the song of harvest home;
All is safely gathered in,
Ere the winter storms begin;
God, our Maker, doth provide
For our wants to be supplied;
Come to God's own temple, come,
Raise the song of harvest home.

All the world is God's own field,
Fruit unto His praise to yield;
Wheat and tares together sown,
Unto joy or sorrow grown. . . .

Joys grew, and so did the small congregation, until backsides of parishioners slid together on quickly shrinking pews.

Couples were wed.

Infants were blessed.

Repentance was preached, the backslidden reached.

Then everything changed.

Where once was joy, sorrow grew. Brother turned against brother, sister against sister, until the only song was discord.

CHAPTER 30

"Why would you want to stay there? After all that, it would be the last place I'd spend the night."

Jillian had only a fifteen-minute break and she had no idea how to explain something to Stella that she didn't understand herself. "I *want* to move out, and I'm going to soon. I just feel kinda bad about leaving everybody at Saint Sans right now."

Stella responded sarcastically. "The way you've described being treated around there, I can certainly see why you're drawn to it. Sounds irresistible."

"Nobody's really been ugly to me but Mrs. Fontaine."

"Yeah, but doesn't she rule the place?"

"Yes, it's hers, but she isn't mean all the time. She's just—"

"A witch, I recall you saying."

Jillian laughed. "I did say that, and I still think that most of the time. I don't know how to explain it. I just feel like I'd be bailing on David. And even on Caryn. Everybody's spooked. I guess there's something about being spooked together."

"Sounds like a blast."

Jillian could tell Stella was annoyed. And she couldn't really blame her. Here she'd practically been begging Stella to take her in, and now that Stella had agreed, Jillian had changed her mind, at least temporarily. "Remember the old woman I told you about?"

"The crazy one?"

Jillian started to correct her, but she thought back on all the times she'd said the same thing to David. "Mrs. Winsee. She's hardly said a word since it happened. It's been three days. Mrs. Fontaine's taken her to the doctor twice already. He's recommending hospitalization followed by . . . I think she said assisted living."

Stella checked her phone with an expression of boredom.

Jillian pressed through. "Mrs. Fontaine says she knows her better than the doctor and that the move from Saint Sans could make her condition irreversible. Clementine's the only one she's responding to, and it would be a mistake to separate them."

"Clementine? Now, which one is that? I thought there were only five of you in that house and the black woman who runs it."

The tone of the last part of that statement irritated Jillian, but Stella was in such a contentious mood, Jillian decided to keep her mouth shut about it. She'd stick with simply answering the question. "Clementine's the cat."

Stella threw her head back with a laugh and cursed. "Listen, if you want to stay in that madhouse, you go right ahead. I'm not looking for houseguests. My place is small. If you want to stay with a blood grandmother you call *Mrs. Fontaine*, have at it. Last I heard, she'd accused you and your mother of killing her son."

The reminder slammed into Jillian's heart like a sledgehammer. "Yeah. She did."

"You're the one who said you needed somewhere to stay for a few weeks."

"I do! I just need a few more days to see if any of this gets sorted out. If the invitation's no longer open, I understand."

"I didn't say it's no longer open. I'm just saying I don't get it. Seems like a no-brainer to me."

Jillian ran out of time before they could settle anything. Instead, she spent the rest of the evening wiping down tables in total frustration. She couldn't decide whether she was madder at herself or Stella. Or Olivia, for that matter. She was the cause of the whole mess.

Stella came by again just as Jillian got off work. "Sorry I was short earlier. It wasn't you. I've got a money problem, that's all. Short on cash for a few weeks, and I was counting on you sharing expenses for a while. The square's a great location for what I do, but it's not cheap. I shouldn't have taken it out on you. I apologize. Do whatever you need to do."

The apology should have made Jillian feel better, but it only made her feel more torn. Now she was going to feel guilty if she didn't move in with Stella and help with expenses. She wished she could wind back time to six months ago and find herself working at Sigmund's and living with Vince like everything was normal. She wished Adella had never called in the first place.

When she let herself into Saint Sans that night after work, she found a note from Caryn propped on the kitchen island:

Jillian—
Gotta pull an all-nighter. Huge exam tomorrow.
You're welcome to sleep in my room again but I won't be there tonight.
See you tomorrow night if you're around!
−C

Jillian blew every bit of breath out of her lungs as she gazed down the hall at the door to Rafe's room. A bulldozer couldn't have shoved her into that room the night she realized it had been Rafe's, and anyway, she had been too scared to sleep by herself after all that had transpired. Caryn had been nice enough to let Jillian sleep on the second twin bed in her room for the past couple nights. But with Caryn out all night, she'd be just as alone there as in her own room. Her other option was another night on the Snapdragon, but she was too scared to sleep in that huge room by herself. What if somebody showed up again on the back porch? Or at the front door?

Her best option was to take her chances back in Rafe's room. Jillian opened the door slowly, glancing behind her to see if the creaking would draw Olivia out of her suite. The coast was clear. She turned on the bedside lamp, shut the door behind her, and dropped down on the edge of the bed. Olivia's words to Sergeant DaCosta about the picture of Rafe and the knife swirled in her head, pinning her eyes to the closet door.

"It's now or never," she whispered, getting to her feet. She opened the closet door, spying two boxes on a high shelf, pushed to the far left. She'd seen them before but never paid any attention to them and now she wondered why. Jillian had always been the curious sort. She hadn't been herself since that day at Sigmund's.

Standing on her tiptoes on the seat of a chair, she struggled to scoot the nearest box off the shelf and steady it to the floor. Inside were three slender photo albums and hundreds of loose pictures. She glanced into each album to determine their order, then sitting cross-legged on the floor, pulled what appeared to be the earliest one into her lap.

Four yellowed pictures were positioned symmetrically on the first page under the cellophane sleeve. A strip of paper in the center of the page had a date handwritten on it in blue ink. Jillian calculated the years and murmured, "Forty-six years ago this coming

December 15." The timing confirmed what she'd already guessed. The photos were from the day of Rafe's birth. The top two pictures were close-ups of a very young Olivia in a hospital gown with a newborn in her arms. Her appearance looked every bit the part of a woman who'd just given birth, but there was a beauty and softness to her that Jillian found almost unrecognizable.

Olivia's smile was weak with obvious weariness but unmistakable just the same. Jillian studied the photographs closely under the direct light of the lamp. The tears in the young mother's eyes would have seemed normal under the circumstances for almost anyone else, but Jillian could hardly wrap her mind around this tender version of Olivia. Both pictures on the bottom of the page were of a newborn in a clear bassinet in the delivery room. *Baby Boy Fontaine, 7 lbs., 10 oz.*

Jillian resented the ache of emotion she felt in her throat. She shut the photo album and pitched it back in the box. Pulling her knees to her chest, she clutched them tightly, letting her mind replay every offense she had against the Fontaine family until the tenderness passed.

She picked up the album again and determined to look through it with greater haste to minimize the emotional fallout. The album tracked Rafe's first twelve months with only a handful of snapshots including his father. Jillian realized when she saw the first depiction of Mr. Fontaine that she'd never spotted a single picture of him around Saint Sans. Then again, there were no family pictures in the main part of the house. If any were on display under that roof, they had to be in Olivia's private suite. Her husband had the look of a man who meant to come across tough whether or not he did. He economized on the smiles and most of the shots depicting him and the baby betrayed a hint of staging.

The only picture of Rafe with both of his parents was at his christening. They were positioned next to the priest in the full-length snapshot, Rafe cradled in Olivia's arms and wearing a long white christening gown. Next to the picture was a small rectangular card embossed with four words in blue calligraphy:

Raphael: God has healed.

Jillian gave extra attention to the picture only because it alone captured the three of them. The christening meant nothing to her and the meaning of the name, in her opinion, had proved preposterously ironic. To Jillian, religion was primarily good for making people neurotic.

Not a single other child appeared among the photographs of Rafe's first year. The album closed with a typical picture of a plump-faced baby covered in white icing.

The second album was no thicker but covered a wider span of time, stretching from Rafe's toddlerhood to early elementary school. He looked about three years old in a snapshot capturing him shirtless and in shorts and cowboy boots. Pictures of each birthday from Rafe's second to his seventh were affixed to the pages, some with a cake, others with a gift. A few appeared to have been taken at small birthday parties, but most depicted him alone, like the majority of the other photos in the albums.

Jillian found herself wondering why Olivia never had any other children and why all semblance of extended family seemed conspicuously absent. Rafe's aloneness seemed so obvious in the pictures. Midthought, the absurdity of Jillian's curiosity hit her. She'd also been raised alone with no extended family. But there was one vast difference: at least Rafe had a dad in his life.

Jillian stared at the last page in the second album, unable to ascertain why the solitary picture yanked at her heart more than all the rest. It was Rafe's first-grade school picture. His plump face was surrounded by the usual blue background and typical white edge. He had a smattering of light-brown freckles across his nose. He was

missing all four front teeth and his hair was endearingly disobedi-
ent and disheveled. The collar of his polo-style shirt was turned up
on one side and his ears stuck out just enough to squeeze a grin out
of any woman with a drop of maternal hormone.

The emotion that shot through Jillian's chest was so new and
disturbing to her that it set her on her feet. She stuck the album
back in the box and closed it without flipping through the last one
in search of the picture with the pocketknife. She climbed back on
the chair and shoved the box onto the closet shelf.

Just before Jillian stepped down from the chair, she reached up
and pressed the edge of the other box with her fingertips. It didn't
budge. She pushed it harder, this time with her palm. It shifted
only about an inch. Whatever was inside was substantially heavier
than the contents of the first box. Curiosity stirred up her soul like
a fork scrambling eggs. She moved the chair as close to that end
of the closet as the door would permit and wrapped her left hand
around the furthest edge of the box. The first try yielded nothing.
On the second try, she nearly lost her balance. For the third try, she
grabbed a wooden hanger and wedged it between the box and the
back of the closet. Adrenaline pumping, she pushed both hands
against the end of the hanger as hard as she could.

The box tumbled to the floor and fell onto its side. The quiet of
the night was disturbed by the sound of glass breaking. Jillian jumped
down from the chair, wincing on her sore foot, to a stack of picture
frames of varied sizes heaped on the floor, facedown, in shards of glass.

Now she'd done it. She needed to get that mess cleaned up in a
hurry before someone came in to see what all the commotion was
about.

She reached for the frame on the top of the heap and turned
it faceup to throw it back in the box. It was a five-by-seven of a
young man holding a dark-headed little girl, her arms wrapped
tightly around his neck and her face pressed next to his.

CHAPTER 31

THE SUNDAY OF BULLY'S BIRTHDAY came with haste. Caryn refuted every excuse Jillian could contrive to get out of going and capped it off with the claim that Bully's big day would be a colossal disappointment if Jillian didn't show up. "How can you let that sweet guy down? Does a hand-delivered pink-iced cake donut mean nothing to you?"

Jillian used the inconvenience of the whole ordeal as a last-ditch effort to dissuade Caryn and threw in a side of fear. "We'd have to walk from the trolley stop to his house and back in the dark. What if that freak has been watching us and follows us?" That's when David added considerable poundage to the pressure by offering them his car.

Jillian instantly protested. "You said you had something to do! Isn't that why you backed out on the party? You'll need your car."

"No, as a matter of fact, I will not," he responded with a mischievous grin. "What I need to do is right here at Saint Sans. I met a man last week who does piano repairs, and he said he'd be willing to look at that old organ and see if there is any resurrecting it. It's not really his specialty but he says he's worked on a few. This evening was the only free time he had. As much as I hate to miss the big occasion, y'all will have to go on without me. But take heart and go in considerable style." He stuck his hand out with his car keys.

Caryn snatched them up like a sixteen-year-old who'd just gotten her driver's license. "Can I run an errand with your car first?"

"Be my guest," David replied.

Caryn returned from the task a couple hours later with a gift bag she presented to Jillian. Carefully folded inside the white tissue was a beautiful cranberry-red cashmere sweater.

"I got myself one too!" she said, laughing infectiously.

"The same one?" Jillian was horrified.

"Nope. A winter-white one, in an ever-so-slightly different style, but I'm planning to look fabulous in it. I've got a red wool scarf I'm putting over it. You want to borrow my black one?"

"And look like twins?"

With that, Caryn turned Jillian toward the mirror over the buffet in the great room and stood right beside her. "Do we look like twins to you?" Jillian gave in to a laugh. "Anyway, the black scarf's plaid. I'll grab it."

Jillian had to admit the sweaters and the colors suited both her and Caryn as if they'd been tailor-made. Even Olivia looked at them with something like admiration on her face, but she stopped short of saying anything. David finally pushed them out the door.

Caryn did the driving as Jillian read the directions off the back of the invitation.

Jillian eyed all the cars parked up and down the street, darkness obscuring the house numbers. "So, which house is Bully's?"

"Jillian, are you kidding me? Head toward the music. That's where you find a party around here."

"I can't believe I let you talk me into this."

Caryn dragged Jillian by the hand up a driveway and into a spacious backyard packed with people laughing and chattering loudly over the music. White lantern-style lights were strung in five directions from a pole in the center of the backyard, and a mesquite fire snapped and crackled. A small band was positioned on the far side, playing music the likes of which Jillian had never heard—or ever dreamed of wanting to.

Jillian had never seen that much food at a party in her life. Long folding tables were covered with platters loaded with fries, hush puppies, coleslaw, new potatoes, and corn on the cob. Steaming over large portable burners were big pots that looked almost like cauldrons.

It occurred to Jillian that Olivia might have fit right in with her broom as long as she didn't have to make small talk with anybody. But a lot of the fun had gone out of calling Olivia a witch. Jillian had somehow started feeling a little guilty about it, though she couldn't imagine why. The antisocialite had earned it.

Mrs. Winsee certainly brought out a different side to Olivia. A strange gentleness had tempered the climate at Saint Sans that week while they all tried to engage the old woman. She was making progress. A security camera had been installed on the back porch, with additional lighting, so Olivia felt confident enough about Mrs. Winsee's safety to let her sleep in her own room. Several days that week Mrs. Winsee sat in a chair in the great room close to the fireplace. She hadn't spoken much except in endearments to Clementine, who regularly rubbed against her ankles and napped on her lap. She hadn't said a word about Mr. Winsee. That was the worst part.

Olivia had been sitting at the dining table with Mrs. Winsee, trying to coax her into eating, when Caryn and Jillian left. On the way out Caryn had said to her, "Mrs. Winsee, I'm about to take Jillian Slater to a *La La*. I gawn teach that girl till she shake a leg!"

Mrs. Winsee's eyes sparkled and Jillian could have sworn she grinned.

That almost made Jillian feel it was worth agreeing to go to the party. But now that she was here, every excuse she'd offered to keep from coming seemed twice as valid.

As if on cue, Bully made a beeline across the crowd, threw his arms around both Jillian and Caryn. "Y'all came!" He scooped them up in a group hug that nearly got their wool scarves in a tangle.

"We wouldn't have missed it! Happy birthday, Billy La Bauve!" Caryn's words were warm. For the next fifteen minutes, Bully dragged Caryn and Jillian all over the backyard, introducing them to people Jillian found obnoxiously friendly. She'd been hugged by at least half a dozen total strangers. Bully's brother picked her right up off the ground, and his mother planted a big kiss on her cheek. She made a mental note to take extra vitamin C when she got home. If she ever got home. This could be the longest night of her new life.

Jillian had never expected to be glad to lay eyes on Officer Sanchez, but since the woman was among the few familiar faces, getting cornered by her was a reprieve. She'd also spared Jillian the obligatory hug, a point in her favor.

"Bully is so happy you guys came, Jillian. Thanks for doing it." Officer Sanchez spoke with obvious sincerity.

"Well, Caryn made me." At least Jillian cracked a smile with the comment.

"I'm glad she did. He's such a great guy. Really, he is. And don't even think his mama doesn't love him."

They both glanced over at Mrs. La Bauve, pouring potatoes in the deep fryer with her face beaming like she was born to throw a party. The whole atmosphere was surreal to Jillian. For one thing, she'd never seen Officer Sanchez out of uniform. Her thick brown hair, usually pulled back in a tight ponytail, was loose and long. She was wearing more makeup than usual and dangling earrings, but then again, so was Jillian. Officer Sanchez was dressed much like Caryn and Jillian, too, in jeans and a sweater, but with a short leather jacket thrown over it.

"Well, now, *that's* something you don't often see," she remarked, with a sideways glace at Jillian.

"What?"

Officer Sanchez nodded toward the gate. "Sarge at a party, and not looking like Sarge."

Jillian almost didn't recognize Sergeant DaCosta. His casual dress and cowboy boots made him look years younger than he'd seemed the first time she'd seen him at Saint Sans. Of course, he didn't have all that bad news weighing down his brow and an angry woman to tell it to. The man sauntering through that gate looked downright cheerful. In the dim light, his caramel-colored hair appeared almost blond next to his brown jacket, and his cheeks were flushed by the cold. Jillian watched him walk over to Bully, shove a small wrapped present into his hand, and hug him. They laughed and talked for a moment. Then he stepped over to Bully's mother and embraced her like they were old friends.

"Don't you think?" Officer Sanchez asked, interrupting Jillian's thoughts.

"Don't I think *what*? I'm sorry. I can't hear over the music."

"Don't you think this is a great backyard for a party?"

"Yeah, it is. Oh, my gosh. Is that Caryn? Who's she dancing with?" Jillian exclaimed.

"I think that's one of Bully's old classmates."

"But how does she know him?"

"She may have just met him. Folks into zydeco have their own special bond. The band starts playing, and if you don't have a part-ner, you just look around and see who's game and get out there and let it whirl. It's not really about the romance of it."

"It's the worst music I've ever heard."

The officer laughed. "It grows on you. You better get used to it if you're sticking around. Are you?"

"Not planning to."

"Well, I know one man who might be a tad disappointed if you don't."

"Who?"

"Who do you think?"

As the question rolled from Officer Sanchez's tongue, Bully came right toward Jillian with a smile on his face with edges that could have met on the back of his head. Worse yet, he was two-stepping, with one hand on his belly and the other hand extended toward her. "Care to dance, young lady?"

"Me? No!" Jillian glanced around, scrambling for a fast excuse. "I'm—I'm *starving*!"

"Well, why didn't you say so? Nobody goes hungry at this house." Bully shouted over his shoulder, "Mama? This girl right here can't dance till she eats. Somebody start scooping."

Before Jillian could think the next clear thought, Bully had shoved her onto a bench right in the middle of a crowded table and set a large white tray in front of her, piled three inches high with crawfish. He couldn't have been prouder if he'd presented her with a soufflé in the shape of a swan. "Mmmmm, mmmmm," he moaned. "You can't do better than that!" He grabbed a mudbug off her plate, shucked the peel, and threw it in his mouth as he gestured to the people on Jillian's left to scoot over so he could sit down.

Suddenly every eye within spitting distance was on Jillian, glar-ing at her like the success of the entire evening hinged on what she did next. The birthday boy's face was one spicy breath to her left.

His shoulders were squared toward her and his gaze was focused tightly enough to bore a hole through the side of her head. Jillian couldn't think of a single time she'd ever used the word *bliss*, but if that wasn't the expression on his face, she was bereft to name it. She had one split second to decide whether or not she had it in her to fail him.

She picked up a crawfish, tried to peel it without looking, squeezed her eyes shut, and stuck it in her mouth. Caryn would later swear that she'd also held her nose but Jillian never admitted to it. What was without question, however, was the longest drawn-out gag reflex that had ever transpired on this side of the French Quarter. Eight people had cleared the table by the time she opened her eyes. To everybody's considerable relief, all that projected out of Jillian's mouth was the crawfish, which landed right in the middle of her tray, inexplicably causing Bully to also gag.

"I felt the legs on my tongue! I really did! Like they were wiggling!"

The laughter could have stopped traffic. As soon as people quit hugging her and slapping her on the back like she'd won a contest, Jillian scooted away from the table and tried as inconspicuously as possible to search for a bathroom. The back door opened to a well-lived-in den of warm colors, worn rugs, and copious couch pillows. Decorative lamps of various shapes and sizes lit the room. That morning's newspaper was folded on an end table. The built-in bookshelves displayed family pictures spanning what appeared to be four generations, from preschoolers who might have been Bully's nieces and nephews all the way to his grandparents.

The house had the same feeling to it that Adella's house had. Love lived in it. Love and laughter. In fact, it seemed that the more these people got to laugh at you, the more they loved you. They were an odd bunch that way.

Hearing voices just outside the door, Jillian resumed her search for a bathroom. She found a powder room just down the hall from the den and resolved to stay in it until she'd formulated an exit plan from the party. A few stragglers tapped at the bathroom door but all it took was an extra-long spray of Mrs. La Bauve's Toodaloo Shoo air freshener and off they went.

CHAPTER 32

"Miss Slater, you okay?"

Startled, Jillian jumped up from the rocking chair. She'd snuck out here to the front porch after nearly choking to death on bathroom spray. She had hoped no one would notice her.

"No, don't get up." It was Sergeant DaCosta, standing at the edge of the yard near the driveway. "I had to get my phone out of the car. I just saw you here all by yourself. Did you lose your way?"

"No." She sat down, scrambling for words. "I was just . . . taking a break for a minute. That's a lot of party going on back there."

"Yeah, it is," the sergeant chuckled. "Bully is about as well-loved as a man can be. Good family." He paused for a moment. "I was surprised to see you here."

Jillian felt defensive. "Officer La Bauve came over to Saint Sans and invited all of us last week."

"No, no. I mean I was *glad* to see y'all. Just surprised. I wouldn't have thought you'd want to come."

"Caryn insisted. That's who I'm waiting for. The car's locked and she has the keys or I'd be sitting in it."

"Well, you might be waiting a little while. Last I saw her, she was out on the dance floor with Bully and they were drawing a crowd."

"Oh, great. We'll be here till midnight." Jillian set her head back on the rocking chair and blew out a deep breath. "Who knew Caryn was such a partyer? I would have assumed she was too serious for all this."

"Serious people are allowed a little dancing on occasion. Don't you think?"

Jillian shrugged. "And I wouldn't have taken Officer La Bauve for being exactly light on his feet."

He laughed. "Did you happen to notice the big man in his midfifties—almost bald—playing the accordion? That is Bear La Bauve, Bully's dad."

"You have got to be kidding. His name is *Bear*?"

"I'm sure it's not his real name, but it's all I've ever heard him called."

"But why?"

He drew back his head and grinned at her. "Are you serious? He's at least six-four. And that one you hear singing right now? That's Bully's big brother."

Jillian shook her head. "This is the strangest place on the planet."

"You mean this particular house or New Orleans in general?"

"No, not just this house. I haven't exactly lost sight of the fact that I'm staying in a dead man's room in a repurposed church down the hall from a woman who looks like Morticia on *The Addams Family*."

"Some of the greatest people on earth live in this town, Jillian. I forget that myself sometimes."

She looked up at him with surprise. She couldn't remember him calling her by her first name before.

"You've had an unfortunate introduction to New Orleans. I'm sorry for that." As he spoke, he took several steps toward the front porch. "The two of you must not have been close."

"Who, me and Mrs. Fontaine? Uh, no. Not close."

"Actually, I meant you and your . . . Well, you refer to him as 'the dead man.'"

"Rafe?" The edge in her voice was razor sharp.

"It wasn't my intention to cross a line. It just seemed odd not to acknowledge anything about the ongoing case or how we know each other."

"We *don't* know each other, Officer." When Jillian saw she'd embarrassed him, she half wished she hadn't said it.

He stood still and silent, staring off in the distance, for what seemed like a solid minute. When he flinched, she expected him to head up the driveway to the party. Instead, he walked toward her, extending his right hand. "Hi. My name is Cal."

Taken aback, she reached out and shook his hand.

Sergeant DaCosta—Cal—stuck both hands in his pockets and started rattling off a bio. "I was born and raised in these parts. I went to elementary school about fifteen minutes from this front door and junior high two blocks from there, where I harbored the deep, dark secret that my mother was making me take piano lessons. I played football and basketball in high school, decent at both, a star at neither. I went to Northwestern State University in Natchitoches and straight into law enforcement. I've never lived outside Louisiana. My dad died of cancer when I was a senior in college, so I felt like I needed to come home and live with my mom for a while after graduation. I lived there until she got back on her feet. I'd saved some money, and a couple of years ago I bought a small house. A fixer-upper. I'm fairly decent with a hammer. I was engaged once. She later married my best friend. I like dogs, but I'm not home enough to have one. I shoot baskets sometimes at a park close to my house. Every couple of years I fish off the coast of Mississippi with some old friends, including the one that married my old girlfriend." He squinted his eyes like he was performing a mental inventory. "And I like books."

"You like books?"

"I like books."

"You don't strike me as the book type."

"Bully didn't strike you as light on his feet, yet I'd lay a ten-dollar bill on the arm of that chair that he's spinning somebody around on the dance floor as we speak. Your turn."

"What kind of books?"

"History, mostly. And biographies. I said it's your turn."

"Fiction or nonfiction?"

"What's with the book fixation? You're stalling."

"I can't really think of anything to say."

"What do you mean you can't think of anything? You were born where?"

Jillian hesitated, wishing she could name any other state. "Louisiana."

Cal's eyebrows shot up.

"My mom moved us to California because she wanted to get away from—" she glanced at Cal and continued—"from Rafe. I grew up in San Francisco."

"And?"

"And that's it."

"That's it?"

"I don't think Caryn's ever going to come looking for me."

"Apparently not as long as the band is playing."

"Well, they're pathetic."

"Bear and his band? To hear Bully tell it, they've played at wedding receptions as far away as Breaux Bridge."

"Oh, well, that changes everything. Like anybody's got a clue what the singer's saying." Jillian leaned forward and glanced at the driveway. She pulled out her phone to check the time. "I don't get what's taking Caryn so long. She can't be having that much fun."

"Bowlegged woman."

"No, she's not! She's just skinny."

"The song. That's what the singer's saying. 'Hey, bowlegged woman.' It's a classic." Cal leaned down her direction. "Come on. You can't crack one small smile over that?"

Jillian touched her upper lip with her index finger to keep from grinning.

Cal didn't let up. "Anyway, you can't say it's no fun if you've never tried it. That's the rule around here. I'll tell you what, Miss San Francisco. Succumb to one lesson, and if you hate it, you hate it. And you win." He held his right hand out to her, palm up.

"What? Are you serious? No. Absolutely not."

"Why not? You got two left feet or something? Or just bowlegs?"

"What I've got is at least a shred of self-respect. The neighbors would see us. I'd feel like a fool."

"Is that all?" Cal walked over to a small bench on the porch with a large fern on it. He placed the plant on the ground, dragged the bench under the porch light, and stood on top of it.

"What are you doing?"

"Gimme a second, will ya?"

Jillian's jaw dropped as Cal unscrewed the two lightbulbs in the fixture.

"There. No one will see you. On your feet, Miss Slater." He took her right hand and pulled her to her feet.

"You're kidding me."

"Nope. Not kidding. But dancing's no fun if somebody's making you do it. How about we make a deal that you get to say when we're done? That work? We'll take it really slow."

"I don't know. I guess." Her heart started beating double-time. "You don't see anybody coming this way, do you? If Caryn sees me, I'll never hear the end of this."

"Driveway's clear." Cal extended his left hand out to the side and opened his palm. "Put your right hand here." She hesitated for a few seconds, took a deep breath, and placed her hand in his. "Now take your left hand and cup it around my shoulder."

"I'm not going to be good at this."

"Fun's the only mission. Remember? This isn't the *Nutcracker Suite*. The pressure's off. Are we still good to go?"

Jillian nodded.

Cal placed his right arm gently around her. "I'm going to teach you a basic little two-step. It's mostly about shifting weight back and forth. The first lesson may be the hardest for you," he said with a grin.

"Ugh. What is it?"

"*Let me lead.* One of us has to, and since this is your first time, the job rightly defaults to me. Unless you'd like to improvise and make it up as you go."

Jillian bit her bottom lip and fought a laugh. "Okay. You lead."

"It's going to go like this, starting with your right foot and my left: *slow, quick-quick, slow, quick-quick.* We're going to add a rock in it in a minute, but let's get the hang of this first. Ignore the music because it's going too fast for a first shot at it. Let that fade out and you listen to me count to eight. Remember: *slow, quick-quick, slow, quick-quick.* The slow steps will be two beats and each of the quick steps, one."

"I'm already getting confused!"

"It's easier to do than to explain. Drop your hands a second and watch my feet." When Cal checked the driveway again, Jillian realized he wasn't exactly uninhibited himself. He shook out his legs to loosen up and then proceeded to demonstrate the steps with a fair enough agility to catch Jillian by surprise.

Rather than admit she was impressed, she limited her comments to "Nice cowboy boots."

"Thank you. Try to concentrate." They both laughed, relieving some of their nervousness. "Now mirror what I'm doing, and then we'll put the arms into it."

To the sparing of her dignity, Jillian got the hang of it after a few tries.

"You're doing great. Give me your hands and let's go at it again and we'll add a rock to it. We'll still do *slow, quick-quick, slow,* but on that last slow step we're going to both rock backward in opposite directions, you on your right foot and me on my left. I'll count to eight and we rock back on seven. Make sense?"

"No!"

"It will when we do it." He walked her through the steps at a snail's pace until she started to pick them up. "See? You're getting it."

"Don't talk or I won't be able to concentrate!" With every step Jillian counted aloud.

"Do you think you can look up from the ground now?"

"I don't know."

"Try."

Jillian looked up from her feet to his face. He was grinning. The light of the lamps streaming through the shutters in the den brought the blue in his eyes to life. She looked away quickly and lost count, stubbing her toe on the point of his boot.

"Ow! What size are those things?" Jillian dropped her hands and grabbed her foot.

"Thirteens. You got something against thirteens?" Cal cocked his head to the side, listening to the music emanating from the backyard. "Come here! This is our song! It's slow enough for us to catch up with it."

Jillian never stopped counting her eights or looking down at their feet, but halfway through the song she was rocking back right on the dot of seven.

"Look at you go, girl! Feet like greased lightning."

They both got tickled. "Shut up or I'll lose count!"

Two minutes later they were still in step. "The music's over," Jillian said.

"Is it?" Cal asked, continuing his lead.

"Yes." Jillian stopped and lowered her hands, her face flushed.

They stood facing each other for a moment in the awkwardness of the silence until it was broken by the sound of Cal's phone. He drew it out of his pocket. "DaCosta." He listened for a few seconds. "Where?" Then, "On my way."

He stuck the phone back in his pocket, glanced down the street toward his car, and looked at Jillian. He took her right hand one more time, raised it over her head, and slowly turned her in a circle.

"Thank you for the dance."

Jillian couldn't get a single word to come from her mouth. Cal opened the front door and motioned her inside so she could go through the house to get back to the party. She stepped into the entryway and he closed the door behind her.

Jillian was about to enter the backyard when she turned around and hurried back to the front door. She swung it open, took several steps down the walkway from the porch, and peered down the street. He was gone.

"You're welcome," she whispered.

CHAPTER 33

ON THURSDAY AFTERNOON, Adella opened the door before the two officers could knock. She'd seen them turn into Saint Sans from the window in the utility room.

"Sarge parked in the back. He reminded me that's where you like us to park when we drop by." Bully was his usual polite, cheerful self. "I'd rather be coming over here for a donut drop like last time, but my favorite shop closes at two o'clock. I don't know why, though. Lots of people like donuts at night, particularly if they're hot. Of course, the cake ones I like aren't usually served hot. Maybe I should have picked up some fried clams." Bully caught a glimpse of his supervisor's expression and redirected. "But anyhow, we've got some business we need to tend to."

"How are you, Mrs. Atwater? It's been a while. You weren't here the night of the fiasco," Sergeant DaCosta said, stepping through the door.

"No, I was not. Contrary to what it seems, I do not live at Saint Sans, Officer, but I'd be lying to say I'm glad I missed it. I'd have had a handful of that man's hide or else. The very idea, terrifying Mrs. Winsee that way. And it's a wonder David's head didn't come clean off and land in the middle of the pond in the park. Do you think he meant to use that knife to break in?"

"Maybe, but I don't think so," the sergeant responded. "I think he meant to leave it on the porch like everything else. But he's gone way past trespassing at this point. I do want all of you to know what we're thinking. Mrs. Fontaine is here, isn't she? We spoke on the phone. She's expecting us."

"I'm here, Sergeant." It was Olivia, emerging from her wing of the house. "I asked Adella to stay for whatever you're here to say. She knows as much about the goings-on around here as anybody. As you well know, she oversees this place, and I want her up on everything."

Compliments were hard to come by with Olivia. For a split second, Adella was flattered.

"Furthermore, I never seem to retell events and conversations to the satisfaction of her interminable curiosity. This will save me considerable energy. I won't have to tell her where everybody was standing and what everybody was wearing."

Bully brightened. "Well, I guess we make your job easier, since every time we show up we're wearing the same thing."

Sergeant DaCosta took a deep breath. "Anybody else who could join us might be helpful."

Adella was the one who kept tabs on everyone, so she spoke up. "Caryn was going to the library after class. David's here, though. I'll knock on his door."

As Adella started down the hall, Olivia called out to her. "Leave Vida be. I hear her television going. If we don't make a big commotion, she'll stay preoccupied. She doesn't need to have all of this stirred back up."

David entered the great room behind Adella and shook hands with both officers.

"You look like you're healing up there," Sergeant DaCosta commented.

David rubbed his cheek and smiled. "Yep, but I think I preferred purple to this odd shade of green I've got left. At this rate, I could be wearing this lovely shade with my tux at our school Christmas performance."

"It's a wonder you got out of that with only a black eye to show for it."

"Well, the bright side of it is that my students were impressed. That first week, all they could do was gawk."

The officer smiled rather uncharacteristically. "Well, I'd say they should be impressed. It took a fair amount of guts to take on a man the size you described. Looking back on it, would you say he was as tall as Bully?"

Bully stiffened his posture for full measure as David eyed him. "Every bit as tall. Yes, he was. And equally—" David paused a moment—"well, hefty. No offense."

"No offense taken! Mama says I came into this world so big that they left the hospital and drove me right to junior high."

Adella wanted to laugh, but Sergeant DaCosta and Olivia were so unamused that she thought better of it. Thankfully, David had manners enough to chuckle.

"Is there anybody else that you want in on this dialogue?" Sergeant DaCosta wanted to know.

"Are we looking for a quorum?" Olivia pulled out a stool from the kitchen island and sat on it. "We've already counted out Caryn and Mrs. Winsee. Unless you mean to question Clementine, that leaves us with Miss Slater. She's about to leave for work. Shall we summon her?"

Bully gave up a *yes* with an air of enthusiasm that could have blown the bird feeders off the limbs. All four of them looked expectantly at Adella.

She turned and headed toward Jillian's door. "If y'all need me to round up the neighbors, just tell me and I'll grab my foghorn out of my handbag."

Adella returned to Olivia, David, and the two officers in under ninety seconds. "Miss Slater will be out in no time. I'm sure she wouldn't mind if we got started."

The sergeant seemed distracted, but he proceeded. "Mr. Jacobs, I'd like to ask you to concentrate again on the night of the incident. Is there a chance you saw the pocketknife in the intruder's hand at any time?"

"No, sir. I didn't see it until you spotted it on the doormat."

"Is it possible that he dropped it or pitched it and it landed randomly in that spot?"

"I suppose it is, but I cannot recall seeing anything leave his hand."

Olivia fidgeted. "Officer, what place of importance does this have?"

"We have a person of interest, Mrs. Fontaine. We lifted a set of prints off the knife and found a match."

Olivia stood. "Who is it?"

"Numerous arrests, but not a single instance of violence. Petty theft, disturbing the peace, that kind of thing. And nothing in recent years. He's been a nuisance as much as anything. At six-three, he fits your description. But this is outside his pattern. He's not really been the type to show up in a residential section far from the quarter."

"Types can change," Adella responded.

"That's true. And that's one reason we're here. We're trying to establish a motive."

"What does this have to do with how the knife got to the mat?" David asked.

Bully interjected, "We're trying to figure out if he came to leave the knife or use it."

The statement made the hair on Adella's arms stand up. "Surely you've interrogated him. What does he say he was doing there?"

"We haven't made an arrest yet. But make no mistake—we will. He's just dropped out of sight for a while. He didn't likely go far. We'll find him." Sergeant DaCosta looked at Olivia as he said those words. "Between now and then, we're compiling facts and trying to find some missing pieces."

Olivia's words came forcefully. "Sergeant, I'll ask you again. Who is it? By that I mean what is his name?"

He fastened his gaze on Olivia like a man who knew he had only one chance to gauge a first reaction. "His name is William King Crawley."

Olivia drew down her brow and stared off into the backyard while everyone else in the circle stared at her.

Adella had to bite her tongue to keep from spewing a stream of questions, but the sergeant was commanding the lead, studying Olivia's expression, and obviously not wanting to rush her to an answer.

Finally he started the inquiry. "Do you know him?"

"My memory is not what it used to be," Olivia responded with a palpable discomfort, "but I am trying my hardest to run that name through every mental file I have, and for the life of me, I cannot recall ever hearing that name."

"Go to the mental file of your husband's relationships and deal-ings, Mrs. Fontaine," he instructed. "Does it ring any kind of bell there? A *William Crawley*? *Bill Crawley*? *King Crawley*?"

Bully suggested, "Think even in nicknames, like *King Craw.* Anything?"

Olivia sat down again and rubbed her forehead. "Nothing. But I was involved in very few of my husband's relationships, business or otherwise."

Adella was the only one in that gathering who could fully appreciate Olivia's level of cooperation with the officers who stood before her. Her vulnerability in front of them was hard for Adella to watch. She sat on the barstool next to her, wishing she could pat her hand, touch her shoulder, or show some kind of support and solidarity, but she didn't dare. Adella knew that a gesture of gentleness would reveal to Olivia that she looked as vulnerable as she felt. She'd withdraw so fast their heads would spin. Adella settled for rubbing her own forehead.

"Perhaps if I could see a picture, Sergeant DaCosta." Now Olivia had actually addressed him by name, a departure Adella took to mean one of two things: either Olivia was having a breakthrough or a breakdown.

Adella shifted in her seat and studied the room. Jillian should have been out here by now. What could be taking her so long? David had remained silent throughout the dialogue, but she knew he was as focused as a bird dog sniffing a covey of quail.

She stared at the three men standing next to one another: two policemen and a choir teacher. In stature David lacked their size, but as a man, he stood toe-to-toe with them and looked them in the eye. Adella hadn't always been a great judge of male character, as her mother might have testified, but since the day Emmett Atwater walked into her life, she'd steadily developed some good taste.

The sergeant glanced at Bully, who pulled a printout from between the pages of a legal pad. Bully placed the page faceup on the kitchen island and carefully slid it in front of Olivia. His approach seemed a sincere attempt to convey that he was friend and not foe.

"I wanted you to focus on name recognition before you saw his picture," Sergeant DaCosta explained. "Recognize him? It's not recent, but it's what we've got, and who knows—it might be better this way if his original connection was in past years."

Three heads immediately dropped over the picture as Olivia, David, and Adella studied the mug shot. Without lifting his gaze from the page, David was the first to speak. "So this is the face behind the mask of the man who hit me."

"Well, we can't say that for sure," the sergeant countered, "but we have plenty for questioning when we find him. We can say this much: this man's prints are on the pocketknife and he fits the size you described. Mrs. Fontaine, does he look at all familiar to you?"

Olivia looked up from the printout with a wearied expression. "No." She slid it back toward Bully.

"I know it's uncomfortable to be the one singled out in this kind of questioning, but you understand why. If he's the one who has pulled the rest of the stunts, it's obviously personal. He has some kind of tie to you. If all these things are connected—a theory we're still sorting through—why would this man in this photo—" he tapped the picture emphatically—"leave flowers at the burial with an ominous card, plant baby paraphernalia outside the house, possess and leave a torn picture of your son, Raphael, as well as a pocketknife your son received as a child?"

Olivia stood, anger flashing across her face. "Do you think I know that? Do you think I am not more anxious than you to get some answers? Or do you think the ice woman is oblivious to the fact that this whole household has been endangered?"

"Nobody's said that," Sergeant DaCosta responded.

"Nobody's thinking it either." Unlike Adella, Bully didn't hesitate to reach out and pat Olivia on the shoulder. "We just want to get to the bottom of it for all your sakes. A necessary part of that is figuring out why this guy right here would do those exact things."

Adella spoke up. "He's obviously playing sick jokes."

Sergeant DaCosta's expression took on a whole new level of seriousness. "He's officially surpassed sick jokes. Mrs. Fontaine, listen carefully to me. We think there is every possibility that the pocketknife was the murder weapon. According to the medical examiner's report, it could be consistent with the wound. We've contacted the office requesting further inquiry."

The face that had been red with anger instantly went white. Olivia walked over to a chair in front of the fireplace and dropped down in it, turning her back to all four of them. "Rafe, killed by his own father's fancy pocketknife."

They remained silent for a moment. David moved toward Olivia and sat on the hearth where he could look her in the eye. His words came barely above a whisper. "His father's father's pocketknife. Isn't that right? Isn't that what I remember you saying— that it had first belonged to your husband's own father?"

Perhaps the difference had little bearing on the case, but Adella well understood what David was doing. However detached or hard-hearted Rafe's father had been, the last thing Olivia needed right now was to think that one of the few nice things he'd done for his son had ended up killing him.

When Adella walked over to the sitting area in front of the fireplace and sat down, the two officers followed suit. The sergeant sat forward on the edge of the chair, his head down and his elbows on his knees. He rubbed his hands together before he looked up and spoke. "They're testing the knife for DNA. There is no visible trace, but they can tell us more than we can see."

"Do you need something?" Olivia's question came across odd.

He glanced at Adella, who gave him a puzzled look. "Of what nature, ma'am?" he asked.

"Do you need something to match it with?" Olivia spoke matter-of-factly.

"Oh no, ma'am," Bully replied too hastily but without a hint of guile. "We still have the clothes we found him in."

A lump welled in Adella's throat when she saw Olivia wince. *"And a sword will pierce through your own soul also."* The words of Simeon's prophecy over Mary, the mother of Jesus, were pulled like a single piece of yarn from Adella's memory and looped in perfect script on the fabric of her mind.

Sergeant DaCosta spoke with a mixture of professionalism and compassion. "What we need most from you is any piece of information, now or in the next few days, that could remotely have to do with this man or this case. For now, is there anything at all that you haven't told us that might help us?"

A door opened and closed in the hall, and Jillian appeared at the entrance to the great room. Bully wasted no time standing and greeting her. Sergeant DaCosta stood as well, but more nervously, brushing some cat hair off his pant leg.

Adella knew the instant she saw Jillian what had taken her so long. Not only had she changed out of her uniform, she'd touched up her hair and, Adella was fairly sure, her makeup. She was a sight to behold in that midnight-blue top and those jeans, but a suspicious one. "Jillian, did they cancel on you? I thought you were going to work."

"I am."

"Where's your uniform?" Adella was perplexed.

"It's in here." Jillian held up a plastic bag. She also had her purse over her shoulder.

Adella craned her neck to look around the dining table at Jillian's feet. She had on a pair of black leather boots, with a hint of Western flair to them, astride at least two-inch heels. Adella had never seen them before, so she was pretty sure they were brand-new. "Your work shoes in there, too?"

"Adella," Olivia said, annoyed. "Jillian is a grown woman. She is perfectly capable of knowing how to get herself ready for work."

"I'll change there," Jillian explained.

"I see." What Adella saw was a young woman who'd spruced up her appearance for somebody in that room, and it was neither Olivia nor her. Adella gave a once-over to each of the officers.

Bully? Maybe they had bonded behind Adella's back when she insisted that Jillian walk him to the car after he'd delivered the pink-iced donut. She wouldn't have taken Bully for Jillian's type because he had such a naiveté about him, but goodness knew opposites attracted.

Adella felt puffed up with pride over Jillian. Look how far she'd come under her tutelage. If Vince—sly, savvy, and self-consumed—had a polar opposite on this planet, Adella supposed it was Bully. But she sure hadn't seen that one coming. She'd really just meant Jillian to be nice to the young man.

When Jillian walked over to the middle of the great room, the gentlemen sat down. The cat seemed to have everybody's tongue.

Bully broke the ice. "We've had some breakthroughs in the case that we'll get you up to speed on. Sarge was just asking Mrs. Fontaine if there was anything she hadn't told us. We're trying to make sure we've heard everything."

Adella tried to keep from rolling her eyes, especially now that she suspicioned something between Bully and Jillian. But the mere thought that those two officers had hopes of a tell-all coming from Olivia would have been laughable under lesser circumstances. Adella was almost certain that everything Olivia had told them was the truth. She just highly doubted she'd told them, or anyone else for that matter, *everything*.

Adella glanced at Jillian, anticipating the expression the young woman always seemed to have on her face when she had fresh cause to look cynically at her grandmother. After all, Olivia was the one on the hot seat, a fact that Jillian had earned the right to enjoy. But at this particular moment, Jillian seemed oblivious. Adella took a good look at Jillian's eyes and followed her path of vision like a clothesline hung taut between two poles. That line led east of the hearth where David was sitting, west of the chair barely holding Bully, and landed right on the face of one Sergeant Cal DaCosta. Remarkably, he had an identical look in his eyes.

"Oh, Lord," Adella whispered louder than she should have.

"Anything at all, Mrs. Fontaine? Anything out of the ordinary, even if it seems unrelated?" Bully brought the wanderers' attention back to the matter at hand.

When Olivia didn't respond immediately, everyone perked up. She tended to be a quick draw with a *no.*

"I'm missing some money. I can't see how that has anything to do with this, but you said—"

Sergeant DaCosta interrupted, "From your purse? Had you left it in plain sight of the back porch?" He was clearly trying to establish whether the perpetrator had entered the house.

"No, no," Olivia responded. "It was not in my purse. It was in my desk drawer in my bedroom. I've kept a little cash on hand ever since the hurricane, in case the banks closed for several days."

"How much cash are we talking about here?" Sergeant DaCosta steered the questioning while Bully jotted a note on his legal pad.

"I'd say a thousand dollars, give or take."

Adella would regret what she did next as much as anything she'd ever bemoan. It was pure reflex, like someone had hit her just below the kneecap and caused her to kick. The instant she heard the amount, she swung her head back with enough force to squeak the chair and looked at Jillian.

Jillian stared at Adella with a look of disbelief. Her eyes jumped from Adella to Bully, from Bully to Olivia, from Olivia to David, and from David to Sergeant DaCosta. By now they were all look-ing back and forth between her and Adella.

"I didn't take it!" In the immediate confusion, no one responded, but the silence masqueraded across the hardwood floor as accusation. "Adella, you told them! I trusted you and you told them!"

"No, Jillian!" Adella jumped to her feet and tried to grab her by the arm. "I didn't! I didn't mean that you—"

Jillian ran to her room and turned the lock while Adella knocked insistently on the door. "Girl, let me in this minute!"

Moments later Jillian sprang from Rafe's room with her bor-rowed suitcase, her purse, and the plastic bag filled to capacity.

"Jillian, I didn't look at you because I thought you did it. I just couldn't believe the coincidence! The desk drawer and all."

Jillian stormed past Adella through the great room where everyone stood with their jaws dropped. Before she slammed the door, she glanced behind her and said, "Nobody better follow me. I never want to see any of you again. I mean it!"

CHAPTER 34

JILLIAN CHANGED HER CLOTHES in the cramped stall of the ladies' room at Café Beignet with tears dripping from the end of her nose. The second she'd arrived, a coworker had asked why she was so dressed up, making Jillian feel twice the fool. She set her dark-blue top on the small metal shelf and, in the twisting and turning of putting on her uniform, knocked it into the toilet bowl.

"You've gotta be kidding." She stuffed the dripping-wet shirt into the plastic bag with her toiletries, put on her work shoes, stashed her things in a corner of the kitchen, and clocked in. Her hands were shaking so badly that her first two orders were practically illegible. A woman at the second table who couldn't have passed a sobriety test if her life depended on it asked Jillian if anything was wrong. That was it. Jillian went straight to the night manager and begged for the evening off.

"Why? You just got here. You sick?" the manager asked.

"Yes." Jillian should have left it at that but she didn't. "The truth is, I'm so upset about something that I'm sick. My stomach feels awful and my head is killing me." Her voice broke.

At first the manager looked perturbed, but her face softened somewhat when tears pooled in Jillian's eyes. "You have the flu?"

"No. I just feel sick all over."

"I think you have the flu. Go. Take your germs out of here. You think I can afford to get sick? Shoo." Jillian knew this was the woman's way of showing her mercy. She'd be less likely to get fired for leaving sick than upset.

Jillian started down the sidewalk with only one place to go. She had enough cash on her for a week in a cheap motel but she didn't know how long she'd need to make the money last. The dollars would stretch further if she could stay at Stella's. More than anything, Jillian needed to buy some time until she could bring herself to do the inevitable: call her mother for help. The one time she'd risked using her phone to call Jade, her usual live-and-let-live mother had flown completely off the handle about Jillian staying at Olivia's. The whole conversation had been so childish Jillian could hardly believe it.

Jade pitching her own daughter into the backseat usually meant one thing: she was having man problems. Jillian had never known her mother to simply like a man. Moderation didn't appear to be a category Jade understood. She was either cold to a man or consumed with him. Nothing in between. Jillian had tried to muster up a little compassion toward her, but sometimes she got tired of being the one in the mother role.

As she started up the stairs to Stella's apartment, she thought about the first time they met and how something about Stella early on had reminded her of Jade. The one glaring contrast was that Stella hadn't spoken of a single issue with a man in the months they'd known each other. But Stella's shock at seeing Jillian at her door, and her reluctance to invite her in, made Jillian wonder if she had male company.

"I've caught you at a bad time, haven't I? Is someone here?"

Stella seemed a little anxious as she looked over her shoulder toward the bedroom door. "No, no. No one's here. I was just . . . doing some cleaning."

Jillian had never seen Stella's bedroom. The door was always shut and the one time Jillian had tried to open it, it had been locked. Now it was open, and Jillian could see that the room was in disarray. A black trash bag, partially filled, was sitting on the bed.

"Listen, I can go to a motel tonight. In fact, I have enough money to stay in one several nights. There's that one just a few blocks from here." Jillian shifted the weight of her bag to her other hand. "I'm sorry I just showed up on your doorstep."

"I was expecting you at some point, Jillian. I just didn't think it would be today. It's okay. Come on in. Everything's just kind of a mess." As she spoke, Stella crossed the living room and shut the bedroom door. "You look like you've been crying. Tell me what happened."

At first Stella still seemed uneasy and distracted, but the farther Jillian got into the story, the more focused she became. She said most of the things Jillian needed a compassionate listener to say until she came up with this question: "So did you?"

"Did I what?"

"Did you take the money?"

Jillian could hardly fathom what she was hearing. "No, I didn't take the money! I've never set a foot in that woman's room by myself. I can't believe you asked me that."

"Well, I wouldn't have blamed you if you did. It's a pittance compared to what she owes you."

"I don't get what you're saying." Jillian had no intention of taking up for Olivia, but she was struggling to follow Stella's reasoning.

"Come on, Jillian. Think what you should have inherited when her son kicked the bucket. You haven't stolen from her. That witch has stolen from you."

Jillian's head was still throbbing. "I never looked at it that way."

"You're kidding me. Why on earth have you been staying over there all this time?"

The answer to that question had gotten more and more complicated and less and less clear even to Jillian, but she well remembered what had landed her back in New Orleans. "To hide!"

"Okay, okay. Settle down, girl. I've told you over and over, I'm on your side. I think they're jerks. That's all. I mean, at this point, they're probably nuts enough to think you've pulled all the stunts."

"They couldn't think that."

"With the money missing? Oh, I bet they do. Think about it from their angle. None of it started until after the first time you came to town."

"But none of it was me!"

"I know that. You don't have to convince me. That's just the kind of people they are. They don't really care about you."

"The man at Mrs. Winsee's window. How could I have had anything to do with that?"

"I'm sure the police think by now that was a Halloween prank. A coincidence. Don't you think?"

"But the pocketknife!"

"Be reasonable, Jillian. There is only one place for that knife to come from—somewhere in that house. I'd bet a thousand bucks that Olivia suspects you found it and put it there at the back door. *I* know you didn't. But that's how people like her think."

Jillian held the top of her head with both hands. What Stella was saying made horrifying sense.

Stella sat down on the couch next to her, put her hands on

Jillian's knee, and leaned in toward her. "Jillian, look at me. You did the right thing. You're out of there."

Jillian nodded tentatively, feeling like her best-case scenario was finding the least-threatening spot in an unstoppable nightmare.

"You're welcome here, and we'll make the best of it. I know it's painful to face the facts, but the sooner you do, the faster you'll get on your feet."

The shift of tenderness in her voice would have brought Jillian to tears had Stella not hugged her. She stiffened instead, unaccustomed to a lingering embrace of comfort. After a few uncomfortable seconds, Jillian patted Stella on the back to prompt some closure. She pulled away from her and said, "Thank you."

And she meant it. She knew that nothing about her showing up that evening on Stella's doorstep was convenient to the woman. It was just that after what had transpired earlier at Saint Sans, she considered Stella the only friend she had in the world, even though Stella was old enough to be her mother.

Jillian's thoughts drifted to Allie in San Francisco. She'd been her best friend in the way most often woven between peers. They'd shopped at the same places for clothes and used the same figures of speech. They knew one another's stories and quirks and phobias. Jillian could use Allie's lip gloss right after her without feeling all freaky about germs. Regret ached in Jillian's chest. She wished she hadn't let Vince come between them. If she hadn't, maybe Allie would have come looking for her.

Given time, Caryn might have become a friend like Allie, but that possibility had just gone up in a puff of smoke. Stella was right. By now, everybody at Saint Sans probably saw her as a crook, if not a total psychopath.

"Here you go, Jillian." Stella handed her a pillow and a blanket and a fitted sheet. "You might try putting together a makeshift mattress from the cushions. You'd at least be able to stretch out on the floor. Here, let me have that and I'll do it for you." Stella reached for the sheet.

Making a bed on the floor wasn't the worst idea. Jillian still remembered the crick in her neck from the time she'd somehow managed to pass out on that couch. The flashback to that odd sleepover with the card reading made her think of Bully, and how he and Sanchez had beaten at the door the next morning. If someone had told her that day she'd be at his next birthday party, she'd have called them crazy. She wished now she'd never gone to the party. Those moments with Cal on Bully's front porch had made today's events at Saint Sans immeasurably more painful and humiliating. A wave of nausea came over her.

"You okay?" Stella asked.

"Yeah. Just spent."

"Hungry? You're welcome to whatever you can find in the kitchen. I'll grab some things from the market tomorrow."

"Thanks, Stella. No worries about tonight. I couldn't eat anything if I had to. I'll chip in on the groceries tomorrow, though."

"Deal. Glass of wine?"

"No. I'm good."

Stella poured herself a glass, said good night, and disappeared behind the bedroom door. At least there was a tiny powder room off the kitchen that Jillian could use. She'd never seen a one-bedroom with an extra bathroom before and she was thankful for it.

In the three-minute interval between feeling accused of robbing Olivia and storming out the door of Saint Sans, Jillian had managed to pack every personal belonging she had. She unzipped the bulging suitcase and pulled out the contents until she found Adella's pajama top and then the pants. As she put them on, the feeling of betrayal nearly swallowed her whole. How could Adella have done that? Or even thought that?

But Jillian felt more than a sense of betrayal. She felt sad, a kind of sadness that soaked through to her bones and drained her of strength. A sadness she'd not even felt over Vince. She turned on her side and curled up into a ball, trying not to separate the cushions beneath her. Squeezing her eyes shut, Jillian attempted to force every emotion out of her heart but anger. It felt best. Hurt the least. But it refused to abide in there alone.

Those five people had been like aliens the first few weeks she stayed at Saint Sans. But at least they were there, always stirring around and coming in and out. Someone was always cooking something. The dryer was always running. Clementine always whining. The smell of dark coffee wafted through the vents at least twice a day. Adella was forever in a twit about this or that, and her stories about her boys could have been water-colored into a comic strip. Of course, Jillian tried not to laugh or show any other signs of warming up around there. Olivia was too cold for much warming up. Jillian had known all along the arrangement was temporary.

But during that short two-month stay, every square inch of the house under the steep metal roof was taken up with life and astir with dust that refused to settle. Jillian had been raised as the only child of a mom who worked hard and long to make decent money. She knew what it was like to be alone and lonely or, maybe worse, in bad company. The way some of them at Saint Sans had gotten into her business annoyed her profusely, but on the flip side, they'd also roped her into theirs. There were the replayed antics of David's students and Caryn's constant fears over flunking out of medical school. Jillian knew more about Mrs. Winsee's honeymoon than anybody under seventy ought to hear.

Olivia abbreviated virtually every good conversation just by walking into the kitchen, but at least she was around. And if she wasn't, signs of her presence were everywhere. Her pruning shears and gardening gloves were always on the back porch and the flowers in the vase on the dining table were usually clipped from her own garden. If, God forbid, the flowers were store-bought, they'd all have to endure hearing what Olivia found wrong with them. Every now and then she'd be in a less contrary mood and freer of speech and they'd all find the rare glimpse mesmerizing.

"There's no telling what treasure is in that vault," David would say. "If we could spike her coffee, think what all we could find out." The whole place was like a padded cell of eccentrics. Almost everything about it was in some way absurd, but the absurdities had not been wholly absent of amusement. There was all the yelling Adella had done over the mouse that scampered behind the refrigerator. She'd made David pull Clementine out from under the Snapdragon by the tail, which he'd done wearing a pair of long yellow dishwashing gloves he'd found under the kitchen sink. Once Clementine was apprehended, Adella threw on Olivia's soiled garden gloves, got down on her knees, and tried to force the cat's wide girth into the narrow space between the fridge and the wall. The combined elation of the residents was immeasurable when the mouse darted out and tried to head up her skirt. A mouse had never ended up deader.

And Caryn had bought them matching sweaters.

Somewhere along the way, Jillian had let her guard down, and this was what had come of it. Pain. The penetrating kind. The kind that bruised a person from the inside out.

She would not let it happen again.

CHAPTER 35

By morning, the cushions had come completely apart under the fitted sheet. Jillian's head was propped on one and her legs were on another, and her entire midsection had sunk to the floor in between. She'd tossed and turned and rearranged the bedding most of the night but finally dozed off out of pure exhaustion just before dawn. Now the incessant beeping and grinding of a garbage truck at the curb below Stella's apartment forced her swollen eyes open.

"Coffee," she whispered. She knew there was a coffeemaker on the kitchen counter, but she didn't feel at home enough to rummage through the cabinets for a filter and something to put in it. Stella might have terrible taste in coffee. What if she liked that chicory? Or what if she made her coffee so weak, a person could see the grounds in the bottom of the cup? The irony wasn't wasted on Jillian that she wished she had a cup of Olivia's coffee to muster the courage never to see her again.

By the time Stella emerged from her bedroom, Jillian had put the cushions back on the couch and chairs and folded the sheet as much as a fitted sheet would agree to fold. The extra pillow from Stella's bed was in Jillian's lap and her hands were folded properly on top of it. She knew that most of the awkwardness she felt was unnecessary. After all, Stella had welcomed her. Still, she felt like a schoolkid waiting to see the principal after getting caught skipping class.

"Hey there. Get any sleep?" From the look of her, Stella wasn't much of a morning person either. Jillian's reluctant host ran her fingers through her tangled hair. She pulled back the curtain to peer at the pouring rain.

"Some," Jillian answered. "You?"

"Some." Stella smiled as she said it but Jillian felt a twinge of guilt. "Sky's falling out there."

"Yeah, it is," Jillian responded, walking over to the window. Thunder clapped in the distance.

"Welcome to winter in New Orleans. If you want snow instead, you're out of luck. I hate the cold, though. I even hate it this cold."

"I like some cold weather if the skies are blue," Jillian added. "To me, it's the rain that makes it miserable." They were talking about the weather. This was liable to be a long day. Jillian would be relieved to go to work later that afternoon.

"I bet you could use some coffee."

"Yes!" It was the best news Jillian had heard since she'd arrived on Stella's doorstep. "I would have made us some, but I didn't know where you kept everything." She followed Stella into the kitchen.

"I told you to make yourself at home."

"I know. I just felt a little weird about it."

Stella opened the cabinet and pulled out a box of filters and a can of coffee. "You'll need to get over that."

The can wasn't the best sign about the coffee to come. A bag would have boded better. But whatever was inside that can was infinitely better than what was in the empty mug waiting on the counter. The coffee turned out to be surprisingly decent, and what it lacked in quality, Jillian made up for in quantity. The pot was empty in half an hour.

"Going to work today?" Stella asked.

"Planning to. The manager insisted last night that I had the flu, so I could probably get away with not going in. But too much time on my hands would give me too much time to think. I wish I could just switch off my brain. This is so embarrassing, but I've got to get one of those prepaid cell phones."

"What happened to the phone the witch gave you?"

"I threw it on the bed when I left. Are you kidding? I wasn't about to keep it. I don't want anything of hers."

"You'll need to get over that, too." When Stella winked at Jillian, she squirmed in her chair trying to decide how to respond. Stella obviously found it unthinkable for Jillian not to push for some of the Fontaine money.

Jillian wanted Stella's approval, but she wanted contact with Olivia even less. The merest hint that Jillian was after money would cause Olivia to claim that she'd been right all along about why the girl had shown up.

"Is she just going to let you become homeless, too?"

The question caught Jillian off guard. She remembered telling Stella about Rafe when they first met, but they'd hardly talked about it since then. In her current situation, the prospect hit so close to home that it terrified Jillian. She already felt like a vagabond. All she needed was for someone to give voice to her fear.

"Isn't that how it happens?" Stella didn't let up.

"What do you mean?"

"The family turns their back on you and leaves you to the streets, while they sleep tucked in their pretty beds?"

The urge to take up for Olivia was an odd twist of emotions that left Jillian rattled. Olivia had certainly not taken up for her the day before. And Jillian was starkly aware that she was at Stella's mercy. She rose to her feet, walked over to the sink, and rinsed out her empty coffee mug. "I don't think it was quite that simple."

"Oh, really?"

"Really."

Both women went dead silent. Jillian was the first to break it. "Man, it's raining cats and dogs out there."

A few minutes later, Jillian worked up the nerve to ask a question she'd dreaded since the moment she'd opened her eyes that morning. "Stella, may I use your shower? I can do everything else in the little bathroom." It had a sink and toilet, but if she didn't have access to a tub, she would have no choice but to check into a motel. At that point her stack of cash would circle the drain faster than her bathwater. She'd started to accept that a call to Jade was coming, but she couldn't handle it yet.

Stella looked surprised, as if the thought of Jillian needing access to her shower had never occurred to her. How on earth Stella had entertained the idea of her moving in a couple weeks ago without considering they'd need to share that bathroom was a mystery.

"Of course." Stella's mouth said yes but her eyes wore an unmistakable no. "It's just a mess in there. I was in the middle of clearing a bunch of stuff out and cleaning everything up when you came last night. You're going to have to give me a little while to straighten things up." She picked up her phone and looked at the time as if she had somewhere she needed to be.

"I don't care if your room's messy. All I need is the shower. Well, and some shampoo. I grabbed my makeup and a few other toiletries when I left Saint Sans, but I didn't think to grab the shampoo. I wasn't thinking very clearly."

"No problem. I get it. But I can't bring myself to let you go in there with everything turned upside down. Just give me a little while."

"I so wish you wouldn't bo—"

Stella had already gone into her room and shut the door behind her before Jillian could finish the sentence. "No bother at all, Jillian. I need to do it anyway," Jillian muttered under her breath.

She pulled a pair of jeans out of her suitcase and tried to remember where she'd stuck her makeup. When the plastic bag occurred to her, she remembered the shirt she'd dropped in the toilet at Café Beignet. She tore open the bag and pulled the top out of it carefully with her thumb and index finger. "Gross." She stepped on the pedal of the trash can in the kitchen, and when the lid opened, she dropped the top in it. At least the makeup was in a sturdy enough plastic bag to be rinsed off without getting her eye shadows wet. She'd found them in the cosmetic aisle at the drugstore near Saint Sans, but they still weren't cheap.

Most of the morning had passed by the time Stella came out of her room. "Have at it," she said, not rudely by any stretch but matter-of-factly.

"Thank you so much," Jillian responded sincerely. As she walked into the straightened bedroom, change of clothes in hand, she noticed Stella pausing at the door.

"I have an errand I've got to run." Stella seemed anxious.

"I hate that you have to go out in this deluge."

"Well, me, too. But I've got something I need to take care of."

"Go right ahead. You sure don't need to babysit me, Stella. I want to be as low maintenance as I can as long as I'm here. I'll just take a shower and do the rest of my getting ready at the sink in the other bathroom. Okay with you?"

Stella looked unsettled. "Yep. I'll be back before you know it." Stella remained at the doorway to the bedroom until Jillian went into the bathroom and shut the door.

Jillian took her shower in record time, hoping to be out of there and in the other bathroom by the time Stella got back. It took Jillian a full minute to realize that the chrome knobs in the shower were reversed. Teeth chattering, she turned the C knob quickly to the right and the icy water warmed up.

She opened the bathroom door the second she was dressed. "Stella, I'm out!" She walked into the bedroom, wrapping the towel around her head, and heard no response. Relieved that she'd gotten out of the shower before Stella returned, she slowed down a bit, caught her breath, and picked up her pajamas from the bathroom floor.

On her way back to the living room, she noticed a book on Stella's nightstand. It was a tattered clothbound antique with the spine split on one end and shredded on the other. The front of the book had a design on it, but the cover was too dark for her to discern the image from across the room. Curiosity piqued, Jillian stepped over to the nightstand and picked up the book. She prepared herself to be impressed if it turned out to be an old classic.

The faded image on the cover was a woman wrapped all the way around with her floor-length hair. She was standing in a garden that looked a lot like the one in Stella's bizarre mural. A large snake was curled at the woman's feet. The picture was disappointingly unoriginal. Jillian didn't know much about the Bible, but it didn't take a theologian to assume the woman on the cover of the book was supposed to be Eve. The title on the spine was unreadable, so she opened the book to check for one inside, sending chunks of brittle pages to the floor.

She squatted down quickly to gather up the sections of yellowed paper and stick them back in place. Wedged in before the last few pages was a close-up photograph of Stella, taken not many years before. Jillian pulled it out and stared intently at it, her heart beginning to pound. The picture in her hand had been ripped in half. Jillian thumbed through the old book, searching for the other piece or a note that might go with it. Not a single other item was tucked in the pages. Jillian's mind started to race. She did not know how it was possible or why it would be so, but she knew as much by intuition as memory who'd been in the other half of that picture. She'd caught a glimpse of it in Olivia's hand.

Jillian's pulse reverberated in her ears. "It can't be," she whispered, trying to back herself out of the madness. "You're putting things together that don't go together, Jillian. Get a grip. It can't be the same picture." She knew her words were sane and reasonable. What were the chances that Stella and Rafe had been in the same picture? But her insides were sounding a frantic alarm.

She jumped to her feet, her eyes darting wildly around the room. The bottom edge of Stella's closet caught her eye. The door was shut tight, but the corner of a black trash bag was protruding about an inch through the opening at the base. Jillian's memory jumped to the bag that had been on Stella's bed the night before. She remembered how nervous Stella had looked, glancing over her shoulder toward her bedroom, leaving Jillian so long at the front door. *She was just cleaning stuff out. Nothing unusual about that,* Jillian told herself. *She was embarrassed about the mess. But why get all nervous about it? And why did I get that weird feeling?*

What she was doing was inappropriate enough, but snooping in a person's bedroom closet was a boundary a true friend would refuse to cross. What kind of friend was she? Right or wrong, a second question welled up within her with such force that it drove her past the war within to a place of no return. What kind of friend was *Stella*?

She quickly perused the room for another bag. Maybe the bag in the closet wasn't the one she'd seen the night before.

Jillian knew this much for certain: the trash bag on the bed last night hadn't been in Stella's hand when she'd stood in the doorway earlier. Jillian placed her palm on the doorknob to the closet and leaned back for an eyeshot of the living room, making sure she was alone. Stella could walk through the apartment door any second.

Adrenaline spiked through Jillian like a geyser. She turned the knob and opened the closet to a maelstrom of clothes and hats and shoes. She shook her head, chiding an imagination that was derailing her rationale like it was a runaway train. Glancing into the living room again, she crouched down to untie the knot in the black trash bag. The knot was stubborn in her trembling fingers. "Come on! Give!" Tearing into the bag would give her away the second Stella opened the closet. Finally the knot came loose.

The heavy rain darkening the windows frustrated Jillian's view. Turning on the light was out of the question. She foraged through the bag, trying to identify the contents by feel, checking and rechecking the front door. Panicking over how long it was taking, Jillian rotated the bag upside down, tumbling out the contents. The items toward the top of the heap were random and meaningless: a few pieces of women's clothing, a towel, an old purse. She dug toward the bottom like a dog digging for a bone. Underneath a stringy terry-cloth robe, she turned up a man's shirt. Next to it she found a faded baseball cap and, beneath it, a card key from a local motel. She drew an old cell phone out of the pile and felt around for a charger, surfacing, instead, a single glossy snapshot.

Jillian snatched the picture and held it above her head to catch as much light as possible. It was the two of them, Stella and Rafe, in a photo apparently taken at the same time as the one torn in half. Her thoughts whirled, trying to snag something that made sense of the sight. She came up on her knees, stuck the photo in her back pocket, and began stuffing the contents back into the bag as fast as her hands would fly. She glanced around her and frantically patted the floor for anything she'd left out of the bag. Her right hand landed on an object that had tumbled to the edge of the dresser.

It was a man's wallet, typical dark leather with time-blackened edges. Jillian picked it up and opened it, butterflies crowding her stomach. Under the clear plastic was an old state of Louisiana driver's license. She blinked her eyes, adjusting her sight to the shadows, glared at the man's picture, and read the small print.

Fontaine, Raphael Weyland

Stunned, Jillian dropped back on her heels and fell into someone standing behind her.

CHAPTER 36

SPRING 1919

THE ORGAN WAS NOTHING LIKE the pipes at Saint Mary's, but it had been donated to Saint Silvanus, and anybody with a lick of sense knew not to look a gift horse in the mouth. To a charter congregation big on cause and short on funds, the instrument may as well have been dipped in gold.

It was a regular pump organ that had been restored some years earlier but never electrified. The owner meant to get rid of it but claimed it just wouldn't leave. More of a parlor variety, it was Victorian-style oak with an intricately carved crown pediment set behind four spindled torches, the latter of which went almost without saying.

The fancy beveled mirror embedded behind the fretwork was a

classic. It served as the eyes in the back of the organist's head. With her back to the congregation and the organ flush against the north wall, she could not only see the soloist she accompanied but faces of parishioners as well. That coveted bench was the best seat in the house, but the options were rather limited regarding who would grace it. Hiring someone was out of the question. The church could barely support the parson's small family. The first volunteer who appeared to know middle C from high C won the bench. The congregants counted themselves fortunate when she happened to be a widow who'd taught piano lessons for longer than many of them had been alive. After all, how different could a piano and an organ be?

The organ pedals were Brianna's favorite preoccupation during prolonged vocal selections when everybody could stand but her. Since she was seated on the front pew of the opposite section, she enjoyed the perfect side view. Each pedal was overlaid with harp-shaped filigreed metal plates that teased as brass. It was a nice touch, certainly, but the ornamentations were a cut above the normal tastes of a nine-year-old.

What Brianna loved best was the way Mrs. Scoggins often slipped off her shoes to pump the organ so as not to scratch the fine filigree, and on no rare occasion, a stocking would get stuck to a rough edge. This was an understandable distraction and one that normally led to an untimely chord as the stocking rarely if ever pulled free on its own. By the time Mrs. Scoggins bent over and rose again, the soloist had moved on and could seldom find her way back.

Brianna's joy was not complete until she shifted her gaze to her father, enthroned on the platform in a tall-back chair with red velvet inserts.

CHAPTER 37

"YOU KNEW HIM!" Jillian scrambled to her feet, trapped between Stella and the closet door.

"How dare you pry into my private things? I took you in and you—"

"How dare *I*? Are you kidding me? Here's a better question: who *are* you?" Jillian's fury exceeded her fear. She tried to step around Stella, but Stella bodily blocked her. Jillian leaned forward, bringing her face only a few inches from Stella's. "You need to move or I swear, woman, I will move you."

"I will move under one condition: you sit down and let me explain. There are things you need to know."

"Oh, I want an explanation alright. Now, move."

Stella hesitated before taking a step back. Jillian bent down and gathered up her pajamas and toiletries and walked around Stella to the living room. Stacking up all her things in the chair closest to the apartment door, Jillian said, "So, talk."

"Sit down and I will."

"I prefer to stand. Actually, I prefer to leave, but you owe me an explanation."

The look Stella gave Jillian was chilling.

Jillian steeled herself and refused to back down. "You knew him. How?"

Stella walked over to the window and gazed into the downpour without saying a word. She placed her hand on the cold pane and spread her fingers apart, squinting as if she were staring through them. A sheet of lightning lit up the room. Jillian fell into the chair and pulled her knees to her chest as thunder clapped right on its heels. Stella never flinched.

"Jillian," Stella finally uttered, still staring out the window, "I need you to go somewhere with me."

"Are you out of your mind? For starters, it's falling a flood out there."

"It's not like a tornado and we're not going to melt if we get wet. It will be worth it to you. You need to see some things with your own eyes."

"What kinds of things? Why don't you tell me what they are first and then I'll decide if I want to make the trip."

"Pieces of the puzzle. Things you need to know about the Fontaines. There's more to all of this than you realize. You don't know that woman at all." Stella paused for a moment, her back still to Jillian. "And there are some things of Raphael's. Things you will be very interested in seeing."

The tone of Stella's voice and the halting cadence of her words were so different from normal that Jillian would not have known it was her in a pitch-black room. Jillian wondered if Stella might have taken something. Either way, Jillian was annoyed that she wouldn't just face her and talk. "Why do you have stuff that belonged to him? Answer me that first."

Stella turned around slowly and leaned her back against the windowpane. Her eyes were now fixed on Jillian's. "We had a thing."

The fact that Stella had insider information on the family was nearly intolerable to Jillian. She was still trying to wrap her mind around an existing connection between them. "A thing. What kind of thing?" Jillian knew what Stella meant, but after weeks of withheld information in multiple face-to-face conversations, Jillian wasn't going to let her get away with the indirect approach. She was quickly losing patience with Stella's whole mysterious air.

"We were together for a while."

"A couple. Is that what you're saying?"

"Yes."

"Hmmm. And exactly when would that have been, since my understanding is that it has been some time since he was sober enough to carry on a relationship?"

"He had his seasons."

"So you two had a 'thing' during one of his 'seasons,'" Jillian responded sarcastically.

Stella stared at her without saying a word. Jillian let the silence hang heavy between them for a while but soon lost patience with what seemed like a game. She stuck her pajamas and her toiletries in her suitcase and zipped it up.

As Jillian turned toward the apartment door, Stella muttered, "His last."

Something about those two words stuck a hook through Jillian's soul. She did not want to go with Stella, but in that moment, she knew she did not have the will to resist it. The curiosity was too much. The gaps in Rafe's story had become the gaps in her own. Those puzzle pieces did not belong to Stella. They belonged to her. Jillian resolved to gather them up, call Jade for help, and walk away from these people forever. "Is it close by?"

"Close enough."

"You have one hour. Then you drop me off at the café. From there I'll check into a motel until I can leave town. Agreed?"

Stella nodded. "Give me a moment before we leave. I need to take some things from here." She paused. "So that you can see it all together."

"I'll be at the bottom of the stairs for two minutes, and after that, I'm leaving."

Stella soon descended the stairs with a bulging purse under her arm and keys in her hand. Despite the umbrella, they were both drenched by the time they got to Stella's car. Jillian hadn't felt much like huddling with her underneath it. It made no difference anyway. The rain was falling diagonally in sheets.

Stella tried the ignition several times before the old car started. It was a small model and quite low to the ground—unnervingly so, given the flooding that had begun in the narrow streets around the quarter.

Jillian tried to keep from shaking all over while waiting for the heater to kick in. The speed of the windshield wipers added to her agitation and the blade on the passenger side was half off, whipping back and forth furiously. The traffic lights were only visible up close. Jillian shoved her right foot into the floorboard as Stella drove through a stoplight.

Lightning split the sky and Jillian braced herself for a clap of thunder that nearly shook the car. "Maybe we should stop somewhere until some of this passes." Jillian was almost at a full-throttle yell, trying to make herself heard over the roar of the downpour.

Stella's response was equally loud. "Where would you suggest?"

Jillian had no idea where they were, but it was clear even through the gray blur that this was not a neighborhood of cafés and convenience stores. Twisting around in the seat in search of friendly shelter, she realized not one light was on in the run-down buildings they were passing. "The electricity must be out. This is freaky. Let's go back."

"We're here." Stella made a sudden right turn that nearly threw Jillian into her lap. The front tire bumped hard against the curb and the car swerved left as Stella overcorrected, nearly careening them into a flooded ditch. By the time Jillian could compose herself, Stella was pulling the car up to an old storage unit on the back side of a lot. Jillian could no longer think of anything that could be behind that roll-up door to make the trip worth it.

Stella got out of the car in the gushing rain without glancing back at the umbrella. She walked methodically around to the trunk and opened it. The trunk slammed and Stella appeared at Jillian's car window and tried to open her door. Jillian hesitated for a moment but unlocked it. After all, whatever they'd come to see was obviously behind that door. As she grabbed the umbrella and cracked the door to unfold it, she saw a crowbar in Stella's hand.

"What's that for?" she yelled over the roaring rain.

"The door sticks." Black mascara streamed down Stella's face.

Stella hit the roll-up door several times with the crowbar and then crouched down to wedge it between the bottom of the door and the pavement. The door gave way, sliding up quickly and bouncing at the top with a bang. A beam of light streamed from the left edge of the unit. Jillian tried to make sense of the sight before her. When the beam jerked side to side, she saw the form of a large man inside the unit wielding a flashlight.

Fear shot through Jillian's body like a bolt of lightning. She scrambled behind the car.

"Jillian!" Stella yelled. "Get in here and out of the rain. Don't be ridiculous!"

"Who *is* that?" His face was blurred by the sheets of rain

between the car and the storage unit but Jillian could see that he had on a thick canvas olive-green jacket and a brown knit cap pulled down to his eyebrows.

"A guy I've been helping out. What's wrong with you? Come here! Do you want to see the stuff I have to show you or not?"

"I changed my mind. I want to go to the motel."

"We came all this way. One box will be enough for you to see."

Jillian circled around the car and tried to open the door. "Stella, unlock the car!"

"Why are you freaking out?"

"I'm not coming in there with anybody else but you." Jillian was drenched and trembling all over. Stella turned to the man and said something that was indecipherable to Jillian. He was a head taller than Stella but the way he nodded as she spoke to him was almost childlike.

The man handed Stella the flashlight and unexpectedly exited the storage unit, jogged around the corner, and disappeared.

"He's gone. You satisfied? Ten minutes and we'll leave." Stella turned her back to her and pushed several tattered cardboard boxes away from the splattering rain.

Reluctantly, Jillian stepped into the unit, spying the blankets on the concrete floor. "He's been sleeping here?"

"Just for a few days. Down on his luck. I offered it to him for a night or two because it was better than nothing."

Barely, Jillian thought. Except for the small floor space that had obviously been cleared for the man to stretch out, the unit bulged with copious water-stained cardboard boxes, several lamps with no shades, plastic crates, and trash bags. Most out of place was a large leather desk chair. Its oxblood surface was weathered and brittle, but at one time, it could have seated an executive.

"Give me a minute," Stella said, "and let me get my hands on the right boxes."

A gust of wind caught the umbrella Jillian had left open at the entrance to the unit. Jillian lunged toward it as it tumbled down the concrete driveway.

"Leave it. We'll get it when we go." Stella's voice was dry and cold. "Here," she said, pulling an old short-legged stool from behind a stack of boxes. "Sit on this and I'll give you some things to look through."

Jillian sat down and waited, her teeth chattering from the cold. Stella's clothes were soaked and her long hair in strings, but she seemed completely oblivious to the elements. Jillian watched Stella shift boxes around and set several on the floor in order to reach the one at the bottom. As she dragged it out of the corner, roaches scattered toward Jillian. She jumped to her feet and hopped in a single bound on the seat cushion of the desk chair. The brittle leather gave way under her shoe and the seat ripped. Stella couldn't have heard it amid the sound effects of the storm but she looked at Jillian disapprovingly nonetheless.

She pulled the heavy box by one cardboard flap over to the stool rather than the chair and said, "You can start with this one."

Jillian didn't want to leave the chair, but she'd come all this way to see what missing pieces were hidden in this storage unit. She squinted and searched the dimly lit floor for anything creepy or crawling before reluctantly returning to the stool. The contents in the box appeared to belong to a man, though Jillian was having a hard time fitting them into the life she'd pictured Rafe living. They were professional items like a silver business card holder, a slender leather box with an assortment of expensive-looking pens, a leather six-ring notebook with a calendar inside. Appointment times, names, and phone numbers were handwritten in various squares.

"These are Rafe's?" Jillian asked.

"Keep looking." Stella raised the flashlight the man had left behind and shone it on the contents.

Growing more agitated by the minute, Jillian dug further into the box and pulled out a wooden plaque with a picture of a Little League baseball team under glass. It was an award thanking *Nolan Property Group, Inc., of New Orleans* for its generous support that season. Jillian looked up at Stella and tried to project her voice over the pounding rain. "I'm confused. What does this have to do with Rafe? Did he work here?" Stella stared at her without answering. "Look, I'm soaking wet and freezing to death in here. I'm not playing games with you. Get to what you brought me here to see."

"Some of it's in there," Stella responded with an odd look of disdain.

Jillian pulled out the top half of the contents and set them on the smudged concrete floor. Flipping through the remains, she came upon two separate newspaper articles, both laminated for preservation. One was an obituary for a Steadman A. Nolan and the other was an article titled "Local Businessman Found Dead in Apparent Suicide." "I still don't get it, Stella. What's this about?"

"Read them."

"I don't want to read them. I don't even know who this guy is. Tell me what this has to do with Rafe!" Fury rose up in Jillian. She shouldn't have gotten in the car with Stella. She had no idea where she was and no way back to the side of town she recognized except in the passenger seat of that old car. She was stuck and she was scared. She'd known Stella was peculiar from the start but the woman standing in front of her didn't just seem strange. She seemed half crazed.

Stella shone the flashlight on her own face, catching the whites of her eyes, and slowly mouthed the words *Read them.* She stepped closer to Jillian and focused the beam on the articles.

Jillian looked first at the article about the suicide. She was too rattled to read every sentence, so she scanned for key words that might link Rafe to the article. She got no further than the third paragraph when the name Fontaine jumped out at her. She instantly recognized the name of Rafe's father. The context was a very public, drawn-out lawsuit that had unexpectedly landed in Fontaine's favor in an odd twist of events, awarding him every asset belonging to real estate magnate Steadman Nolan. The next morning a housekeeper discovered Nolan's body hanging from a belt.

Turning her attention immediately to the obituary, she found the typical biographical information including the dates of the man's birth and death and references to his schooling and his contributions to the community. The obit made no mention of the trial or cause of death, of course. It was the usual depressing stuff. Why Stella couldn't have told her this story back at the apartment was puzzling and maddening, and she still couldn't piece together a direct link between the newspaper features and Stella's relationship with Rafe. She skipped several paragraphs and moved straight to the end.

Mr. Nolan was preceded in death by his wife, Marilyn Reeves Nolan, and is survived by his daughter, Stella Nolan. In lieu of flowers, donations may be made to Steadman A. Nolan Memorial Fund.

Jillian's body was shaking violently, her mind awhirl. She tried to control her voice but fear and anxiety broke up every syllable until her words sounded to her like static. Finally, clearly enough for Stella to understand, Jillian said, "This was your *dad*?"

"They gave five hundred dollars." Stella's tone was ice.

"Who?" Jillian couldn't follow her.

"The donations. They amounted to five hundred dollars. It didn't even cover cremation. That's what I got. Five hundred dollars."

"That's awful, Stella. Terrible. But what does this have to do with Rafe?" Jillian began to rock back and forth on the stool, trying to rub the cold off her arms and the foreboding off her bones.

"Can you believe he thought he was too good for me? A drunk? He'd been coming in and out of my place for several months, sobering up or sleeping it off. He'd work some, then crash again. I'd fed the fool. Harbored him. Stored his stuff. And all while biding my time. Finally I decided I'd waited long enough. I said to him, 'You know what we ought to do? We ought to get married.' Would you like to know what he did?"

Jillian froze. She wanted to say no but she couldn't form a single word on her tongue. She shook her head weakly.

"I said," Stella persisted, taking another step closer, "would you like to know what he did?"

"What?" Jillian managed.

"He *laughed*. In my face. Said I sure was funny. It was everything I could do not to strangle him that night in his stupor. The next time he showed up, I brought up the idea of meeting his mom. One guess what he said to that."

Jillian shook her head again, trying to stop the tirade and wishing she'd never opened that closet door in Stella's apartment.

Stella wouldn't shut up. "He said, 'I don't want to put her through that.'" She began laughing maniacally. "Imagine! He didn't want to put *her* through *that*! After everything those—those *crooks* had put *me* through!" She raised the flashlight and brought it down hard on the plaque, shattering both the glass over the team picture and the lens of the flashlight.

Jillian covered her head, terrified that Stella would hit her next.

"Crawley!" Stella shouted. "Now!"

Jillian heard a man's voice booming behind her. "Don't want to!"

266

"Crawley, do it! If you don't, I'll turn you in to the cops so fast, you won't see the light of day for a decade!"

Lightning split the sky and Jillian whirled around to see the big man who had been sleeping in the storage unit towering over her with a crowbar in his left hand, sopping wet, shaking his head and murmuring, "Crawley don't want to."

She scrambled to her feet and lurched into the pouring rain, running as fast as her shoes would slosh through six inches of water. She'd almost made it to the corner when a shock of pain shot through her skull.

CHAPTER 38

ADELLA WAS INCONSOLABLE. Nearly twenty-four hours had passed since Jillian stormed out of the house feeling all accused. She'd thrown some hissy fits since that day Adella met her in baggage claim, but something felt different about this one. Jillian had lost face in front of someone she'd taken a liking to.

Throughout the day as they waited for news, Adella had whispered over and over, "Jesus, help her."

According to Bully, Jillian's boss at the café reported seeing her the evening before but only for a few minutes. She had been sick, so the night manager had sent her home. She'd failed to show up for her shift today, and no, she hadn't called in.

The situation hadn't warranted anything official. Bully's involvement was personal. Everybody knew he had a soft spot in his heart for Jillian. He'd also become a presence at Saint Sans.

Something about him made a person feel like the world wasn't as awful a place as it threatened to be. He was proof that not everything big was bad.

Officer Sanchez had repeatedly beaten on the door at Stella's apartment and gotten no answer. It was the most logical place for Jillian to go, and it was within walking distance of the café. The officer said she'd pressed her ear to the paneling but the thunder had made it impossible to hear any activity or conversation coming from inside. Bully told them Officer Sanchez had left her card in the crack between the door and the casing with a note for Stella to call her ASAP. They'd not heard a peep from her yet.

Adella had tried calling Jillian right after it happened last evening, but her heart sank when she heard the cell phone ringing in Rafe's old room. Then she had tried to run after her. After all, Jillian had said, "Nobody better follow me. . . . I mean it!" and that was like waving a red flag at a bull. But in this case, the bull was wearing her Sunday spiked heels, not because it was Sunday but because the navy-blue slingbacks had gone perfectly with her outfit. All to say, the spikes kept punching holes in the grass in the front yard and Adella's feet kept coming out, probably on account of the baby powder she'd sprinkled in them that morning thinking her feet might swell by early afternoon. She'd finally pulled the shoes off entirely and slung them clear to the neighbor's live oak but the young woman had vanished before she could make it barefooted to the corner. The officers were still in the house at that point, having no idea what had just hit them.

Adella had a terrible time trying to explain Jillian's outburst without spilling the beans about that money in San Francisco. She didn't outright lie. She just took a mighty long way to the truth. She hem-hawed and loose-jawed in so many circles that the whole lot of them got as dizzy as kids coming off a carnival ride. She'd stopped short of feigning a seizure, thinking that might come in handier at another time. Luckily, Olivia had done just what Adella hoped. She'd finally gotten exasperated and said, "That'll be enough, Adella. Thank you."

She'd hung around and tried to busy herself answering business e-mails for the next couple of hours, but Olivia finally talked her into going home. Now that Adella had learned that Jillian never showed up at work today, she was determined not to budge an inch from Saint Sans until they knew where she was. The roads were too flooded anyway. Emmett had offered to come get her in his pickup, but she told him the biggest favor he could do her was to look after the boys. She wouldn't have had to ask.

Olivia was characteristically tense and tight-lipped except to reassure Mrs. Winsee that Jillian was just fine. The old woman wasn't herself yet but she was more lucid than she'd been the first few days after the Halloween fiasco and had begun communicating with one-word responses or questions. She'd stood at a window in the great room for over an hour today watching the downpour despite the thunder vibrating the glass. She'd occasionally turned toward Olivia and stammered with a pained look on her face. The only word they could make out came in the form of a question. "Jilly?"

Olivia had finally coaxed her into taking a nap, but she moaned something fierce every time Olivia tried to close her door. Mrs. Winsee's protests won out and Olivia ended up leaving it wide open. When David came home from school and learned there was still no news, he too refused to get out of earshot. He was sitting at the kitchen bar trying not to get on his landlord's nerves while grading geography exams for a fellow teacher with a new grandbaby.

Olivia's phone rang loud enough to scare the fur off a cat, and obviously recognizing the number, she answered, "Officer?" Seconds later, "Hmmmm," then, after another moment or two, "I see."

When she turned her back to the dining table for a little

privacy, Adella popped out of her chair, circled around in front of Olivia, and mouthed with excessive emphasis, "Did they find her?"

Olivia motioned like she was swatting a cloud of killer bees. Adella thought it would have been considerably less trouble to respond with a simple yes or no.

"I'm assuming you've checked to see what flights have departed."

David looked up from his papers and locked eyes with Adella as they each attempted to piece together the information from Olivia's side of the conversation.

She suddenly became refreshingly wordy. "My question, Officer Sanchez, is how she would have paid for a cab to get to the airport and then purchased an astronomical same-day ticket." Both David and Adella nodded with approval. Olivia paused for a moment. "I am absolutely certain, Officer. My granddaughter is not a thief." Their eyes nearly popped out of their heads. The phone call ended with Olivia firmly stating that she'd expect to hear from them soon. After exhausting all those extra words, she saved her breath on "Bye." Adella had long since suspected that Olivia got away with the cheapest cell phone plan in the free world.

When Olivia turned around, she came within an inch of stepping right on Adella's foot and David might as well have been pinned on Adella's shirtsleeve. "The two of you look like an ice cream cone with two scoops. One chocolate and the other the whitest vanilla I have ever seen in my life. David, you could use some sun. I can only assume that you're vitamin D deficient."

David glanced at his hands. He'd talked about getting some of that sunless tanner over the summer, but one of his students was bound to call him out if he showed up six shades darker in the middle of winter.

Adella was in no mood to play games. "Well? Out with it!"

Olivia set the phone facedown on the table, put her hands on her hips, and said, "Could you two step back far enough for me to get a little air?"

"Are you trying to kill me, Olivia, or just punish me?"

"Officer Sanchez finally heard from the woman Jillian has stayed with before, the one she left her card for, with a note insisting that the resident call her right away."

"Stella, right?" David was holding his own competing with Adella for answers.

"Yes, I believe that's the name the officer used."

"What did she say?" Adella blurted out, elbowing her way right in front of David.

"I'm getting to that, if you two will let me. The woman said Jillian had stopped by yesterday evening but only to say good-bye. She told her she was leaving New Orleans and flying back to San Francisco. According to whoever this woman is, Jillian had called her mom—on whose phone, I do not know—and the two of them agreed it was time for her to move home. She'd assured her she'd pick her up at the airport."

"Jillian's mother?" Adella was incredulous.

David shook his head. "How would Jillian get a flight out in this weather?"

"The officer suggested she might have had time last night to get as far as Houston before this weather blew in. They're making phone calls. But Jillian's an adult, however irresponsible, and since there's no reason to suspect foul play, the options for retrieving personal information from a flight roster are limited. They're going to call me when they learn something."

Olivia sat back down at the dining table, turned her phone faceup, and tapped the screen with her fingernail. Adella sat down across from her and had half a mind to do the same thing but decided to tap her foot instead. David sat back down at the kitchen bar and tapped his red grading pen on the counter. Had Mrs.

Winsee been back to herself, she'd have come alive and danced a little jig.

Nobody said a word for several minutes, which was just about as long as Adella could last wide-awake. When she stopped tapping her foot, David stopped tapping his pen. He spun around on the stool and eyed the two of them at the table. Adella took a deep breath and then took the plunge: "She didn't take that money, Olivia."

"Of course she didn't." Then Olivia said something Adella wouldn't have believed if she hadn't heard it with her own ears, even if someone swore to it on a stack of Bibles. "Get me Jaclyn's number. Or Jade or Jam or Jewel or Juice or whatever Jillian's mother is calling herself these days."

Adella had no idea how to find it, but miracles seemed to have been flying around that house like hummingbirds, and she figured she was liable to catch one.

CHAPTER 39

CAL'S LEFT FOOT HIT THE PAVEMENT almost before he threw the squad car into park and turned off the ignition. When he pushed through the front door, Frank and Sanchez were both on their feet waiting for him.

"Where is he?"

Frank spoke first. "Room one."

"Bully?"

"Pacing outside the door." Sanchez looked like she'd seen a ghost, and she was not an easy woman to scare.

Cal had rushed back to the office during his lunch break as soon as he got Bully's phone call saying they had brought William Crawley in for questioning. A patrol car had been summoned by a hot dog vendor to the intersection of Decatur and St. Peter, where a man—who turned out to be their suspect—was reportedly shouting nonsense and tearing off his shirt. The vendor had to yell to make his voice heard on the 911 call. "I think that's blood on his T-shirt!" Cal had ordered that no one question Crawley until he got there.

As soon as Cal turned down the hall of the interrogation room, he could hear a man yelling maniacally. Bully's back was to the door, his face deep red and his jaw clenched. Cal glanced over his shoulder and saw Sanchez and Frank right on his heels.

Something was wrong. Something was usually wrong. It was the nature of police work. But this particular noon something was very wrong. Cal's ears were ringing from the whoosh of blood pumping through the arteries in his neck.

As Bully's big hand clutched the metal doorknob and turned it, the seconds dropped speed to Cal and ticked in slow motion like a hall clock chiming midnight. The man's voice muffled into the background and Cal could hear the sound of his own shoes hitting the floor. His right heel first. The ball of his foot. His left heel. He reached up slowly and pulled the collar of his shirt away from his neck and heard the crackling of heavy starch. He blinked like a shutter on a camera moving through thick syrup.

As Cal crossed the threshold and entered the room, the seconds found their feet and leapt back on the clock. The man's wrists were in handcuffs pinned to the table but he'd kicked the chair to the left side of the room. Both shoes were off and in opposite corners. Flailing his upper body back and forth violently and kicking the wall behind him with the bottom of one foot, he yelled continually, disturbingly, "Crawley didn't want to!"

Cal tried to yell over him, "Pipe down! And sit down!" He gave a look to Bully and shot his eyes over to the fallen chair, signaling the officer to grab it, come around the table, and force the man into it. Bully was the only one with the size and muscle to do it. William Crawley was enormous. In order to calm the man, Bully was forced to do what Cal knew was the last thing he wanted to do: talk kindly to the man and comfort him.

"It's alright, buddy. It's alright. How about some water? Want a glass of water? Looks like you haven't slept in days."

Crawley stiffened and Bully, wedged right behind him, patted both the man's shoulders. "It's okay, buddy."

Cal lowered his head just enough to get Bully's eyes on his own. Police officers who worked in tandem had to learn how to read one another's expressions. Too many occasions arose when words mustn't be overheard or would take too much time when every millisecond counted. Cal's stare was one of extreme caution, meant to convey that Bully better tighten his stomach muscles because he might be about to take the elbow of a crazed Samson right in his diaphragm. Bully slid his grasp from Crawley's shoulders to his elbows and he tugged them downward. The big man's bones became like rubber and he slouched in the chair like a levee collapsing in a flood. He put his face on the table and wept.

Cal released the breath pent up in his lungs and sat down in the chair opposite Crawley. Bully stepped over to the side of the table so he could see the faces of both men.

"You William Crawley?"

He kept sobbing but an affirmative answer was still clear enough for the video camera in the upper corner of the room to pick it up.

"Sir, would you sit up please and help us out? We'd like to get you cleared for anything you haven't done and help you work through what you didn't want to do. But you're going to have to tell us what that is. Can you do that?"

He slowly raised his head, mumbling disjointed syllables. It sounded like nothing but *bah bah bah* to Cal and he couldn't make heads or tails out of it. He knew full well that the officer from psych was behind the glass making an evaluation and he could already see the handwriting on the wall. A judge would rule this man incompetent to stand trial. The guy smelled like he hadn't had a bath in a while but he didn't smell like liquor. It could be drugs, but Cal had a feeling the dude's system was as clean as a whistle.

Cal hated to have to say this, but the shape the man was in, he knew it was necessary. "Mr. Crawley, am I understanding correctly that you waived your right to an attorney and you're willing to answer some questions?"

Bully stiffened as if to brace himself. He wasn't the one who brought him in. Steve Gates was, and he was one infraction from nine weeks in anger management.

Crawley didn't appear roughed up. He had a busted lip, but with all the flailing, it was probably self-inflicted and it was a wonder he hadn't cracked his head like a hard-boiled egg. The bruising around his wrists already threw a stark contrast of painful-looking deep purple against his dark-brown skin. The oddest part of his appearance was what was left of his T-shirt. The neckband and short sleeves were still intact but the whole front was torn off, exposing the man's expansive chest. The rest was dangling like a little boy's superhero cape.

"Don't want no lawyer. Crawley goin' away fo' a long time." The tears streaming down his cheeks caught the fluorescent light and looked like the slender fingers of a river under a noon sun.

"Why do you think you are going away for a long time, Mr. Crawley?"

The man again broke out into loud sobs.

"It's hot in here!" Cal yelled. "Can somebody turn up the air?" Bully glanced at the mirror behind the sergeant. Somebody on the other side of it better be jumping up and making haste to the thermostat. Cal tried to compose himself. When Crawley dropped his head on the table and cried, Cal got a good look at the back of his

T-shirt. The vertical tear had an inconsistency. The bottom six or so inches had a straighter edge, like it had been cut with a knife or a pair of scissors.

"Officer La Bauve, where is the rest of this man's shirt?"

Bully responded, "It's been bagged as evidence. It's gonna need to go to the lab right away, Sarge."

Cal had a bad feeling that he heard Bully's voice break at the end of that sentence, right there in the middle of an interrogation. Whatever was going on was still mud to Cal but it was becoming plainer by the minute that Bully either knew more than he did or had imagined something he hadn't. This much Cal was sure of: he wasn't about to put up with a pair of grown men crying in that room, especially a pair with a combined weight in excess of four hundred and sixty pounds.

"Officer La Bauve, do I need to get another officer in here?"

"No, sir." Bully put his shoulders back, his hands behind him, and straightened his spine like a soldier at parade rest.

"Good, because I better not need to. Mr. Crawley, I'll ask you again. Why do you think you are going away for a long time?"

The man's face was still pressed against the table but he'd gone dead quiet. His shoulders were so massive they covered his ears.

"Mr. Crawley!" Cal picked up the volume.

No response.

The rise and fall of the man's back was almost imperceptible. Maybe Cal had been wrong about him. Maybe he had taken something. Maybe he'd taken *a lot* of something. Cal shot Bully a look of concern. He reached over and nudged the man's right shoulder. "Mr. Crawley?"

Crawley threw back his head and howled so loud, everybody within earshot nearly jumped like skeletons clean out of their skin. Cal had had enough. He scrambled to his feet, kicked his own chair out from under him, slapped his palms down hard on the table, and said, "Stop it. Get control of yourself and talk to me like a man."

With his palms still flat on the table, Cal dropped his head, squeezed his eyes shut, and swallowed hard. He had no idea where his next words came from. Nobody could have thought they were more out of character for him than he did. "William? Or is it Willy? Did they call you Willy? Willy, what would your mama say to you right now?"

"My mama? Or Miss Earnestine?" Saliva had collected on his bottom lip.

"Who?"

Crawley looked over Cal's shoulder to something miles beyond the wall. His mind seemed to follow his gaze straight into a wormhole. "Miss Earnestine. She care fo' me. She take me in."

Cal righted his chair and sat back down. "That's good. That's good, Willy. What would Miss Earnestine say to you right now?"

"She say, 'Tell the truth, boy. You bettah tell the truth.'"

"That's right, Willy. You better tell the truth. That's always best. It can set a man free. What is the truth, Willy?"

"That woman tell me—" Crawley stopped in the middle of the sentence and his eyelids hung to his pupils.

"Willy, you talking about Miss Earnestine?"

"No! Not Miss Earnestine!" Agitated, Crawley pounded his fists against the table. "Miss Earnestine a good woman. She a churchwoman! Ain't you ever met a churchwoman?"

"Then who? Who is that woman who told you something? That woman who ain't no churchwoman?"

"You know who!"

"No, Willy, I don't. Help me. Tell me who."

"She play cards."

"At the casino, Willy?"

"No, man. You ain't listenin'!"

"I'm trying to. What do you mean by cards?"

"Devil cards! She say they tell me to."

"The cards told you to do something?"

"She say they did."

"I need a name, Willy. What's that bad woman's name?"

"She play like she like me. Like she gon' be nice to me. She gimme money. Say, 'Go eat, Crawley.'"

Cal spoke calmly and quietly. "And what did you say to her, Willy? What did you say to the woman who gave you some money and told you to go get something to eat? Right after she gave it to you, Willy. Think. What did you say?"

"I say, 'Thank ya, Miss Stella.'"

Cal sat back with his brows drawn, tilted his head, and stared at the wall, his mind scrambling to connect dots that, five minutes ago, hadn't been on the same page. It could be a different Stella. It was a common enough name. The trouble was, the square wasn't a very big square. Without moving anything but his eyes, he shifted his gaze to Bully's face and followed the young officer's dead stare to Crawley's.

Cal bolted straight up in his chair. "Willy, what did she say the cards told you to do?"

"No, no, no! Crawley say he don't want to!" He began thrashing again, screaming something incoherent. Before Cal could anticipate the move, Bully lurched behind Crawley, wrapped his left arm around his neck, pressed his forearm to his Adam's apple, and without tightening his grip, hollered as loud as he could in the man's ear, *What did you do?*"

"Crawley don't wanna kill dat girl!"

Cal scrambled to his feet, lunged for the door, and yelled, "Sanchez! Get me a search warrant!"

She was already flying through the hall.

CHAPTER 40

SUMMER 1921

REVEREND BRASHEAR had promised his daughter an outing. She'd had a touch of pneumonia the month before. Tonsillitis prior to that. The doctor had told Raymond privately that the child's frequent ailments and increasing fatigue did not bode well toward a normal lifespan. Though Raymond knew that Evelyn Ann had to have shared his doubts that they'd ever see her grown, he'd strangled all the volume of his dread and voiced only confidence. Now he didn't know how to break through the protective cocoon his wife had spun around herself and their daughter to convey the unwelcome news.

Evelyn Ann had grown increasingly detached from everything and everyone but Brianna, and Brianna's world had gotten smaller and smaller until it fit snugly, safe from all alarm, in the palms of two hands. With painstaking patience and effort, Evelyn Ann had created a world within those walls woven in embroidery threads, slathered in watercolors, and alive in storybooks. Still, the child's immune system weakened as though it required the contamination of community to survive.

The doctor let Brianna overhear him tell her parents that the girl could use some fresh air. It was all the permission she needed to bleat like a calf and kick against the stall. "The lake!" she cried again and again, referring to Pontchartrain, a body of water she'd seen only a handful of times. Brianna had been infatuated with water all her life, swimming in her imagination where she could not walk. The fact was, she could swim better than she could walk, a feat she'd mastered out of mildly strong arms and raw determination.

"Out of the question, Brianna. Don't even entertain it!" her mother replied. The trip was doable in a day, but it would be a long one and too taxing on the child.

"Then, the river!" she countered.

An argument ensued between her overprotective mother and her overindulgent father, a rarity right in front of her, and Raymond declared that he'd take her by himself.

One of his church members owned a small boat and they'd fished from it on several Saturdays. The older parishioner had seen little promise of a fisherman in the man of the cloth, but he'd seen something of perhaps greater value. He'd seen the reverend submit his bravado to the great deep, quiet his command, and lower his volume. Maybe the parishioner was making too much of it, but he'd been known to comment loudly enough that the sermons after a good fishing trip were particularly fine. The man had offered the boat to Raymond whenever he wanted it, teasing that it was "for the sake of the flock."

He'd never taken him up on it, but he was doing so today. The winds were calm and cotton clouds with kind intentions scattered themselves across the blue sky. Evelyn Ann went along, miffed and brooding, only to see to it that they didn't drift too far from the shore. Soon she'd loosened her grip on the edges of the boat and let herself bask in the child's mirth.

The sun slid down the auburn locks of Brianna's hair and brushed her ivory cheeks with dashes of pink. She was frail of body but abundantly alive with expression and imagination. She caught sight of a mama duck in the distance with five ducklings paddling behind her and squealed with delight.

Raymond reflected on how long it had been since they'd all laughed like that. This was a good idea. They'd all needed the gentle breeze in their faces. He winked at Evelyn Ann, and he could have sworn she blushed like she had when they were courting on her daddy's front porch. She'd pulled so far away in the last several months and he'd let her. He knew today that had been a mistake, and he planned to woo her again. He must fight for her, especially if their fight for Brianna could one day be lost.

CHAPTER 41

THE DOOR TO STELLA'S APARTMENT gave way to Bully's shoulder on the first try. Bully headed into the kitchen and Sanchez checked the small bathroom. Cal stormed toward the bedroom, yelling, "Police! Get your hands up!" He kicked the door open with his weapon drawn. When Bully came through the bedroom door, Cal signaled for him to open the closet door while he aimed his weapon at it. With it clear, Cal threw open the door of the master bath.

"She's not here." He holstered his gun.

"Sarge?" It was Sanchez, standing in the doorway to the bedroom with a stainless steel kitchen trash can in her hands.

"So, what's the significance?"

She set it down and stepped on the pedal, and the lid popped open. With her thumb and index finger, she carefully lifted a crumpled piece of fabric from the can. As Cal walked across the room to study it, Sanchez held up the garment by two shoulder seams so he could get a good look at it. The bottom edge was silted in coffee grounds but there was no mistaking it. It was the dark-blue top Jillian had on at Saint Sans two days earlier when Cal and Bully were there. He nodded. "That's hers." He paused a few seconds to steady his mind and temper his anger. Then, "Tear this place apart."

Sanchez instantly turned the trash can over and spilled the contents out on the floor. An empty tomato sauce can rolled under the bed. Bully got down on his knees, grabbed the can, pulled everything else out from under the bed, and started for the closet. Cal dialed his phone with one hand and rummaged through a drawer in the bedside table with the other. "Frank, whatcha got?" He'd left him and another officer behind at the station to see if they could get anything else out of Crawley. "That's not going to cut it. When are they going to let you back at him?" Bully and Sanchez stayed on task, trying to work both quickly and carefully, but they quieted down enough to hear the sergeant.

"Well, until they do," Cal continued to Frank, "replay that video feed as many times as it takes to catch any syllable in all that babbling that has any significance. Some of it has to mean something." Cal listened for a moment, grimaced, and responded, "No, no blood. At least none yet, but we're not done." They talked a few more minutes, and right before Cal ended the call, he said, "Thanks, man. I know y'all are trying. Call me with absolutely anything you come up with, even if you're not sure it has anything to do with the case." He stuck the phone back in his shirt pocket, pulled aside the curtain in the living room, and stared out the window at the curb.

Cal addressed Bully and Sanchez. "We need to know if she has a car and the make and model. That's priority one."

"I can do that, boss," Sanchez responded.

"And then I need a detail over at Mrs. Fontaine's. She's not going to like that it's none of us, but I can't spare you yet and I'm not sending Bully." Cal saw Sanchez glance over at her partner. "Get a car over there and have the officers tell her that you'll be there as soon as you can make it."

"How much do they tell her?"

"Only what we know for certain. We've made an arrest of a suspect whose prints were on the pocketknife. According to the suspect, he had an accomplice, and the accomplice is still at large. Tell them it's just an extra precaution. The officers can stay outside if she doesn't want them in the house as long as they stay on that property."

"They're not to mention Miss Slater, I'm assuming."

"Not in regard to the suspect or anything he implied. But they need to keep constant tabs on whether or not anyone is hearing from her or hearing anything about her. Also have them question each one again about where they think she might have gone. They might have thought of something since yesterday." Cal hesitated for a moment. "The officers may as well go ahead and tell them that an airline ticket has not been purchased under her name since the time of her departure from Mrs. Fontaine's two days ago. That doesn't mean she hasn't left the city, but it means that she didn't likely fly. I also want all the residents at that house for the next twenty-four hours or until we release them. And, Sanchez?"

"Yes, sir?"

"Find out what's holding up the detective. I needed Sparks over here fifteen minutes ago."

Sanchez already had her phone to her ear.

Sparks walked through the door five minutes later pulling on nitrile gloves. Cal motioned him into the kitchen. "Start bagging here," Cal instructed. "We might get lucky with one of those coffee cups."

"Got it. Officer Sanchez mentioned a shirt."

"Yep, it's over there in that bag. It's damp, like it's been submerged, but it'll turn up something."

"Any visible sign that the resident was trying to rinse blood out of it?"

"You'll know that better than me. I'll let you do your job." Cal glanced around the apartment to check the progress and caught both Bully and Sanchez glaring at him inquisitively.

Cal updated them matter-of-factly. "Frank confirmed that the blood on Crawley's T-shirt isn't his own." Nobody had been convinced it was, since the man lacked sufficient injuries to explain it. Still, they would have welcomed the news of a bad nosebleed. Cal replayed bits and pieces of the interrogation from memory. "You two have been around long enough to know that we don't have any evidence yet that the *girl* Crawley referenced in his last outburst is Miss Slater. Quite possibly, it's not."

"That's right, Sarge," Sanchez responded. Bully looked over at Sparks bagging the coffee cups for forensics.

"Due diligence is all," Cal insisted, knowing Bully wouldn't buy it, but it still needed to be said because it was true. They were all three jumping to conclusions based on a bad feeling, and a bad feeling could prove right . . . or shoot an entire investigation down a rabbit hole.

"You telling me, boss, that Crawley could not cough up one single description of the girl? Not hair color? Not height? I mean, he couldn't have even held up his hand to estimate how tall she was so we might at least know if he was talking about a young woman or a child?"

Sanchez shook her head as if a chill had gone up her spine. "The only scenario more horrifying than what we're fearing is if that blood belongs to a little girl."

Bully dropped his head.

Sanchez rarely exhibited blatant sentimentality on the job. Female cops typically had to remain tough if they wanted the same respect the males got. This time, however, proved exceptional. She walked over to Bully, put her arm around his shoulder, and said, "It's awful either way."

Cal pulled out his cell phone to make sure he hadn't missed a call or text from Frank or anyone else involved in the investigation. He made sure the ringer was turned all the way up and double-checked that the phone was getting decent reception in the building. He stuck it back in his pocket, aggravated that no one from the district had updated him. Even a **No update yet** would have been better than nothing. By this time Sanchez had let go of Bully, and Cal could think clearly enough to answer his questions.

"According to Frank, Crawley hasn't said an intelligible word since we walked out the door. Said he was near catatonic. Psych was about to come in and do a face-to-face evaluation. Everybody knows what's at stake."

Bully shook his head and rolled his eyes.

"Yes, they do. If Crawley conveys the least clue, we'll hear from them. Sanchez, any word on a car yet? You're killing me."

She turned the face of her phone toward him, showing a text on the screen. "Nothing matching her name yet. Most of the residents on the square get around on public transportation." She continued sorting through a box of random papers and magazines Bully had pulled out from under Stella's bed. Suddenly she threw her fist up with something in her grasp. "Look at this!"

Cal stepped over and grabbed it. It was a snapshot with a close-up of Stella's face on it and seemed recent enough to work. "You know for sure that's her?"

"Absolutely!"

"How?"

"After Bully and I were here before, I started keeping an eye out for her."

"Why didn't you tell me you were suspicious of her?"

"It was more of a personal thing. It never occurred to me that Jillian could be in any physical danger. It was a psychological thing to me. No, that's not true. It was a spiritual thing. I wanted to—well, I don't know any other way to say it except how they'd say it at my church. I wanted to test the spirit. I wanted to get close enough to Stella to see if she was predatory. If she felt, you know, *evil*."

"I'm listening."

"Do you believe in that kind of stuff, Sarge?"

"What? In evil? Are you kidding me?"

"I mean, do you believe there are forces out there? A war between good and evil beyond what human eyes can see? Between light and darkness, I mean. That kind of thing."

"Spit it out, Sanchez. I want that woman in custody by midnight and I want Jillian Slater ruled out as a victim of any violence whatsoever within the half hour. What are you trying to say?"

"I guess I'm trying to ask if you believe there is a God and a devil."

Cal's eyes shifted over to the mural on the wall behind the table. "What does that have to do with this case?"

"Something really dark is going on here. I've never said a word on the job about any of this, have I, Bully?"

"No, ma'am, you sure haven't."

"And I won't," Sanchez pledged to Cal. "All I've done is pray about it, but I've done that a lot."

"Tell me this," Cal requested. "Did Stella know you were on her tail?"

"No, I can't imagine she did. I was careful, and believe me, you couldn't have picked me out in a lineup. I wasn't in uniform. I never inquired about her by name, but I hung around the square a couple of nights and engaged in a few casual conversations about who could read cards around here."

"Sanchez knows her cards, Sarge," Bully interjected. "Her aunt was all into it and taught it to her."

"Yeah, I know enough of the lingo to get people talking. Teased a couple of merchants that I was thinking about setting up shop around there. Stella's name came up in no time. They're territorial, you know. I was told where she camped. I got a very good look at her soon after that."

That was enough for Cal. He stared at the snapshot again, handed it back to Sanchez, and said, "Send it." Within no time at all, that picture was distributed electronically to officers all over town. Cal instantly sent a message to Frank to watch for it, print it out, and have it shown to Crawley. Twenty-five minutes later Cal received a call from him confirming that the picture elicited a strong enough reaction to assume for now that the woman in the picture was Crawley's Miss Stella.

"I don't know if it would stand up in court, but it's enough to establish her as our best lead," Frank said. He also told Cal that Psych cried foul at first and insisted that Crawley be shown an assortment of women's pictures. They ultimately agreed that his strongest response seemed to be centered on this one. The best news was that they'd snuck a picture from Jillian's California driver's license into the mix and couldn't conclude that he recognized her.

When Cal responded to Frank with a measure of relief, Frank lowered his voice. "I'll be honest with you, buddy. That dude was so thrown by the one woman's picture, I'm not sure he ever really focused on the rest of them. His mind snapped. I don't think there's much doubting that. When it happened exactly, who's to say?"

"Well, surely somebody can!" Cal responded.

"What do you mean?"

"He's hung around this part of the city for years, Frank. Been here all his life based on everything we've gathered. Get the officers dispatched on the square to ask around about him and find out if his big display today at Decatur and St. Peter was a surprise."

"I'm on it. I'll do it myself. It's all I can think about anyway."

Cal thanked him, ended the call, and shouted for Sanchez.

"Here, Sarge!" She peeked her head around the bedroom closet door, where she'd dismantled every garment and pair of shoes in it.

"Good job on the picture. Well, on the whole afternoon. We've got undercover personnel watching for her in the area and in a café at the corner in case she tries to come home. Heard anything from the detail we sent over to Mrs. Fontaine's?"

"Oh yeah. You were right. They were not greeted warmly."

"Fine by me. People need protecting in a situation like this whether they want it or not. Was she steaming?"

"Who, Mrs. Fontaine?" Sanchez asked.

Cal nodded.

"No, they said she went straight to her room and shut the door, and they haven't seen her since. It was Mrs. Atwater that nearly fried them up like a chicken. She's already called me twice."

"What did she say?"

"I'll let you hear it for yourself." Sanchez brought up the screen for her voice mails and pushed Play.

"This is Adella Jane Atwater, wife of Emmett Isaiah Atwater III, and I happen to be the manager of Mrs. Olivia Fontaine's historic residence, which—hear me clearly—is nothing less than a landmark in this city and has been turned tee-totally upside down with every officer in the entire NOPD except the very ones we actually know. The exact same ones, I might add, who promised to keep us informed on every development involving our missing resident who has all but fallen off the face of the earth but why in tarnation would we expect answers regarding an actual human when we cannot even get to the bare bottom of a baby rattle? Perhaps the competency discharged to this residence might best be judged by the fact—"

"That's enough." Cal rubbed his forehead. "How long does she go on?"

"There's another minute and a half of that one and a second message similar to it, except with more adjectives. Frank forwarded me a text from one of the officers over there. Would you like to see it?" Sanchez held out her phone.

"No, ma'am, I would not. You call her back yet?"

"No, sir." Sanchez winced. "She'll drag every piece of information out of me that I've ever known, suspected, or feared about Jillian Slater."

"Yeah, I know. I better call her back myself."

"Boss, wait a second." It was Bully.

"What is it?" Cal glanced down the *A*'s in his contacts on his phone.

"We're getting close to being done here. I've only got one more drawer to go through and I bet Sanchez would cover that for me. I'm going crazy here and I'm not doing any good anyway. Let me go to Saint Sans. I'm the one that's been over there the most. The officers who are there can keep an eye on the house from the outside and I'll hang out with the residents. I'll pick up some food and take it over there so they'll have some supper. And I'll just sit with them. I don't care if it's all night. Let me do it."

"Billy La Bauve, I'm telling you that if you shed one tear over there, I swear I'll—"

"I won't!" Bully put his hat on, bolted out the apartment door, and started down the stairs.

Cal followed him as far as the door. "And don't bring up what Crawley said. *Or* what was on his shirt. Don't mention anything that vaguely rhymes with *blood*!"

"I won't!"

"And call them and tell them you're on your way before Mrs. Atwater leaves another voice mail."

Bully had disappeared from the stairwell before Cal could get that last command out of his mouth. From somewhere outside, Cal heard the words "I will!"

CHAPTER 42

"WHERE IS SHE?" Cal shouted, pounding on the door of the psychiatric unit where Crawley had been transferred for assessment.
Cal had been in a fury from the moment forensics confirmed
that the blood on the man's T-shirt was Jillian's. He'd held on to
the reasonable notion that the blood could have been anybody's,
including Stella's. Over the last few months he'd made an effort to
be less committed to the conviction that everything worked out for
the worst. With one piece of information, the mentality fell back
on him like a pitch-black hood over his head.

Frank grabbed Cal from behind and pulled him away from
the door. "You're going to end up getting yourself cuffed—or at
the least, thrown off this case. You better calm yourself down or
nobody's going to cooperate with us here. What's wrong with
you, man?"

Cal elbowed him forcefully and beat on the door again. "It's been three days! *Where is she?*"

A security guard appeared in the hall with two police officers. Personnel on the other side of the locked door were scrambling, some on their phones summoning help and others ducking for cover into the hospital rooms of patients. It wasn't every day that a security threat came from an armed police officer.

"Where'd you leave her, you—?"

When the security guard and the officers picked up the pace and started running their direction, Frank went for Cal's ankles and pulled his feet out from under him, sending him facedown to the floor.

"We're good here, fellas!" Frank called down the hall, his full weight pinning Cal to the linoleum.

"Looks like you are!" one of the policemen responded sarcastically. "What's the problem here?" As he walked closer, he bent over and looked at Cal. "Sergeant DaCosta?"

Frank leaned over Cal and spoke right into his ear. "You gonna settle down or are you gonna make me call the captain?"

"Let me up," Cal growled.

By the time Cal made it to his feet, several hospital administrators had walked onto the scene demanding an explanation. The police officer who'd recognized Cal spoke up first. "Nothing but a misunderstanding here. Looks to me like these officers aren't getting the cooperation they need for an active investigation. I'll let you explain, Sergeant DaCosta."

Cal's voice boomed through the corridor. "There's a man in there who holds a piece of information somebody's life depends on. His name is William Crawley. We need access to him. Every second we stand in this godforsaken hall increases the odds against finding the woman alive. Let us in *now*."

The chief of staff studied the screen of his phone and responded,

"It is my understanding, Officer, that he was admitted in a highly agitated but incoherent state and is presently under sedation so that further tests can be administered without harm to him or to medical personnel caring for him. We appreciate the difficulty of the situation, but he is incapable of answering questions."

Cal was on the verge of exploding. "This blood is on your hands."

"No, sir," the administrator replied, "this *patient* is on our hands. He is under guard by one of your own, and the moment he has been assessed and deemed to be in a proper condition for questioning, we will let—"

"You will let *me* at him first." The woman seemed to materialize out of thin air. "I have been appointed by the court to represent Mr. Crawley. Here is my card, Officer."

Frank placed his left hand on Cal's chest and reached out with his right hand to take the card from the attorney. Texts came in simultaneously on Frank's and Cal's phones followed by calls. Cal unlocked his glare from the face of the chief of staff and glanced at the caller ID. It was Sanchez.

"Talk," Cal spoke into the receiver.

"Sarge, we have the make and model of the car."

"Plates?"

"Yes. It was registered under a different last name but same first name, Stella. A neighbor confirmed it's the vehicle he's seen her drive."

"Distributed?" Cal had no intention of wasting time with unnecessary words.

"Done. If the text came through, you should already have it."

Cal glanced at the screen of his phone. Frank followed suit, having an almost-identical conversation on his phone with another officer in the unit.

"Call me with anything else," Cal responded, turning back

toward the administrators, officers, and lawyer congregated outside the locked doors of the psychiatric ward.

"Sarge?" Sanchez spoke up with urgency. "You still there?"

"Yeah?"

"I found something."

"Speak, Sanchez! I need to get into that hospital room posthaste."

"An old bill to a storage unit. Past due. I have no idea if she still—"

"Address, Sanchez!" Cal pushed through the exit door to the stairwell with a bang and started down the stairs. Frank was right on his heels.

"I'll text it right away. Tracking down the unit number now."

Halfway between the third and second floors, Frank's voice echoed, "Where are we headed?"

"Gentilly!"

"Give me more than that, buddy!"

"Follow me!"

Sirens blaring, their tires squealed right on North Rampart and left on St. Bernard. Cal veered right onto Tureaud for almost a mile and then onto North Broad. It was just after 6 p.m. and darkness was falling faster than the rain. The 610, on the other hand, was barely moving, but Cal and Frank wouldn't be on it long enough to make much difference, particularly since Cal was flying up the shoulder. This wasn't a great day for traffic to pull over to the right at the sound of a siren, especially with the limited visibility. The police cars pulled off in tandem at Elysian Fields, hardly pausing at intersections. Cal led Frank right over a curb and onto the broken concrete driveway of an old storage facility.

"I need the unit, Sanchez!"

She shouted back so she could be heard over the siren. "Thirty-six, boss! Three six!"

"We've got numbers missing here." Cal was alternately flooring the accelerator and throwing on the brakes as he tried to read the unit numbers. He turned off the siren, rolled down the window, and motioned for Frank to silence his.

"There should already be a squad car there, Sarge. Dispatch sent one ahead of you to get the door open."

Cal turned down a narrow alley between units, came to a T in the road, and looked both directions. "There's no car here!"

"Frank says it just pulled in behind him. But we've got a picture up and located the unit. If you're facing the back, take a right at the T. It's the fourth one with a full-size roll-up door."

Cal took a sharp turn to the right, hit the brakes, and jumped out of the car. He motioned to the door as the other officers pulled up behind him. The trunk of the third squad car popped open. An officer retrieved several tools from it and headed toward the unit.

"Now, now, now, *now!*" Cal shouted.

The officer tossed a crowbar to his partner and they headed to opposite ends of the roll-up door. In less than a minute, the door gave way and rattled and clanged its way to the top. Boxes and overstuffed trash bags were stacked all the way to the edge. Cal scanned the dark unit with his flashlight and blew out all the air in his lungs. He'd banked on some sign of Jillian. Some shred of evidence that she was alive. The blood on Crawley's T-shirt was hers, but he'd seen a lot of bloodshed in his years on the force without anyone turning up dead.

Frank patted Cal on the back. "What do you want us to do here? Start pulling that stuff out?"

"We've got to find that car."

"Yeah, we do. And we will. We're combing the city for it and alerts are going up on screens all over Louisiana. As of today, Stella's picture is plastered everywhere. We'll get her."

Cal nodded slightly. He wanted Stella in custody alright, but what he wanted more than anything was Jillian Slater alive and in one piece. His hope was hanging by a three-inch-long thread. "Okay, guys, let's get into this stuff and find something to go on."

One of the officers already had his head in a box. "I've got a couple articles of women's clothing here, but it stands to reason that they're the suspect's."

"Pull them out anyway," Cal said. "Keep them dry, though. Then find me something better than that." He set several boxes on the floor. Something the officer had just pulled out of the box caught his eye. "Let me see that!"

The officer pitched Cal the item.

"That's hers! That's her boot! That's what she had on when she left Saint Sans."

"You sure, buddy?" Frank asked.

"Do I look sure?"

"Throw me that whole box!" Frank shouted. He drew out a pair of women's pajamas, some old wool gloves, a coat, and a blanket. "Recognize any of this, brother?"

Cal picked up the coat and looked at it carefully. He shook his head. "But that doesn't mean it's not hers."

Frank looked at the other two policemen, who were navigating their way through stacks of meaningless paraphernalia. "Let's speed it up here." They'd pulled up one of the squad cars and shone the headlights into the unit so at least they could see what they were doing.

Cal took several pictures of the contents of the box that had held the boots so he could text them to Bully. Cal had all but moved Bully into Saint Sans until they could either locate Jillian or come to a confident conclusion that Saint Sans was no longer under threat now that Crawley was in custody. The connection between Stella and Crawley was still unclear and no one had been able to come up with a plausible explanation as to how Jillian found herself in harm's way between them.

So far the police had nothing concrete on Stella. She'd admitted on the phone to Sanchez that Jillian had stopped by on her way out of town, so all traces of her in the apartment were easily explainable. Forensics found no trace of blood on the blouse discovered in Stella's kitchen trash, but if some of Jillian's belongings *were* in that storage unit, they'd have something to go on. Cal needed to know if the clothes in that box were Jillian's. And Bully was in the perfect place to find out.

"Sarge, you better take a look at this."

The contents of a black trash bag were in a heap at Frank's feet and Cal could see that he had a man's wallet in his hand. Cal fought off the agitation crawling up his spine like a garter snake. He wasn't looking for a man's belongings. He was looking for a woman's. *One* woman's. The last thing he needed was another player in this whole pileup.

Cal reached out and took the wallet, opened it, and turned it toward the headlights of the squad car. He tried to shake the confusion out of his head and read the Louisiana driver's license again. He looked at Frank, who was nodding his head.

"It's our corpse, boss."

There, in black-and-white, was the name Raphael Weyland Fontaine. And beside it, his picture, with eyes wide open and alive. Cal dropped his hand to his side and stared into the distance as bits and pieces of the last four months with the Fontaines became metal filings finding a magnet.

"Did you get Bully's text?" Frank asked.

"What?"

"Did you get Bully's text?" Frank stepped closer to him and tilted his head toward Cal's phone. "He just sent it to me to double-check because he expected you to reply immediately."

"Didn't hear it come in. What is it?" Cal read the words on his screen at the same time Frank relayed it to him.

"Mrs. Atwater recognized these pajamas. They're Jillian's."

"Is she sure?" Cal asked, trying to get his thoughts to land in one place.

"She says she's certain because she gave them to her. They're Jillian's. She thinks the boots are too, but she's positive about the pajamas. Bully asked her to keep it to herself for now but he says she's about to come unglued."

"Get all this stuff sorted *now*," Cal shouted to the other officers. "And get another team over here to help. We're wasting time here, and we haven't even made a dent in this mess. We need that woman's car, Frank!"

Cal looked for something in that storage unit heavy enough to give his excess adrenaline an outlet. He threw two boxes off the seat of the biggest thing in there: a large leather office chair. He grabbed it by the bottom lip and jerked the chair forward, causing it to tip and fall. Cal threw an old lamp out of his way, grabbed the legs of the chair, and dragged it forward and all the way past the squad car. It was everything he could do not to cuff it and throw it in the backseat. He was itching to make an arrest.

He wiped the rain off his face and stared almost mindlessly into the open space left by the missing chair. His eyes were so tired he felt like they were playing tricks on him. He hadn't had a wink of sleep in thirty-six hours. He rubbed his eyes with the heels of his hands.

"Officers on the way." Frank stuck his phone in the clip.

Cal could hear a siren in the distance. "Thanks. That'll help." He stepped back into the unit and stared at the wide path he'd left in the dirt on the floor when he dragged the heavy chair out. He shifted to one side, allowing the beam from the headlights to illuminate the whole space. He took another step forward and peered at something on the floor catching the light.

It was the sole of a bare foot.

CHAPTER 43

AFTER ADELLA'S SEARCH turned up a phone number with a San Francisco area code, Olivia got in touch with Jillian's mother. She uncharacteristically held her acidic tongue for a solid twenty minutes while Jade gave her the tongue-lashing she'd obviously saved up for a solid twenty years. It was the very kind of conversation Olivia would have done most anything to avoid, but the wretched dialogue at least answered the question. Jillian had not gone to California to her mother's place. Not yet, anyway.

Bully was practically living at Saint Sans, the place was under constant surveillance, the residents had been asked not to leave the premises unless absolutely necessary, and who could blame them for going stir-crazy? Everybody but Olivia hovered around the great room to stay in the loop and to keep one another company in all the infernal waiting. Earlier today David had chopped up every vegetable in the kitchen and tossed the whole heap into a pot with some stew meat, mild spices, and a couple of fresh bay leaves. Whether or not anybody ended up with enough appetite to eat, something simmering on the stove offered a fixed point to congregate.

When Bully took Adella to the side to show her some pictures he'd just received from another officer and she identified the pajamas as Jillian's, he asked her to keep the discovery to herself until they had more information. He said those were Sergeant DaCosta's orders. Keeping things to herself wasn't exactly Adella's forte, particularly in matters that could tie a square knot in a pair of intestines, but she'd assured Bully she'd comply in order to save the rest of them considerable panic.

She'd fully intended to keep her word, but Olivia came out of her quarters before she could properly feign a stiff upper lip and quit beating the Snapdragon with her purse. Olivia took one look at her and demanded with the choicest words for Adella to spit out whatever had her hollering, "God help 'em if I get my hands on 'em!"

Technically, Adella didn't break her promise about not telling Olivia. She made Bully tell her.

Before Bully could bring the pictures up on the phone to show Olivia, he might as well have been flypaper and Mrs. Winsee, David, and Caryn flies. Now they all five knew, and a strong sedative wouldn't have been a waste on any of them. Somehow the uproar over the pajamas even jolted Mrs. Winsee back to her old self and maybe smack-dab into one of her old stage plays.

"Ransom money!" she'd yelled. Everybody, including Bully, stared at her quizzically. She grabbed hold of Olivia's shoulders and commanded, "Get the money!"

"What money are you talking about, Vida?" The tank of patience Olivia seemed to reserve solely for Mrs. Winsee sounded down to the dregs.

"Pay them off!" she insisted.

"Pay *who* off, Mrs. Winsee?" Caryn tried to help.

Mrs. Winsee shook Olivia like a rag doll. "The heiress's kidnappers!"

They all looked at David, who shrugged in confusion. "You've got me." David was normally the one who could call out, in perfect charades style, the name of the play Mrs. Winsee was reliving in her mind. Without his help, they were stumbling around in the dark on an unknown stage.

"Get the money!" Mrs. Winsee barked once more, grabbing Olivia by the arm and dragging her down the hall, past Rafe's old room, into the private suite. Adella followed right behind them, Bully right behind her, and David and Caryn right behind Bully.

"I put it in a safe place." Whatever Mrs. Winsee had done, it was clear that she was pleased with herself.

The expression on Olivia's face at having all five of them in her private space would have caused demons to tuck tail and run, but human curiosity could be indomitable.

"Scat, you lazy grimalkin!" Clementine yowled as Mrs. Winsee shoved her off the end of Olivia's bed. Before Olivia could get a word of protest out of her mouth or pick up her chin from the floor, Mrs. Winsee lifted a corner of the mattress and pulled out a stack of cash. "Here! Ransom money!"

When Olivia froze, Adella took the stack of money and flipped through it to estimate the sum. "It's the money I accused Jillian of stealing."

"You didn't accuse her." David's words were thick with compassion.

"But I may as well have, because she believed I did. And that's why she left and now we don't even know—"

Bully made a quick interception. "How to thank you, Mrs. Winsee. That money might really come in handy."

"How much did they demand? Is it enough?" Mrs. Winsee's voice leapt an octave with the second question.

Bully responded respectfully. "I bet anything Jillian has checked into a hotel and bought some new pajamas and clothes and no telling how threadbare her bank account is getting. This may be just what she'll need to borrow when she comes to her senses."

Mrs. Winsee looked woefully dissatisfied with his uninspired answer. He went on, "But if I get a ransom note, for sure this will be enough." With that she nodded and exited Olivia's room stage left.

Adella held the cash out to Olivia. She took it and folded it in her hand and said dryly, "She must have found it in my drawer and moved it when she stayed in here after the Halloween ordeal."

Bully tried to reassure them that any shred of mystery cleared up under that roof could put them one step closer to finding Jillian.

They all dispersed after Mrs. Winsee's dramatic revelation of the money she'd hidden under Olivia's mattress. David returned to the stove and minded the stew with a wooden spoon. Olivia did the usual, but not before reminding Bully for the hundredth time that he was to knock on her door the moment he knew something.

Adella couldn't remember sitting down for hours. She was about to do so when she realized that Bully was outside on the back porch and Caryn was holding the door open, talking to him. Poor man probably needed a breath of fresh air after being cooped up all day with the inmates. The fireplace in the great room was blazing and popping a bit enthusiastically for a big man in a heavy uniform.

"The meat's tender," Caryn was saying, "and David and I are going to go ahead and have a bowl of beef stew. Want to come in and have some with us?"

Adella couldn't quite hear Bully's response, but the next thing she knew, Caryn was back in the kitchen filling a thermos bottle with coffee. When she reached in the drawer for the measuring spoons, Adella had to ask. "Girl, what on earth are you doing?"

"Bully likes three teaspoons of sugar."

"Well, I don't think he meant you had to measure it to a T. What he means is sweet."

"I want to get it just right. You think level teaspoons or heaping?"

What Adella thought was that something was curious. But she didn't say so. "Heaping. A man doesn't grow that size leveling a teaspoon."

It wasn't Adella's fault Caryn left the door ajar when she headed back to Bully with the thermos. Anybody the slightest bit down-wind could have overheard their conversation. What was she supposed to do, bring her earplugs with her to work?

Caryn sat down on the bench next to Bully. Since they both had their backs to Adella, she didn't see how it would hurt to open the door a little wider even with David giving her that look. Nobody could tell Adella he didn't secretly want her to. Caryn's words to Bully came with seriousness and a twinge of tenderness.

"You know that everybody here appreciates what you're doing, don't you? We are aware that you have taken it upon yourself to attend to us. You did not owe us that. Even Adella knows it. She's mostly bluffing out of pity for Mrs. Fontaine, who'd about rather stick needles in her pupils than let strangers in this house."

Bully's response was soft. "I wish things had gone different from the start. I wish none of this heartache had befallen this household. I wish this were a different world. That's what I wish."

"Well, me too," Caryn answered. "But there are no stars out tonight and nothing to wish upon, and this is the world we've got. And in this mean world, Officer Billy Bob La Bauve, we get to meet some good people along the rocky path. You are one of them. So is Officer Sanchez, and for that matter, Sergeant DaCosta."

Adella had to agree with that. She wasn't sure where this whole thing was going, but one thing was certain. Those officers meant well no matter what Olivia thought. David stepped over to the door, gave Adella a curious look, and stuck his head outside. "Caryn, you coming? Your stew is turning into a Popsicle. Bully, we'd be so happy for you to join us. You sure you don't want some?"

"Thank you, sir, but I better wait. The officer patroling out front could probably use a little break about now. I'll take his post awhile and have a look around. But maybe if Caryn doesn't eat it all," he said, looking at that skinny thing with a grin, "I'll have a bowl after that."

When the two of them stood to their feet, Adella and David gawked. The backs of both their pants were dripping wet. How they had managed to have an entire dialogue on a bench cushion soaked by rain was a mystery to Adella, but she wasn't sorry. Not one bit. And neither was David. It was the best sight they'd beheld at that fine house since the launch of two baby cardinals.

"I'll get a couple of towels," David whispered, trying to recover a straight face.

"Take your time" was all Adella could say, bent over the way she was.

CHAPTER 44

CAL CHARGED FULL FORCE into the storage unit, yelling and shoving boxes and crates out of his way. Frank shouted to the other officers, "Make some space! We've got a body here!"

Cal dropped to his knees and slid his left hand under Jillian's shoulders and his right hand behind her neck. He pressed his face to hers. She was cold—but not the cold of death. He lifted his head and bellowed, "She's still alive! Get me an ambulance!"

The whole place erupted in light and sound. The officers were shouting and the siren of the approaching police car was earsplitting.

"Careful there, buddy," Frank spoke from behind him. "We don't know the extent of the injuries. Keep your head."

Cal cut the duct tape off her ankles and wrists and winced for her as he removed the strip across her mouth. She showed no reaction.

He cupped his hand under her left ear and said, "Hey, girl. You're safe. You're gonna be okay. We've gotcha." He dropped his head on her shoulder. "*I've* gotcha." He wiped a smudge of dried blood from her forehead. "Hey, talk to me. Insult me. Come on, I know you've got something to say." He checked her pulse and gently patted her face, trying to elicit a response. "You see that, Frank?"

"What, boss?" Frank was leaning over him, his hands on Cal's shoulders.

"Her eyes twitched."

Frank took a few seconds before he responded. "I think I did." Cal would learn later that Frank had lied, but he was glad he did. He wouldn't have wanted to hear what those three officers thought her chances were.

"Where's that ambulance?" Cal shouted without taking his eyes off her.

"On its way."

"She did it again!" Cal put his hands on her cheeks. "Jillian, you're not getting off this easy. You've got some scores to settle. Heck, you still have at least one more dance lesson to endure. I feel like you've got some potential. I'd bet a plate of crawfish on it."

She began shaking violently. Cal tore off his jacket and put it over her. "Frank, there was a blanket in that box. Throw it to me." He tucked it around her and rubbed her arms as briskly as he thought she could stand. He slipped his hand behind her head to see if he could determine the size of the wound. Her hair was caked with blood, but at least she wasn't lying in a pool of it. He could hear the ambulance getting closer, so he craned his neck for any glimpse of it. Even with red-and-blue lights flashing in his eyes, he could tell a small crowd of officers had joined them on the scene.

When he looked back down at Jillian, he saw her lips move slightly. He leaned over her. "What is it? Tell me one more time, a little louder." He could hardly discern her breath, let alone any sound. He shouted to the officers, "Could you get this place quieted down? I think she's trying to talk!"

It was no use. The squad cars were silenced but the ambulance was screaming bloody murder. Medical personnel were on the property and out of the vehicle, heading with a stretcher into the storage unit, in what seemed like seconds. "Let's get out of their way, boss," Frank coaxed. "Let them to her."

Cal carefully removed his hand from under her head and got to his feet. A paramedic circled around him before he could step to the side. "What do we have here, Officers?"

Frank answered. "We suspect a blow to the back of the head. There may be other injuries. That's as far as we got."

As the paramedic checked her fingertips, toes, and the bottoms of her bare feet, he glared at the raised flesh around her ankles. Cal saw him glance at the same red rash on her wrists and around her mouth and quickly survey the vicinity. Cal knew what the paramedic was looking for. "Frank bagged the strips of tape. Need to see them?"

The man shook his head, searching for a vein that hadn't collapsed. Another paramedic flattened the stretcher, moved in beside him, and handed him an IV kit.

Jillian had been left in the dark and exposed to the cold for over two days. Crawley seemed convinced she was dead, but once Stella realized she wasn't, she obviously left her alive on purpose. Considering the condition she left her in, compassion could be ruled out as a motive.

Cal shook his head with frustration when the first three attempts at an IV proved unsuccessful. "Officer," one of the paramedics said, "if you could give us a little wider berth here, it might help. You're blocking some light."

"Well, could you talk to her or something? Tell her what you're trying to do?"

The man swung his head around, looking like he was about to take Cal's head off at the shoulders.

"Her name's Jillian," Cal stated and moved out of the light.

He never heard the paramedics say her name, but he heard both of them reassure her even in her unresponsiveness. When they found a workable vein at the ankle and inserted the line, Cal was certain he saw her foot jerk and he lurched toward her. Without turning around, one of the paramedics motioned him to step back and Cal complied. With the drip started, the medics bandaged her head, moved her carefully onto the gurney, and strapped her in.

The moment they raised it, Cal stepped in beside her and took every step the medics did. The rain had grown thin but a large drop from the eave of the roof hit the back of Cal's neck as they exited the storage unit. It rolled down his spine, raising the hair on his arms. He swallowed hard against the acid creeping up his throat and considered the possibility, as foreign as it was, that he might be about to throw up. "They're going to take good care of you, Jillian. They'll get you to the hospital and get you warm."

Frank joined Cal a few feet away from the ambulance. "Let's let them get her where she needs to go. We've got a suspect to find. That's what you and I can do for Miss Slater."

Cal nodded and stepped away from the stretcher as they slid her inside and one of the paramedics joined her in the back. Taking one last look, Cal piped back up. "Wait—I think she's trying to open her eyes."

"We've got her, sir. She needs to get to a hospital."

Frank slapped Cal on the back and yelled over the siren, "I've got to take this call. This should be an update on Crawley." He jogged toward his car so that he could close himself inside and hear the caller.

Cal paused, waiting for the ambulance to take off. A minute

later when it still hadn't budged, he shouted even if no one could hear him, "What are you waiting for? Go!" He hit the side of the vehicle twice with the palm of his hand, hoping to signal the driver that all was a go.

The siren ceased and the back doors of the ambulance reopened.

"She's dead," he whispered. Cal knew the assumption didn't add up. He knew, had she coded, they would have taken off all the faster and performed emergency procedures en route.

"You Cal?" the paramedic yelled.

"Yeah! What's the holdup?"

"The patient's saying your name. Hurry it up. You've got ten seconds and we're taking off if you want her to ever say it again."

Cal jumped into the back of the ambulance and knelt right beside her. "Jillian, it's me. It's Cal."

She seemed to be trying to open her eyes.

"What is it? Talk to me."

Jillian moved her lips but made no noise.

"I can't wait any longer, Officer. You better disembark and let us get out of here. Track us down later and I'll tell you if she says anything."

Jillian made an attempt to lick her lips and uttered, "She."

"*She*? Is that what you said?" Cal put his ear as close to her mouth as he could. He sat back up and stroked her face gently with his thumb, looking for some hint of green between her eyelids. "Jillian, talk to me. *She* what?"

Again, "She."

"Okay. I got that part. *She* . . . ?" He leaned in closely again.

"Killed."

"Pulse is erratic, Officer. We need to go."

"Jillian," he said quickly, "they're about to make me get out of this ambulance. Tell me what you want me to know. Say it. Whatever it is, take a stab at it."

With those last few words, she clenched her eyes, grimaced, and mouthed the words "Killed . . . my . . . dad."

"Out, Officer! Her pulse is spiking."

The siren wailed, and in less than twenty seconds, Cal was out the door and the ambulance on its way.

As it took the curb and turned out of sight, he dropped to his knees, threw back his head in the pelting rain, and cried like Bully.

CHAPTER 45

THE TROLLEY STOPPED just down the block from Saint Sans, and
Bully saw several people disembark. What he'd give for Jillian to be
one of them and for all of this to turn out to be a huge miscalcula-
tion. Crawley could have been hallucinating about doing harm to
Jillian. It seemed to Bully that she could have run smack into his
big barrel chest and busted her nose. A nose could bleed like
nobody's business, he didn't care what anyone said. And somehow,
with all that blood, Crawley feared her good as dead. Thought he'd
even killed her. Stranger things had happened. What was to say she
couldn't have taken off on a road trip with Stella with, at the worst,
a crooked snoot?

    He leaned forward and took a good look at the people who'd
gotten off the trolley. Two of them were well on their way down
the sidewalk, but one was loitering a bit like she was waiting for

someone. On the other hand, maybe she was lost. Best Bully could tell, it was a girl. It was well after dark, and he'd never been keen on women being alone after sundown near a city park. He'd just go over there and check. He didn't know this area like the Eighth District, but he was pretty sure he could help her get where she was going.

Bully crossed the two streets and the neutral ground in between and walked her direction. He called out to her from about a hundred yards to keep from scaring her. "You need some help?" Sure enough, she was turned around. Bully was familiar with the bistro she was trying to find to meet some friends. It was only a few blocks away and around the corner to the right. "I can walk you as long as I can still keep an eye on that house right there." She couldn't have been more than nineteen and was as nervous as a cat. She actually thanked him and let him see her to the second corner. He watched her until she was out of eyeshot. She waved and so did he. That was something else about this part of town. The waving.

Bully walked back toward Saint Sans wishing he had another update from Sarge or Frank, either one. Last he'd heard, they hadn't turned up anything else suspicious at the storage unit. The residents might have another long night ahead of them with no news. Bully hoped not, for all their sakes, unless no news was good news. Sarge had Sanchez sitting tight at central, keeping tabs on all the incoming and outgoing information. Others on the force could do the same thing but the sergeant had taken such an interest in this case that he wanted somebody in his own unit deciphering what was significant and what was not.

Squinting from a block away on the opposite side of St. Charles, Bully studied the curb adjacent to Mrs. Fontaine's driveway. He hadn't seen that car there earlier. Or had he? He focused as hard as the drizzling rain would let him. On second thought, he couldn't have missed a car parked that close to Saint Sans even with the headlights off. In all probability, it belonged to somebody visiting a neighbor. He quickened his pace and pulled out his flashlight just the same. He'd have to knock on a few doors to find out. Bully was pretty sure the neighbors were getting tired of police cars and inquiries, but the way he saw it, they could consider themselves safer than they'd been in years. Some neighborhoods paid a fortune for extra security. Theirs had come compliments of Mrs. Olivia Fontaine, who some might say had the tightest rich fist in all of New Orleans.

He crossed the street and the neutral ground with the tracks and walked down the westbound edge of St. Charles toward Saint Sans. At a good hundred feet away, Bully shone the light on the windshield, and even with the glare, he could see that the car was empty. At least the front seat appeared to be. He swiped the beam over the hood of the car and down the fender to identify the color and model and started toward the neighbor's front door to ask about it.

A shot of adrenaline went through Bully like a geyser. He turned around and started jogging toward the parked vehicle, trying to hold his phone steady enough to bring up information from the APB distributed earlier. The car was a match. Bully radioed the officer inside Saint Sans as he ran toward the car to confirm the license plate. About twenty feet from the vehicle, the rumbling of a motor competed with the sound in Bully's ears of his own labored breathing and hammering pulse. When the beam of his flashlight caught the steering wheel, he saw a woman sit up. The motor revved loudly, and before Bully could process the sight and leap out of the way, the gas pedal was floored.

It was strange how Bully never felt the impact. He was deafened to the sounds. He tasted no fear. He smelled absolutely nothing. All of his senses deferred to his sight. He watched the flashlight twirling in the air in slow motion, carving circles of white into the dark night.

CHAPTER 46

THE ELEVEN-YEAR-OLD stretched out her thin arm, reaching for a mossy stick floating nearby.

The outing, though begun in conflict, had become a peaceful interlude for the family. Raymond felt confident he had been right to insist upon it. The air was comfortably warm with barely a breeze to chill his frail daughter. He and Evelyn Ann both reveled in hearing the child's giggles and exclamations of delight. One might almost believe she had never been ill.

As the mild current swept the twig farther from Brianna's fingertips, she stretched for it. Unexpectedly, the boat lurched. Raymond jumped to his feet to steady her, lost his balance, and they both went overboard.

He would never be able to remember what happened next. His memory became as murky as the waters that sucked them into its depths.

He was a strong swimmer. The boat had capsized in water only a few feet deeper than an average man's height. He could not explain why he'd been unable to save the girl, who could not have weighed more than seventy pounds, except that panic had flooded his lungs.

He had no memory of Evelyn Ann hitting the water, though clearly she had.

Reverend R. J. Brashear alone emerged alive on the shore that day. He bore bruises and scratches from his attempts to save his daughter and his wife, though exactly how he'd tried had completely escaped his mind.

The congregation of Saint Silvanus Methodist Church flocked to his side, wept with him, stood beside him, and held him on his feet as his family was laid to rest. All mourned, and every hymn in the chapel found its pitch in a minor key.

The sentiment of the psalmist was the salt of their tears.

> *By the rivers of Babylon,*
> *there we sat down, yea, we wept,*
>
> *When we remembered Zion.*
> *We hanged our harps*
> *upon the willows in the midst thereof.*

CHAPTER 47

Jillian heard voices around her and tried to pry open her eyes. Her lids felt like they were coated in molasses and her body like deadweight, heavy as lead on a concrete floor. Maybe she was having a dream. She'd tried to awaken herself from dreams before that became dark rooms with no doors where she'd found herself trapped and alone. All four walls would start closing in around her with a screech as maddening as nails on a chalkboard.

She braced herself, anticipating the wave of terror that always engulfed her with an unfolding nightmare.

Oddly, it didn't come. There were no walls. Nothing closing in. She could tell the room was brightly lit, even with her eyes closed. *Don't move,* she told herself. *Just open your eyes.* She willed her eyelids upward and peered through the slender opening. A form was there. Something moving.

No, not *something. Someone.* Nodding, maybe. The sounds

were muffled, but they harkened back to something familiar. She blinked her eyes in slow motion.

"Jillian? Can you see me?"

No, but I can hear you, she thought loudly, wondering if she'd managed to make a sound. She squeezed her eyes shut as tightly as she could, attempting to rouse them from their slumber and remind them to work. When they responded to the prompt, she gave equal force to popping them open. A face as rich as milk chocolate was inches from hers. She flipped through a mental Rolodex of names. Adella. That's who it was. She couldn't tell if Adella was smiling or frowning. Jillian felt the woman's warm hand on her forehead and then the gentle brush of fingernails combing back her bangs.

"Jillian, can you see us?" It was another voice, equally familiar. Another brown face alongside Adella's. This one was definitely smiling. It was Caryn.

Beside her face, a paler one. A man's face. A kind face, also smiling. "We're right here."

Jillian's mind scrambled for a moment, trying to land on a name.

Always the gentleman, he saved her the struggle of placing him by filling in the blank. "It's David."

Yes, David. She liked David so much. Jillian hoped she was grinning. She was trying to, anyway.

A voice from Adella's left. "Mr. Winsee wanted to come too. But he was indisposed with the *Times-Picayune* and Olivia was chomping at the bit. She nearly drove over David's foot pulling out of the driveway. Caryn opened the door while we flew in reverse and he dove in like Clint Eastwood. You should have seen the audience running for cover. At the first stoplight, I tugged my seat belt so tight my girdle felt loose."

Trying not to move her throbbing head, Jillian willed her gaze to follow the voice. Mrs. Winsee's hair was done and her lip pencil was the least awry Jillian had ever seen it. An unexpected lump knotted in her throat. She didn't know why. She felt happy as far as she could tell, but her heart didn't seem to know what to do with it.

Adella's and Caryn's faces moved apart and a new one came into view.

No one spoke for a few moments, and then she heard someone clear her throat. "Jillian?"

She tried to make a sound of response, and if her ears weren't deceiving her, she thought maybe she'd been successful.

"It's Olivia."

Jillian stared at her for a moment, trying to reconcile the strange concoction of emotions crowding her chest. She shifted her eyes all the way to her left and rehearsed every name as she moved her gaze slowly to the right, one face at a time. *David. Adella. That's Mrs. Fontaine next. First name, Olivia. Caryn is beside her. Then Mrs. Winsee.*

One or more of those people—if not all five at once—were in Jillian's hospital room for the next four days. Her first forty-eight conscious hours were battered by relentless bouts of nausea. Strewn thoughts were sewn together piece by piece as she gradually made sense of the source of her agony.

She'd sustained a fierce concussion that had written its jagged signature in fifteen stitches on the back of her head. She overheard one nurse say that most people would never wake up from a blow like that, and if they did, they'd never know it. Jillian's whole body was so sore that she felt like a slab of deep purple from head to toe. She'd also entered the ER perilously dehydrated.

Her memories of the events that had landed her in the critical care unit were hazy, like a porch light up the block on a foggy night. They'd caught Stella, but that was all she was told except that she was no longer in danger.

Jillian awakened once in the middle of the night to her elbow touching someone beside her on the bed. She lifted her head to turn it without putting pressure on her wound and saw Caryn sound asleep next to her, cradling a small plastic bowl. Of the five, only Caryn was small enough to fit beside her comfortably on the narrow mattress. She was apparently keeping the bowl in close proximity for Jillian's next round of nausea. Even the sight of it made her queasy.

She heard a soft snore but it wasn't coming from Caryn. She lifted her head again and looked across the small room at the green vinyl couch right beneath the window. David was folded up on it like an accordion. How he could sleep in that position was a mystery, but she was strangely comforted by it.

The first time Jillian was able to find her words and muster enough volume to be heard, Adella was kneeling beside her hospital bed, lips quivering uncontrollably as she spoke. "Jillian, forgive me. Please forgive me." She dropped her head on the edge of the bed. "If I hadn't looked at you the way I did that day, you wouldn't have left, and none of this—"

"No . . . don't," Jillian said hoarsely. She reached for the glass of water on her bedside table and sipped through the straw. Mouth moistened, she spoke again, this time more clearly. "Wasn't . . . your . . . fault."

"Yes, it was."

"No." Jillian did something she'd never done before. She reached out and grasped Adella's hand. "They would have kept coming for us."

Jillian sat up as tall as she could without reawakening the searing pain at the crown of her head. Her memory had fully awakened to the scene in Stella's apartment when she discovered Rafe's belongings. She'd also remembered getting in the car with her. What she knew so far about the storage unit was based almost entirely on what she'd been told. She could say this much to Adella with absolute certainty: "Somebody was going to get hurt." She drew a deep breath and, exhaling, added, "Sooner or later."

"But this way, everybody got hurt."

The doctor burst through the door, abbreviating their

conversation. Jillian used every ounce of energy she could muster to answer his questions.

"How's the dizziness?"

"Better, I think."

"They're getting you up some, right?"

"Yes. Starting to."

"You're not attempting to walk without assistance, are you?"

"No."

"When was the last time you vomited?"

"Only once during the night. Improving."

"Scale of one to ten, ten being the most intense, how would you rate your pain?"

"Six," she said.

The doctor helped her sit up and lean forward so that he could examine her stitches. "Swelling's going down but I'm not going to let you out of here until your temperature is normal for twenty-four hours."

"How long do you estimate that might take?" Jillian was glad Adella posed the question. She wanted to know too, but was too spent to ask.

"Don't hold me to this, but at this rate, you'll probably take her home in forty-eight hours or so. It's stabilizing at a low grade."

Home, Jillian thought. *And where will that be, exactly?*

"Dr. Sutherland, Jillian's mother lives in San Francisco and wants her on the first plane home the second she's ready to travel. Can you give me some ballpark estimate to pass along to her?"

Jillian shot her gaze toward Adella. She didn't know they'd heard from her mom. She scooted back up on her elbows. "When did you talk to her?"

"You talked to her too, Jillian. Just a little. We put the phone up to your ear soon after you regained your wits. You responded to her with a couple of words."

"I don't remember." Jillian turned on her side toward Adella to avoid returning the back of her head to the pillow.

"Is it any wonder, after all you've been through?" Adella asked. "She's called several times. She's very concerned."

The doctor glanced at the time and reentered the conversation. "Let's concentrate on getting her pain and her temperature completely under control and getting her out of here. Then, based on her progress, we'll revisit a flight plan. Jillian, I'm only overseeing the medical concerns. There are other considerations that I won't be able to control for much longer. Needless to say, the police are pushing hard to question you."

Needless to say? The police? Her stomach flipped. Maybe it was needless to say to everybody else in earshot, but it was news to Jillian. "Why?" The rational side of her mind knew she was victim and not perpetrator in the nightmare with Stella, but her less rational side still feared getting caught and exposed as the real loser.

"They want to conduct an interview, as I understand it, to ascertain whether additional criminal charges should be filed. As you probably know, the judge denied bail, so the woman is not going anywhere anytime soon. I've kept them at bay, insisting on sufficient time for you to work through the fog of thought and speech common in your type of head injury. You are one of the lucky ones, Miss Slater. You're doing well. But therein lies the problem. You may have to deal with them soon."

Dr. Sutherland patted her on the foot and smiled. "Of course, they'll have to deal with your grandmother first. I don't envy them that. So far, from what I hear, the score is three to zip." The doctor finished tapping a note into Jillian's computer file. He glanced back her way and spoke at a hurried pace. "I'm going to change your pain medication and see if we can get you more comfortable. Is there anything else you need from me?"

Jillian shook her head and winced as her bandage brushed against the pillow.

Struggling to process all the information and to stay alert on the new pain medication, she grew quiet over the next little while. She sensed herself slipping into that familiar hole, but for the first time she didn't want to. With her eyes still closed, she whispered, "Talk to me, Adella."

"Who, *me?*"

She smiled. "No, the other Adella. You see one anywhere?"

That was all the invitation a woman with Adella's caliber of verbal skills needed. She stayed several more hours and small-talked non-stop about everything under the sun. Jillian knew she wasn't herself when she didn't mind listening to it. Emmett sure would have come up to see her if he could have, she told her, but Olivia equipped that guard at the door with a very short list and in no uncertain terms did she mean for him to abide by it. Adella explained that this was one of those rare occasions when she had a mind to do what the woman wanted. After all, she'd gone all tae kwon do on one nurse who'd tried to kick the five of them out the night Jillian was admitted. She'd also threatened to skin Clementine with a potato peeler if she got under her feet again. Who knew what else the woman was capable of doing? Adella grinned when she said it and nobody grinned as well as Adella.

Then she started into, "What you need, young lady, is a manicure. It looks like you've been scratching a gator's back. You been running some of those swamp tours on the side? Is that where you've been going all this time? And there I was, thinking you were making big-nits." She marched to the end of Jillian's bed and uncovered her feet. "Oh, lawdy, look at those toes! Naked as the day you were born. I haven't had pol-ish off my toes in twenty years except for a color change. That does it," Adella said. "We're going to Nail Estelle on the way home."

"Adella?"

"What, honey?"

"Do I have any clothes to go home in?"

Adella paused for a moment and stared at the fluorescent light over Jillian's bed. "You will when it's time to check out of here. I promise you that. Sound good?"

Jillian nodded. "What about my pajamas?"

Adella wrinkled her nose like she smelled something awful. "Those big old things? It's time you had some new ones. I'll get some at the Walmart on my way home and put them through the washer with some Downy so they'll be good and soft."

"I don't want new ones."

Adella went a little quiet after that, but she kept patting Jillian's hand, so that was fine by her.

David came on duty next, and he scooted a chair as close as he could to Jillian's bed and they watched a movie on his laptop. Well, he watched the movie. She dozed off and on, secure in occasional bursts of his laughter. "Think they've got any popcorn in this place?" Jillian asked at one point.

"You finally hungry?" David asked, jumping to his feet. "I'll be right back." A catnap later, he returned to the room with his arms full and a frown on his face. "Well, I failed, but not from lack of trying. I was told by Nurse Ratched that you need popcorn like you need—may I be blunt?"

"Yes," Jillian said, grinning.

"Like you need another hole in the head. Since she had that much right, I thought I better go with her on the popcorn. However, I have not come back empty-handed."

"I can see that."

"Three puddings: vanilla, chocolate, and . . . wait for it."

She cut her eyes his direction and he held up the third container. "Butterscotch for the win!"

"I'll have that one."

"I thought you might. And for dessert I got you Boston cream pie."

"I'll have the chocolate pudding for dessert. You have the pie."

"Don't mind if I do."

And that's just what they did.

CHAPTER 48

JILLIAN AWAKENED to an empty hospital room for the first time. She looked at the clock. It was ten past seven, but was it morning or evening? *Morning,* she decided. *This time of year, it would be dark if it were evening.*

She rolled over so she could see if anyone was in the bathroom. The door was ajar and the light was off. Loneliness dropped on her like it had been chewing its cuticles to the quick, chafing to be welcomed home.

A nurse with a familiar face walked into the room to check Jillian's vitals. "How's our girl this morning?"

"Okay, I think."

"According to your chart, your temperature stayed down during the night. How about we get you up and to the shower?"

The task seemed insurmountable, but Jillian had to admit that a shower and a crisp, clean gown would feel really good. She pushed the button to raise the head of her bed and then slipped her feet over the side and slowly to the floor.

"I'm going to hold on to one arm, but very lightly this time," the nurse said. "I want to see how well you can walk on your own. Let's give it a try. You'll have to bring your friend with you." She nodded toward the IV stand.

When Jillian made it around the bed, the nurse cheered for her. "Look at you go! You're going to be blowing out of here before you know it! We need to get you out in the hall today so you can get some distance on your feet. Where's that posse of yours? You finally run 'em off?"

Jillian's heart sank. "I don't know. I guess I must have."

"Good for you. I don't know how you've gotten a moment's peace."

Jillian didn't know how to tell her that having them there *was* her only moment's peace. While she waited by the sink, the nurse turned the shower on and gauged the temperature. She put a loose shower cap on Jillian's head to keep her stitches dry.

"When can I wash my hair?" Jillian was just becoming alert enough to care.

"Not yet, but ask the doctor when he comes in today." The nurse stood right outside the shower curtain until Jillian was finished, and then she helped her dry off her feet and get dressed. After she got back into bed, the nurse took her blood pressure once more and checked the tape on her IV.

"I'm gonna go grab you a fresh bag of fluids. I'll be right back. Feel like trying to eat some solids this morning for breakfast? Scrambled eggs, maybe?"

Jillian grimaced. "Toast?"

"Toast it is." And out she went.

Jillian had barely gotten her pillow situated and her sheet and blanket smoothed out when the door flew open again. "Wow, that was fast."

"Well, fast for you, maybe, but I could have gotten here quicker skateboarding on a box turtle. I have been sitting in traffic for a solid hour. I blew my horn every chance I got just to have something to do."

Had Olivia not turned her back immediately to set a couple of bags on a counter, she would have caught Jillian looking like she'd seen a ghost. Jillian tried to think whether or not the two of them had been alone in that hospital room since she'd regained consciousness. She couldn't quite remember, but if they had, Jillian knew she couldn't have been very alert. The two of them alert and alone with one another held all the peaceful promise of two sticks of dynamite with tangled fuses rolling toward a campfire grill. They were Old Smokey and Spitfire and somebody always got a good barbecuing.

Jillian leaned as far left as she could without falling out of the bed to catch a glimpse of whatever Olivia was unloading. She watched her pull out a large plug-in kettle with one hand and a small thermos with the other and set them both on the counter. Then Olivia retrieved an object about the same size as the kettle but this one was wrapped in a kitchen towel tightly secured by a large rubber band. Olivia slipped off the rubber band and unveiled what might have, to date, been the loveliest sight Jillian had seen in all of New Orleans. It was Olivia Fontaine's most valuable personal possession: her French press.

Either Jillian's new pain medication was kicking in, she thought to herself, or she'd suddenly found a reason to live. She sat straight up on the hospital bed like she didn't have fifteen stitches in her head. The next thing she saw Olivia lift from the large bag was a tall mason jar filled to its neck with gorgeously brown and perfectly ground coffee.

"You brought *coffee?*"

Her back still to Jillian, Olivia held up her left hand to indicate that she wasn't finished yet. Jillian grinned and waited.

Next, Olivia reached into the smaller bag and carefully unwound gold tissue paper from two china cups and saucers. Then came a long-handled spoon. Jillian watched carefully as Olivia pulled a large bottle of water out of the big bag, poured most of it into the kettle, then plugged it in and flipped the switch. Two dessert plates of the same china pattern as the cups and saucers materialized. Last, Olivia reached all the way to the bottom of the large bag and removed a medium-size plastic container with a red lid. She pulled two croissants out of it and set one on each plate.

"Hmmm." Olivia put both hands on her hips and glared at the occupants of the two plates. "They've lost a few flakes. I fear they may have taken a bit of a beating when I drove over a curb trying to get around an idiot waiting for a better shade of green at a traffic light. The bag fell over and they landed on the floor."

"They look great to me," Jillian responded awkwardly, sipping her water through a straw. She wasn't exactly sure what to do with what was unfolding in front of her, but if Olivia was willing to act out of character, she was too. Those croissants looked good, and nothing sounded better than a decent cup of coffee. She studied Olivia's strong hand as she shook the coarse coffee grounds from the mason jar into the floor of the French press and picked it up to see through the glass if it looked like the right amount.

"I ground the beans at Saint Sans. It's a shame that was necessary, but the bag was already too heavy. I had to make the unfortunate choice between the grinder and the bottle of water. The mere thought of tap water from the bathroom sink of a hospital was . . . well," Olivia said, "don't make me go on. We might as well draw it from the bathtub. We'd probably swallow a tadpole."

Jillian dropped her straw out of her mouth and set down her

water. This was precisely why she'd always preferred to limit most of her water intake to coffee. It was reasonable to expect that the temperature killed most of the germs and surely a tadpole couldn't survive it. No telling what that elixir was going to do to Jillian's stomach, but she had every intention of taking the risk.

She obviously wasn't the only one feeling awkward. Olivia had been in her room going on seven minutes and still hadn't looked at her. Waiting for the water to boil and the kettle to turn itself off would have offered a person with average social skills the opportune moment to turn around and chat. Instead, Olivia stood over it with both her palms flat on the counter and the little finger on her left hand tapping like it was taking all day.

"What is it they say? Something about a watched pot?" Jillian asked, trying to poke some holes through the silence.

With that, the kettle switched itself off. "And like many other things you learn along the way, they were wrong."

The next four minutes filled the room with a fragrance she'd once heard Olivia describe to David as "too good to be of this world." She'd said, "The coffee bean, David, may indeed be man's most persuasive argument for the existence of God." He hadn't argued. In those days Jillian wouldn't have smiled over something Olivia said for all the money lost in Harrah's Casino, but somehow she felt like doing it today. That was the kind of thing a head injury could do to you, she guessed.

"Sorry it took me so long!" The nurse was back with a replacement bag for Jillian's IV. She stopped in her tracks. "Did Dr. Sutherland say you could have coffee, young lady?"

Olivia did an about-face toward Jillian as both women answered in unison, "Yes."

"And when was he in here, may I ask?"

"At half past a party pooper," Olivia quipped. The timer went off on her phone and she gave the nurse a look that would have sent a lesser woman running for the hills. "I need to press this coffee right this minute, and perhaps I'm giving you too much credit, but based on that stain on your top, I'm guessing you're a coffee drinker. If you can manage to come up with a cup, I might consider filling it half-full. But only half. And then I'll expect you to go about your business."

Jillian grinned while the nurse glanced back and forth between the two of them. It was the aroma that did it. Jillian was sure of that.

The nurse responded, "I'll raise you a pinch of croissant and you win."

"Deal!" Jillian all but shouted.

Olivia looked disgusted but conceded under one condition: the nurse better get a move on it or that coffee was going to cool off and the scene was liable to get ugly. With lightning speed, the nurse switched out the IV bag, returned with a disposable cup, and held out her napkin for a pinch of croissant. Olivia rolled her eyes and held out the plate. The nurse wrapped the napkin around an end of a roll and pulled. Half of the insides came out.

"A pinch, not a pull!" Olivia chided.

The nurse turned on her rubber heels and exited the room, waving half a croissant over her head and chuckling.

Olivia glared at the door for a moment. "Styrofoam."

"I saw it."

Olivia shook her head. She placed both the cups and saucers on Jillian's table and poured steaming coffee from the French press into each one and a bit of cream from the thermos. One day Jillian was going to learn how to pour coffee into a china cup in such a way that it swirled like a whirlpool.

Fifteen minutes later and two cups each, the two of them had barely exchanged a word beyond an inexplicably uncomfortable *thank you* and *you're welcome*. Jillian couldn't bring herself to say,

"That's the best coffee I've ever had in my life" one more time even though it was. Three times was enough and the repetition would only make the obvious twice as obvious.

"The television doesn't work in this room. Can you believe that?"

"Purely barbaric" was all Olivia said.

Jillian thought about pretending to fall asleep as a mercy to them both but the coffee had her so wired she could barely blink.

After ten more discomfiting minutes, Olivia finally broke the silence. "Does it hurt?" Her tone lacked tenderness but the question itself at least defied coldness.

Jillian tried to answer similarly. "Yes."

Olivia nodded and stared at a few stray coffee grounds in the bottom of her empty cup.

"But not as bad as it did," Jillian added.

Olivia sucked in her top lip for a moment. She stood and took both coffee settings to the counter and set them down. When she kept her back to her for more than a few seconds, Jillian's heart sank. *We're back to this. We're always back to this.*

She was taken by surprise when Olivia turned around suddenly, leaned back against the counter, and held the edge of it with both hands. "I've never been successful at this, Jillian. I don't expect I'll be successful now, but I don't think I can make it much worse. Do you?"

Jillian didn't know what to say. She wasn't certain she was following Olivia's train of thought.

"I mean us. The two of us together." Olivia sucked in her top lip again. "I don't think there's much of a chance of breaking something that never was fixed. Do you?"

"Uh, no. I guess not."

Olivia continued. "So what I'm wondering is whether, years from now when you look back on this awful time, this tragic season when you suffered for someone else's—" Olivia winced. "I'm wondering if it could mean something that a stubborn old woman came to a place where she was willing to try." She paused, keeping her gaze toward the floor. "Even if, when all was said and done, she never got it right." Olivia looked up at Jillian as if to test the waters and see whether she should continue ankle-deep or jump back to shore. "I wonder if we could come up with anything at all."

"Like what?" Jillian was so nervous, her windpipe felt the width of a coffee stirrer and the question came out with a squeak. She tried to clear her throat and asked it again.

"Your mother is demanding you home. As well she should. I wonder if you would be willing to stay at Saint Sans until you go. These next days are promising a storm. A lot has happened. You'll need a place to sort through the worst of it. Saint Sans is not such a bad place, is it?"

Jillian shook her head.

"That old house has remained standing for a hundred years," Olivia said, "and who knows why? Maybe to spite the storms. If you'd rather go to a hotel, I have money. It's all I do have, but I have a mound of it. It's up to you. But you're welcome to stay with us."

Before Jillian could respond, Olivia turned back toward the counter and amended her last two words. "With *me*."

CHAPTER 49

JILLIAN WAS RELIEVED when Adella proved true to her word about bringing clothes for her to wear home from the hospital. She came strutting into the room on release day, accessorized with a black plaid scarf and charcoal derby hat, rolling a sizable suitcase behind her. "It's yours, and I do mean the whole suitcase. If I have to see you using that ratty old suitcase of mine one more time, I'm going to zip somebody up in it and it's liable to be you."

"Look at you, all dressed up, Adella. You must be going somewhere."

"Where I'm going is to Saint Sans with you. Do you think the hat's too much?"

"No way. You look good." Jillian grinned as she said it, but not because she didn't mean it. She'd just never known anybody in San Francisco exactly like Adella. She bent down to lift the suitcase onto the bed.

"Don't you even think about it!" Adella heaved the case up to the mattress and opened it.

Jillian's eyes popped wide open as she discovered three pairs of jeans, four tops, one pullover sweater, two pairs of shoes, and a jacket. "You spent too much money!" she protested. The marvel was that she didn't particularly despise any of them. The fake rabbit fur on the collar of the coat was probably removable. At least it wasn't fringe.

"I was on your grandmother's dime, and I don't mind saying I twirled on it. I felt so festive and free that, for an encore, I pulled out my debit card and treated myself to the ensemble you're blessed to behold this morning. Fifty percent off at Dillard's."

Before Adella had started growing on her, it used to annoy Jillian to no end that the woman pronounced *Dillard's* like *billiards* with a *D*. She'd felt the need to correct her the second time she heard her say it, but Adella had looked at her like she'd left a pair of Q-tips in her ears and said loudly, "That is exactly what I said. *Dilliard's.*"

Jillian pulled out each piece of clothing and held it up for a good look.

"I may as well be honest," Adella confessed. "Caryn went with me."

"She did good," Jillian replied.

"You think they'll fit? Girl, I bet you've lost ten pounds."

"They'll fit just fine," Jillian answered. "I'll grow back into them." She placed them on the bed and paused a moment. "Thank you, Adella."

"Thank your grandmother."

"I'd rather thank you."

When Adella retorted, "I bet you would," they broke out in matching grins.

"Whoa!" Jillian held up a new bra with the tags still on that had been tucked under the jacket. "I don't think this is gonna fit!"

"Well, we'll stuff it with coffee filters till I can get you another one. How was I to know? Do you think I signed up for all I've gotten into with you? I only have sons!"

As recently as ten days ago, Jillian would have gotten good and offended by that. But after the way Adella had tended to her over the last week, it would be embarrassingly childish. Adella meant that kind of thing as an endearment, and accepting it took a lot less energy than taking exception to it.

"Then you better have a thick stack of filters." When she saw the new pajamas at the bottom of the pile, her expression changed. She tilted her head and frowned at Adella.

"Oh, for pete's sake!" Adella exclaimed. "I do not know for the life of me why you are fixated on my old pajamas. If you'll hold your horses, you'll get them back. I've harassed the authorities all I can. Right now your luxury sleepwear is being processed by our friends at the police department as evidence."

"Evidence? Why?" Jillian was getting panicked over this memory blackout and no telling what was ahead with the police. Olivia had somehow managed to keep them out of Jillian's room for a record-setting seven days, insisting they could come to Saint Sans and meet with her once she got settled there, but she knew she couldn't avoid them forever.

And then there would be a trial, and what if she had to testify but couldn't remember anything? And what was she going to do if she had to see Stella face-to-face? Anxiety surged through every artery in Jillian's body and her stitches began to throb.

Adella blew out a breath of exasperation. "Can you just let your poor head have a minute's peace? You're making *my* head hurt. When you're not trying so hard, it'll all come back to you. We'll have to deal with it soon enough. For now, get in that bathroom and put on some of these clothes and let's see if we can light a fire under those nurses and get them to break you out of here."

Adella reached into the suitcase, unzipped a compartment, and pulled out a small bag. "As soon as you feel like it, we'll go back to the store and you can pick out your own, but this will do until then. It's time you came back to the land of the living, and I, for one, don't know how on earth a grown woman can do that without some color on her lips."

Jillian glanced into the bag and saw a tube of mascara, an eye shadow palette, an eyeliner pencil, some blush, and a tube of lip gloss. Her eyes widened when she opened the eye shadow.

"Bold, huh?" Adella was clearly pleased with herself. "Turn it over and look at the name underneath. It's called Winter Greens. Perfect for your eye color. You use that shimmery gold shade right under the eyebrow to break it up. You don't want to brush those greens all the way to the brow. Less is more with the bolder shades. Well, unless it's New Year's."

That was almost enough to make Jillian chuckle, if only her head wasn't throbbing so much. "Good to know. Okay then. If I'm supposed to get this kind of ready, you may be waiting awhile." Dr. Sutherland had told her the physical exhaustion was normal and that, actually, she was doing astoundingly well considering what she'd been through. His biggest concern, he said, was that she'd overdo it. She needed calm and quiet for a while to let herself heal.

Glancing at her phone, Adella announced, "You have fifteen minutes. That's about how long it will take me to answer a few e-mails, and then we're busting out of this joint."

When Jillian stepped out of the bathroom half an hour later, Adella broke out in a smile and clapped her hands. "Well, look at you!"

Jillian returned the smile with a weaker one and sat down in the chair by her hospital bed. "I can hardly stay up on my feet that long without feeling like I'm going to collapse. If I get back in that bed, I could go right to sleep."

"Save that nap till we get you to Saint Sans, young lady. I mean for them to get us out of here on the double. You wait here while I get the nurse." Adella pulled the curtain in front of Jillian as she left the hospital room.

Adella was Jillian's designated driver to Saint Sans by Olivia's appointment, she'd told Jillian. There was a fair ruckus in the hall as arrangements were made for which elevator she'd ride and which first-floor exit she'd be allowed to use.

"According to hospital regulations, you have to use the circle drive at the front. That's patient pickup," the nurse insisted.

"I don't care if it's patient stickup, that is not where Mrs. Olivia Fontaine made arrangements with your chief of staff to have her granddaughter exit," Adella argued at considerable volume. "We have special permission to depart by a less public door."

"What difference does it make?" Jillian asked under her breath, anxious to leave by whatever means was most expedient. She was quickly coming to the conclusion that Olivia was being even more eccentric than Mrs. Winsee.

The sound of a male, authoritative voice entering the dialogue brought Jillian to her feet and she peeked around the curtain to see the face it belonged to. Her thoughts raced at the sight of the security guard. Conjuring up scenarios—none of them good—that could explain why he was stationed back at her door, Jillian missed what was said. That Team Fontaine had won the match was clear, however, when the guard walked in a few minutes later beside a nurse pushing an empty wheelchair.

Adella entered the room behind them jingling her car keys and reaching for Jillian's new roller bag. "I'm going to get your ride while this nice gentleman will see you down the south tower elevator to a side door where I will pick you up posthaste. Then it is straight to Saint Sans with you, young lady."

"We're not going to Nail Estelle?"

"Not today. Your grandmother has rerouted us, and she is in no humor for a detour."

Jillian sat in the wheelchair and propped her feet on the metal footrests.

"We got everything?" Adella asked, casing the room for any overlooked personal items.

"The flowers!"

"Jillian, those flowers are deader than my great-granddaddy. I've got the cards in my purse. That's all you need." When Jillian responded with an unusually agreeable *okay*, Adella relented. "Oh, good grief, if you're going to act like that about it, we'll take them."

Adella loaded all three arrangements onto Jillian's lap and the small herd headed into the hall. Jillian said her good-byes to the personnel at the nurses' station and the one who'd particularly captured Jillian's fondness leaned over and folded her up in her generous arms. "You're gonna be alright. You hear?"

"Thank you," Jillian responded, trying to mask the emotion knotted in her throat. She had yet to grow accustomed to those kinds of hugs.

As they made their way through a maze of halls, Adella said, "Good thing we went to the trouble of arranging a secret exit since what we have here, ladies and gentleman, is the floral edition of Hansel and Gretel. Shall I just ask them to make a public announcement that we're departing the building?"

Jillian glanced behind her at the trail of yellow petals that had rendered the chrysanthemums in the red vase all but bald. "Nobody cares. I don't know why you're making such a big deal about it."

The nurse hadn't uttered a word in five solid minutes but she picked this exact opportunity to pipe up. "We haven't seen them today anyway. Maybe they've moved on to something new."

Out of the corner of her eye, Jillian saw Adella shoot the nurse a quelling look.

"Who are you talking about? Who haven't you seen today?" Jillian asked.

Instead of answering, the nurse transferred her attention to the last turn. "We're almost there. We'll take a right at the end of this hall and come to a set of double doors. Mrs. Atwater, we'll let you pick her up there. Pull up under the green awning where the sign says Outpatient Surgery."

After issuing the nurse a "Thank you ever so much" with sharp enough sarcasm to slice a steak, Adella stomped out the door and into the large parking lot in search of her car. Her jaw was moving faster than her feet.

"She's giving somebody a piece of her mind," the nurse said with a smirk on her face that only a fellow smart aleck could adequately appreciate. Fortunately, she was in the right company.

"Oh, I know exactly who she's giving a piece of her mind to," Jillian said. "I just don't know why. You want to give me a clue?"

"I think I'll leave that to her, except to say that no few people are itching to get to you."

With that the guard's tongue was untied long enough for him to suggest with an impressive measure of frankness that the nurse stick to her job description.

Jillian shook her head and began surveying the people in the outpatient surgery waiting room. One guy was sound asleep with his mouth wide open. An older woman no bigger than Caryn was dressed in a purple tracksuit and reading a Bible. At least it looked like a Bible to Jillian. There was one on the bookshelf at Saint Sans that looked just like it. A young man was playing a game on his phone, and the woman next to him was lost in a book. Jillian tilted her head and squinted her eyes so she could decipher the title between the woman's fingers. *Last Dance, Last Chance.*

A middle-aged man yawned loudly as he picked up a copy of the *Times-Picayune*. He crossed his legs and disappeared behind its full length and width. Jillian perused the headlines facing her. Then she lurched as if the wheelchair had rolled over a live wire and looked again to be sure she'd read it right.

Hope Growing Dim for Critically Injured Officer La Bauve

She scrambled to her feet, only dimly registering the nurse's warning that she needed to sit down before she fainted. The guard grabbed her arm to hold her steady, but she beat her fists against his chest. "What happened?" she shrieked. "What happened to him?"

CHAPTER 50

"WHY DIDN'T ANYONE TELL ME?" Jillian's tears were rivers.

It had been everything Adella could do to keep the hospital from readmitting the young woman. She'd managed to get Jillian into the car by threatening that they were going to wheel her right back to that hospital room if she didn't straighten up. Then Adella nearly hanged herself on her plaid scarf wallowing all over the car with Jillian, trying to buckle her seat belt. On top of that, Adella had sailed through every yellow light between there and Saint Sans with the girl rocking back and forth and wailing at the top of her lungs. It was a safety hazard. That's what it was. She couldn't have heard an ambulance in a convertible. Then, to top it all off, when they finally made it to Saint Sans, she had to threaten a pack of local reporters within an inch of their lives if they did not get their tail ends out of the driveway—only, looking back on it, she had a bad feeling she hadn't said *tail ends*. Well, if she hadn't, it wasn't her fault. They'd pushed a God-fearing woman to the edge of the uttermost.

David had met Adella at the back door and helped negotiate Jillian down the hall and into Rafe's room while Olivia tried to settle Mrs. Winsee. She was wailing her head off with Jillian without the least idea why.

After they finally got Jillian into bed, Adella sat on the edge of the soft mattress. She let go of a sigh from somewhere so deep and tired that it nearly bruised her lungs on its way up. A few minutes later, Olivia joined them, pulling up a chair on the other side of Jillian's bed. Both women had known all week that the question was coming. Adella went ahead and took the lead. "We couldn't, Jillian. Dr. Sutherland even agreed. You've been through so much trauma yourself. You didn't need another thing to worry about until you could start to recover."

"When were you going to tell me?" Jillian asked through broken sobs.

Olivia responded this time. "When you got here and we had a little privacy, so you could process it without an inquisitive audience. Obviously, things did not go as we hoped. Adella, could you explain to me how Jillian came upon this information? We went to substantial lengths to hold that off."

"She saw a newspaper while I went to get the car. She read a headline."

Still crying inconsolably, Jillian looked up at Olivia and choked out the words "Is Bully going to die?"

A chill shot down Adella's spine.

Olivia rubbed her lower lip and then tapped it. Adella had been around her long enough to know what that meant. She was searching for words from a Scrabble grid of *Q*s and *X*s, *Y*s and *Z*s. Adella took her turn from a grid with more vowels to buy Olivia a little time. "Jillian, your grandmother has been up to see Bully's mama every day since it happened, wearing the soles of her feet to calluses between the two hospitals."

Only a person who knew Olivia's history could appreciate what those hospital visits had cost her. Withdrawal had always been her defense against the fodder her late husband hand-fed the media. He'd thrived on it. She'd died on it. Olivia would have shaken the dust of New Orleans off her feet before the man's body cooled had her only child not been out there somewhere on those streets. Remaining reachable had been her only means of keeping vigil. And now the media hounds were not only feeding on the fresh meat of a brand-new Fontaine docudrama. They were also gnawing on rotted meat: all the old footage and all the old articles about the lawsuit, the suspected mob connections, and the suicide of Steadman Nolan. The story going full circle was a media dream come true. And Olivia had subjected herself to it day after day, just so she could walk into that intensive care waiting room to sit with a family she'd never met, to try to say words she had never said.

Mrs. Fontaine, how do you feel about what happened to Officer La Bauve?

Do you feel responsible for it?

Can you comment on Stella Nolan?

What is your memory of the Nolan suicide?

Is it true that your late husband had mob connections?

How do you feel about Stella Nolan being cheated out of her inheritance?

Is it true that your own heir died penniless on the street?

They held screens right in front of Olivia's face replaying the footage of Sergeant Cal DaCosta leading a handcuffed Stella Nolan from the backseat of his patrol car into the police department. She looked into the camera and yelled like she'd rehearsed every syllable, "Lock me up. Hang me like my father. It won't matter! Death and destruction will still come to the Fontaines and all they touch. They are a brood of crooks and murderers. A curse is upon them!"

And louder and louder, over and over, until the sergeant dragged her through the door. "A curse on you, Olivia Fontaine! A curse on your blood! A curse on all that belongs to you!"

Adella was certain that none of it had been harder on Olivia than this moment, sitting beside her lost son's bed, trying to explain the inexplicable to all that was left of him.

"When I made the choice to hide from you what happened in front of this house to Officer La Bauve, I determined that, when the time came to tell you, I would disclose it in full. I will tell you everything you want to know about that night and about our history with . . ." Olivia paused and clenched her eyes shut.

Adella leaned across the bed. "Your head hurting again, Olivia?"

Olivia winced. "About our history with the Nolans. When you're ready. For now, let me answer your question about the officer's prognosis. The La Bauves have been told to prepare themselves for his passing. According to the specialist, his organs are giving indications that he won't hold out much longer. Had his body not been so formidable, he wouldn't have lived through the first night. He has never regained consciousness and he is primarily being sustained by artificial means."

Jillian put her hands over her face and sobbed.

Olivia stood, smoothed her slacks, and said, "Adella, I'm going to check on Vida and then make us all some of that tea Jillian likes. I think coffee might be too much for tonight."

The next several days were piecemeal with pain and sadness, with quietness and questions, with moments of gentleness, brutality, and beauty. There was no normalcy. There were no established roles. No rules to go by. No being excused. They'd all been skinned alive. All of them at Saint Sans. All of them at Bully's bedside. All of them at the Eighth District. There was no cover. There was no doing it especially well. There was only the enduring. Thanksgiving came and went with as little fanfare as Adella had ever seen. Yes, they all had more to be thankful for than they could shake a stick at, but no, they didn't have the time or the heart or the energy for the traditional celebration.

Adella came early in the morning and stayed as long as she could after work hours without AJ and Trevor Don bellyaching. Emmett Atwater was as fine a man as God made these days, at least in Adella's book. Emmett told her she had his blessing to spend several nights at Saint Sans if she felt like she needed to. "I'll bring you over an air mattress. I don't mean a plastic one. I mean Army-grade. I'll even blow it up for you." Emmett always had a twinkle in his eye when he was about to do somebody good.

"Sheets?" Adella asked. She wouldn't get a wink of sleep without sheets.

"Off one of the boys' beds. He'll never notice. Do you think Jillian would mind if you put it on the floor in her room?"

"No, I don't expect she would." Adella took a moment to think about it. "In fact, she might be glad. She does better in the day than in the dark. Between her own memories starting to resurface and her picturing Bully over and over getting hit by that awful car, the girl can hardly shut her eyes. I'll find out if Olivia would be relieved for me to stay a few nights with her."

But she never asked her. When David heard of Adella's plan, he shook his head. "She reads to her at night."

"What do you mean she reads to her?"

"I mean Mrs. Fontaine sits in the chair next to Jillian's bed and reads to her."

"What on earth does she read to her?"

"Jane Austen."

"*Pride and Prejudice?*"

"*Emma.*"

"Then what?"

"Well," David responded, "if every night is like last night, she reads to Jillian until she starts nodding off, then Mrs. Fontaine gets up, turns out the lamp, and goes out."

"Huh. Well, I never." Adella was flummoxed.

"And that's not all."

Adella slid the utility room door shut and turned the dryer on so nobody could hear them. "Spit it out."

"She turns on a small lamp in the foyer between their rooms and . . ." David raised his eyebrows all the way to his receding hairline.

"And what?" Adella slapped the top of the washer with both words for special emphasis.

"And leaves both their bedroom doors open all night."

"Boy, you watch yourself, messin' with me."

"You heard me."

"You're telling me that she leaves the door to her private suite open all night."

"Correct."

"How do you know?"

"I set my alarm for 3 a.m. last night just to check. Wide open."

"She must be skimming off Mrs. Winsee's medication."

As it turned out, Adella learned, Olivia did considerably better in the night than the day. Actually it made sense when she thought about it, since there was less talking involved. Reading wasn't the same as talking. The officers coming and going nearly drove Olivia to drink bleach, and the way they drilled Jillian with the same questions they'd asked the day before made her want them to, she confessed.

Olivia was not a little perturbed that Officer Sanchez wasn't among the police officers sent to question Jillian. "She doesn't know these men," she complained to Adella. "She shuts down with them." Officer Lamonte was the only officer familiar to Jillian. Nobody watching could say he wasn't trying. For that matter, so was Jillian. He'd been kind and patient and she'd been cooperative. Just unusually soft-spoken.

"They said Officer Sanchez is taking some time off," Adella reminded her. "That's understandable, since she's Bully's partner and all. I heard the whole unit is completely undone."

"I saw her twice over at the hospital where Officer La Bauve is."

"In the ICU waiting room?" Adella asked.

"Once."

"Did you talk to her?"

"No," Olivia responded brusquely. "She was in regular clothes. She looked different."

"That explains it." Olivia was hands down one of the oddest people Adella had ever known. If she was taking some of Mrs. Winsee's medication, Adella felt like suggesting she might try a higher dose.

"The other time was on the first floor."

Since Olivia rarely offered information on the bloodless side of a tooth-pulling, she had to be after something. She owed Adella a debt of gratitude for agreeing to play along. "So where did you see her on the first floor?"

"Going into the chapel." When Adella didn't respond by the count of three, Olivia added, "You know, the kind they have in some hospitals."

"Yes, I do know. And . . . ?"

"And that's all. There was no more to it."

"Okay then."

Olivia studied her. "You think she's religious?"

"Who?"

"Who were we talking about, Adella? Officer Sanchez."

"I have no idea. Why?"

"Just wondering."

Olivia never just wondered about anything.

"Many people reach out for God when they're in a crisis," Adella said, "and thank goodness they do. Nothing is at all unusual about that. And his ears are open to their cries."

"He must have gotten an earful from Officer Sanchez."

The woman was exasperating. "What are you getting at?"

"She was still in there an hour later when I left."

"I thought you'd only seen her twice. That would have been three times."

"Well, aren't you quite the math wizard? Try this math: sixty-four minutes in the hospital chapel. *Sixty-four.*" Olivia gave her a pointed look.

Before Adella could come up with a suitable response, Jillian appeared out of nowhere. "I need to go to the hospital."

Adella jumped to her feet, and Olivia exclaimed, "What is it? Did you have a seizure? Blurred vision? Let's see, disorientation?"

Had Jillian not stopped her, she would have continued in perfect order through the checklist of maladies Dr. Sutherland told them to call him about immediately. "No. I need to go to Bully's hospital. With *you.*"

"Me?" Olivia looked like she'd just seen her own picture on the back of a milk carton.

"You."

CHAPTER 51

FOUR DAYS HAD PASSED since Olivia had last come to this waiting room. Her hands had been so full with Jillian she couldn't leave Saint Sans. She'd also feared that, if she dropped the least hint of where she was headed, Jillian would insist on joining her. Olivia had no intention of taking that chance. She'd not let Jillian be subjected to the media that had been hounding her.

Yet here they were. This was the reason Olivia was going to have to let Jillian go back to San Francisco without a hint of resistance. She needed to be away from this place. From this history. From this curse.

Olivia had no idea how far a curse could reach, but it would have a harder time getting its bony hand around her neck in San Francisco than at Saint Sans. It had moved right into Saint Sans, taken its shoes off, and walked around bare and bold. Look at all that had happened to Jillian since she'd been there. She was going to have to go. That's all there was to it. The sooner the better.

"Mrs. La Bauve, I'm sorry. We must have come at the wrong time. There's no one else here." Olivia felt her face scald with embarrassment.

Bully's mother patted the seat of the chair right beside her. Her exhaustion was palpable. "Nonsense. It's the perfect time. Bear is in there with Billy. The nurses make occasional exceptions, but the hard-and-fast rule is one visitor at a time."

Olivia's feet were stuck to the floor. In her wildest imagination, she had not pictured sitting right by the grieving mother and having to come up with something comforting to say. "Where are my manners? Mrs. La Bauve, this is my—"

"I know exactly who this is. Jillian, aren't you a sight for sore eyes, you lovely thing?" She patted the chair on the other side of her. "Come. Tell me how you're feeling. We were frantic about you."

Jillian did something she might not have felt as free to do had she been a little older. Olivia guessed she just couldn't help herself. She burst into tears, threw her hands over her face, and said, "I'm so sorry! I'm so, so sorry, Mrs. La Bauve!"

"Mrs. Fontaine, bring that child right here—" she patted the seat again—"and let's you and me talk some sense into her and dry her tears."

Olivia was taken aback.

"Right here." More patting.

Even Olivia had sense enough to know that the most grief-stricken person in the room ought not have to do so much patting. She got Jillian by the elbow, led her to the chair beside Bully's mother, and sat down on the other side of her. Perhaps Mrs. La Bauve had missed the discomfiture.

"How is he?" Jillian sobbed.

"He is about the same. His doctor said he's got the strongest heart they've ever seen."

Jillian nodded and sniffed several times.

Olivia held the Kleenex box right under Jillian's chin, and before Jillian could reach up to pull out a tissue, Mrs. La Bauve snatched one with a whoosh.

"Here you go, dear," she said, holding it right under Jillian's nose.

"Thank you, Mrs. La Bauve."

"Honey, go ahead and call me Bootsie. Mrs. Fontaine, you, too. That's what my friends call me. Well, and Bear. He started it."

Jillian's nose was barely dry when a mountain of a man walked through the door with a younger man behind him who looked vaguely familiar to Olivia.

"Bear, Mrs. Fontaine's been kind enough to come back to see us, and her granddaughter just barely out of the hospital. Look how well she's doing. Did you get to meet Jillian that night at Billy's party? Or did you put that accordion down even once?"

Jillian stood and stretched out her hand, and he took it in both of his. "Mr. La Bauve," she said tenderly and earnestly, "I am so very sorry."

"Thank you, Jillian." His eyes were as glassy as the Gulf.

He reached behind him and pulled the young man out front. "Look who I found in the hall again, Bootsie."

Mrs. La Bauve scolded him with a smile. "Cal DaCosta, I told you I better not see you up here today."

He hugged her and kissed her on the forehead. "You know I had to come."

"This young man has been up here every day at least twice." Mrs. La Bauve put her hand on his cheek. "He's been in there with Billy as much as Bear and I have."

"Mrs. Fontaine," Cal said, extending his hand to Olivia. He offered his hand to Jillian and said her name softly. Olivia noticed something about their eyes and a slight hesitation before they shook hands.

"You look well. Really well. Are you feeling good?" Cal asked.

The room was suddenly stuffy. No telling how much body heat a man Bear's size probably gave off.

"I'm okay," Jillian responded. "It's Bully." She struggled to get the words out of her mouth. "I didn't know what happened until the day I left the hospital."

"They had you shut in there pretty tight." Cal's eyes met Olivia's. "We sure tried to get in."

Olivia didn't utter a syllable.

Jillian lifted her gaze and looked into his face. "I'm so sorry, Cal."

Cal? What happened to Sergeant? Olivia picked up the box of tissues and goosed Jillian in the ribs with it. "Here, Jillian. Blow your nose."

"It's my fault," Cal stated with a strident conviction that no one in the room could ignore.

"Cal," Bear said, "don't start that again."

"It is. Nobody can tell me it's not. I should never have let him go over to that place."

Olivia couldn't exactly pride herself on emotional perceptiveness, but even she heard the hiss of that blade. Something about the way he'd said the words *that place* with such distaste, like it was somewhere terrible. Shameful. Olivia saw every drop of blood drain from her granddaughter's face.

Jillian stood motionless for a few seconds without blinking an eye. Something or other was said but Olivia's ears were ringing too loudly to hear it and Jillian looked like she'd turned to stone.

"I think this girl has had enough activity today," Olivia announced. "Dr. Sutherland would have my head on a platter if he knew I'd pranced her all over town. We'd best go."

Jillian collected herself and leaned over and hugged Mrs.

La Bauve. "I won't stop thinking about Bully or any of you for a single moment. No one at Saint Sans will."

Mrs. La Bauve reciprocated the embrace, a tear spilling from each eye. "Pray for us, honey. Pray for Billy. We don't know what we'd do without him."

"I will," Jillian whispered through her own tears.

Neither Jillian nor Olivia said anything on the way down the elevator. Something awful and heavy and painful sat down on Olivia's heart. This was what happened when you opened yourself up to people and sat by their beds and tended to their wounded heads. A terrible wave of nausea engulfed her. "Jillian, I'm going to have to go to the ladies' room. I don't want you to walk to the car without me. Can you wait here for me?"

Jillian nodded.

When she came out of the restroom a moment later and Jillian wasn't where she'd promised to be, Olivia spun into a frenzy. She rushed back into the ladies' room and called her name, glancing under the stalls. She darted into the cafeteria and checked every corner.

An elderly woman spoke from behind the information desk. "Is that who you're looking for?"

It was Jillian, standing in the doorway to the chapel.

"Yes." Olivia cleared her throat and blotted the perspiration on her upper lip. "Thank you." She headed toward Jillian, but when she reached her and caught the focus of her attention, she stood next to her in silence.

"It's Officer Sanchez," Jillian whispered to Olivia.

"Yes."

"She's praying."

"Yes, Jillian. She is."

Jillian took a step forward and Olivia took her gently by her little finger. "Let me take you home. You've done too much today."

"I promised Mrs. La Bauve." Jillian tugged her hand from her grandmother's grasp and walked down the aisle to the second pew, where Officer Sanchez knelt.

The officer looked up at her with surprise and started to get to her feet. Olivia could see that Jillian dissuaded her, shaking her head and whispering something Olivia couldn't hear, before kneeling beside her.

Olivia watched from the doorway, blood rushing to her face. The awkwardness she felt on her granddaughter's behalf was agony. She had no choice but to put a stop to it. Jillian was overwrought. It was as simple as that. Just as Olivia started forward to gather her up and take her home, Officer Sanchez smiled at Jillian and held out a hand to her. Jillian hesitated but eventually placed her hand in that open palm.

Officer Sanchez bowed her head. Olivia watched her granddaughter. Jillian's gaze moved like a searchlight from one wall to the next, from picture to etching, from fixture to floor. Olivia thought how she'd give almost anything for a chance to look through the lenses of Jillian's eyes right that moment. What did she see? Or what didn't she see that she longed to see? The room was simple and the walls were stark. The atmosphere was pleasant enough. But expecting God to show up in a hospital chapel was like expecting a gourmet chef to show up in the hospital cafeteria.

Jillian lifted her chin and stared at the ceiling. Then she did the strangest thing. She looked over her shoulder at Olivia. *What does she want from me? Rescue?* Then, just like that, Olivia knew what Jillian's eyes were saying.

Come with me.

Olivia's stomach flipped and her chest constricted. She drew down her eyebrows and shook her head. *No.*

Jillian peered at Olivia a few seconds longer. Then she faced forward and bowed her head.

CHAPTER 52

DURING THE FIRST SEVERAL WEEKS following the tragedy,
Reverend Brashear walked through his days in a fog. The pastors of
other churches came and paid their respects. Some tried to befriend
and counsel their fellow servant of God. Even the unredeemed tipped
their hats with pity when they passed the grieving reverend on the
streets. Loss was no respecter of persons. The holy and unholy alike
could enter the horror.

As he began to fumble his way back to life, a lovely young
woman began coming to Saint Silvanus. Was it a coincidence? Was
there a direct connection? No one knew for certain. But it was
around that time the preacher began to heal.

As is often the case, there were those who believed they knew exactly what was happening, and they were not shy about sharing their insights with the unenlightened. Someone said the woman had been seen at the front door of the parsonage—after dark, no less. Perhaps she was only delivering a meal, but who could tell? Did she cross the threshold? There were varying opinions. Soon the idea began to circulate that she had a questionable reputation. A few declared, now that they'd had time to reflect on it, that they were certain they'd seen her on the back row of the chapel on a Sunday before the tragedy.

Rumors piled like kindling, sparks were fanned into flames, and eventually the Reverend R. J. Brashear was charged with the double murder of his wife and child. Not by the sheriff, let it be said, though under civic pressure, he'd circled by a couple of times with questions. No, Reverend R. J. Brashear was charged by the jury holding court on the pews of Saint Silvanus Methodist Church. A handful had remained by his side, calling the ordeal a godless farce, but they could neither pay his modest wages nor shield him on the streets from shame.

CHAPTER 53

JILLIAN FELT CAUGHT in a loop of cartwheels she couldn't stop.
She'd gone with Olivia to the hospital brokenhearted over Bully and
come home from the hospital brokenhearted over Cal. Of course, she
couldn't tell anyone that. She'd feel too silly. Looking back on it now,
she realized she'd made too much of that dance on Bully's front porch.

An odd thing was happening between her and Olivia. They were
getting a little more practice at being alone, just the two of them.
They didn't have to do it much because somebody else was usually
close by at Saint Sans, but it was no longer awkward enough to avoid
at any cost.

Olivia came into her room with her bifocals on and wearing her
floor-length housecoat. She picked up the novel off Jillian's nightstand and opened it to the page with the bookmark.

Jillian couldn't get her mind off Cal or, for that matter, off
Bully, so she rolled over on her side toward the nightstand and said,
"I don't feel much like reading tonight, O." She'd been trying to

use Olivia's new grandmother name as much as possible so that she could stretch the elastic out in it where it wouldn't feel so tight.

It had been Olivia's suggestion that Jillian call her something other than Mrs. Fontaine.

"What would you like me to call you? How about Grandma? Or Nanny?" she'd asked, tongue in cheek.

"I don't think so," Olivia had said. "Somebody you call Grandma or Nanny, well, you have pictures with her that are in frames. That's not really us."

Jillian didn't have any other ideas. "What do you want me to call you?"

"The way I see it, it's not for me to say. It's about what you feel comfortable calling me. If it's Olivia, we'll go with that. If that's all that's true, then that's all we've got."

"Oh," Jillian said.

"Hmm," Olivia responded. "Give me a second to think on it. It's not too bad. Come to think of it, it's got a nice ring to it. Well, that was easier than I thought it would be."

"Huh?"

"I like it. Let's go with it. *O* it is."

So that seemed to settle it.

Olivia was utterly undeterred by Jillian's statement that she didn't feel like reading tonight. "Well, that works just fine," she said, "since you're not the one reading." She sat right down, got right to it, and Jillian stayed awake the whole time.

Olivia's reading was mesmerizing. As smooth as silk. She knew just when to speed up and just when to slow down. It was an odd thing to Jillian that Olivia could do it so well with someone else's story but she could rarely find the right words in the middle of her own. Jillian mustered up the courage to pay her an unsolicited compliment. "You could hire out to publishers to do their audiobooks. I love the way you read."

It must have embarrassed Olivia because all she said in return was "You're not asleep yet."

"I know."

"Then how am I supposed to know when to turn out the lamp?"

"I'll turn it out in a few minutes. You go ahead."

"What happened today keeping you awake?" Olivia asked.

"Which *what happened*?" Jillian was mortified that Olivia might know how she felt about Cal, especially after he'd spoken so disparagingly of Saint Sans.

"Whichever *what happened* is keeping you awake."

"My stitches are itching." It was all Jillian could think to say, and it wasn't a lie.

"Friday and they're out. In the meantime, I saw somewhere on the Internet—"

"*You* get on the Internet?" Jillian couldn't help herself.

"Yes, Jillian, I get on the Internet. Do you think I'm stuck in the Stone Age? As I was saying, I saw somewhere that according to recent laboratory studies, popcorn has certain properties medically proven to stop the itches of stitches."

Jillian bolted out of bed. Olivia popped corn the old-fashioned way with a big heavy pot, its bottom blanketed in oil. After the first pop, she kept the pan moving so the kernels wouldn't burn. She did it rhythmically to-fro, to-fro, to-fro, to-fro like a metronome. A savory fragrance matching no other, that pan of popping corn wooed all three of the other residents out of their rooms. Olivia oversaw Jillian as she made a second batch.

"Slower, Jillian! And get that fire down!"

"I'm doing it slow, O!"

"Well, slower!" she barked. It was their way. And to them at that moment, their way was sublime.

After the pops were fewer and seconds apart, Jillian pulled the pan off the burner. Olivia took off the lid to inspect it and steam coated her bifocals and everybody laughed. She poured it into a large bowl, set down the pan, looked at Jillian without the least grin, and said, "Perfect corn." Butter and salt flowed like milk and honey.

Jillian collapsed in her bed as the clock in the great room struck midnight, ending an odd concoction of a day and beginning a new one. She dropped off to sleep with two sentences competing for space in her stitched-up head.

"I should never have let him go over to that place."

"Perfect corn."

The next morning Jillian took her coffee out on the back porch. She felt warm and safe. As he left for work, David had seen her there and brought out his grandmother's quilt to wrap around her.

She closed her eyes and felt the mild winter breeze tickle her nose and blow her messy morning hair. Suddenly a shock of words reverberated from somewhere nearby.

"Death and destruction will still come to the Fontaines and all they touch. They are a brood of crooks and murderers. A curse is upon them. A curse on you, Olivia Fontaine! A curse on your blood! A curse on all that belongs to you!"

Adrenaline shot Jillian to her feet. Stella! But she was supposed to be in jail.

Jillian tripped over the quilt and landed on her hands and knees. Her heart was pounding. She looked frantically at the gate. Stella wasn't there. She looked through the back glass of Saint Sans into the great room. Stella wasn't there either. Where was she?

A tall bush on the other side of the fence started shaking and the limbs started rattling. Between the slats in the fence, she saw a figure—a person—run toward the front of the house. Jillian ran through the back door and screamed, "She's here! She's here! Call the police!"

"Jillian, who?" Olivia cried out loudly, her face instantly radiating alarm.

"Stella!" The name came out of Jillian's mouth so shrill and chilling it sounded like the cry of a screech owl.

"Girls, get in Caryn's room *now*! Shut the door and lock it!"

Caryn grabbed Mrs. Winsee by the hand and flew with her down the hall screaming for Jillian to follow them.

After several minutes of untethered hysteria, Olivia called the three girls out of Caryn's room. Jillian could see Olivia's pistol weighing down the right pocket of her housecoat. Her cell phone was in her hand.

"I just got off the phone with Officer Sanchez. Stella is safe and secure in custody under constant watch."

"But it was her! I heard her! I know her voice!" Jillian had no uncertainty.

"I believe you, Jillian. We all do," Olivia reassured her. "Now, tell us how you know it was her."

"She must have thought you were out there with me, O. She screamed at you."

"What did she scream at me, Jillian? Tell me what she said."

"It sounds crazy but she was screaming, 'A curse on you, Olivia Fontaine!' She kept shouting weird stuff about curses. 'A curse on your blood' and stuff like that. She's nuts!"

Olivia stumbled, and Jillian reached for her, afraid she was about to faint. She and Caryn helped her sit down.

"Vida?" Olivia lifted her face and spoke to Mrs. Winsee. "Vida, are you listening to me?"

"Yes, Olivia. I'm listening."

"Everything is fine here. This was just a fire drill. We should have told you in advance before we practiced."

"You surely should have. And you should have told Mr. Winsee.

If this had been a real fire, was he supposed to crawl out the window, him with that bad knee?"

"Vida?" Olivia persisted. "After all that drama, we could use a snack. Don't you think?"

"I'll whip up something!"

"Thank you. Why don't you make us a beautiful spread of yogurt and berries and walnuts? No one can make a yogurt parfait like you."

As Mrs. Winsee began rummaging through the refrigerator as happy as a lark, Olivia looked at Caryn and Jillian with an expression so serious, the hair stood up on the back of Jillian's neck. With a nod of her head, she indicated the far end of the room.

Jillian and Caryn settled on the Snapdragon and Olivia took the chair nearby. "Jillian, what you heard was a recording. One that had obviously been meticulously remastered by a reporter for full volume and effect."

"What are you talking about?"

So Olivia told her everything, including how they now knew Stella had been the one who'd left the flowers with the card that said *Atonement*.

"What does it mean?" Jillian asked, hanging on every word.

Olivia could generally pummel a paragraph into its frankest phrase to convey what she wanted to say. This time, however, she hemmed and hawed with a rare lack of coherence.

"She said you were cursed. Is that creepy or what?" Jillian inquired.

"Stupid nonsense," Caryn said.

Jillian tended to be more superstitious than Caryn, more frightened of the dark and far easier to spook than her scientific friend. "I don't know. It puts chills up my spine."

Later in the day Olivia asked if she could speak to Jillian privately. They stepped into Rafe's room and closed the door.

"I want you out of here as soon as possible, far away from this place."

Jillian's heart would have been irreparably damaged except for the fact that Olivia's expression and the tone of her voice conveyed something entirely different from her forceful words.

"It's the curse thing, isn't it? You think it's real."

"Jillian, that woman was younger than you when her father, Mr. Steadman Nolan—" She stopped for a few seconds, like she was reading her granddaughter's expression to measure how blunt she could be. She picked back up uncensored—"hanged himself over losing that lawsuit. A few months later we started getting a string of anonymous letters making those same claims. The letters went on for a year. In fact, I believe it was a year to the day."

"You think it was her," Jillian returned.

"Yes. I know it was. Back then I thought it was religious nuts threatening us with the vengeance of the Lord. Many were out-raged by the court decision over the lawsuit," Olivia explained. "Those threats could have come from any number of people."

"Did you believe in those curses at the time?"

"Not when I was in a rational state of mind. But as time went on, our lives got worse and worse. Rafe, sinking into alcoholism, until he was no longer able to work, no longer able to—" the words looked brutal for Olivia—"to stay sober, even with continual bouts in rehab. I did everything I knew to do until his father demanded I stop."

"Tough love," Jillian said.

"Jillian, do not give your grandfather that much credit. No, I don't believe that was his motive. Nevertheless, Rafe ended up on the streets, Mr. Fontaine further and further into questionable business deals and practices, and me deeper and deeper in . . . well, in what-ever I'm in. Nothing went right. Not one thing unless you count a mound of money—made by God only knows what means. Then Mr. Fontaine died, then Rafe. Slowly. One day, one drink, at a time."

"But Stella killed him," Jillian interjected. She didn't want Stella absolved of a single ounce of culpability.

"Yes, she did. One way or the other. By curse or blade. And then you came, Jillian, and look what has happened to you. I'm certain that woman was laying a trap for you from the moment you first wandered into her neighborhood. Heaven knows how she found out who you were, but I tell you I won't have it. I want you packed up and gone the second Dr. Sutherland says it's safe for you to travel."

They'd learned that Jillian didn't have a warrant out for her arrest. O had always insisted there wouldn't be. She said she knew from experience that it usually took a whole string of crimes to get arrested, and even then, a lot of people got away scot-free. So at least Jillian no longer had that fear hanging over her.

But even knowing Olivia's motive for wanting her to leave, the words cut like a knife and stung like the knife had been soaked in poison. "I'll have to come back for trial."

"Yes, and we'll deal with that then. You are not safe here."

"Neither are you, O. Come with me."

Those three words again.

"I can't. My place is here. Here in this old house."

"I love this old house," Jillian said, tears burning in her eyes. She'd never said it before, but she realized it was true.

Olivia took her to see Dr. Sutherland as planned on Friday, and after a thorough checkup, he removed her stitches and proudly announced that she was free to fly.

Jillian and Olivia were both quiet in the car on the way home. Olivia shocked Jillian by taking her to a phone store, getting her a new phone, and putting her on a good plan. "I insist on paying for it," Olivia stated flatly. "It's the only way I can make sure you'll feel guilty enough to keep in touch with me."

Jillian's first call was to Jade, to tell her she could come home and that O was going to pay for the plane ticket. She just needed

to know what day and time. Recalling how adamant Jade had
been about her getting back ASAP, Jillian suggested Monday. She'd
looked at flights and told her she'd picked one with an early evening arrival time so Jade wouldn't have to leave work early.

"Who?" Jade asked, missing the whole part about Monday evening.

"Olivia."

"Oh," Jade responded.

"Yes, O. That's her grandmother name."

That had not gone over particularly well but Jade hadn't pressed
it as much as Jillian would have expected. She soon knew why. Jade
had a little tweaking she needed to do with her and Jillian's plans.

"I've got a business trip I absolutely must make. The gallery is
sending me to France to be their eyes on a few pieces they might
want to bring in."

Jillian was completely caught by surprise. "Right now at
Christmastime?"

"Oh no, no, no, silly. I'll be back before Christmas and I want
you home before I even open my suitcase!"

"What day do you want me to schedule the flight?"

"They are still nailing that down. Can I get back to you on that
in the next forty-eight hours?"

"Okay," Jillian answered, trying to wrap her mind around what
had just transpired between them. She knew her mother loved her.
She'd just have to get used to her way again.

More buoyance from Jade. "I can reach you at this new number,
right?"

"Right."

After they hung up, a familiar feeling fell on Jillian like black
lead-weighted wool. It was the one she'd had more times than she
could bear to count within the walls of Saint Sans and, really, well
before that. That feeling that she didn't know where to go. Like her
time had run out in one place before she could line up another.

It preyed on secret fears of homelessness she'd had even in adolescence when her mom reminded her what a loser her father had been. She hadn't done it often. Just when it was convenient. Just when somebody new was moving in and Jillian asked, "Why can't it just be you and me? Why do we have to have a man?" It was always Rafe's fault. He was too big a bum to pay child support.

Her stomach in tight knots, Jillian mustered up the courage to tell Olivia that she'd talked to her mom. She knew Olivia wouldn't put her out but she also knew how anxious the woman was for her to leave.

Olivia dropped her chin nearly to her chest and blew out a deep sigh.

"I'm sorry, O."

Olivia looked at her. "I've never been more relieved in my life."

"You haven't?"

"No. But I'd just as soon you keep that to yourself."

"What about the curse?" Jillian was completely confused.

"Oh, make no mistake, young lady. I have not changed my mind." The determination Jillian saw in Olivia's eyes well supported her words. "I have no intention of keeping you here longterm. It's just that it felt a little rushed."

"But you said yourself the moment Dr. Sutherland released me."

"Yes, I did, and I meant it. But I didn't mean Monday. Well, I did mean Monday, but once it was decided, I meant it less. I thought maybe another few days and then we would undoubtedly be driving one another to distraction. And see what's happened? By the time Jewel gets back—"

"Jade."

"By the time Jade gets back, we'll be on each other's last nerve. Don't you think?"

"Undoubtedly."

"We won't even be speaking by then. Let's do it right then."

CHAPTER 54

Adella was as nervous as a cat.

"Woman, you're going to wrench your neck with all that strain-ing and ogling and craning." Emmett was seated on the end of the pew with AJ several empty spaces down from him and Trevor Don several empty spaces down from him. Tonya, the new love of Trevor Don's life, was right next to him, where she'd been most every service since they'd gotten sweet on each other.

"Where under the heavenly hosts are they?" Adella showed Emmett the time on her phone. "I told them to be early. Wait!" she exclaimed, slapping him on the shoulder. "I see them!"

It was all Jillian's doing. She'd seen the flyer Adella had thumb-tacked on the bulletin board in the utility room and pointed out that the date, December 15, was Rafe's birthday. His first birthday since they'd buried him. Jillian had the idea—both brilliant and insane, in Adella's opinon—of inviting Olivia to the Christmas program. Never mind that Adella had been posting a similar flyer every year for the past eight years and Olivia had never batted an eyelash at it. Never mind that church was the last place on earth Adella ever expected to see Olivia Fontaine.

When she expressed her misgivings to Jillian, the girl had shrugged and said, "Stranger things have happened. Like Bully. Caryn says the doctors believe he is responding to stuff they're saying to him."

"Like Bully, sure as the world." Adella had to give the girl that. It was a wonder if she'd ever seen one.

"Do you think that's a miracle, Adella?"

"I do, honey. I sure do. And you're going to need one yourself if you're hoping to show up at that church on December 15 with your grandmother in tow."

Until Adella saw Olivia Fontaine with her very own eyes in the back of that church sanctuary, she still believed they'd more likely have a pair of giraffes singing second soprano in the choir that night than Olivia planted in a pew.

But lo and behold, Jillian's plan had worked. She'd reported every delicious detail to Adella. She'd front-run the whole thing by going to David and Caryn. She sat them down on the edge of Caryn's bed and delivered them a moving address on the day's significance, getting them all lathered up with sympathy. Then when they were all soft and squishy, she dropped the catch on them: they'd have to come too. Of course, they'd balked and squawked and whined, but they couldn't deny that the chances of getting Olivia there in a group was a far sight better than getting her there in a pair. Jillian knew Mrs. Winsee would be a piece of cake. She loved outings.

Jillian waited until all five of them were in the kitchen deliriously happy over a huge pot of Uncle Wayne's Winter White Chili and nearly drunk over the smell of chopped fresh cilantro. She brought it up casually while grating a pound of Colby. "Since I'm leaving on the twentieth, I thought maybe you four could give me an early Christmas present." She'd grinned and most had grinned back. According to Jillian, Olivia instantly looked suspicious, and it was little wonder to Adella, though she didn't tell Jillian why. Olivia once told her that the girl was the hardest person to give anything to that she'd ever met.

As planned, the inquiry was made regarding Jillian's specific wish for her early Christmas present.

"A night out! All five of us!" she announced with ill-fitting enthusiasm.

Mrs. Winsee hopped to her feet to grab her purse. Caryn and David shouted out guesses with performances that could have qualified them for a game show. Jillian launched into a sentimental oratory about what all Adella had done for her and how she had no way to repay her kindness and how Adella had put that flyer up every year for eight years in a row, but understandably, none of them wanted to go. They'd all nodded at this point because they hadn't. Well, all except Mrs. Winsee, but she couldn't very well go by herself, the way she'd been going out the front door in her slip.

"Why couldn't we do it this one time for Adella?" Jillian had presented, and from what David reported to Adella, she might as well have had a cellist playing behind her. David and Caryn couldn't act too anxious or they'd give themselves away, so they grumbled and complained until Jillian stared them down for over-doing it. They turned on a dime and announced that, for Adella's sake, how could they possibly say no? Mrs. Winsee applauded zealously. And Olivia took a bite of Uncle Wayne's Winter White Chili, swallowed it, and looked thoughtful for a moment before asking if anybody else at the table thought maybe Jillian had mis-calculated the cumin.

"Please say yes, O!"

"Not going."

"Why not?"

"Don't want to."

"Do you always have to do everything just like you want to?"

"Yes. That's what old widows get to do if they have the cash."

"You're not that old."

"I'm too old to go to a church Christmas program. Next you'll ask us all to wear matching Christmas sweaters."

No thought on earth could have delighted Mrs. Winsee more. She was up, lickety-split, looking through her closet. The other three glared at Olivia, trying to will sufficient guilt on her.

"Not going." That was that.

But here she was in Adella Atwater's very church, looking surlier than ever. Adella waved like she was starting a car race. She leaned over to Emmett and whispered, "I can tell you right now what got her here."

"What?" he asked.

"Vida Winsee, that's what."

"And Jesus," Emmett added with appropriate emphasis.

"No doubt about that, Emmett Atwater. And tonight Jesus has come to Benton Avenue Baptist Church wearing Vida Winsee's eyebrow pencil."

Emmett got so tickled that he had a fit of coughing, causing Adella to dig through her purse for a cough drop, which she was unable to find before her five guests filed up to the pew with all the Christmas cheer of prisoners walking the plank. "Here!" she said, handing him the only thing she could find.

And Emmett, being the gentleman he was, stood and stepped into the aisle to greet their guests and invite them to take their seats. Somehow, in the confusion, he handed David the plastic jar of multicolored fiber-supplement gummies instead of shaking his hand. David, being equally the gentleman, sat down on the pew, the whitest man who had ever darkened those doors, and cradled them in his arms with conscientious bewilderment.

AJ scooted down by Trevor Don, who was more than happy to scoot closer to Tonya. Caryn sat next to AJ, then David, then Jillian, then Mrs. Winsee. Olivia snarled like a bulldog next to Mrs. Winsee and Adella perched on the verge of an anxiety attack next to Olivia. Emmett closed the row per Adella's request. His legs were so long, an uncomfy patron of the religious arts might be less apt to attempt an escape with him guarding the exit.

The lights went down and a single violin played the slow and haunting melody of "O Come, O Come, Emmanuel." A two-hundred-voice choir wove in the lyrics as the instruments responded to the violin's irrepressible call to worship.

The program was to be an extravaganza, just like every year. The whole choir was participating, and the worship team and the band members and the organist and the keyboard player. They even had a small orchestra, complete with a harpist. The stage—for that matter, the whole church—was all done up for Christmas. There was a black velvet backdrop with electric twinkling lights so it looked like nighttime and a stable right on the stage that looked so real Adella could swear she smelled hay. And she couldn't wait to see Flo Deever's grandbaby as this year's baby Jesus. Flo's daughter had just come back to Jesus last June and here she was, playing the Virgin Mary. That right there was just how God was.

The spotlight shone on the stable as a young woman walked onstage with a baby cradled in her arms and Sister Liz Anne began the narration. The little one kicked his legs and fussed right on cue while the audience oohed and aahed.

Adella bent forward, looked past both Olivia and Mrs. Winsee, and whispered, "Psssssssst! Jillian!" Everybody within eight square feet heard her except the one she was after.

Undeterred, Adella leaned across the curmudgeon's lap. "Mrs. Winsee, get Jillian!" That Olivia had not offered a hearty narration all her own right there in the house of the Lord was no small sparing.

Then Emmett had to stick his nose into it. "Shhhhh, woman! You're disturbing the peace."

Adella batted at Emmett with her left hand, and with her right, she motioned to Mrs. Winsee to punch Jillian. Jillian leaned forward and cocked her head at Adella, who pointed toward the stage and said, "Flo Deever's girl! She's the one I told you about. That's her son, Jesus."

The whole row all the way down to Trevor Don and Tonya swung their heads toward Adella. "What I mean is," she said, clearing up any blasphemy, "that's her son *playing* Jesus."

Olivia shot her eyes toward Jillian and back toward Adella. When Adella caught a glimpse of Jillian's alarmed expression over Olivia's shoulder, she realized she'd let the cat right out of the bag concerning the setup.

Adella sat back so fast she nearly gave herself whiplash, but what she got instead was a hot flash. She grabbed the prayer sheet out of her purse and fanned herself wildly, stopping just short of blowing Emmett's necktie. Emmett turned his head down toward her and whispered in her ear, "Unless you can find your name somewhere on the program for tonight's presentation, may I suggest you leave the narration to Brother Cecil and Sister Liz Anne?"

Sister Liz Anne started up again like she was doing it to Adella out of pure spite. "Mary sat down and leaned against the outside of the stable, propped the baby on her lap, and taking a strip of linen and tying back her hair, she began to stare into his tiny face."

Flo Deever's girl did exactly that. Emmett sat up tall and looked around the audience, obviously trying to spot somebody. He whispered to Adella, "Don't you know Flo's as pleased as a kitten with a ball of wool?"

"Shhhhhh, man!" Adella responded with no small satisfaction. "You're disturbing the peace. With you jabbering and jawing, not a soul for three rows can make out a word Sister Liz Anne is saying." Adella knew good and well he was trying to make up with her after closing her spirit.

"Mary had never seen the moon so bright. The night was nearly as light as the day. Only hours old, the baby's chin quivered. His eyes were shaped like almonds and were as black as the deepest well. She held him tightly and quietly hummed a song she'd learned as a child. She had been so frightened of this moment, so sure she would not know what to do. She had never held an infant so small, and he was God, wrapped in soft, infant flesh, with bones so fragile she felt like he could break. But every fear, every doubt, every inadequacy was momentarily caught up in the indescribable rapture of a mother's affection."

Adella felt Olivia jerk like she'd had a sudden stomach cramp and then shift around uncomfortably. Adella picked her purse up off the floor and whispered, "I've got a roll of antacids somewhere in here. Need it?" She rummaged around in her purse.

Olivia curled her lips in a most unflattering fashion and mouthed the word *no*.

Sister Liz Anne kept on and on like no one at all had a stomach cramp. "Mary remembered asking Elizabeth things she dared not ask her dad and mother. 'What am I to do when he comes?' Her cousin's reply would remain etched upon Mary's heart long after her son had saved the world. 'He will tell you what he needs from you. Beyond what he needs, all he wants is for you to embrace him and talk to him.' She looked into his delicate face and watched him closely as he seemed to stare deeply into the moonlit sky. And she began to talk. 'Sweet baby boy. Do you know who your Daddy is? Do you know your name? Do you know why you're here?'"

Olivia made a strange sound. Adella couldn't quite put a name to it. It was almost akin to a grunt, only slightly more ladylike, but nothing short of a hand grenade was stopping Sister Liz Anne's narration.

"A tear dropped from Mary's chin to the baby boy's. He yawned and made such a funny expression she grinned, wiping her face on the yellowed rags she'd draped around him. The fussing calf had obviously found its mother. Not a sound was coming from inside the stable. The earth stilled. The infant slept. She held the babe next to her face, and for just a moment, all the world silenced to the breath of God."

The odd sound happened again but this time louder. Maybe Olivia was choking. Adella leaned over to Emmett and said, "Olivia's having some kind of spell. Stay on your toes in case you have to do the Heineken maneuver."

Emmett looked past his wife to Olivia and then back at his wife and said, "*Heimlich.* She looks fine to me." He pointed to Sister Liz Anne. "Pay attention."

"Mary closed her eyes and listened, stealing time like a hidden metronome. As high and as wide as she dared to think, she still could not begin to comprehend. She, a common child of the most humble means, who had never read the Scriptures for herself, was embracing the incarnate Word. The Son of God Most High rested in her inexperienced arms, sleeping to the rhythm of her heart."

David's eyes nearly popped out of his head when a children's choir, cherub-faced and robed in white with big red bows, filed onto the stage to share the spotlight with a soloist. Adella grinned, knowing precisely what was coming. She knew that woman's voice could melt the bones of a bull moose and give the likes of Mariah Carey a run for her money. With no small satisfaction, she watched David close his eyes and press his palm to his chest as if the sound transcended what a human heart was built to bear. With the fever pitch of the final lines, David looked so overwrought Adella thought he might throw himself into the aisle in a fit of somersaults.

The spotlight returned to the stable, where the young woman sat beneath the twinkling stars, the baby snug in her arms. Sister Liz Anne spoke one last time. Adella didn't mind, seeing how Flo Deever's girl was doing such a fine job up there on the stage. She intended to tell Flo—and mean it—that she'd never seen a better Virgin Mary.

"This time Mary hummed a song she did not know, a song being sung by the choir of angels hovering over her head but hidden from her carnal senses. The deafening hallelujahs of the heavenly hosts were silent to mortal ears except through the voice of a young woman who had unknowingly given human notes to a holy score. The glory of God filled the earth. Heaven hammered a bridge, but one young woman sat completely unaware of all that swelled the atmosphere around her. The tiny baby boy had robbed her heart. *So this is what it feels like to be a mother,* she mused. She crept back into the stable, wrapped him in swaddling clothes, and laid him in the manger. Just down the path, the sun peeked gently over the roof of an inn full of barren souls who had made him no room."

The mic went to Brother Cecil, whose commanding voice popped the words right off the page of Saint Luke's second chapter, gave them legs, and sent them leaping into the atmosphere and landing on eager listeners.

"'And in the same region there were shepherds out in the field, keeping watch over their flock by night. And an angel of the Lord appeared to them, and the glory of the Lord shone around them, and they were filled with great fear. And the angel said to them,

"Fear not, for behold, I bring you good news of great joy that will be for all the people. For unto you is born this day in the city of David a Savior, who is Christ the Lord. And this will be a sign for you: you will find a baby wrapped in swaddling cloths and lying in a manger." And suddenly there was with the angel a multitude of the heavenly host praising God and saying, "Glory to God in the highest, and on earth peace among those with whom he is pleased!""""

With that the narration ceased, and more than two hundred voices and twenty instruments burst into song with volume enough to blow the halos off the heavenly hosts. Notes shot heavenward like fireworks.

O come, all ye faithful, joyful and triumphant,
O come ye, O come ye to Bethlehem;
Come and behold Him, born the King of Angels;

O come, let us adore Him,
O come, let us adore Him,
O come, let us adore Him,
Christ, the Lord!

David jumped to his feet, sending the supplements rolling. All over the room people stood and applauded and raised their hands. Some of the women waved white hankies. Mrs. Winsee yelled, "Bravo! Bravo!" and nobody acted like she shouldn't. David grabbed Jillian's hand and pulled her to her feet, wrapped his arms around her and squeezed her tight.

Everyone stood as far as Adella could see. Everyone except Olivia.

Olivia sat with her jaw fixed, her back rigid, and her hands firmly planted on her knees. Suddenly her head dropped forward and a sound came out of her mouth with a volume that could have curdled blood if not for all the clapping.

Startled, Adella bent over her and asked with ample volume, "Are you alright?" When Adella put her hand on Olivia's shoulder and felt her breath break and spasm, the realization hit her hard. The concrete dam had broken wide open and so had the heart of a mother of an only son. Olivia began to wail.

Adella whirled around and glared panic-stricken at Emmett. "Do something!" she said. So he did. He stepped around Adella, sat down next to Olivia, put his arm around her, and gently pressed her head to his shoulder. She buried her face in the lapel of his suit coat and cried the kind of cry that erupts from somewhere way down deep after being pent up way too long. He pulled a white handkerchief from his inside coat pocket and handed it to Olivia while Adella patted him on the shoulder to keep him at it.

Whether or not the rest of the row was fully aware of the spectacle was unclear to Adella, the way Mrs. Winsee had gone to hula dancing. Adella never saw Olivia look Emmett in the face or speak a word to him but she knew that man of hers. He had need of neither. Toward the end of the song, Emmett took Olivia by both her shoulders and prompted her upward to her feet. He braced her by one arm just in case.

Pastor Sam walked onto the stage with an infectious smile that stretched a country mile. Brother Cecil handed him a mic, and he greeted the joyful throng saying, "Glory to God!" with every syllable standing on its own, none weaker than the last: *"GLOW-REE TO GOD!"*

The congregation broke into a rousing applause of unpretentious love.

"Welcome, congregation, friends, and guests! How many of you are glad that you came to this house of the Lord tonight?"

The audience cheered. Well, most of it did. Adella spied the

whole row and surmised that if Trevor Don and Tonya even knew
where they were, she was a monkey's uncle. Caryn and AJ laughed
and high-fived. Adella intended to find out what that was all
about when she got that boy back in the truck. David looked one
breeze shy of a bodily rapture. Jillian's eyebrows were raised and her
expression uncertain, but she didn't look unhappy. Mrs. Winsee,
having grabbed Emmett's sopping wet handkerchief from Olivia,
was waving it with enough vigor to black somebody's eye. Olivia
had recovered somewhat and reset her stoic jaw, and Emmett was
standing tall and looking straight ahead like nothing had ever
happened.

Adella put her arm around his waist. "Remind me," she whispered up toward his ear nice and loud, "to marry you all over again."

Accompanied by the keyboard, Pastor Sam said to the congregation, "I'll just keep you good folks on your feet for a moment if you'd be so kind. We've come under this roof for one reason tonight. We've come to celebrate the birth of King Jesus, the holy Christ, the Son of God."

*Amen*s and *hallelujah*s sprang like leaks from pipes bursting with living waters.

"But Jesus didn't come just to live," Pastor Sam continued. "Jesus, the spotless Lamb of God, came to die. By divine plan from before time began, Jesus came to give his perfect life on a cross, bearing all our sin and shame, so that whosoever will—"

Cheers of "Whosoever will!"

"I said, whosoever will!"

Folks looked around at one another, nodding. *"He said whosoever will!"*

Pastor Sam picked it back up. "So that whosoever will, let him come, turning from his own way and believing on Jesus' name, embracing his free gift of grace that no one can earn. . . .

Does anybody in the house understand what I'm saying to them tonight?"

Shouts of affirmation all but shook the chandelier.

"That man or that woman, that boy or girl, whosoever will confess Jesus as Lord, in that very moment will be saved. And nothing—no demon from hell—can snatch you from his Father's hand. No matter what you've done, where you've been, what you've seen, or who's your kin, I mean *you*. Has anybody in this house besides me found out the hard way that your own way led you the wrong way? Anybody in this house besides me found out you can't save yourself? Anybody in this house besides me found out that no other human on earth, try as he may, could save you either?"

Hands waved wildly.

"We'll not tarry long," the pastor promised, "but we'd be terribly remiss not to give you a chance to respond. In the apostle Paul's letter to the Romans, he told us just what to do." Pastor Sam opened up a Bible and read it word for word, his eyes sparkling as bright as the lights on the black velvet backdrop. "'If you openly declare that Jesus is Lord and believe in your heart that God raised him from the dead, you will be saved. For it is by believing in your heart that you are made right with God, and it is by openly declaring your faith that you are saved. As the Scriptures tell us, "Anyone who trusts in him will never be disgraced."' The tenth chapter and the thirteenth verse says it just like this: 'Everyone who calls on the name of the Lord will be saved.' Did I say *everyone*, congregation?"

"You said everyone!"

"But nobody can come to Jesus for you. Brother Isaac is going to keep playing that keyboard for a few more minutes, and if the gift you want this Christmas is Jesus, he's yours for the taking. Whether you've done well at love or failed at love, you've never in your life been loved like Jesus loves you. Will you receive it today? Will you have the boldness to step out of that row and walk right up front, right now? We won't embarrass you. I'll just pray a simple prayer with you and bless you to go on your way, a new creation, saved and secured by the blood of the Lamb."

Adella normally loved this part. But now she fidgeted, shifting her weight from one foot to the other, wondering if Pastor Sam's version of "not tarrying long" was causing anybody else's ankles to swell. She glanced up to see Emmett smiling and nodding, so she knew folks were going forward. She saw a light come on in her purse and opened it with the toe of her shoe. It was a text from AJ. She knew that because she'd enlarged the text font till she could have read it on a billboard a mile off. **I'm starving. When is this going to be over?**

She leaned forward to give him the awful look he'd earned and there was Jillian, looking past Mrs. Winsee to mouth something to Olivia. Adella squinted her eyes to see if she could read the girl's lips.

Come with me.

All Adella could see of Olivia was the back of her head, but even from the back, she could tell that head was shaking. Jillian mouthed the word *please*, and this time, Olivia's head didn't move at all. Adella's jaw nearly came unhinged when Jillian excused herself in front of David, Caryn, AJ, Trevor Don, and Tonya and stepped into that aisle.

Before Adella could get her wits reassembled, Mrs. Winsee trailed right behind Jillian down the row and out into the aisle. Adella threw her hands on her hips, knowing good and well exactly what had happened. Lodged between Jillian and Olivia, she'd thought Jillian was talking to her. David looked like he'd seen a ghost and Caryn leaned forward and mouthed, *Want me to go grab her?*

"Good Lord." This came from Olivia, who stepped on nearly every pair of feet between her and the aisle before heading down front in hot pursuit.

No one dared ask what happened up front when Jillian, Mrs.

Winsee, and Olivia returned, particularly since Olivia hadn't made it in time to fetch Mrs. Winsee back to her seat before Pastor Sam led them in prayer. They all avoided looking at each other even when Pastor Sam told them to extend the right hand of fellowship and say *Merry Christmas* to all and to all a good night.

As the residents of Saint Sans joined a sea of congregants in the aisles toward the exits, the choir sang a most robust benediction with a glorious gospel music flair.

> *Joy to the world! the Lord is come;*
> *Let earth receive her King;*
> *Let ev'ry heart prepare Him room,*
> *And heav'n and nature sing,*
> *And heav'n and nature sing,*
> *And heav'n, and heav'n and nature sing.*
>
> *Joy to the world! the Savior reigns;*
> *Let men their songs employ;*
> *While fields and floods, rocks, hills, and plains*
> *Repeat the sounding joy,*
> *Repeat the sounding joy,*
> *Repeat, repeat the sounding joy.*
>
> *No more let sins and sorrows grow,*
> *Nor thorns infest the ground;*
> *He comes to make His blessings flow*
> *Far as the curse is found,*
> *Far as the curse is found,*
> *Far as, far as the curse is found.*

CHAPTER 55

"I KNOW YOU HATE TO SEE HER GO." Adella was in the kitchen with Olivia, who was looking over an e-mail of an estimate for the cost of pouring a new driveway. She knew Olivia wouldn't want to talk about it but somebody had to.

Olivia kept her eyes fixed on the screen. "Since I hated to see her come, I suppose it's fitting. Did you have any idea cement could cost this much?"

"Olivia, you've done well."

"Don't be ridiculous. We both know better than that."

Adella pulled out a stool and sat down right next to her. "I want you to listen to what I have to say to you, Olivia Fontaine, and see if you can find it in your heart not to make me walk away from here feeling like I wasted my breath."

Olivia didn't look up, but she did at least fold her hands beneath her chin and stare past the laptop screen.

389

"Do you remember six months ago when you walked into this very room and saw that young woman standing here, not three feet from where we're sitting?"

"Unfortunately, my memories of that day are crystal clear."

"That same young woman who stood in this room, a stranger to her father's house and as hostile as a prickly pear cactus, will hug at least half a dozen people good-bye tomorrow in a puddle of tears. She will fly out of this city a different person than she came—and leave all of us changed."

"I hate good-byes."

"I know you do. I'm not all that kindly disposed to them myself, but as Emmett says, learning to say good-bye is a necessary life skill. And anyway, it won't be forever."

"Oh yes, it will. With the Nolan woman taking that preposterous plea bargain, there will be no trial requiring Jillian to return to New Orleans. She'll get to San Francisco, go on with her life, and never look back. As well she should."

Adella, like the rest of Saint Sans, had been horrified by the plea bargain. The prosecutor insisted that a guaranteed twenty-five years for Stella Nolan behind bars was better than taking the chance on a jury getting sentimental over how the Fontaines had wronged her and left her desperate. The woman insisted she never saw Bully in front of her car that night. The reason she'd been in a hurry, she said, was that she'd had a change of heart. She was rushing off to free Jillian and then turn herself in. All she'd meant to do when she took Jillian to the storage unit, she claimed, was to show her proof of the connection between their two families. Assaulting her and tying her up had been William Crawley's doing. He'd supposedly threatened to kill Stella if she told anyone where Jillian was being held. It was he who'd planned to demand ransom money and run with it. It was also he who had found Rafe's pocketknife in an alley. Stella had no earthly idea who'd stabbed Rafe. All she'd known was that it wasn't her. She could never have hurt him. She loved him too much.

Adella knew better. The woman had been eaten alive by her quest for revenge. Like so many, she clung to the belief that money would fix the wrongs done to her and her family. Since her father's wealth had gone to the Fontaines through Olivia's husband's shady business dealings, she tried to get her hooks into Rafe. Then when Rafe rejected her, she apparently determined to destroy him and his family. No telling how long Stella had plotted, and when Jillian showed up in town, the plan easily expanded to draw her in.

But Stella's carefully woven claims won the day, especially since Crawley was in a psychiatric unit, unable to string ten intelligible words together. Of course, no one with half a brain believed a word of it, but the prosecution would be carrying the burden of proof in an oil-slick courtroom. The prosecutor's concerns about potential sentimentality seemed chillingly validated by a public outcry demanding special protection for Stella Nolan after her lawyer stated that she feared reprisals behind bars from members of law enforcement.

"The world's gone crazy and we with it," Adella had told Emmett the day the plea agreement was signed. "Her raggedy tail is getting away with murder."

"You know better than that, Dell. There's a higher court," he'd said.

The consolation—and no small one—was that neither Jillian nor Olivia would be subjected to a long, drawn-out trial or the media circus that would surround it. Jillian would never have to lay eyes on Stella again and Stella wouldn't soon lay eyes on Orleans Parish. The irony right that moment in the kitchen with Olivia was that this meant they might never lay eyes on Jillian again.

"She's planning on coming back for Easter," Adella reminded Olivia.

Olivia looked at her. "She thinks she will, but by that time, she'll have moved on. She'll have better things to do."

"Better than the Easter cantata? What, I ask you, could be better than the Easter cantata? If you think the Christmas pageant was spectacular, just wait till you see this. Last year's Jesus was so convincing, I nearly—"

"I'm still recovering from the Christmas pageant, Adella." Olivia put her hand up as she said it, but Adella was almost positive she was suppressing something akin to a grin.

"I'll shut up with this. When that stone rolls away right there on that stage and he comes strutting out of that tomb alive, well, we'll just see if you can keep from throwing a shoe. You better have a spare pair because I'm telling you right now, it doesn't get better than that. Jillian won't miss it for anything. I'm going to pray about it. He who has begun a good work between the two of you—and I'm talking about the real Jesus here and not some actor—he will complete it."

Olivia rubbed her chin and nodded. "Thank you." She woke up her laptop and looked back at the estimate. "Well, we'll make the best of it tonight."

"You still going with the stuffed flounder?"

"No, she changed her mind."

"Again?"

"As of last night at bedtime, she'd settled on creole shrimp and cheese grits."

"The one with the andouille sausage?"

"Yes. Imagine that."

"It should be some mild consolation to you that the girl will leave with good taste. Dessert?"

"She wants to take a container of pralines home with her on the plane. I told her I'd send her some, but she insisted on my making them right in front of her so she'd know just how to do it. We'll make those together later this afternoon. Our formal dessert is David's rum cake. He made it last night so it could soak for twenty-four hours."

"You're messin' with me now."

"You're welcome to stay. You may as well see it through. You brought her here."

Adella supposed those last four words conjured up as many mixed emotions for Olivia as they did for her. How Adella and Olivia had survived that whole debacle with Jillian was anybody's guess but God's.

"David and Caryn have offered to take her to the airport tomorrow morning. At least I won't have to go through that ordeal."

"*What?*" Adella couldn't button her lip to save her life. "Olivia Fontaine, you thank David and Caryn kindly for the offer, but you tell them in no uncertain terms that you will take your own granddaughter to the airport." She wasn't about to let her get away with regressing like that.

"I don't think I can do it. It would be too awkward there on the curb. I don't know what I'd say. We've all got our limitations, Adella. You'd get along better with the rest of humanity if you'd recognize that."

"You drive me crazy, Olivia Fontaine. Stark raving mad. No wonder Mrs. Winsee runs around here in her unders. I've got no problem with limitations, I'll have you know. But I do have a problem with renaming preferences 'limitations.' Here's what you say on the curb, plain and simple: 'I love you, Jillian. I'm glad you are my granddaughter. I don't want to lose touch with you.'"

"It's easy for you to say stuff like that, Adella."

"No, it's not! It's *worth it* to me to say stuff like that. You don't say that kind of thing because it's easy. You say that kind of thing because it's true and you want the person to know it. You look them in the eye and say it even if your face turns red and you break out in a sweat."

"I don't think I can do that without making a fool of myself."

"Why? Because you just might shed a tear? So what? What would be wrong with her seeing that your heart hurts to see her go?" Adella stood and put her hands on her hips. "My grand-mother Waddell and I stood at my granddaddy's casket together when I was sixteen years old. I was trying to stay strong and keep a stiff upper lip for her sake, but she wasn't buying it. She took me by the hand and said, 'Baby girl, you let those tears fall and I'll let mine, too. The pain of a hard good-bye is the heart's tribute to the privilege to love.' We stood right there, hand in hand, and cried together with no shame. To this day, it is the sweetest memory I have of my grandmother. Now, stop feeling sorry for yourself, and let your sorrow pay tribute to the privilege you've had to get to know this young woman and like her enough to wish she didn't have to go."

The front doorbell rang. Adella walked toward it in a huff and never gladder to be in one. She'd felt like crying all the way over here today thinking about saying her own farewell to Jillian. What she needed was to get good and mad at Olivia, and then she wouldn't feel so sad. In fact, she had a good mind to spend this very day recollecting all the ways that woman had nearly put her in a padded cell.

Come to think of it, Jillian herself had been as big a pain in the neck as Adella guessed she'd ever had. Just the thought of how that girl acted when they pulled up in front of Saint Sans for the first time was enough to churn up the acid in Adella's stomach. Then there was all the stomping off and the stolen money and the pregnancy test and the what all and what for and every conceiv-able what-on-earth. It was nonstop theatrics. Always something to worry about.

And why else had Adella been late to work that morning except that she had to go to the police station to get those ridiculous pajamas? She was going to have to wash and dry them right there at Saint Sans because they stank to high heaven from who-knows-what-else was in that evidence room. And then she was going to have to go hide in the garage and wrap them in tissue and put them in the gift bag she'd picked up at the Walgreens. That's how it had been from the first day she'd laid eyes on that girl.

Adella rubbed her tingling nose on her sleeve and opened the front door just in time to see the UPS truck rolling away from the curb.

"You expecting a Christmas order?" she asked Olivia as she walked back through the great room with the package.

"I can't recall if I'm expecting anything else or not. What's the store?"

Adella read the return address. "Huh. It's not from a store at all. It says it's from Saint Andrew's."

Olivia glanced at the box. "Is that a hospital?"

"No, it's that old Methodist church on North Rampart."

"The Vieux Carré?"

"That's what it says. What do you think it is? It's fairly heavy."

"My telepathic abilities don't kick in until after my second pot of coffee, Adella. You'll either have to wait until I have consumed it or open the package for yourself." Olivia got up and turned on the flame under the water kettle.

Adella pulled a slender knife out of the acacia block, sliced through the packing tape, and opened the flaps of the cardboard box. "Whatever it is, it's been wound in enough bubble wrap to take me till Christmas to open." After fiddling around inside the box, she added, "It's two different items they've got mummified here." She set them both on the counter, still wrapped tight, before pulling out a sealed envelope and waving it toward Olivia. "And here's this." It bore the printed return address for Saint Andrew's, but it wasn't addressed to anyone.

Olivia reached for the canister of coffee beans. "Read away. I'm listening."

Adella tore the envelope open and pulled out the sheet of letterhead. "It's addressed 'To whom it may concern.'"

"Are you concerned?" Olivia asked dryly.

"You know full well that I can hardly bear the suspense." That was the truth if Adella had ever told it.

"Then get on with it."

> To whom it may concern:
>
> These items were found recently in a storage room that had to be emptied for renovations. The large closet unfortunately had not undergone inspection in many years and had become a dust-collecting depository for articles with unclear destinations. Most of the contents were taken to the Dumpster, where they belonged. Thankfully, our custodian had the wherewithal to retrieve these two articles before they were never to be seen again.
>
> We have no idea how these items came into our church's possession. Our guess is that they were sent to us by the Methodist council when the doors of St. Silvanus were permanently closed. We felt that it was appropriate to send them back to their proper home. They are treasures indeed to those who hold such things sacred. If you have no use for them, please contact us at the number above, and we will happily drop by and pick them up. Several of us would be pleased to see what you've done with the old church anyway.
>
> Blessings to all of you this holiday season.

"The letter is signed by the pastor's admin," Adella stated, as curious as a cat.

"Well, don't tarry then. We might as well see what the good people of Saint Andrew's consider 'treasures indeed.'"

Adella had already cut the tape on one of the items and started unrolling a laborious stretch of bubble wrap before Olivia could say *indeed*. "Would you looky here?" She held up a rather sizable gold-plated chalice. "Isn't it gorgeous?"

Taking it from her hand, Olivia studied the cup carefully.

"This right here can only be one thing, shaped this way," Adella deduced, picking up the other item. "It's got to be the bread plate."

Sure enough, it was. Olivia slid her palm along the bottom of it and then held the plate eye-level, studying it from the side. "He has a few small dents in him, but most one-hundred-year-olds do, I'd say. They call this a paten, don't they?"

"Yes'm. That's correct. Why do you suppose they think these belonged to Saint Silvanus?"

Olivia gave Adella an innocuous look and turned the plate over. The words were engraved in the center.

Saint Silvanus Methodist Church
Est. 1918

"Well, the cup says no such thing." Adella turned it over to prove it. "It just has a small—"

"SSM," Olivia interrupted. "Which just might correspond with Saint Silvanus Methodist. Adella, you may as well go ahead and give in to the reading glasses more than once in a blue moon when you think nobody's looking. They're coming to take you over sooner or later."

"*SSM* also corresponds with Sister Smart Mouth, and my confusion was understandable since it would have been addressed to the same residence."

Both women were so preoccupied with the relics, they didn't

hear Jillian walk into the great room until she set her phone down forcefully on the kitchen island. "I'm not going," she announced, sounding as mad as a shot hog.

"You're not going where?" Olivia inquired, getting back to the business of coffee beans.

"I'm not going to San Francisco."

"Of course you are. You're just getting the jitters." Olivia turned on the grinder.

"I do not have the jitters, O!" Jillian yelled over the loud whir.

Olivia shut off the grinder, poured the grounds into the French press, and turned to face her granddaughter. "Whatever you have, you'll be over it by morning, because I promised your mother you'd be on that plane and on that plane you'll be."

"You can put me on a plane if you want to, O, but it will not be to San Francisco. I don't care where else you send me. Put me on a plane to Haiti. But I don't want to go to San Francisco. Please, O."

Adella started to butt in but Olivia gave her the stop signal with the palm of her right hand and appeared serious about it.

"Jillian, let's turn down the histrionics a bit and talk reasonably." Adella could tell Olivia was measuring every word and trying to stay calm. "Tell me what happened."

"Look for yourself!" Jillian picked up her phone and handed it to Olivia.

"Hmmm" was all Olivia said.

Adella looked good and hard at Olivia and then did the same with Jillian. Throwing both her hands up, she said, "Don't either one of you mind me. I'll just stand here and get the twisted gut."

"May I?" Olivia asked Jillian, holding the phone tentatively toward Adella.

"Be my guest!"

Adella snatched the phone out of Olivia's hand and read the texts not once but twice.

Hi, Mom! Hope you're getting over your jet lag. I'm almost packed. Heading to the airport late tomorrow morning. Looking forward to seeing you. Feels like forever. Did it work out where you can come get me? It's OK if you can't. I can take a cab. Just let me know.

Hi Jillian! Still jet-lagged but deliriously happy. I have a surprise for you! Someone I'm anxious for you to meet. He's coming with me to pick you up. We'll be the ones in baggage claim looking like newlyweds.

As much as she hated to admit it, Adella could think of only one thing to say. "Hmmm."

"Can you believe it?" Jillian's voice was at fever pitch. "*That's* what she was doing in France after she'd demanded that I come home as soon as the doctor said I could fly. She was on a honeymoon!"

Adella muttered, "Well, that's a fine kettle of fish. One fine kettle of fish."

Olivia sucked in her top lip and jutted out her chin. "Adella, if you wouldn't mind meditating silently for a moment while I remind Jillian how undone her mother was over all she's been through. Your mother loves you, Jillian. You can take my word on that one because it doesn't come naturally to me to take up for—"

"Jewel." Adella couldn't help herself. The licking she'd like to give that woman with her purse right now wouldn't be fit to be rated PG-13.

"*Jade,*" Olivia corrected. "Adella, don't you have something to do?"

Jillian hardly took a breath. "I didn't say she didn't love me, O. I know she does. She always has. But I don't have it in me right now to move in with her and another new man. It's too much." She shook her head. "I am so tired of being the extra person in the house. I'm so tired of bouncing around and not belonging anywhere. I just want my own place." She turned and walked back toward her room, defeat rolling from her shoulders like she was five decades older. "No worries. I'll go to San Francisco."

"Oh no, you won't!" Adella and Olivia said the words in unison as if they'd practiced for months. They were so shocked by their perfect synchronization, they glared at one another like they were looking into a carnival mirror.

Adella was glad Olivia spoke first. After all, she had no claim on Saint Sans except on her knees in her prayer closet.

"Jillian, this is your home. You belong here. You are not an extra. Not anymore. You can live here as long as you want. And when the day comes that you want a place of your own, this will still be your place to come home to. That room will be yours as long as I'm alive."

Jillian had stopped to listen but she didn't turn around. With her back to her grandmother, she apologized. "I've put you in a difficult position, O. I'm so sorry. What other choice did I leave you but to say that?"

"Jillian Slater, you have plenty of money to get a place of your own. It is in an account with your name on it as we speak. It won't buy you a mansion unless you want to spend every dime of it right off the bat, but it will afford you a small place with ample character that will be more than sufficient. The money was your father's, and you are his sole heir. The banker is awaiting your signatures on the appropriate documents. I'd planned to have you sign them before you flew out in the morning."

Jillian turned and stared at Olivia with equal parts shock and confusion. She shifted her gaze to Adella.

"Don't look at me, honey. This is the first I've heard about any of this."

Olivia took a deep breath. "You have enough to check into a hotel in San Francisco until you find a place to live as long as you don't tarry. You have my blessing to do that, Jillian. Or there might be another city you prefer. A city, say, for instance, with a poorer view than the Golden Gate but embarrassingly better food. You have options." She cleared her throat. "The only thing you *don't* have is no place to go. You don't have to decide right away. Take some time to think about it."

Jillian held her chin up and met Olivia's gaze. "I don't need time, O. I want to live here. With you and David and Caryn and Mrs. Winsee. With Adella in and out all the time and with Clementine rubbing against my legs and getting cat hair on my pillow. I want you to read me every book in your library. I want to finish college. I want to know the difference between a gardenia and a camellia. I want to learn to cook like you."

No one moved for a moment. Then Olivia brushed off her slacks and walked to the refrigerator. Pulling out a pound of salted butter, she said, "That's asking a lot. The cooking and all." She set the butter on the counter with a nice, crisp whack. "Go get your stuff unpacked and hide that suitcase under your bed, and put on the closest thing you have to some praline-making pants. But before you do one bit of that, I want you to call your mother."

Jillian instantly looked at the screen on her phone.

"Did I say *text* your mother? I did not. I said *call* her. You make it right with her."

"Jade doesn't know anything is wrong," Jillian protested.

"That's fine, but if you're going to stay, it's got to be with her blessing, whatever that may look like between the two of you. You can't make a home anywhere you've moved out of spite."

"Very good, Olivia!" Adella was impressed, plain and simple. For all she knew, Olivia might have learned that from her. She'd ask Emmett later if he'd ever heard her say such a thing.

Adella stopped by Jillian's room before she left that afternoon and found her organizing her closet.

"Why have you got your purse, Adella? Aren't you going to stay for supper?"

"No, baby. I thought I'd get on home to my three men, seeing as I'm not having to say good-bye to anybody in particular tonight."

Adella could tell Jillian was a little disappointed, but she knew this was the right thing to do. Her place was in her own refrigerator. "But I brought you something." She handed Jillian the silver gift bag with a bright-red ribbon on it.

"Should I wait for Christmas?"

"I think today will be just fine. It's nothing fancy."

Had Adella known what Jillian's face was going to look like when she pulled out that old sleepwear, clean and pressed, she'd have had her camera ready.

"My pajamas!"

Jillian threw her arms around Adella and cried like a baby. Between sobs, she caught her breath and blurted out, "Thank you. For everything."

Adella held the young woman tight and patted her back. "Oh, now, you quit that crying and get in there and help your grandmother with those shrimp and grits. You can at least fry some bacon, can't you?" Jillian smiled and nodded, her face dripping like a dishrag. "I'm gonna go home and rest up. God only knows the refereeing I have ahead between you two Fontaine women now that this has gone at least as semipermanent as my old double-wide. Don't think I won't be asking for a raise either."

Adella made it to the car and shut the driver's-side door just in time. Had she not turned up her Donnie McClurkin Christmas collection, no telling who would have heard her squalling and carrying on. At least this way somebody not minding their own business might think she was singing.

CHAPTER 56

THE SUN SET ON CHRISTMAS EVE at Saint Sans as the temperature
rose in busy ovens. Olivia was busy in the kitchen with David and
Jillian offering what help they could. Had Olivia not had the forethought to equip that kitchen with one full-size oven and another
half and a freestanding electric turkey roaster, they'd have been
forced to suffer the shame of a single entrée.

The whole house was astir with last-minute preparations.
They'd expected to have a perfectly horrible Christmas, with Rafe's
room the cleanest it had been in six months and Olivia shut in her
suite like the days of yore and Jillian long gone to San Francisco
without a single glance back. That's not what they'd gotten.

"Jillian, if you eat another chunk of praline off those sweet
potatoes, we may as well have dumped yams from a can," Olivia
scolded.

"Why haven't you said a single word to David while he's downed at least four cloves of roasted garlic from the brussels sprouts?"

"Seriously? You're tattling on me?"

"The first one that breaks off an edge of that pastry on the Wellington is going to supply a head on a platter for entrée number three," Olivia threatened, and she hadn't minded giving them the stink eye when she said it. She'd saved enough dough to shape two S's on top, and they had come out posing for a *Louisiana Living* photo shoot.

"Vida, is the table about ready?" Setting the table was her job since she didn't need to be anywhere near a burner, particularly when she lacquered down her hair, which she always did at Christmas. Olivia set out the Spode Christmas plates on the buffet adjacent to the dinner table in advance to shorten the distance and reduce the breakage. So far only one saucer had jumped to its demise.

David leaned over and whispered under his breath, "Mrs. Fontaine, you might want to double-check the table."

She glanced up between heaping spoonfuls of jalapeño cranberry sauce into petite crystal bowls. "Looks splendid to me!" And it did, alive with color, festive in mood, and bursting with flavor before a single morsel had graced it. "Excellent taste in placement, Vida. And the chrome chargers are perfect with all the silver trim. And haven't we become quite the crowd? Look at that full table."

"My point exactly," David whispered. "Does the table look slightly more populated than usual to you?"

When she looked at him, confused, he held up six fingers. Olivia glanced back at the table. David was as right as rain. Six place settings. Olivia's only wonderment was why on earth this would have amounted to an iota of confusion in this house. "Will Mr. Winsee be joining us tonight, Vida?"

The elderly woman responded with complete surprise like it was the most absurd thing she'd ever heard. "Mr. Winsee? Don't be ridiculous."

Olivia and the others all froze, holding their breath, terrified that she'd realized he was dead. Not one among them was prepared to let him go, particularly not on Christmas Eve.

Wagging her finger at Olivia, Vida said, "You know as well as I do that he's in bed again with the croup." They all breathed a sigh of relief. "David, I can't imagine you've gotten a wink of sleep either with these paper-thin walls. All that cigar smoking you two boys have been doing is catching up with him. And don't think it won't catch up with you either."

David shrugged his shoulders, wide-eyed.

"Just listen to that hacking." When they all inclined their ears the direction of Vida's room, she offered a disclaimer. "Don't let him fool you. He's resting quietly right now so he can be ready to cough up a lung as soon as I crawl into bed."

"So, who's the extra place setting for?" Jillian inquired this time.

"What? Are you talking about this one?"

Vida pointed to a spot on the other side of the centerpiece. Olivia caught a glimpse of the top of the goblet and realized what she had done. "Uh-oh." She pitched the spoon onto the counter so she could make a beeline to the table for a quick intervention.

Before she could clear three steps, Vida had already come out with it. "It's the Lord's Supper."

It was the Eucharist serving pieces, as plain as day.

Crowded among the red-and-green confetti of five Christmas Spodes was a gold-plated paten. Beside it, a large matching chalice. While Vida stood behind the Lord's chair gratified and near misty-eyed, the others stood by, speechless.

"Will you be adding utensils?" For the life of her, Olivia could not think of another thing to say. Between the salad forks, dessert forks, dinner forks, steak knives, regular knives, butter knives, regular spoons, coffee spoons, and teaspoons festively framing the other plates, the Lord's setting appeared conspicuously stark.

Vida looked at Olivia like she didn't have sense enough to come in out of the rain. "Olivia, the Lord eats with his hands."

The timer went off on one oven for the cajun oyster dressing and the other oven for the popovers. There was nothing left to be done but eat.

After they said grace, that was. Caryn brought it up. "I feel like we should say a blessing or something." This she said with her eyes shifting toward the Lord's plate.

No one could argue, nor did anyone volunteer.

"Caryn, since you brought it up, why don't you say it?" The request seemed reasonable enough to Olivia, particularly since the popovers would get stone cold if somebody didn't get a move on it.

"Uh, okay. I guess I'll say what my daddy always says." She bowed her head and then glanced back up to see if any other head was following suit. At that subtle signal, every chin dropped.

"Bless us, O Lord, and these thy gifts, which we are about to receive from thy bounty, through Christ, our Lord. Amen."

"That was lovely, Caryn," David said.

"It was," Jillian agreed.

The others nodded, and all of them flew into a feast of unfettered joy.

Oh, how they did eat. The whole oval table was elbows, passing plates and platters and sweeteners and grinders of salt and pepper. The five of them chattered and chewed and mouthed off and mused and ate and ate till they ached.

Two hours later, all five were on their feet clearing the table, covering the leftovers, rinsing the glasses, and scrubbing the plates. The only thing fuller than their bellies was the dishwasher. It groaned like it had dreaded this day for months. They'd promised

Olivia that the kitchen would be spotless and the table empty before they reposed in front of the fireplace with hot cocoa.

And it was soon empty. Except for the Lord's plate, with one lone popover right in the center of it.

David stood at the table, holding the dishrag he'd used to wipe off the last few crumbs and scattered salt. "Mrs. Fontaine, what would you have me do here?" he asked with an impressive balance of practicality and reverence. "He hasn't eaten a bite." He leaned over and peered into the chalice. "Nor, from what I can tell, has the Lord had a single sip."

What to do wasn't all that simple, seeing as how Vida was standing arm's length from Olivia, ears attuned to every word.

Olivia always did her level best not to take the wind out of the sails of Vida Winsee, and not just because she had made that promise to Mr. Winsee before he passed. In a wretched world, selfish and shriveled, that old woman was as full of hope as a sky-high balloon is full of hot air. One day Vida Winsee would go to sleep and not wake up, but thanks be to God, it hadn't been today. And this was Christmas Eve.

"Just leave it, David," she instructed with a wave of her hand. "I'll tend to it later."

Caryn and Jillian sat on the hearth with their hot cocoa. Olivia, with hers, sat in the gold-and-red wingback, Clementine asleep in her lap. Vida was audaciously cheerful in an armchair with a half-moon of whipping cream on her upper lip. David walked back into the circle carrying five Christmas gift bags.

Everyone instantly protested. "We said we weren't doing presents!"

"These are not from me," he claimed. "They're from Adella. She asked me to distribute one to each of us tonight, and that's precisely what I intend to do."

Vida said, "That little dickens," and Caryn, "She's so sweet."

"*Sweet*," Olivia interjected with a perfect smirk, "is not the exact adjective that comes to my mind when I think of Adella Atwater." Everybody laughed.

"How about *thoughtful*?" Caryn returned.

"I can go with *thoughtful*. And *mouthful*. To Adella," Olivia said, lifting her gift bag like a glass of champagne.

"Hear! Hear!" the others chimed in and lifted theirs.

It was no easy feat to win a prize in absentia for best white elephant gift, but Adella had managed to accomplish it. Their presents were identical: framed pictures of the five of them walking into Adella's church the night of the Christmas pageant. A photographer had been stationed in the foyer to capture the gleaming expressions of expectant gatherers come to hear glad tidings.

Having fought a cold for three days, David had never been paler or the end of his nose redder, which explained why he was picking at it. Something had gone badly wrong with Caryn's hair to make it look that much like an isosceles triangle, and it didn't help that she, a virtual teetotaler, looked three sheets to the wind. Olivia could only guess that Vida had sniffed out the photographer since her likeness was captured bent at the waist, head thrown forward, taking a bow. Jillian appeared to be patting her head and rubbing her stomach, and somewhat vigorously at that, although she claimed she'd undergone an attack of severe itching. Olivia looked like she'd been caught in a stampede under the very hooves of Dasher, Dancer, Prancer, Vixen, Comet, Cupid, Donner, and Blitzen—and had come back crazed with vengeance.

Four of them howled and one of them grinned until most of them spilled their cocoa. They told stories on Adella and on one another and how they'd each ended up at Saint Sans.

Finally it was getting close to midnight and the firewood was embers, so all agreed to call it a day. Olivia swept Clementine to the floor, got to her feet, and picked up her empty cup and Vida's.

"What was that?" Jillian asked, straightening her back.

"What was what?" David responded.

Jillian sat still for a moment and her eyes grew wide. *"That!"*

Olivia glanced at David and saw that he was as perplexed as she was.

Caryn put her hand on Jillian's wrist. "Do you hear something outside?"

After the last six weeks, they'd all earned the right to get spooked. But Olivia hadn't heard anything out of the ordinary.

As if echoing Olivia's thoughts, Vida sat up and looked around her. "All I hear is some thunder."

A rumble vibrated the floor. Jillian picked up her feet, squeezed her knees to her chest, and ducked her head between them. A clap of thunder followed. "No, don't!" she cried out, shaking all over.

Olivia was bewildered. Jillian had never reacted this way to a storm before.

"Jillian," David said gently, "everything's fine. It's just a typical winter thunderstorm. We have them all the time."

With the next bolt, the lights flickered off and back on. Jillian whimpered.

"There, there," Vida said tenderly. "Don't be afraid. We're perfectly safe in—"

Lightning split the sky, lighting up the garden as if it were day. Rain hammered on the metal roof. Thunder cracked like a massive branch breaking off a mighty redwood.

Jillian let out a bloodcurdling scream.

CHAPTER 57

The chapel was pitch black when Reverend Brashear turned the key in the lock of the side entrance to Saint Silvanus. Instead of turning on a light, he reached into a drawer and pulled out several long matches and walked methodically to the pine altar near the pulpit.

It was a moonless night, not quite midnight, though the clock in the parsonage was unwound and mute. The first match refused to strike, and after several tries, the thin stick broke in his hand. The second match lit with a burst of white and held its flame for all six slender candles. Shadows shivered and jerked like uneasy spirits scared of the dark.

He turned slowly and faced the empty pews. He pictured the faces of his congregants, the grim and the gracious, in their established places.

As early as the third Sunday of Saint Silvanus's abbreviated existence, families had already claimed their territory. What God appeared to lack in dependability, they made up for in predictability, both in seating and in countenance. Those who smiled, smiled every service. Those who grunted and growled never ceased. Those who yawned could never catch up on their sleep.

Raymond hadn't minded the claiming of the pews in the early days. Colonizing seats was the signature of a community staking its claim on a house of God they felt they co-owned. He'd looked forward to the young church's rite of passage since the day he'd been ordained. But the familiarity also meant that, when pews began to empty one Sunday at a time, Reverend R. J. Brashear knew at a single glance precisely who was missing.

His gaze was drawn to that front row, where he'd seated Brianna next to Evelyn Ann every Lord's Day she was strong enough to come. The leg at the end of the pew bore nicks from the braces of her shoes, though it was out of view in the dark. He'd run his hand over them for the first time a few days before. He knew they were there before he looked. At times when he'd pause between superlatives in a sermon, he'd hear a knock of her heel against the wood. Evelyn Ann, eyes never wavering from the pulpit, would reach over with her eyelet-laced glove and gently pat Brianna's knee. Both gestures had been a strange comfort to him.

His special graces, in pools on the front row, tended to wane in a thin tide toward the back. Old man Woffard tapped his empty pipe on the armrest if the preaching went too long—and not rhythmically either. Mildred Cunningham made a honking sound when she blew her nose, which she did incessantly into her husband's handkerchief every Sunday. But the annoyances were not always audible. Milt Mahachy twisted the end of his beard during the sermon, and by the end of the service, it looked like it would spear the open page on his hymnal.

This had been his congregation. This and a smattering of other saints, long-suffering and sentimental, full of faith, full of hope. It had been harder than he'd supposed. And it had been better. And woefully worse.

He forced his gaze away from the front pew. Candle wax had begun to collect on the marble top of the pine altar. His eyes had adjusted to the darkness now and he made his way to the small kitchenette just off the chapel. He reached into a cabinet and withdrew a carafe of wine and picked up the loaf of bread from the countertop. When he returned to the altar, he poured the wine into the chalice, hands steady, the room motionless, soundless.

He broke the bread and uttered the words he knew by heart.

"'For I have received of the Lord that which also I delivered unto you, that the Lord Jesus the same night in which he was betrayed took bread: And when he had given thanks, he brake it, and said, Take, eat: this is my body, which is broken for you: this do in remembrance of me. After the same manner also he took the cup, when he had supped, saying, This cup is the new testament in my blood: this do ye, as oft as ye drink it, in remembrance of me. For as often as ye eat this bread, and drink this cup, ye do shew the Lord's death till he come.'"

He dipped the bread into the wine. He lifted his chin and stared at the stained-glass image of Jesus, the rocking boat, and the daring disciple. Then he took the bread.

Not a single ear was open when the gun went off.

Suspicion taints sorrow like few other poisons. Once it is offered in a silver chalice, full and tipping, most people cannot help but sip. Held on the human tongue long enough, its rancid taste turns sweet. Swallowed, suspicion sinks so deep into the mire of bored and fickle hearts that it resurfaces as fact. It killed Saint Silvanus Methodist Church, and at last, it killed her pastor.

Over the years, several valiant efforts were made toward resuscitating the church. But no matter how promising the man at the pulpit, fate seemed to forbid it. It was not a question of God. If God had ever been there, he had vanished without a trace.

No one remembered who first nicknamed the church Saint Sans, but it stuck like storm shutters to broken windows. Some argued that it was a kindness. They could have called it Ichabod.

CHAPTER 58

Olivia took several steps in her granddaughter's direction. "You're perfectly safe, Jillian. All of us are."

The house rumbled and Jillian continued wailing and screaming. "No, no, stop it! No!"

Caryn's lip quivered and she looked at Olivia with the face of a scared little girl. "What's wrong with her, Mrs. Fontaine?"

Motioning for Caryn to scoot from the hearth, Olivia sat down next to Jillian and placed her hand on her back. She could feel the girl's heart hammering. "Tell me what's the matter. Talk to me right now."

When the electricity went off and the house went black, Jillian threw her hands over her head and yelled, "Run! Everybody, run!"

Olivia held her as tightly as she could and David sat down on the other side of her and wrapped his arms around them both. Vida stood flailing her arms frantically and started toward the front door.

"Caryn!" Olivia called. "Tend to Vida. Right now." Caryn jumped to her feet and charged toward her. "Don't let her out that door!"

Competing with the crackling thunder, Olivia struggled to maintain the calm in her voice that Vida required in an episode like this. "Vida, come over here by me and let's you and I talk to Jillian. She's a little upset."

Panicked, Vida turned the lock on the front door while Caryn tried to pull her away from the door by the waist. "I don't think I can hold her!"

When David let go of Jillian so he could help Caryn with Vida, Jillian grabbed on to Olivia's shirt with both fists.

Olivia was as far outside her comfort zone as she had ever been. "Shhhh, now. I've got you." The house was pitch dark. The sheets of lightning were their only eyes. "David?" she called out. "What's that song Vida sings sometimes?"

"I don't know which one you mean, Mrs. Fontaine!" he responded, sounding like he was in pain. What was Vida doing to the poor man? "Mrs. Winsee, I beg you to let go. You are about to scalp your good friend David! Mrs. Fontaine, is it 'Chapel of Love'?"

"No, the hymn!" Olivia scrambled through her memory for the scattered words. "You know the one. The 'walks with me' one. Sing it to her, David."

"*Now?*"

Another clap of thunder. Another scream from Jillian.

"Now!"

The words were a little muffled at first, but David sang.

> *"I come to the garden alone,*
> *While the dew is still on the roses,*
> *And the voice I hear, falling on my ear,*
> *The Son of God discloses."*

Vida began to sing with him, just a few words here and there at first.

"And He walks with me, and He talks with me,
And He tells me I am His own;
And the joy we share as we tarry there,
None other has ever known."

Olivia rocked slightly back and forth with Jillian and hoped against hope that maybe she was listening.

David stopped singing. "Caryn?"

"I'm right here," she answered.

"Are you okay?"

"Yeah. I think so."

"Can you come here and sit with Mrs. Winsee for a moment?"

Olivia could hear David walking toward the front doors and wondered what on earth he had in mind. Her question was answered when she heard whooshing pumping sounds and a few reedy notes from the old organ. So he had gotten the thing working again.

David found the chords and continued the hymn.

"He speaks, and the sound of His voice
Is so sweet the birds hush their singing,
And the melody that He gave to me
Within my heart is ringing."

Vida's quavering voice joined in on the chorus, this time word for word and with full vigor.

"And He walks with me, and He talks with me,
And He tells me I am His own;

And the joy we share as we tarry there,
None other has ever known."

The lightning kept flashing, but the thunder grew shy and hid behind the organ. Jillian's sobs were quieter now.

Olivia looked down at her face and followed her gaze all the way up to the stained-glass window. The light flashed continually behind it, making the foam of the waves a frosty white and swirling iridescent blues through the waters. The hand of Jesus extended toward the storm-battered boat.

Jillian's words were so soft, Olivia couldn't make out what she was saying. The organ quieted and so, for a moment, did Vida and David.

"Help us. Please help us," Jillian was whispering toward the man walking upon the sea.

Olivia squeezed her eyes shut. She felt the crash of a thousand waves against her chest and the weight of a lifetime of anchorless storms.

The clicking sound of a lighter drew the attention of all to Caryn, standing beside the dining room table. "I don't know why I didn't think to do this earlier." She lit each of the six red candles. "I just couldn't think. Here are a couple of flashlights, too." She'd retrieved them from under the sink.

Like moths to the flames, Olivia and the others went to the table where Caryn stood. No one said, "Let's all sit down," but one by one they did.

They took their best shot at making small talk. "Man, that was some kind of lightning!" and "How much rain would you bet we got?" to avoid "Mrs. Winsee nearly pulled every hair out of my head" and "What in tarnation was all that yelling about?"

Jillian spoke the quietest of all but her words hushed every other. "I woke up in there."

Every head turned toward her.

She kept her eyes fixed on the flame of a single candle and spoke again. "In the storage unit. Stella's."

No one said a word.

"I didn't know that's where I was. It was too dark. Such black darkness I thought maybe I was blind. That whatever awful thing was hurting my head had blinded me."

"Oh, Jillian." Tears welled in Caryn's eyes.

Olivia found herself blinking too, but only from the candle smoke, she was certain.

"I told myself I didn't have to see. All I had to do was feel my way around and I could find a way out. That's when I realized my wrists and my ankles were bound. With what, I had no idea."

"Dear God," David said, lowering his forehead into his hand.

"Keep talking, Jillian." Olivia would rather lay down her life in that bed of ashes than hear what Jillian had to say, but she'd lived long enough to know it was the only way. If Jillian could endure the horror of it, they could buck up and bear the telling of it.

Jillian cleared her throat and covered her quivering bottom lip with her fingers. "Something crawled on my feet." She paused to catch her breath. "I tried to scream, only my mouth was bound too. I wiggled my toes and bent and straightened my legs frantically, and whatever it was fell off."

A hand, creased and speckled with advanced age, reached across the table to hold Jillian's.

Jillian lifted her chin and peered into Vida's eyes and reciprocated the grip of her hand. "The thunder," the young woman said. "It just went on and on. I screamed and screamed inside my own mouth, *Somebody help me! I'm in here! Can anybody hear me? Please help me!* I felt something with my toes. I could tell it was cardboard and figured it was a box. I kicked my feet against it as long as I could, trying to make noise."

Jillian looked at Olivia, and Olivia, perceiving that she needed affirmation to proceed, nodded.

"But you were not alone, were you, Jillian?" It was Vida.

"Yes, I *was*! I was so alone. I was terrified. The pain in my head. It was excruciating. I could tell my hair was wet and I knew it was blood. Nothing could hurt that bad and not bleed. And I was freezing." She caught her breath and shook her head like she was trying to toss the memories somewhere far away. "It was unbearable."

Tears spilled down Jillian's cheeks as well as Caryn's and David's.

Olivia watched the peculiar way the candlelight shimmered in the streaks on their faces. Tears pooled in her own eyes, but she willed herself not to set them free. She fought to keep her jaw strong and her face dry. Her grandchild needed courage to reach in and draw out whatever words remained on the floor in that black darkness. She'd withheld too many things from Jillian in the last twenty years out of nothing but pure spite. She would not with-hold the one thing she had to offer her: iron in her blood.

Through the equal gift of shared sobs, Caryn spilled out the words "I don't know how you stood it."

Jillian stared back at the flame, transfixed, like she didn't hear her. "And then it was over," she said.

David spoke next. "Over how, Jillian?"

"All of it. The thunder. The pain. The terror. It was just over."

"You went into shock," Caryn explained.

"I guess I did. But I'd never heard anyone describe it like that. I guess you hear this all the time, Caryn, but it felt just like a heavy blanket. So warm. So real. Like something I would have sworn at the time I could feel on my skin. It was so vivid that I thought, *Someone's in here with me!* I told myself to be afraid because no one good knew where I was. But I couldn't muster up my fear. I couldn't even muster up my pain. I think it was the shock, like you said."

Caryn offered no response.

"Then what, Jillian?" Olivia prompted. "Tell us every single thing."

"Then I must have fallen asleep."

"What do you remember happening next?" Olivia had no intention of letting her stop until that black hole was an empty well.

"I heard voices. I opened my eyes and saw Adella. Then you, Caryn. And you, David. You, Mrs. Winsee." Jillian glanced at Olivia, held her gaze, and reached out her other hand. "And you, O."

Olivia fixed her jaw but several tears fought their way free. She placed her hand on Jillian's.

"Tonight," Jillian said. "Tonight I remembered."

"Christmas is the time for remembering." It was a strange thing for Vida to say. No proper time for Merry Christmases. But everyone there knew the old woman's heart. This night had been hard for her, too.

Olivia looked at David, who, with elbows on the table, had dropped his face into his hands. He didn't appear to be crying. His shoulders were still. He was just sick at heart, Olivia supposed, like all of them were.

They all sat silently at the table for what seemed a good while. Both hands on the mantel clock had now reached twelve. Olivia opened her mouth to suggest they blow out the candles and get to their rooms with the flashlights. The electricity would surely come back on before morning.

Before she could say a word, David spoke. "'For I received from the Lord that which I also delivered to you: that the Lord Jesus on the same night in which He was betrayed took bread; and when He had given thanks, He broke it.'"

David reached over to the gold-plated brass paten and pulled it over in front of him. As the others watched wide-eyed and puzzled, he lowered his chin, whispered the words "Thank you," and tore the popover into five pieces. He took one piece and handed the plate to Caryn. She stared at him questioningly. When he nodded, she took a piece and passed the plate to Vida. The paten shook slightly in the old woman's hands, but she steadied it with one hand and took her portion with the other. She passed it to Jillian, who knew nothing to do but imitate the others. With one piece of bread remaining on the plate, Jillian passed the paten to Olivia.

David spoke again. "'And the Lord said, "Take, eat; this is My body which is broken for you; do this in remembrance of Me."'"

He put his portion of bread in his mouth. The others hesitated for only the briefest moment before they followed suit.

Once more David spoke. "'In the same manner He also took the cup after supper, saying, "This cup is the new covenant in My blood. This do, as often as you drink it, in remembrance of Me."'"

He reached for the chalice, cupped it in both hands, and held it just below his chin. Unable to look away, Olivia studied David carefully and watched him squeeze his eyes shut. His jaw tightened for several seconds and he pressed his forehead to the lip of the cup. Then he opened his eyes and sipped from it.

When he passed the cup to Caryn, she did not hesitate. She lifted the chalice, took a deep breath, and drank. She held the cup out to Vida, and when she took it in her trembling hands, Caryn wrapped her own hands around the woman's and helped guide it to her mouth. Vida turned toward Jillian, smiled the warmest smile, and extended the cup to her.

Jillian took the gold-plated chalice in both hands. That she carefully and meticulously reenacted David's every move was lost on no one at the table. Jillian squeezed her eyes shut and pressed her forehead to the lip of the cup. After holding it there for several seconds, she opened her eyes and sipped.

At last the chalice passed into Olivia's hands. She stared at it for what felt like a full minute. She lifted her eyes first to David. She shifted her gaze to Caryn. Caryn's eyes met hers and the young woman smiled. Olivia next studied the lined and kind face most familiar to her at the table. Then she looked at the face that most resembled her own, the face of the only one who'd been a stranger to her just months ago.

Lastly Olivia stared at the place at the table Vida had set for an unseen guest. And she took the cup and she drank it.

CHAPTER 59

CHRISTMAS WAS THE FIRST DAY Jillian and Olivia had ever spent
alone together at Saint Sans.

David had told Jillian he always spent the day with a circle of
unmarried friends who'd migrated together from the school district. Some had kids, and some on occasion brought dates, but
all had a place and an annual assigned dish. Heralded the Nobel
laureate of world-class eggnog, David was in high demand. Mrs.
Winsee's great-niece from Slidell always sent a driver for her on
Christmas morning and sent her back Christmas night pleased
as punch with a thermos of virgin wassail. First- and second-year
medical students did grunt work at city hospitals all Christmas
Day, so that was where Caryn would be celebrating.

Exhausted and completely wrung out, Jillian slept late that
morning. The electricity had come back on around two o'clock,
turning on nearly every light in the house just as she'd fallen asleep.

They had gingerbread cookies for breakfast and, between them, one full pot of French press and half of another. Over the last cup of coffee, Olivia brought out a gift meticulously wrapped in gold foil paper and red satin ribbon. When she placed it in front of Jillian, she said, "Next year, if you're still here, we'll get a tree. I should have gotten David to fetch us one this year once I knew we'd have you for Christmas."

"No worries, O. My mom and I really didn't do that kind of thing either."

That seemed to perturb Olivia to no end. "Do you think any lots are open today?"

Jillian didn't know Olivia well enough yet to read whether or not she was serious. "Probably not, but anyway, what kind of shape do you think the trees would be in by this time?"

Olivia picked up the gift and set it down forcefully in front of the large flower arrangement on the kitchen island. "There," she said. "Make like that's a tree and I'll have you one no later than December 1, next go-round."

Jillian hopped up from the stool and hurried into her room to get the two gifts she had for Olivia. "I didn't know if I'd have guts enough to give these to you or not. David let me use the gift wrap he had left over."

Olivia appeared to be completely taken aback. "You shouldn't have gotten me anything."

"Why?"

"You just shouldn't have."

It was nearly a scolding, tempting Jillian in the worst way to shift into her defensive gear with a dramatic "Well, forget it then." Instead she said, "Well, I did. It's not store-bought, so relax."

Olivia's lips were pressed shut like they'd been superglued. Jillian lifted the tape gradually on the gold foil wrapping of her gift and unfolded it with such care, she could have reused the paper. Inside she discovered a printout of a registration confirmation under her name for the spring semester at the New Orleans School of Cooking.

Jillian was slack-jawed. "What? Are you kidding?"

"Does that sound like anything you'd want to do? I didn't know if it would be presumptuous."

"It's perfect! I can't wait!" She scanned the page again. "I can't believe this. Thank you, O!" She stopped short of hugging her for Olivia's sake. "I start in just two weeks!"

"I'm pleased that you like it." Olivia pulled a key out of her pocket. "This is the extra key to my car. At some point, of course, you will want to get your own car. But until then we can share mine. Much of what I have to do away from Saint Sans is flexible. We'll have to work around each other a little, but I think we can manage it just fine."

"I can take the trolley."

"You can. But it must get exhausting thinking about the street-car schedule when you need to run to the grocery store or pharmacy. Or want to go out with friends."

"I don't really have any friends outside Saint Sans." Jillian didn't say it with self-pity. She just stated it as a fact.

"Well, you will at some point."

Taking the key, Jillian said, "That's very kind of you. I probably would enjoying using it some. I won't overdo it." Butterflies fluttered in Jillian's stomach as she slid the two gifts she'd wrapped for Olivia in front of her. "Your turn."

The butterflies intensified to something nearer to panic when Olivia unwrapped them and looked at the two framed five-by-sevens without uttering a single syllable or cracking the least smile. In her right hand was Rafe's first-grade picture, freckled face and front-toothless. In her left hand was a picture of an older Rafe holding a curly-haired, dark-headed little girl whose arms were wrapped tightly around his neck.

Someone needed to break the silence and Jillian was pretty sure it wasn't going to be Olivia. "I found them in the closet in Rafe's room. Gosh, I hope *this* wasn't presumptuous. It seemed like a good idea at the time." Jillian squirmed, feeling queasy.

"He was about your age here," Olivia said, looking at the picture of Rafe and Jillian. "You were, if I'm remembering right, about three."

Jillian paused to muster some courage. "O, can I ask you something?"

Olivia turned her head toward her without answering. Jillian had never known anybody who seemed more comfortable saying no, so she took Olivia's silence as a yes and pounced headlong where angels might fear to tread. "Are there others?"

"Other children?" Olivia looked aghast. "No. Of course not."

"No, not other children. Are there other pictures? Of me—" Jillian hesitated—"and him."

"Probably. I haven't looked in those boxes in a good while."

Needing to give some measure of recognition to the other picture, Jillian pointed toward it and said, "He was cute. The hair and all."

Olivia abruptly scooted back the stool and stood. "Thank you for the gifts." With that, she turned on her heels and started in the direction of her room.

Jillian's face burned with embarrassment and disappointment as she watched Olivia walk away. She paused at the edge of the great room, however, just before she got to the hall. She set the photo of Rafe and Jillian on the buffet across from the dining table and appeared to inspect it. After a tad of rearranging, she left it there before walking to her room and closing the door.

Flummoxed, Jillian retreated to her room as well and spent the next little while showering and getting dressed and replaying the scene over and over in her head. By the time Jillian heard pots and pans clattering around in the kitchen, she was in a stew. She knew what she'd do. She'd march herself right into that kitchen and demand an explanation.

Even if Jillian had done the wrong thing, wasn't it supposed to be the thought that counted? What terrible ulterior motive could she have had for framing those pictures and giving them to her own grandmother? She wanted answers. She intended to force the woman to talk about it. Jillian worked herself into a lather and whirled around her bedroom door, heading toward the kitchen for a confrontation. And then she stopped dead in her tracks. She stared at the bookcase in the foyer between their two bedrooms. There was Rafe's first-grade picture, him plump-faced and smiling wide, the collar of his polo shirt sticking up on one side.

The two women unloaded the overstuffed dishwasher like nothing had ever happened, and then they contrived the best turkey and Swiss sandwiches on rye that Jillian had ever put in her mouth. Olivia insisted they wouldn't be worth the trouble to chew if she didn't grill them in butter on a hot iron skillet. "I'm not even going to think how many calories are in that thing," Jillian commented.

"Good, because it's Christmas, Scrooge."

After their late lunch, Olivia stirred up a fire in the hearth and sat down with a book in the wing chair, while Jillian collapsed on the Snapdragon with the laptop to peruse the New Orleans School of Cooking website.

When the doorbell rang late in the afternoon, Jillian rolled to her feet and said, "I got it, O."

"Who on earth would drop by somebody's house on Christmas Day?" Olivia asked, abundantly annoyed.

"Normal people, Grandma Grinch."

"Humph."

But nothing seemed vaguely normal to Jillian about the person standing on the other side of that front door.

Olivia came to her feet in record time. "Sergeant DaCosta, what brings you here?" Her question came with an air of seriousness and dread that Jillian couldn't really blame her for. His face six months earlier had not been a welcome sight.

Jillian, on the other hand, tried to fight the welcome sight of that particular face. She didn't want him to be handsome, not to her anyway. She didn't want him to look like he cared. She didn't want to see him on any front porch again. She wanted to accept that ridiculous encounter at Bully's house for what it was and for- get all about it.

"Don't let me alarm you, Mrs. Fontaine. I'm here on a personal matter, not police business." Dressed in a button-down shirt and jeans, he glanced over his shoulder at his pickup truck parked at the front curb to offer proof.

"I see." Olivia sounded unconvinced.

"Can I come in for a moment?" Cal asked.

Jillian tried to regain some composure and take up a little slack left by her grandmother's inhospitality. "Of course, Officer."

She meant it to be formal and his expression suggested he hadn't missed it, but what caught her off guard was the way he came right on out and admitted it. He walked past her and said at a volume she alone would hear, "Alright. I deserved that."

"Your Christmas, Sergeant," Olivia spoke matter-of-factly. "How has it been?"

"Good, thank you. I had coffee with my mom this morning and took her to my brother Daniel's house just before noon. We had lunch with him and Stephanie and the kids."

"I understand from the *Times* that he's running for city council." Olivia's statement stunned Jillian. She had no idea her grandmother kept up with current events like that, and it certainly never occurred to her that Olivia knew Cal had a brother.

"Yes, ma'am, he is. And if I know him, he'll win." Cal grinned and asked about Christmas at Saint Sans.

Olivia cut to the chase before Jillian could get off the starting block. "Our festivities were last night. Jillian and I have had the day to ourselves, which we've both enjoyed immensely." Jillian raised her eyebrows, but apparently nothing short of a general anesthetic was going to stop Olivia. "To what do we owe this unscheduled visit?"

"I want to apologize for the way I managed to sound when we ran into each other in the ICU waiting room with Bully's parents."

"Whatever do you mean?" Olivia asked. "I can't say as I recall anything at all that you said."

Jillian rolled her eyes. "What my grandmother means is that we're not sure why you'd feel the urge to come and tell us this today. You didn't say anything wrong anyway."

"It wasn't what I said so much as how I said it. And even that wasn't intentional. It just sort of boiled up to the surface."

"Who could blame you, after what happened?" Jillian glanced away. "After what happened to Bully." She would not avoid saying his name just to avoid the extra pain.

"Well, Bully's mother. That's who. I went by the hospital today after I dropped Mom off at home. Mrs. La Bauve very kindly cornered me out in the hall and asked if I'd seen you since then."

"And why would you have?" Olivia asked.

Jillian was fairly impressed when Cal was intent enough on saying what he'd come to say to ignore Olivia's attempts to unbalance him.

"I told her that I hadn't, and she said something that really threw me. She said it sweet because she knows no other way to be, but she said it straight so I'd get it."

Olivia put her hands on her hips. "I'm assuming you'd like to tell us what that was."

"To answer Jillian's question why I showed up here today, yes, ma'am, I would."

"What did she say? I do want to know," Jillian interjected.

"She said, 'So that's how you left it, then? With them feeling like you'd insulted their home. And after all they'd been through. That's beneath you, Cal.' I'd like to ask forgiveness from you both."

"Bootsie said that, did she?" Olivia grinned. "I don't recall an insult. Still, we appreciate the thought and thank you for coming by, don't we, Jillian?"

"Yes, you do recall it, O, and so do I."

With Jillian's words, Olivia crossed her arms over her chest and took as loud a breath as humanly possible.

Jillian trudged forward before Olivia could derail the conversation again. "Though I did not blame you for how you felt, your apology is accepted. You surely know that we could not be sorrier for what happened to Bully because of us and that we do feel responsible." Cal tried to interrupt her, but she gave him the stop palm she had learned from Olivia. "Our hearts were shattered. You can't imagine how glad we are to hear about his progress almost daily from Caryn."

"What's happening with him is pretty mind-blowing," Cal responded. "Mr. and Mrs. La Bauve said that several specialists have flown in to study him. They are convinced he's going to come out of this thing. It's astonishing."

"It's a *miracle*," Jillian emphasized.

"I'm not sure I can argue with that." Jillian suspected he had tears in his eyes.

"Oh, for heaven's sake, I'm about to fall sound asleep standing up." It was vintage Olivia Fontaine. "I'm going to have to make a pot of coffee. Since you're here, Sergeant, you may as well have one with us."

And he did. He asked about how they'd celebrated Christmas the night before and Jillian showed him the menu and told him just about everything prior to the first clap of thunder. She leapt over the bad part for all their sakes and landed right on David playing the organ and singing with Mrs. Winsee. "But that's right—you took piano lessons when you were a boy."

"Good memory there, Miss Slater." Cal paused for a moment and looked into her eyes. "I hope that's not all you remember."

Olivia went into such a coughing fit, Jillian had to jump to her feet and pound her on the back. Then just as suddenly, Olivia recovered. She stood, glared at the mantel clock, and said, "Look at the time! I'm so sorry we have to cut this visit short, but Jillian and I have to get a move on or we're going to be late."

Jillian glared at Olivia with confusion.

"Remember, Jillian? You promised your dear O a good movie!"

Cal and Jillian somehow managed to get out the front door without dear O joining them. "I'm sorry," she said, walking him to his truck. "I know she seems rude, and honestly, sometimes she is, but right now she's just being protective."

"I don't blame her. The woman's been through it." Cal took a few more steps. "Jillian, please let me say something before you make me get in that truck." He reached out and took her by the wrist. "I've thought about you constantly. I have. It started months ago. The first I realized it was that late night Frank and I were at the café and you spilled the coffee. I've tried to stop myself over and over from going down this path by rationalizing that it would never work, but still, I can't get you off my mind."

"I don't know how you could say that. You never stopped by to see how I was."

"That's not true. Ask your grandmother how many times I tried to get in that hospital room."

"To question me."

"You know better than that. That's why the others who had their heads on straight were there. That's not why I was there."

"But you never came by here after they brought me home."

He sighed. "The whole thing with Bully really messed me up. What I meant that day when I said I should never have let him come over here was that I knew—we all knew—he was personally involved. That he had personal feelings for you. We'd known that for weeks. I just kept thinking if I'd never let him come, he'd never have gotten hurt. The night he got hit was the same night we found you. I'd just confronted how strongly I felt about you when I got the news. There I was, about to go after the woman he had his eye on, when he was fighting for his life. What was I supposed to do with that?"

"I get that. But then why are you here now? Why not just call and apologize and leave it at that?" Tears stung Jillian's eyes.

"Because of what Mrs. La Bauve said. She didn't send me over here just to apologize. She sent me over here to see *you*."

"How do you know that?"

"I just know. I looked her in the eye and said that I was doing right by Bully. And she looked me in the eye and said, 'Don't you worry about Bully, Cal DaCosta. You think God is doing all this for his body and nothing for his heart?' She knows, Jillian. She knows what we're too proud to admit."

Jillian looked away as a tear spilled down her cheek.

He wiped it away with his thumb. "Please? Let's just see. I won't push. I won't rush. Give me the chance to spend time with you and get to know you."

She took both of his hands in hers. "Cal, I need you to listen to what I'm about to say and let me get it all the way out while I have the strength to say it."

He nodded. "Okay. I'm listening."

"I want to say yes so badly, but for once in my life, I'm going to say no. I have been lost for twenty-five years, trying to find out who I am and where I belong. The only part of myself I know in the least is Jade's daughter, and I'm glad to be that. But I don't know Rafe's daughter. The guy lived on the streets and died on a sidewalk filthy and famished. I've just begun to know Olivia Fontaine's granddaughter. I don't know Jillian Slater, the grown-up. I've made so many mistakes. If you knew even half of the stupid things I've done—"

"You think I haven't done stupid things? Who hasn't?"

"You promised not to interrupt."

"Okay, go on, but I don't like where this is going." Cal shook his head.

"I've confessed those mistakes and asked God to forgive me and I'm trying to believe he has. Adella says Jesus has made me brand-new. How do you know you'd like the brand-new me? I don't even know if I'm going to like her. I need to find out who she is. I just need some time for all of that before starting a new relationship."

"Jillian?" It was Olivia, sticking her head out the front door. "If you still want to see that movie—"

Jillian would have stalled her if she'd thought there was anything left to say, but there wasn't. "I'm sorry, Cal. I wish so many things had been different."

And he turned and walked away. Not a word. Not a single glance back. Just the sound of an engine rumbling down St. Charles.

CHAPTER 60

IN MARCH, Jillian and David went for a long walk at Audubon Park, both trying to take off a couple of pounds of nothing but pure creamery butter that Olivia's cooking had slathered on their behinds during the winter.

"I know a secret about you," David said.

Startled, Jillian wondered which aspect of her past was about to come back to haunt her.

"I heard you're getting baptized sometime over the next month," David went on.

Relieved, Jillian asked, "Who told you?"

"You know who told me." And she did. She knew good and well it was Adella whisper-hollering in the halls at Saint Sans and she didn't care.

Jillian had insisted on going to Adella's church even with Adella insisting that she might feel more comfortable at another. Olivia had chosen one not three blocks from Saint Sans because it was big on liturgy. The worship within those traditional walls supplied words to a woman who often struggled to find them. She also wanted to blend in. Her granddaughter, however, did the very opposite of blending in.

"I don't want to start from scratch, Adella. I want to go to BABC." And she made sure to pronounce it just like the insiders did: *Babsy.* "I already know four people there: you, Emmett, Trevor Don, and AJ." Jillian had immersed herself quickly in that family of God out of fear that loneliness and heartbreak would otherwise welcome back her past insecurities and she'd fall right back into her old patterns.

"What made you decide to be baptized?" David asked.

She told him how God had hemmed her in, starting with Mrs. La Bauve's request, then praying with Officer Sanchez, then hearing the invitation that night at the Christmas pageant and walking the aisle. They talked about that harrowing Christmas Eve night and the awful flashbacks Jillian had and how she was certain, how she knew beyond a shadow of a doubt, that if she did not get out into the brightest light, the darkness would engulf her. It wanted her. It was calling for her. She knew it. "It wanted all of us," she told him. "Darkness lurked in that house, David. We couldn't get rid of it. It was too big for us. It knew the past and it knew *our* pasts and it claimed our futures. Only God could defeat it."

He went silent for a while, and she let him. A little while later she spoke again. "David, can you tell me another secret?"

"If I know it."

"How did you know what to say on Christmas Eve, when you had us pass around the plate and the cup?"

They took several steps before he answered. "It's complicated." He paused again. "It was like Mrs. Winsee said that night. Christmas is the time for remembering. Let's just say I remembered."

"You remembered it word for word. I know because I asked Adella where you got all that, and after I described it to her, she got that Bible off the shelf in the foyer and showed it to me."

"It came back to me just that way, out of the blue. I'd memorized it years ago."

"Why?" Jillian was completely mystified.

"It was a lifetime ago. I was a whole different person. A very naive person. But a person who loved Jesus."

Jillian stopped right there on the sidewalk and turned toward him. "You're kidding me. What happened?"

"I began to believe he hated me. It's hard to keep loving someone you think hates you."

That appeared to be all David was willing to say on the subject, so Jillian let it rest. She couldn't begin to guess how he'd come to that conclusion. All she knew was that his suffering as a result had been great.

Three weeks later, David joined the choir at BABC. He had a little trouble keeping step right at first, but he got the hang of it pretty quickly, proof of which came the Sunday he sang "If It Wasn't for the Lord" as part of a quartet. He was as red as a beet at the end of it when everybody cheered.

Sometimes Jillian took three steps forward and two steps back, but it didn't take a math wizard to realize that was still one steady step forward. At the same time, she was flourishing in her cooking classes at the New Orleans School of Cooking. After all, Jesus didn't have anything against good cooking. He was always up for a feast.

All the residents came to the service the day Jillian was baptized just like they'd accidentally come the day she met Jesus. Olivia drilled her the week before the baptism about whether or not she was doing it out of pressure or if she thought maybe it was too much too soon. "No one's pressuring me, least of all Adella. She's too scared of you to pressure me. No, I don't think it's too soon. I've been to classes. I understand what it means and how I'm publicly identifying with Christ. I have a lot to learn, but I've got that part down."

The baptistery at BABC was just above the choir loft, normally concealed behind a heavy red curtain. The congregation knew they could expect to witness the sacred rite of believer's baptism when the curtain was open. There was no quiet buzz among the congregants that Sunday morning when the red curtain was wide open at the beginning of the service, Jillian was nowhere to be seen and the Atwater row was packed to the gills with guests. Even some of her classmates from the New Orleans School of Cooking were there.

After three songs and a round of greeting one another in the name of the Lord and another round just for greeting guests, Pastor Sam appeared in the baptistery. "We have two candidates for baptism today, brothers and sisters!"

Everybody hooted and hollered and shouted, "Praise the Lord!"

"First we have Mr. Jackson Wayne Bradley. He's nine years old and he wants everybody to know that he has accepted Jesus Christ as his Lord and Savior, don't you, little brother?" Jackson looked straight out at the congregation, nodding and smiling so big, he lit up the whole room. "Family and friends of Jackson Wayne Bradley here to support him in this profound occasion of his public identification with Christ, we invite you to stand in his honor." And they sure did.

"Hi, Mama!" he yelled.

"Hi, Son!" she yelled right back.

And he made quite a splash, too, when somehow the happy notion hit him to swim out of the baptistery instead of walk. And, my, how he could kick when he swam. One thing was for certain. That boy had been baptized and so had Pastor Sam.

"Our second candidate for believer's baptism is Miss Jillian Slater."

When Jillian walked into the water, wearing a white choir robe and a white turban around her head, half the congregation gasped. Adella told her later, "You looked just like royalty, like a Christian Cleopatra! So beautiful and radiant with that deep-olive skin against that white garb." Every jaw on the entire Atwater pew went slack to the ground.

When Pastor Sam invited family and friends of the candidate to stand, the residents of Saint Sans managed to come to their feet all self-aware, but then a fair ruckus broke out in the sanctuary as people stood up all over the room, even in the balcony. Jillian blinked away a pool of tears in her eyes over the unexpected outbreak of affection.

"Miss Slater, do you confess your belief in Jesus Christ as your Lord and Savior before these witnesses today?" Pastor Sam asked.

She nodded and said yes, her lip quivering.

"And do you wish to profess your love for him and your commitment to him as you identify in his death, burial, and resurrection?"

She spoke louder this time, full of conviction, iron in her blood. "Yes. Yes, sir, I do." When he nodded at her, giving her the signal, she cupped both hands over her mouth and nose.

"Miss Jillian Slater, my little sister, it is my great honor to joyfully baptize you this day in these sacred waters. I do so in the name of the Father who gave his Son for you, the Son who gave his life to make you his spotless bride, and the Holy Spirit who dwells within you and seals you unto the day of redemption. Buried with Christ in baptism—" Pastor Sam ducked her head briskly under the water so she'd never forget it, and as he lifted her head drenched and dripping with grace, he proclaimed loudly, "Raised to walk in newness of life."

The whole place erupted.

⚜

The Fontaine fortune took a hard hit in June. It was all Zacchaeus's fault. The pastor at Olivia's church read the story of the repentant tax collector on the Sunday just before the first anniversary of Rafe's passing. Olivia didn't even stay for the sermon. She came straight back to Saint Sans and paced the great room floor. The second Jillian and David walked in the door from Benton Ave., they all ate fried shrimp po'boys with Mrs. Winsee.

They'd barely wiped the grease from their chins when Olivia asked to speak with Jillian alone. "I'm going to my banker tomorrow to find out how much financial gain came to the Fontaine trust from the Steadman Nolan lawsuit years ago. And I do mean all of it, interest and everything. And I'm going to give it away. I've made up my mind. I'm not asking your permission. I'm just telling you because we're family."

Jillian could hardly pick her jaw up off the floor.

"Thank God, your money is safe and sound in separate accounts that all belong solely to you," Olivia added. "Your father's inheritance was established before the Nolan gain and never profited from it. It's unalloyed. The irony is not lost on me that I've rarely been angrier with anybody on this earth than I was with your grandfather when he refused to put a single penny of that win into our only child's hands. All those years ago, God foresaw this day and protected that money just for you."

"Oh, my gosh, O. My mind is spinning. How much do you think it will be?"

"I expect it to be at least half. I think it's safe to say we were twice as wealthy after that lawsuit as we were before."

"How much will be left?"

"That's not for you to worry about."

"Then we'll share mine! O, I will always take care of you just like you've taken care of me."

"I believe you, Jillian, but I am confident it won't come to that. I haven't been a big spender. I won't be rich, but I will be a long way from poor."

One day late in August, Jillian pulled out of the parking lot in Olivia's car, leaving her final cooking class of the summer term.

The location of the school had caused her to face the old haunt over and over again where she'd first run into Crawley and gotten tangled up with Stella. It seemed to be God's way with her: *Let's take it head-on, Jillian, you and me.* This particular day, she took a corner right by a man crumpled, sun-worn, and passed out cold on the sidewalk. It was a common sight in certain sections of the city. She had no real explanation why this one moved her like it did. Maybe it was his age. Maybe it was something about his big mop of hair. Maybe it was the way he looked dead before he really was.

Whatever it was, it moved her to take the next left instead of a right and head toward one of the most famous cemeteries in New Orleans. She'd have to search to find his grave. She'd never been there and wasn't certain her grandmother had been since the burial. They'd not gone on the anniversary of his death. They'd gone, instead, to put cashier's checks in Steadman Nolan's name on desks at homeless shelters, rehabs, food banks, and various ministries to the poor like free legal advice and aid for the mentally ill.

But today was Jillian's day to stand at that grave. She parked the car and began her search. She saw no office in sight nor a single other soul. Finally she spotted it—the Fontaine family monument.

Jillian stood right there in front of the graves of three generations of her paternal line: her father's grandparents, her father's father, and next to him, a marker that read *Olivia Constance*

Arseneaux Fontaine. Underneath was the date of her birth, a dash, and a space left blank. Jillian's heart bled warm through her veins. "Please, Jesus," she whispered, "see fit not to be in a rush to fill that in."

Jillian shifted her gaze to the marker next to her grandmother's. She knew it would be right there. She knelt down and traced the etching with her index finger.

Raphael Weyland Fontaine

Under the date of his birth and his death were five words that so unsteadied Jillian, she sat all the way down on the ground.

Rest now, my beloved son

"Dad," Jillian whispered so quietly, she could hardly hear her own voice. "It's me, Jillian." It wasn't that she thought he could hear her. She no longer believed in ghosts or lingering souls of the dead. She knew they all had someplace to go. But some things just needed to be said.

"I wish we'd known each other. Your mom told me I loved you when I was a little girl, and from the pictures, I think she's right. I wish we'd never left you. Dad," she whispered again, tears dripping from her chin, "I'm sorry I hurt you. And I know you're sorry you hurt me. I want you to know I forgive you. I also want you to know that I'm getting to know you. I thought it was too late, but I've realized it isn't. I'm finding bits and pieces of your life. I don't have much, but I know this: you're not who I'd imagined you to be. I'm so sorry your life was so hard."

She placed her forehead on her knee and wept. "I have just one more thing I want to tell you today. Your mom. She loves you so much. She just trapped her love for you deep in her heart and closed it up tight so it could never escape and so no one could ever touch it. Don't think ill of her. She's extraordinary. That's all I really have to say right now."

She came to her feet, stared a moment longer at the marker, then turned around and screamed as she ran right into an old man.

"Sorry I scared ya, miss. I ain't stood there long but I didn't want to disturb your vistin'. I was afraid you'd get away before I could give you this." The man handed Jillian a rubber-banded bundle of a smudged envelope and several small, folded pieces of paper. Jillian was alarmed at the sight of her name written on the envelope. "I been keepin' an eye out for ya for months. I'm the groundskeeper."

"I don't understand. You're really scaring me. Who is this from? Who would know I'm here?"

"I figger the card'll say all that. It's off with me then."

Jillian rushed to the car. She unlocked the door, jumped in, and relocked it. Her hands were shaking as she opened the envelope and pulled out a note card.

January 25

Dear Jillian,

It's been one month to the day since you told me you needed time. I've rehearsed pounding on your front door a hundred times and not taking no for an answer. But something tells me that's not what you need. Something tells me you need a man who will take no for an answer. So I'm waiting.

I've done some praying myself—and not just about you but about a lot of things that needed sorting out. I asked God how I was supposed to know when you were ready. All that ever came to me was that you'd be well on your way to finding out who you are and why you're here the day you show up at your

father's grave. Maybe I'm wrong, but I felt like God put that
on my heart as a sign. So if it's true, and you're on your way
and you're ready to get to know a man still drawing breath who
wants to know you, I'll be waiting.

Cal

Jillian dropped her head on the steering wheel. Seven months had come and gone since the date on this letter. Surely Cal had moved on with his life since then.

Jillian couldn't bring herself to read the other notes. She drove home praying and trying to profess her faith out loud like she'd been learning to do. All the way back to Saint Sans, she thought back over the last eight months. She headed toward the back entrance of Saint Sans, stopping off at the trash can to pitch in the wad of papers. One fell open.

April 25
Still waiting.

It was Cal's handwriting. Jillian's heart jumped into her throat as she retrieved the notes from the trash and laid them on the small table on the back porch. There they were, in order.

February 25
Still waiting.

March 25
Still waiting.

April 25
Still waiting.

May 25
  Still waiting.

June 25
  Still waiting.
  Got a puppy.

July 25
  Still waiting.
  Really bad puppy but I like him.
  He's keeping me company in the meantime.

The last one was in ink that couldn't have been more than forty-eight hours old.

August 25
  Still waiting.
  Still hoping.

CHAPTER 61

OLIVIA TIED THE SASH on her robe and slipped her feet into the house shoes at the edge of her bed. She ran a brush through her hair and clipped it back with a barrette. Eyeing the full-length mirror on her closet door, she chided herself, "The day's half gone, Olivia Fontaine. You should be ashamed of yourself."

She couldn't recollect the last time she'd slept until eleven. She'd been up most of the night with Vida, who'd worried her half to death with a low-grade fever and a terrible cough. She'd had her in the doctor's office the afternoon before and was none too pleased that Doogie Howser didn't seem more alarmed and she didn't mind saying so. She'd have her back in that office this afternoon whether they had an opening or not.

"I'm allergic to cigar smoke," Vida had said some hours ago from the bed, her voice as weak as herbal tea. "If I've told that man once, I've told him a thousand times."

Olivia put an extra pillow behind her head and fluffed it. "I'll have a word with David. I feel sure he's the instigator. We need to keep you at an incline just like this, so don't rearrange these pillows, okay? Nod your head like you're listening to me."

"Well," Vida had warbled instead, trying to talk with the thermometer under her tongue, "I fear he's got a willing accomplice. Where's our Jilly Bean?"

"Sound asleep. It's 4 a.m. No classes tomorrow, so I'm hoping she gets to sleep in. She's been going a hundred miles an hour." Olivia took the thermometer out of Vida's mouth, held it steady right below her bifocals, shook it back down, and jotted *100.2* on a small pad of paper.

Vida gazed off somewhere wonderful. Olivia could tell that by the expression on her face. Then, afoot, Olivia supposed, in that land far away, the old woman whispered, "Sweet, sweet dreams, our little Jilly Bean."

"It's time you were having sweet dreams yourself."

Vida closed her sleepy eyes.

"I've got your monitor on nice and loud in my room. That prescription cough medicine should be working better than this. I intend to ask the doctor this afternoon if you could handle something stronger. I've about had it with him treating us like a pair of eight-year-olds."

Vida didn't respond. Olivia sat beside her on the bed and put her hand on hers, and instead of patting it this time, she rubbed it gently for a good long while until her own eyelids grew heavy.

Olivia sure hadn't meant to sleep until eleven. "Why didn't you wake me up?" she asked Clementine, who yawned as if two old women had kept her up all night poking her with knitting needles. "We better go check on our patient. I think I hear her stirring around in there." Olivia walked over to her monitor and turned it up to its highest volume.

"And use the air freshener when you're done in there, mister! Sometimes I can't go in there for a week!"

Olivia smiled and shook her head. "I'd say they're both up. Let's go make me some coffee and open you a can of tuna." Clementine stretched everything from her nose to the tip of her tail before hopping off the bed and scurrying in front of Olivia to beat her to the kitchen.

Olivia walked by Jillian's wide-open door and stuck her head in to say good morning but stopped short when she caught no glimpse of her. Rounding the hall into the great room, she came to a screeching halt in her house slippers at the sight of an enormous mess on the dining room table.

"Good grief. This is what I have to get up to after going to sleep at 5 a.m.?" She pulled her glasses out of the pocket of her robe and slid them on. Her heart skipped a beat. She picked up the piece of paper propped between the salt and pepper shakers and read the note punctuated entirely with exclamation marks.

Don't kill me, O! I'm coming back to all of this and I'll have it all cleaned up before dinner! Don't move anything! I have a system! I'll be back soon! A friend dropped by unexpectedly and we're grabbing something to eat!

  I love you!

"Since Caryn's at the library," Olivia said to Clementine, "I'm guessing Jillian's out with the Virgin Mary again." What that meant was Flo Deever's girl. She and Jillian had become good friends at small-group Bible study, being the youngest and all. "I guess they've got Jesus with them." He'd been over at Saint Sans just last week crawling all over the place and pulling the cat's tail and eating fuzz out from under the Snapdragon. Olivia had had to excuse herself to her room to avoid a nervous breakdown. She had nearly been in the clear, with her bedroom door shut, when she'd overheard Vida saying, "I've got a great idea! You two girls get out of here and go have you a little fun and Olivia and I will babysit!" With that, she'd headed back to the great room.

Olivia folded up Jillian's note and stuck it in her pocket as she stared at the table. A cardboard box half full of pictures and family paraphernalia was at one end and most of the remaining surface was covered with snapshots and school pictures, certificates and report cards, homemade valentines, juvenile artwork, and the like. Olivia picked up a small booklet and opened it. The pages were filled out with dates of infant immunizations in the familiar penmanship of an awfully young mother.

Olivia inhaled all the way to the bottom of her lungs and exhaled. She hadn't seen any of this in years and supposed she'd never seen it all at once like that, spread out on the table for the world to see. Clementine rubbed against Olivia's ankle, mewing for some breakfast.

Three new photo albums were in a stack on the table. The two on the bottom were still sealed with plastic wrap. Olivia opened the top one at the middle and tilted her head to look inside. The page was still blank. She slipped her fingers under a few other pages closer to the front and took a peek. They were blank as well. Jillian had obviously just gotten started.

Almost without thinking, Olivia opened the front cover of the album, expecting to find the same. She laid it all the way open and stared at the page. It was as far as Jillian had gotten. Affixed to the center of the page was a small rectangular card. On it were four words embossed in blue calligraphy.

Raphael: God has healed.

Olivia lifted her chin as the noon sun sprayed the garden, making velvet of yellow rose petals and satin of purple moons. Clementine jumped on the windowsill and swatted at a dragon-fly perched unbothered on the opposite side of the glass.

CHAPTER 62

"Morning, Lieutenant! You getting used to that new rank yet?"

"Nope. And I hope you're leaving the *good* off the front of that *morning* to save words, Dolores," Cal said back to the dispatcher. "Or are you trying to keep from saying it's a bad morning?"

"It's a New Orleans morning, sir. Just around the block they'd call that a crapshoot."

"Yes'm, they sure would."

"But I can tell you it's a hot morning and you can bet every dime you've got that it'll be a scorcher today."

Cal glanced at the gauge on his dash for the outside temperature. "Yeah, I heard it's supposed to hit 103 today." He grinned. "That weather report came compliments of Emmylou DaCosta telling me I needed to stay hydrated." He knew Dolores would appreciate the source since she had adult children of her own. He'd

455

seen his mom that morning when he dropped off Buford, who was, best as Cal could tell, the worst-behaved puppy in the state of Louisiana. Thankfully, his mom had grown just about as attached to that boxer as he had.

"And I'll know you're a decent son, Lieutenant, if you can tell me right now that you have a bottle of cold water in the cup holder of that unmarked car."

"I'll get to a convenience store before the morning's up and see to it, since I'll have to face the woman before the day's out."

"Well, then, you might as well go to the one at St. Philip and Decatur," the dispatcher directed. "That's where your unit is. It was a holdup. Cashier dead. Appeared to be the only employee in the store."

"Not a good morning for one family."

"Sure isn't, sir."

"On my way. Thanks, Dolores."

When Cal pulled up and parked, the perimeter was marked off with yellow tape and the scene was hopping with law enforcement. Cal walked behind the counter and saw the man facedown in a pool of blood. "One shot?"

The officer nodded. "My guess is, the killer asked for a pack of cigarettes. The cashier turned his back and the dude drew his weapon and shot him. Where it hit, he'd have gone down instantly."

Cal glanced up at the corner of the ceiling. "Camera working?"

"Yep. Baseball cap but one frame caught a pretty fair shot of his profile. Jawline's distinct."

"Witnesses?"

"Woman next door heard the gunfire," the officer expounded. "A business owner down the street says he's nearly positive the perpetrator walked right by his storefront. Said he noticed him and knew he was up to no good. Hid behind some merchandise but watched him. His description might prove more helpful than the videotape."

"Not a bad start to an investigation."

"This one shouldn't be hard to close, Lieutenant."

"That's what I want to hear." Cal felt his phone vibrate in his shirt pocket and pulled it out. Before he glanced at the screen, he asked, "Anybody got ahold of the management?"

"Owner's on his way!" Sanchez called from the rear of the store.

"Good. We'll need an approximation of how much money he carried off."

"Should have that by midmorning, sir."

Cal glanced at the screen of his phone. Taken aback, he stepped into an aisle of the convenience store to read it. **Hi. My name is Jillian. I'm an only child and an only grandchild. I was born to Jaclyn Slater, a single mom, in Baton Rouge, Louisiana, about 75 miles from here. She relocated us and raised me in San Francisco, about 2000 miles from here.**

"Boss?" Another one of the officers.

"Is it urgent?" Cal asked, a bit on the edgy side. "I need to finish something here."

"Just need a thumbs-up when you're ready for us to contact the nearest of kin and how much you want us to tell the media."

"Proceed on nearest of kin. Hold off on media for now."

Cal stared back at the screen, reading and scrolling down with his heart pumping like he'd just run a 10K.

We stayed in the city but moved around quite a bit. I went to 3 different public elementary schools, 1 junior high, and 2 high schools. I loved art like my mother did and spent most of my time drawing and coloring and sketching. By the 4th grade, I could pencil an impressive horse. Always wanted one. Never ridden one. I liked to swim. I played on the volleyball team in 7th and 8th grades, A team, 1st string. My coach said I was the best setter she'd ever had. I didn't get to play in high school because we changed districts twice and I got behind and the coaches already had their key players. The team my senior year

came in 2nd in the district. I sometimes liked to think that, if they'd let me on the team, maybe we'd have come in 1st.

"Lieutenant?"

Cal rubbed his forehead. "What is it?"

"We think we have a name for the suspect."

"Excellent. Lock it down tight and go find him. Good job this morning." Cal walked around to the next aisle and crouched down behind the beef jerky.

I finished 2 years at City College waiting tables. I planned to pursue an art history degree but didn't go any further when I got hired at a popular restaurant called Sigmund's. My dad's name is Rafe Fontaine. I'm told he loved me and that I once loved him. He died a year ago in June. I want to be a great chef someday and maybe own my own restaurant in New Orleans.

I love flowers. I love to read. I love movies. I go to BABC and really like it. My best friend's name is Caryn. I live with my grandmother and am assistant gardener at Saint Sans Apartment House. I have a crush on a guy I haven't seen in a long while. Way too long a while.

Cal stood, headed past the coffee thermoses and the hot dog condiments, and yelled, "Got something urgent I've got to attend to. Good job this morning, everybody. Say a prayer for this man's family today. Bully, can you take this one from here and wrap it up?"

"You know I can, boss!" The man still grinned like a nine-year-old boy.

"Alright then." Cal walked past him and patted him on the back. "It's about time you got that weight put back on you. I don't know what to do with you this slim."

"Working on it, sir!"

"See that you do." Cal pulled a twenty-dollar bill out of his wallet. "Sanchez, buy that man a twelve-inch shrimp po'boy later when he can stomach it, you hear?"

"Will do," she answered, sticking the bill in her pocket.

Cal walked out the door of the convenience store and headed toward his car, picking up the pace. He gave way the last ten yards and ran. He flipped the ignition, threw the car into reverse, backed out, then put it in drive and headed up Decatur. Traffic was still congested and the drivers all looked stupefied by the heat. Every single one of them was reacting with the enthusiasm of a sloth. He laid his head on the steering wheel. "Come on, folks."

By the time Cal had sat through two green lights at one intersection and advanced four car lengths, he'd had enough. He turned the steering wheel hard to the right and headed down an alley, slowing just long enough to glance back at the text to make sure he hadn't dreamed it. It was there alright. Not one word in all these months, and then all of a sudden today.

He'd paused before he'd written that late August note, his heart weighing heavy in his chest, wondering if a wiser man would give on up. He'd written it anyway. What did he have to lose? If he never heard from her, he'd lost her months ago. When he'd gone to the cemetery with the note in his pocket and the old groundskeeper looked at him with so much pity, Cal almost couldn't muster the courage to give it to him. Feeling a little ashamed, he'd said, "By now I guess you're thinking I'm a crazy man, looking for the living among the dead."

"I ain't stood workin' here all these years 'cause I think what's dead ain't never raised."

Cal pulled the note out of his pocket and handed it over. That wasn't even a week ago.

He snapped back to attention when he saw something dart in front of his fender in the alleyway. When he swerved and threw on the brakes, a wiry gray-and-white dog scurried to the end of the alley, unharmed and not overly alarmed. Cal blew out a breath of relief and rolled his window down. "Boy, what are you doing way over here?" It was the stray that hung out with a homeless man Cal had often seen. The same dog he'd found Jillian feeding behind the café months ago.

The dog stopped for a few seconds, panting with his ears perked up and his tail high, then took off like a shot. Cal made his way down the alley and took the one-way street left, detouring around the traffic on Decatur. He glanced to the left before rolling up his window and spied the stray again. There it was, plain as day, in front of an old church, tugging playfully at the end of a broom in the palms of a man sweeping the entryway stairs.

"Can't be," Cal whispered under his breath. He was almost sure he'd seen that man before—one of the many homeless panhandlers on the corners of the quarter. But now the man's weathered face was freshly shaved and his silver hair combed and slicked straight back. And his clothes? Well, they might have been secondhand—or more likely third—but they were clean as a whistle.

When the man began to sing through a mouth of missing teeth, the lieutenant recognized the voice. He'd heard it echoing late at night from that condemned monstrosity on Iberville.

Passing by slowly with his window still down, Cal took one last look at the man sweeping the steps. Then he glanced above him at the modest marquee to the right of the church's front door.

Saints and sinners
Welcomed home
Hurry on now
Past done gone

A decent man knows when to heed advice. Lieutenant Cal DaCosta of the New Orleans PD turned on the dash lights on his Taurus, gave his siren a yelp, and made haste to a houseful of reluctant saints.

A NOTE FROM THE AUTHOR

Dear reader,

Thank you for the privilege to serve you through the pages of this novel. It's novel to me in every sense of the word because I'm a nonfiction writer. But even as a child, I loved crawling into a corner from time to time and scribbling something creative. This was my chance to just go with it. To start weaving a story and see where it would take me.

I prayed hard through the process of writing this book just like I've prayed for every other one I've written. I am driven to the marrow of my bones by a calling, and I have zero interest in wasting time on something of little eternal value. I asked God over and over to please dry up the story if it wasn't something he could bless. Meanwhile, I wrote a fifteenth Bible study and a nonfiction book called *Audacious*. But during every breather, the characters of Saint Sans would start bouncing the dust off the Snapdragon again and off I'd go, chasing them down St. Charles until it was time to get back to Bible study. Until the last few months of writing, I really did not know if I'd ever finish. Then one day I knew how it was supposed to end.

The story line is fictional, but the Savior is not. I have

experienced no greater reality in all of life than Jesus Christ. My own story is different from Olivia's and Adella's and Jillian's, but parts of it have been just as messy and much of it, equally complicated. Their stories were safer to tell than mine, precisely because their families aren't real and their relatives can't call them. (I write these words with a smile.)

I'd like to have been the kind of person who could write a lighter story than what you found within these pages, but I haven't lived a story like that. A writer has to be true to her experience, even in fiction. I have had many joys in this life and shared deep bonds—true and lasting loves—and laughed until my side hurt. I've also found life almost unbearable at times. No few times. Amid unending variables and uncertainties, I have found one constant. One absolute game changer. One perfect hero. He is more than I can keep to myself.

Jesus created and perfected the art of storytelling. Over and over, he told stories to illustrate divine realities like the love of God, the Kingdom of God, the power of prayer, and the impact of faith. Those who first heard them, as well as those who read them now, are able to picture themselves in the parable, even shifting from character to character within a single scene to understand something deeper about God. The same person who might first see himself as the older brother in the Luke 15 parable of the Prodigal Son might meet himself in the mud with the pigs in the next go-round, still smelling to high heaven when he's welcomed home by his dad. The invitation to relate is the beauty of it. The ultimate goal in Scripture is to allow us to relate to the one who offers redemption through his Son.

Thank you for spending so much time with me. I don't take it lightly. I hope you felt welcomed through the doors of Saint Sans. I hope you can picture yourself in an apartment down those halls. If you can't fathom Jesus pursuing you as surely as he pursued these characters, my pen skidded dismally off the page.

Jesus loves us. He is not scandalized by our failures. He is not limited in what he can do with what's left after family disasters. Nothing is beyond his redemption when he is invited in. No one with a whit of breath left is beyond the reach of his grace. My prayer is that his relentless love for you reverberated from the rooftop of Saint Sans and landed securely in your soul.

Love,

Beth Moore

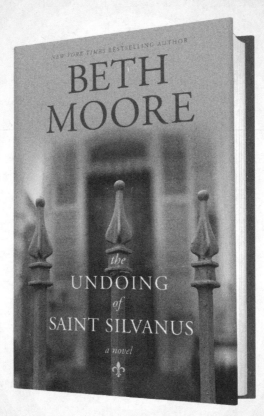

ACKNOWLEDGMENTS

I'M A DYED-IN-THE-WOOL BOOK ADDICT. But no matter how anxious I am to crack the next spine, I rarely skip an author's acknowledgment page. I think perhaps it's because I'm a relational sort and find satisfaction in the symbiosis required in any major body of work. It's God's way, a slice of divine paradox, that we are unable to fulfill our own separate callings alone. In the words of 1 Corinthians 12:21-22, "The eye can never say to the hand, 'I don't need you.' The head can't say to the feet, 'I don't need you.' In fact, some parts of the body that seem weakest and least important are actually the most necessary."

So many people proved necessary for this book to come to print. My heart sinks with the certainty of forgetting some, having written the manuscript piecemeal between Bible studies over an extended time. Forgive me in advance for every oversight.

My mother, Aletha Rountree Green, liked to read more than she liked to eat. She was a two-hander, scouring a book in her right hand, holding a backup in her left. She loved both nonfiction and fiction and fostered this unquenchable affection in all five of her children. My father, Albert B. Green, ran movie theaters after retiring from the military. Our fate to forever love a story was sealed.

I'm deeply grateful to Karen Watson, associate publisher at Tyndale House, who asked me casually across a table some five years ago, "Have you ever thought about trying your hand at fiction?" She somehow managed to make me feel safe enough to try it. By safe, I mean she agreed to these terms: "Karen, if you let me publish something terrible, I'll absolutely murder you." So if it's awful, I blame Karen.

Someone needs to pin a gold medal on Kathy Olson, my editor for this project. Because I wrote the manuscript in edges of time over several years, I paid no attention to its length. By the time I handed it over to Tyndale, it was a whopping 160,000 words. It fell to Kathy to trim this baby down by tens of thousands of words, and she did so with tremendous care. I have savored every exchange and learned so much from her. Her insight has been invaluable and her manner exactly what I needed for this project. She was a pleasure from beginning to end.

I'm deeply grateful to Mark Taylor and Ron Beers for the opportunity to partner with Tyndale House in this novel. I have such a great respect for them both.

Evangeline Williams was my head cheerleader throughout every moment of the on-again-off-again writing process. I do not believe I would ever have finished it without her encouragement, her unrelenting prayers, and her steadfast conviction that God cared about this book.

I am almost without words to thank the original band of women from Franklin Avenue Baptist Church, including Evangeline, who embraced me, stole my heart, and caused me to fall in love with New Orleans. I will treasure them forever for throwing their arms wide open to this white girl. I'm grateful to Elizabeth Luter for her deep prayers for this manuscript and for taking the chance years ago of inviting me to serve the women of her church. I'm grateful to Karen Bias for adding some rich color to my understanding

of Louisiana culture. I owe such a debt of gratitude to Caryn
Rodgers-Battiste, Mary Frances Harris, Noel Braud, and Evangeline
Williams for reading the manuscript and offering fabulous insights
and helping me adapt my terminology in strategic places.

I greatly appreciate retired NOPD officers Louis Colin and
Greg Elder for the time each of them spent with me on the phone.
They were vastly interesting and delightful.

I love my friend Kathie Waldheim, who welcomed me to hide
away in her family's river house near Austin to gain some traction
toward finishing the manuscript. I also thank the McElreaths for
allowing me to rent their condo in Galveston to concentrate on the
final chapters.

A monumental thank-you goes to Kimberly McMahon, my
personal assistant at Living Proof Ministries. She helped me in a
thousand different ways throughout the course of this project. For
the life of me, I don't know how I'd get anything written without
my staff at LPM. I'm deeply grateful for all my coworkers and for
a small handful of friends I swore to secrecy but asked to pray.

Tears burn in my eyes every time I come to a place to thank my
family. There are simply not enough words. The family of a writer
pays a price. Mine has done so with tremendous grace and affection. I have the inestimable blessing of being married to a man who
grabs me by the shoulders when I'm frantic over a project or in a
cycle of self-doubt and says, "Woman, you can do this." My first-
born's particular love for fiction blew wind in my sails throughout
the project. Amanda Jones would have been very involved in ideas,
edits, and final readings had she not been busy at the time bringing
my third grandchild into this world and into our anxious arms.

I'll wrap up these acknowledgments with words of gratitude
for Melissa Moore, my final-born and my co-laborer in a number of nonfiction projects. Handing a manuscript of any kind
over to a first reader is always difficult, but the vulnerability I felt

with this fiction work was almost paralyzing. I'd carefully chosen a first reader outside my usual world for the sake of damage control. When he was unable to follow through, Melissa looked me straight in the eye during a walk in the woods and said, "I'm your reader, Mom." I argued that she'd have too difficult a time critiquing it and being honest if it needed to be trashed. "Mom, I'm your reader," she repeated adamantly. "I can do it."

And she did. She read every last word of it. Chimed in on it. Told me what she liked, helped me catch some inconsistencies, steeped perfect French-pressed coffee, and offered a toast of two words: "Publish it." With that, I had guts enough to e-mail all 160,000 words to Karen Watson, who'd leaned across that table all those years earlier and asked, "Have you ever thought about trying your hand at fiction?"

Jesus, if you can make wine from water, you can make a fiction writer from a nonfiction writer long enough to find one more way to say how wonderful you are.

Learn to say
good-bye
to insecurity.

So Long, Insecurity Group Experience

Perfect for small groups and Bible studies

NEW YORK TIMES BESTSELLER!

So Long, Insecurity Devotional Journal

Journal with guided questions, Scripture passages, and prayers

The Promise of Security

A portable booklet to carry anywhere

MORE FROM BETH MOORE

BIBLE STUDIES

- *A Woman's Heart: God's Dwelling Place*
- *A Heart Like His*
- *To Live Is Christ*
- *Living Beyond Yourself: Exploring the Fruit of the Spirit*
- *Breaking Free*
- *Jesus, the One and Only*
- *Beloved Disciple*
- *When Godly People Do Ungodly Things*
- *Believing God*
- *The Patriarchs*
- *Daniel*
- *Loving Well*
- *Stepping Up: A Journey Through the Psalms of Ascent*
- *Esther: It's Tough To Be A Woman*
- *James: Mercy Triumphs*
- *Sacred Secrets*
- *Children of the Day*
- *Entrusted*

NONFICTION

- *Audacious*
- *Believing God*
- *So Long, Insecurity*
- *Get Out of That Pit*
- *Feathers From My Nest*
- *When Godly People Do Ungodly Things*
- *My Child My Princess*
- *Whispers of Hope*
- *Praying God's Word*
- *Things Pondered*

DVD TEACHINGS

- *Wising Up Wherever Life Happens*
- *The Inheritance*
- *Here and Now, There and Then*
- *The Law of Love*
- *Breath: The Life of God In Us*